LEAVING SMALL'S HOTEL

Also by Eric Kraft

Herb 'n' Lorna

Reservations Recommended

Little Follies

Where Do You Stop?

What a Piece of Work I Am

At Home with the Glynns

LEAVING SMALL'S HOTEL

ERIC KRAFT

Picador USA
New York

The advertisements on page 84 originally appeared in the February 1953 issue of *Popular Mechanics* magazine. All the other illustrations have been drawn by the author or cobbled together by the author from clip art.

Several of the episodes of *Dead Air* that are incorporated in *Leaving Small's Hotel* were originally published in *Exquisite Corpse*.

Picador® is a U. S. registered trademark and is used by St. Martin's Press under license from Pan Books Limited.

Library of Congress Cataloging-in-Publication Data

Kraft, Eric
    Leaving Small's Hotel / Eric Kraft.
        p.   cm.
    ISBN 0-312-18689-4
    I. Title
PS3561.R22L4 1998
813'.54--dc21   98-5725
                                                              CIP

First Picador USA Edition: May 1998
10 9 8 7 6 5 4 3 2

For Mad

In the actual world—the painful kingdom of time and place—dwell care, and canker, and fear. With thought, with the ideal, is immortal hilarity, the rose of joy. Round it all the muses sing.

Ralph Waldo Emerson, "Love"

When reality is folded over to cover the ideal of which we have so long been dreaming, it completely hides that ideal, absorbing it in itself, as when two geometric figures that are congruent are made to coincide, so that there is but one.

Marcel Proust, *Within a Budding Grove*

It exists, my dream world, it must exist, since surely there must be an original of the clumsy copy. . . . There time takes shape according to one's pleasure, like a figured rug whose folds can be gathered in such a way that two designs will meet.

Cincinnatus, in Vladimir Nabokov's *Invitation to a Beheading*

Preface

listen:there's a hell
of a good universe next door;let's go
e. e. cummings

WHEN THINGS GO WRONG, I sometimes wish that I were someone else, somewhere else, living a different life. I wouldn't be surprised to learn that you sometimes feel that way, too. In my case, it isn't necessarily a *better* life that I wish for—my life is rich, surprising, and, on the whole, quite pleasant, and I recognize that—but a *different* life, in the hope that by studying the differences I might learn something, not only about my life but about myself and even about my place in "it all," in the scheme of things, in all that is, and in the hope that by measuring my own life against another I will be reminded of the specific bits and pieces that give mine the flavor I used to enjoy and so come to enjoy it again every bit as much as I once did. I suppose that all I want, really, is to be away from my life long enough to grow homesick for it, so that I will want to return to it, to pick it up where I left it off and carry on with a renewed appetite for it, with renewed vigor and stiffened resolve. I want a vacation, in other words. I want, for a while, to vacate the place where I presently dwell and inhabit some other place, as some other self.

For years, I have found these other places and other selves within myself, in my imagination. It is the cheapest place to visit, the nearest getaway, and I go there often, with the result that there are so many other selves residing there now that when I make the inward leap, I find all those other selves there waiting for me, clamoring to tell me what they've been up to while I've been back at home trying to keep Small's Hotel from collapsing into a pile of old lumber. Like a family reunion, these visits can bring on a headache, and sometimes I find myself packing my bags and heading back to Small's Island before I had intended to go, pleading the thousand things that I have to do at home, arguing that the tide is favorable, the time is right, and when I have returned I find that the trick has worked, that I've been refreshed, that I see my life in a different light, that I'm ready for the next thing, as ready as I'll ever be.

I have used that trick, the inward leap to somewhere else, for as long as I can remember, but I have another, younger, trick up my sleeve, a trick that I discovered about thirty-five years ago, when I was a young man temporarily stuck in a romantic funk. (I had originally intended this romantic funk as a kind of costume, to add a little mystery to the first impression that I made, but like the grotesque faces that our mothers warn us against making, I had gotten stuck with it and couldn't figure out how to get rid of it.) I was sitting on a bench at the town dock, trying to drift into one of my other selves, when, instead, another self came drifting into me. A long time passed before I realized that I had made an outward leap instead of an inner one, that I had imagined yet another self, but this time a self who assumed that he had imagined me. Over the years I have developed this other, outer, self into an alter ego and persona who, within *his* world, has devoted himself to the exploration and elaboration of *my* world and *my* self, for motives much like mine, since for him my world and my self are another place, another self, a vacation. He has become a useful fiction, but much more than that—don't think me mad for saying this—a friend.

Here is his standard version of the story of our first meeting:

I first met Peter Leroy one cold afternoon in the winter of 1962, in Lamont Library at Harvard, where I was a sophomore. I was sitting in a chair at a large table, studying a German lesson. I had my chair tilted back, my legs crossed, with my feet up on the edge of the table and the German textbook in my lap. The library was crowded, the room was warm, and I was tired. I dozed.

When I woke up, I was lying on the floor. My books were scattered around me, people were laughing, and I was embarrassed. I gathered my things and rushed out of the library, and in the cold air the memory of a dream returned to me. In the dream, or at least in the memory of the dream, I saw an island, a small one, and on that island a nameless little boy sitting on a dilapidated dock in the sunny warmth of a summer day, dabbling his feet in the water, playing a game: he was trying to bring the soles of his bare feet as close as he could to the surface of the water without touching it. The memory of that dream has never left me, and even all these years later the dream and the world that has grown from it continue to surprise me. The center of that world is Peter Leroy, the character who grew from the little boy on the dilapidated dock.

I have told that story so many times now, altering the details in the telling, that I'm no longer certain which parts of it are facts and which are inventions, but the point of the story has never changed, and that point is its single essential fact, its truth: that the memory of that dream has never left me, and that even all these years later the dream and the world that has grown from it continue to surprise me.

My version is a little different. One cold winter afternoon, I was sitting on a bench at the town dock, looking toward Small's Island, feeling desperate and alone, and I let myself drift into a daydream. In the dream, I was about seven. I was sitting on the dilapidated dock on the island, in front of the abandoned hotel, dabbling my feet in the water. A sudden sound surprised me, and I raised my head. There, in front of me, not more than a few yards away, was a young man in a rowboat, staring at me. He wore a puzzled look. I waved and smiled. He seemed to be astonished to see me, and at first I couldn't understand why, but then I began to realize that it was because he hadn't expected to see me in his daydream any more than I had expected to see him in mine, and that is when I understood that he and I were having the same dream.

That night, lying in bed, I figured out what must have happened. On that cold winter afternoon I somehow insinuated myself into the mind of the young man I saw in the rowboat, a student at the time, dozing over a German lesson in a college library, sitting in a chair propped precariously on its back legs. Suddenly he woke up and found that he'd fallen to the floor. People were laughing, and he was embarrassed, so he gathered his things and rushed out of the library. Outside, in the cold air, the memory of a dream returned to him, surprising him. He recalled seeing a little boy sitting on a dock in the summer sun, dabbling his feet in the water: me.

I have been living in his mind ever since. He calls me Peter Leroy. I call him Eric Kraft. He thinks he invented me. I think I invented him. He thinks that his interpretation of the facts is correct, but I am convinced that my interpretation is correct, since from my point of view all the evidence tells me that it must be true. From *his* point of view, matters are a little different, something like the situation that he suggests when he begins readings from my work with this invitation:

> Imagine, please, an island, a small one, not in some pellucid subtropical sea, but in a gray bay, shallow, often cold, and on the island imagine an old hotel, where an aging dreamer, Peter Leroy, lives with his beautiful wife, Albertine Gaudet.
>
> Albertine runs the hotel, and Peter spends much of each day sitting in a room on the top floor, writing *The Personal History, Adventures, Experiences & Observations of Peter Leroy,* his life story.
>
> If you could look over his shoulder and watch him at work, you would be likely to find that he was *re*-writing an episode from his past, making of his life a story that it never was, because when he reminisces he finds that he's as interested in the possibilities as he is in the facts, and also because memory, like an old radio receiver, picks up a lot of static.

It is a curious kind of partnership, Kraft & Leroy. The usual descriptions—author and character, ventriloquist and dummy, left brain and right brain—are inaccurate and inadequate. When we were just beginning to work together, Kraft may have thought that in me he had merely found a way to write about himself, and I may have thought that I had found a ventriloquist who was willing to play the straight man while I got the laughs, but as time has passed, each of us has found himself liberated by the other, and each of us has found that to a certain degree he has become what he is through the agency of the other. We are not the same person, though we share a mind.

In the thirty-five years that have passed since that afternoon in the library, there have been many days when he has wished that he lived where

I live, on Small's Island, days when the world he lives in has disgusted him and he would have liked to live apart from it, in this little spot that he supposes he has imagined for me, a place where he imagined that I was living an ideal life (though it has turned out to be the case that boats leak and bills come due in my world as often as in his). In a sense, of course, he *has* lived here, in what is for him that other place, a place apart from the place where he really lives, for at least a little while every day, because he has come to think of "Peter Leroy" as the name he gives to his imagination, and of "Small's Island" as the place within his mind where his imagination resides, and every morning, when he takes his place at his computer, he goes there, comes here. Sometimes the trip is easy, and sometimes it takes him a while, and sometimes worrying over the household budget or some other crap keeps him within himself for a long time, but he always manages to break free eventually, and when you turn the page, you will find that he has made the inward leap, that he's exchanged the painful world of time and place for the world of immortal hilarity, that he's escaped to Small's Island. I think he's on his way here now. You come too.

Peter Leroy
Small's Island

Small's Hotel

"The Little Hotel Without a Slogan"

*A Special Invitation . . .
from Albertine Gaudet, Innkeeper*
❦

If you have ever stayed at Small's, you know that occasionally we provide entertainment in the lounge after dinner. Usually, it's nothing much—sometimes I play the piano, and now and then one guest may attempt to levitate another, but this fall we have something special planned. The memoirist Peter Leroy (who happens to be my husband) will read *Dead Air*, the latest installment of his personal history, adventures, experiences, and observations, in its entirety, over the course of fifty consecutive nights, finishing on his fiftieth birthday. Each reading will be a self-contained episode, so you can "get" any one of them without knowing any of the others. (Of course, you would derive the greatest pleasure from them if you stayed with us for fifty nights and heard them all. Inquire about our special rates.)

This is a once-in-a-lifetime opportunity! Don't miss it!
❦

*Small's Hotel
Small's Island, Babbington, New York
555-SML-ISLE*

Small's Hotel

"The Little Hotel Without a Slogan"

Schedule of Readings

The Daughter of Mr. Yummy

> An author ought to consider himself, not as a gentleman who keeps
> a private or eleemosynary treat, but rather as one who keeps a pub-
> lic ordinary, at which all persons are welcome for their money.
> Henry Fielding, *Tom Jones*

I STOOD AT THE WHEEL of the leaking launch, approaching the dock
on Small's Island and the end of my fiftieth year, throttling down, gaug-
ing the speed of my approach and the severity of the impact if the engine
should stall when I shifted it into reverse to bring the launch to a halt. I
expected the engine to stall when I put it into reverse, because it had been
doing that lately, so *when* it stalled I wanted to be moving slowly enough
to drift into the dock without doing too much damage to the launch or the
dock or the guests, but I was trying not to look concerned, since I have
learned during my fifteen years as assistant innkeeper at a small hotel on a
small island that it isn't a good idea to upset the guests before they even
set foot on the dock.

I had three passengers in the launch, a disappointing number. Three
would have been a disappointing number at any time, but it was particularly disappointing on this trip because Albertine had advertised my mar-
athon reading of *Dead Air* in the hope that she might attract a crowd.
Actually, to be precise about it, we couldn't have accommodated a crowd,
since we have only thirteen rooms and three cottages, but she—well, we,
to be precise about it—had hoped to draw a full house, something we
haven't seen in years.

Ahead, I spotted Albertine running along the path from the hotel to greet the guests when the launch struck the dock. I eased the throttle down another notch, came slowly to the dock, and reversed the engine. It stalled.

"Grab hold of something," I said in the even tone of an unflappable captain. "We'll be coming into the dock." If you had been aboard the launch with the other passengers, you would have thought that everything was as it should have been, that Cap'n Peter probably always brought the launch into the dock this way. I'll bet you would have. Of course, when the launch hit the dock and both shuddered, and you were sent staggering and grabbed for the nearest thing that would help you keep your feet, and the launch rebounded back toward Babbington whence you had so recently come, you might have had second thoughts about your captain, but if you had looked his way you would have seen him smiling, waving to Albertine, preparing to throw her a line, and the twinkle in his eye would have convinced you that the rough landing had been nothing more than a matter of style. It would have. I'll bet it would have.

I threw the line to Albertine, and she snubbed it around a piling and arrested the rebound. She rolled her eyes at me, I shrugged (but not enough for you to have noticed), and she extended a hand to the nearest of the passengers. When they were all safely off the boat, she delivered a speech of welcome, her usual speech of welcome, with, as usual, a few impromptu additions and alterations.

"Welcome to Small's," she said. "It's a pleasure to have you here. I'm Albertine Gaudet, the Innkeeper.

"I hope your journey was pleasant—or, if you came on the Long Island Rail Road, I hope that at least it wasn't too unpleasant. You have my sympathy. I've always thought that it would be nice if there were a private Small's Hotel car, with cocktails and swing music, at least during the summer season, but—well—there isn't. I apologize for the launch too, by the way. We call it a launch, but it's really just an old boat, isn't it? We used to bring people from the mainland in a handsome old Chris-Craft runabout. You would have liked that. It was a fine boat, and everyone loved it, especially my husband, Peter, whom you've met—the launch captain, formerly the Chris-Craft captain, and also Assistant Innkeeper—but it was expensive to maintain and so we sold it for—well—for a nice piece of change, though not as nice a piece of change as we had hoped it would bring us and not as much change as we needed.

"Well, anyway, I hope that while you are here you will consider yourselves my guests. Of course, you're paying for the privilege of being my guests, which might seem to put us in a relationship rather less *intime* than that of hostess and guest, but don't we all, in one way or another, wind up paying our hosts for their hospitality? If we're invited to dinner, we're expected to pay with conversation, aren't we? Some gossip? Maybe even a little wit? And if we're invited to spend the night—well.

"I hope you will find your accommodations satisfactory. All of the hotel's thirteen guest rooms are located on the second floor, and every room has a view of the bay, as you might expect in a hotel on an island as small as this one. (The third floor, by the way, is our living quarters. Enter only if invited, please.) If you're not happy with your room, just let me know. Obviously, we have more rooms than guests—currently, at least—so it will be a simple matter to move you around until you end up wherever you want to be. If you're not happy in the main building, you might like to take a look at the cluster of cottages at the water's edge. The rates for the cottages are a little higher than for rooms in the hotel because the cottages are larger than the rooms in the hotel, and because they offer more privacy, and also because we transported them to the island from the mainland at great expense of money and labor. My husband will be glad to tell you the story. Just ask.

"While I'm on the subject of privacy, let me assure you that you are not required to be sociable while you are here. We will not urge you to participate in any group activities. There *are* no group activities. Well, none except for the readings that Peter will be giving, but I assume that you've come for those, so they don't really count as group activities, not in the same way. I wouldn't think so. They're a special case, a category of their own, *sui generis.* Other than that, though, no group activities. Except for the morning mud wrestling. Just kidding. Really, no group activities.

"You are not, of course, enjoined from *organizing* group activities on your own, if you feel you must, but on the whole we assume that you have come here to be alone and to be left alone. While you are at Small's, you are an island dweller, an isolate, and I urge you to live like one. Take refuge in our old hotel, on our island. Absent yourself from the world awhile. Relax. Go rowing or sailing. We have a rowboat and four small catboats for the exclusive use of our guests—but—ah—you should know that the rowboat and three of the catboats leak—a little—not too much. First come, first served. If you don't like boats—and it's surprising how many people who come here *don't* like boats—you can perambulate the shoreline, take a swim, sit in the lounge and read, or do nothing more than sit on the dock—though I'd watch out for splinters and nails—dabble your feet in the water, watch the moonlight play on Bolotomy Bay, and let the world rattle on without you for a while.

"Of course, if you really want to be left alone, you should move into one of the cottages. They're not that much more expensive, and they're very romantic, the perfect place for a honeymoon, an anniversary week-end—or a discreet affair, for that matter. If any of you decide that you'd *like* to move to one of the cottages, just let me know.

"All your meals are provided, of course, and that includes midnight snacks. In a small refrigerator in the kitchen you will find 'leftovers.' We call them that, but I assure you that our chef makes these 'leftovers' fresh daily, specifically for snacking. I want to make it clear that although they *resemble* leftovers, they are deliberately made to resemble leftovers and are not actually left over from anything. (Some people have a very difficult time understanding this concept, which is why I'm explaining it, and I ask you please not to be offended by the explanation if you understood the concept before I began explaining it.) You may tiptoe from your room in the middle of the night to snack on these goodies—indeed you are encouraged to tiptoe from your room in the middle of the night to snack on these goodies, for if you do not, they will just sit there in the refrigerator and go uneaten, and by the next day they will actually have *become* left-overs, and then what would we do with them?

"Well! That's everything, I think. Go on up to the hotel, why don't you, and Peter and I will follow with your luggage."

The guests started on their way up the path toward the hotel, and Albertine and I begin piling their bags onto a couple of our red wagons, the kind that Dick and Jane used to pull in primers.

"What have we got?" Albertine asked.

"Well, the couple—" I began.

"The fun couple, Dick and Jane."

"You're kidding."

"Not their real names," said Albertine with a wink and a smile.

"Ohhh," I said, raising an eyebrow and slipping into what I like to call my Franche accahng, "hohn-hohn-hohn."

"I told them that we are very discreet."

"Oh, we are, we are."

"And that if they want to be called Dick and Jane, we will comply."

"Oh, we will, we will."

"They're likely to be easy guests."

"The grumpy guy, on the other hand—"

"Oh, great," she said. "Mr. Abbot. Cedric R. Abbot. 'Call me Lou,' he said on the phone. 'Everybody does.' But you're already calling him the grumpy guy?"

"I'm afraid so. Maybe I'm wrong, but I think he's one of those grumpy guys who's always got a smile on his face, but when you look at that smile you know it's a lie—you know the smile I mean?"

She smiled the very smile I had in mind, the smile that she uses when her picture is being taken in spite of her having made it perfectly clear that she does not want her picture taken.

"Uh-oh," I said, responding to the smile. "What went wrong while I was gone?"

"I've had some adventures in repairs and maintenance."

"What now?"

"The boiler again."

"Did you call the Tinkers?" I asked. For nearly all of the fifteen years that we have been running Small's Hotel, we have turned to the Three Jolly Tinkers when we've needed major repairs. Sometimes the Jolly Tinkers have fixed things; sometimes they have not; and sometimes the repairs undertaken by the Jolly Tinkers have become continuing projects, and some of those projects have been in continuous operation for nearly the entire fifteen-year span of our relationship without showing any signs of coming to a successful conclusion—repairing the boiler, to name a single example.

"I did," she said, "but they can't come out until tomorrow, because—" She stopped.

"Because what?" I asked.

She turned toward me. There was a tear in her eye. "Because the Big Tinker died," she said.

"Oh, no."

"There's a curse on this hotel," she said. "It's a nightmare."

I said nothing to that. We hauled the luggage to the hotel, and I distributed it to the guests' rooms.

IN THE EVENING, I had one drink too many before dinner, and, after dinner, in the lounge, I began the countdown to my fiftieth birthday by reading the first installment of *Dead Air*. I began by saying, "There are two epigraphs at the start of *Dead Air*. The first comes from the correspondence of Denis Diderot, but I found it in P. N. Furbank's biography of Diderot, so I'm going to read it as I found it:

> It was [Diderot's] impression . . . that every tendency was to be found in the heart: noble, base, healthy, perverse, exalted, lustful and homicidal. . . . This, he once told Mme Necker, was the "secret history" of the soul. "It is a dark cavern, inhabited by all sorts of beneficent and maleficent beasts. The wicked man opens the cavern door and lets out only the latter. The man of good will does the opposite."

The second is from *The Two Thousand and Six Month Man* by Carl Reiner and Mel Brooks:

> INTERVIEWER: Do you remember the national anthem of your cave?
>
> THE 2000-YEAR-OLD MAN: I certainly do. I'll never forget it. You don't forget a national anthem in a minute.
>
> INTERVIEWER: Let me hear it, sir.
>
> THE 2000-YEAR-OLD MAN (sings): Let 'em all go to hell . . . except cave seventy-six!

And now, 'The Daughter of Mr. Yummy,' episode one of *Dead Air*."

ONE NIGHT, late in the spring, thirty-eight years ago, when all of the summer and most of my life lay ahead of me, fertile as a field growing wild, five of us were spending the night in my back yard: Rodney Lodkochnikov, Marvin Jones, Rose O'Grady, Matthew Barber, and me. Rodney was known as Raskol, and Rose called herself Spike. The rest of us used our real names. We were sitting around a fire toasting marshmallows.

We had been talking about the difference between the ideal and the actual—along the lines of "why don't the insides of the frog they give you in science lab match the drawing in the book?" In the aftermath of that discussion, a silence had fallen. Within it, we toasted the marshmallows and waited for a new topic to suggest itself.

Matthew's marshmallow burst into flame. He pulled it from the fire and, as he rotated it to char it on all sides, asked, "Can you imagine being someone else?"

"Who?" I asked.

"Nobody in particular. Just not being yourself. Being someone else."

"Yeah, but who?" asked Spike.

"Anyone," said Matthew. "Someone who doesn't exist, but might have existed. Somebody new." He blew the flame out and began waving the marshmallow in the air.

"Come on," said Raskol, stirring the fire.

"Okay, okay," said Matthew. "I mean, what if some other sperm had reached your mother's egg before the one that did?"

"What are you getting at?" demanded Spike. She clenched her jaw and squinted at Matthew.

"Well," said Matthew, "what I mean is—"

Spike interrupted him. "What *I* mean is, are you suggesting something about my mother?" She leaned toward Matthew. The fire separated them, but even so Matthew pulled away.

"No," he said. "No, of course not. I mean, I am suggesting that she gave birth to you—" He paused, smiling, hoping for a laugh, but Spike didn't even return the smile. "—and to do that she had to have some sperm—"

"Do you want a fat lip?" asked Spike.

"No, I do not want a fat lip, thank you."

"Then stop saying things about my mother."

"I'm not saying anything about your mother. I mean, except for—"

Spike leaned closer. The flickering flames lit her from below. "I'll defend my mother's good name against all comers," she said.

"I'm sure you would," said Matthew.

Spike squinted at him again. "Are you suggesting that it needs defending?" she asked.

"Oh, come on, cut it out," said Marvin.

Spike grinned and shrugged and said, "Okay, okay. I was only kidding." She tossed some twigs into the fire so that it flared dramatically, shrugged again, and added, "For all I know, I'm the milkman's daughter."

The rest of us thought about this in silence for a moment. Mr. Donati, the milkman in Spike's part of town, was a short, bald man, heavy, always sweating, with black hair everywhere. Spike looked nothing like him.

I said, "Nah."

Raskol said, "Not a chance."

Marvin said, "Highly unlikely."

Matthew squirmed in place and scratched his ear. When he had something to say he could not allow himself to say nothing, however prudent that might be. Finally, he said, "Mr. Yummy."

None of the rest of us said a thing. We studied Spike, sidelong, and, trying not to let it show, compared her with Mr. Yummy.

He had been delivering the Yummy Good brand of baked goods in Babbington, where we lived, for as long as any of us could remember. His route took him around Babbington and round and round again, and because he worked at his own pace, no one could predict when he would arrive with his tray of Yummy Good goods. His appearance at the back door, rap-tap-tapping in a jazzy way he had, was always a pleasant surprise. Whenever my mother heard his rapid tapping, she would call out, "Just a minute!" and run into the bathroom to fix her hair and lipstick. His customers called him Mr. McDougal, but their children called him Mr. Yummy. He was ageless, and he was handsome. He had a big smile and freckles, like Spike.

"Now you're talking!" she said. "Look at these freckles. Look at this smile."

She smiled her smile, and in the firelight the truth gleamed. Spike was the daughter of Mr. Yummy. There could be no doubt about it.

"I never noticed before," I said, shyly.

"Maybe you never saw me in the right light," she said, and that must have been the case, because after that night she became, in my mind, the daughter of Mr. Yummy, and Mr. Yummy became the father of all those things in life that I misunderstood, a role that he still plays.

WHEN I finished reading, my audience sat in awkward silence for a moment, until I said, "Please hold your applause until the author has completed the reading of all fifty episodes."

They laughed at that and gave me a round of silent applause. Then Lou, the grumpy guy, turned to Jane, of the fun couple, and said, "Life is full of surprises, isn't it?"

Her only answer was a smile.

Encouraged by her smile, Lou asked, "Can *you* imagine being someone else?"

"To tell you the truth," she said, leaning closer to him and whispering, although he was the only person in the room who didn't know her secret, "I'm pretending to be someone else right now."

"Are you?" asked Lou, raising his eyebrows as he asked.

"Yes," she said, nodding as she answered.

"Puts a little spice in the marriage to get away from ourselves now and then," said Dick. "Run away to someplace away from it all and become a couple of people we don't know."

"Well, let me tell you something," said Lou, glancing quickly from side to side as if checking to see that he wouldn't be overheard. "You had me completely fooled." The three of them laughed at this, but I saw Dick and Jane exchange a questioning glance, as if they wondered whether they ought to be laughing at a joke that might have been made at their expense.

Lou wandered over to the bar. Because Small's no longer employed a bartender, a card on the bar said "Bartender temporarily out of order. Please serve yourself." It was supposed to be amusing. Lou read the card, did not laugh, stepped behind the bar, and poured himself a cognac. He invited Dick and Jane to join him, but they declined, put their heads together for a moment, and then approached me, hesitantly, looking embarrassed, as if they felt that they ought to say something about my reading before they retired to their room, as if they felt that it would be both impolite and terribly obvious if they just ran from the lounge and dashed up the stairs to their room (where, I suspected, their thoughts had already preceded them and were tumbling amorously under the comforter). "Thank you," they said, nearly simultaneously, and then again, for good measure, "Thank you," before they turned and ran from the lounge and up the stairs to catch up to their thoughts.

THE WIND began to rattle the shutters, and a heavy rain began to fall. Albertine and I battened the hatches and took to our bed. On the edge of sleep, I urged my thoughts backward, back to my own back yard, where I lay supine, looking at the stars on a summer night, looking back in time as far as starlight could take me—and a drop of water fell on my forehead.

"What's that?" asked Albertine.

Another drop.

"What's what?" I asked.

"That sound."

"Sound?" Splat. "You mean that sound?"

"The roof is leaking, isn't it?" she said, and she sighed.

"There's nothing we can do about it tonight," I said, hoping that she would agree.

"Are you sure? Couldn't you put a tarp over it or something?"

"The wind would blow it off the roof. In fact, the wind would probably blow me off the roof. You'd see me flying past the window, holding on to the tarp, headed for the open ocean."

"Okay. Forget it."

"Remember the night the library ceiling fell down?" I asked.

"I remember," she said, "but I'm not going to get nostalgic about it."

"Are you saying I'm getting nostalgic about it?"

"Yes. You've got that tone."

"Tone? What tone?"

"That poignant tone that you use when you start exploring any memory older than a week and a half—any memory, good or bad. It really is a kind of homesickness, because you're in love with the past, in love the way other people are in love with the places that they think of as home, and maybe that's because the past really is your proper home. Maybe you don't belong here. You shouldn't be here now. You'd rather be there then."

"I just wanted to make the point that problems come and go."

"Lately, they come but they do not go. The roof is leaking, the boiler is—is—cantankerous, we're completely broke—"

"Actually, we're broker than that. We—"

"It's not funny, Peter," she said, and there was a weariness in her voice that made me feel that she was right. "Everything is falling apart, and we can't afford to fix anything. The more things fall apart, the fewer guests we get—the fewer guests we get, the less money we have—the less money we have, the more we go into debt—the more we go into debt, the less we can afford to keep the place up—"

"Okay, I get it. Enough."

Silence.

"I'm sorry," I said. "I'm sorry I brought you here. I'm sorry I got you into this."

Silence.

"In the morning," I said, "we'll put the place on the market."

I waited for her to say something, but she didn't say a thing. In a while she began to breathe evenly, and when I turned toward her, I saw that she was contentedly asleep, and smiling. I moved closer to her, away from the leak, and I pulled the quilt over my head to hide myself from the dripping present.

September 11
The Rock at the Mouth of the Cave

What fresh hell is this?
Dorothy Parker

I WAS UP EARLY the next morning, as always, but when I entered the kitchen I found Cedric "Call Me Lou" Abbot already there, chatting with Suki, the cook, and making himself a breakfast sandwich from the meat loaf in the "leftovers" refrigerator.

"Good morning!" Lou said when I walked in. "Coffee's almost ready." He was smiling, but that didn't change my conviction that he was a grumpy guy, because I have learned that many a grumpy guy will smile in the company of strangers.

"Morning," I mumbled, hoping that Lou would conclude from my mumbling that I was one of those people who do not like to converse before they have had their coffee. I turned quickly toward the door and said, "I'll go see if Dexter brought the papers," employing the same significant mumble.

"Swell idea!" said Lou, who apparently had no ear for a significant mumble. "I'll come along." He followed, carrying the sandwich. Together, we headed down the path toward the dock. Along the way, I decided, after a quick survey of my personal history conducted while walking with my head down, my eyes on the ground, and my hands in my pockets, that Lou was probably the first person I had ever heard actually use the word *swell,* or, if I was wrong about that, certainly the first person I had ever heard use the word *swell* so early in the morning.

"This Dexter," Lou asked, "who's that?"

"Dexter? He's our mailman, paperboy, delivery service—"

"Hardworking fellow?"

"Hardly working, as we say around here. He does some fishing and some clamming, except on days when he would rather not, and on his way out to the bay he drops off our mail and our newspapers—"

"—except on days when he would rather not," said Lou, chuckling.

"Right," I said, not chuckling. "I have come to suspect that Dexter does not like delivering our mail and newspapers."

"And why have you come to suspect that?" asked Lou.

"I have come to suspect that because Dexter does not exhibit any apparent desire to see that the goods actually reach us. He brings his boat within what seems to him to be flinging distance of our dock and then from that distance he flings a plastic bag in our general direction. Sometimes he puts enough effort—technically, we call it 'oomph'—into the fling to get the bag onto the dock, and sometimes—"

Lou and I had reached the dock. We stopped there and stood in silence for a moment, looking at a plastic bag floating just out of reach.

"Sometimes he does not," said Lou, chuckling.

"Yeah," said I, not chuckling.

I stretched out on the dock and began trying to snag the bag with a boat hook while Lou ate his meat-loaf sandwich. After a short while Lou said, "What a great morning!"

I twisted my head around and looked up at him to see if he was being sarcastic. He didn't seem to be. He pointed to the bag of papers and mail and said with a smile, "Looks like it's sinking."

"Oh, yes, it is," I said. "It is sinking, slowly but surely."

"Why don't we start up the launch and go out and get it before it goes under?"

"Why don't we?" I said with a sigh. "I'll tell you 'why don't we.' Because after a damp night—and last night was a very damp night—the engine tends to be a little reluctant to start, and also because the launch leaks, and before I leave the dock in it I like to pump it dry so that I've got a better chance of staying afloat for the duration of my journey."

Lou clapped me on the back heartily, as grumpy guys will when they are desperate to hide their gloom, and, pointing toward the bag, said, "It's not going to sink between here and there. Tell you what—why don't I get into the boat and you just shove me out in the direction of the bag while you keep hold of the line, and then pull me back in after I snag the bag?"

"Swell idea," I said, and that was what we did. Then we carried the dripping bag between us all the way back to the hotel and began laying the things out to dry. When Albertine came into the front hall, she found it covered with newspaper.

"'What fresh hell is this?'" she asked.

"It's the paper," I said, "and the mail, and the magazines."

"And it's all over the whole damned place?"

"Just the ground floor," said Lou, beaming. He handed me a limp envelope and the letter that had been in it. "This doesn't look like the kind of thing you'd want lying around for everyone to see," he said.

He was right. It was a letter from the publishers of The Unlikely Adventures of Larry Peters, a series of books for children or young people or "pre-adults" that I had been writing for years, and the news was not good. "In the face of a continuing decline in sales," they wrote, "we have decided with extreme reluctance to write *finis* to the series." There was no mention of a wake with open bar, hot hors d'oeuvres, and a jazz band.

"Oh, this is swell," I said. "This is just swell." I sank instantly into a foul mood, and I was still in a foul mood that evening, when the time came to read the second installment of *Dead Air*.

ONE SPRING NIGHT, thirty-eight years ago, I was camping in my back yard with my four friends Rodney "Raskol" Lodkochnikov, Marvin Jones, Rose "Spike" O'Grady, and Matthew Barber. Spike had brought our meandering conversation to a sudden end when she suggested that she might not be the daughter of Mr. O'Grady, her apparent father, but of the man who delivered the Yummy Good brand of baked goods door to door in Babbington, the man we called Mr. Yummy.

In the embarrassed silence that followed, Spike stirred the fire while the rest of us tried to think of a way to change the subject. This wasn't easy. The thought that Spike might be the daughter of Mr. Yummy stood in the way like a fat man in a narrow tunnel, as plump and sticky as "Little Yummy," the cartoon fatty who promoted Yummy Good's products on television. We sat there, working hard to squeeze past the thought and on to something else, working our jaws over our gum, ruminating vigorously.

When the ideas came, they seemed to come all at once, as if we had squeezed past Mr. Yummy and tumbled into a vestibule from which many passageways radiated. Each of us scrambled into one and asked whatever question he found there.

"Any more potato chips?" asked Raskol.

"Will good eventually triumph over evil?" asked Matthew.

"Are flying saucers real?" I asked.

"Do all hermits live in caves?" asked Marvin.

"Do they fake those nudist-camp pictures?" asked Spike.

Another silence fell. I spent some time wondering about whether the potato chips were all gone, about the likelihood that sweetness and light might eventually prevail over the forces of darkness, whether life was present elsewhere in the universe, and whether all hermits were troglodytes, and I suppose that the others thought about those things, too, but when we finally spoke, we all asked the same question: "What pictures?"

Grinning, Spike produced a folded magazine from her back pocket.

After we had looked at the pictures very thoroughly and tried to explain how the photographer had made the black rectangles stay in place on the people's faces, fatigue settled over us, and we ran out of conversation.

"We can still catch a little of Baldy," I said to Marvin. His question about hermits living in caves had been inspired, I knew, by listening to "Baldy's Nightcap." This was a radio program hosted by a dummy, Baldy. His ventriloquist, Bob Balducci, had been relegated to the background as file clerk, gofer, and yes-man—or in Bob's case, yeah-man. Part of Baldy's routine was the pretense that he lived in a cave.

"Okay," said Marvin. He turned his radio on.

I coveted Marvin's radio. It resembled a small piece of luggage, with a real leather case. The radio took a while to warm up, as radios did in those days, so the sound of Baldy's voice came upon us gradually, as if he had been waiting outside the bubble of firelight and now, when we summoned him, joined us there, within the shrinking sphere. Baldy was bringing his show to a close, ending, as he always did, with the news:

"The hour is growing late," he said, "It's time to see what's going on in the hideous world outside the cave. Bob?"

"Yeah?"

"Did you roll the rock in front of the cave?"

"Yeah."

"Good boy, Bob. Let's see . . ." There was the sound of rustling newspaper. "We've got the war in Korea . . . some bombings . . . refugees . . . a little corruption here and there. . . . Here's something: 'Ferry Sinks, Ninety Dead.' What is it with these ferries? They go down like rocks! Bob?"

"Yeah?"

"Bring that ferry file to me, will you?" A pause. "Thanks. Nice work, Bob. What have we got here? A hundred orphans on their way to a free lunch . . . ninety lepers going to a clinic . . . two hundred virgins off to dance around a maypole. They always take the ferry! And down they go! Let me tell you something, boys and girls: if you see a ferry pulling away from the dock with a hundred nuns on a pilgrimage, stay off it! That boat is headed for the bottom! Bob?"

"Yeah?"

"Make sure that rock is in front of the cave."

"Yeah."

"Well, it's time to say good night, boys and girls. Remember what Baldy says: stay in the cave. It's a nasty world out there."

Baldy's closing theme came on, and Marvin clicked the radio off. Silence fell into the dying light. I squirmed lower in my bedroll and pulled the blanket over my head—to make a little cave.

JUST BEFORE Albertine and I started up the stairs to bed, the phone rang. At that hour, Al generally preferred to let the machine take all calls, but I still had hopes that I would find on the other end of the line a representative of a vast extended family calling to inquire about taking the entire hotel for a reunion, desperate to find a place that suited their needs, willing to pay whatever I wanted to ask.

"I'll get it," I said.

"Oh, please don't," said Albertine.

I did. It was a woman who identified herself as a Satisfaction Specialist from the *Babbington Reporter* calling to see whether Mr. Leroy had received the paper.

"Yes," I said. "We received it, but—"

"Was it on time?" she asked.

"Yes, it was on time, but—"

"What's this?" asked Al.

"The *Reporter*," I said.

The Satisfaction Specialist asked, "Would you say that the credibility of our journalism was equal to your expectations, lower than your expectations, or in excess of your expectations?"

"Your credibility?"

"Equal to your expectations, lower than your expectations, or in excess of your expectations?"

"Well, to be honest with you, my expectations are not very high. You see, I've been reading the *Reporter* for quite a few years, so I've come to expect—"

"Give me that," said Albertine, and she took—it would not be unfair to say snatched—the phone from me. "Listen," she said into the mouthpiece, "I am probably your biggest single subscriber—sixteen copies— no, *seventeen*—every day—and I want to tell you that the *imbecile* you employ to deliver that rag—Dexter Burke—right—well—oh—really?— then you have my sympathies, Mrs. Burke, believe me. The man is an idiot—and *my aged mother* has got a stronger throwing arm than—oh, yeah? Well, the same to *you*, sweetheart!"

She handed the phone back to me and said, shaking her head, "I've got to get out of this town."

Have You Ever Wondered Why Microphones Don't Resemble Ears?

IN THE MORNING, Albertine called three real estate agencies to list the hotel with them, and in the afternoon I ferried a dozen realtors out to look the place over. They spent more than an hour with Albertine, going through the buildings, walking along the beach, and listing the assets and appurtenances. Every time I crossed paths with the group, one or another of them was using the word *charming,* so it came as quite a shock when they suggested an asking price considerably lower than what we had invested over the years.

"Is that just for the hotel," I asked, "or—?"

"That would be for everything," said Jeffrey, a fat and florid fellow who had assumed the role of spokesrealtor for the group.

"The hotel *and* the island?" I asked. Jeffrey laughed as if this were a joke, and I developed a strong negative attitude toward Jeffrey. "Does that mean yes or no?" I asked.

"It—um—it means yes," said Jeffrey.

"The cottages, too?" asked Albertine.

Jeffrey nodded. No one said anything for a while, and when the silence had grown embarrassing, Jeffrey shrugged and grimaced and said, "Of course you can ask more if you like, but I understood that you were eager to sell."

"We are," said Albertine.

"But not that eager," I said.

"Well," said Jeffrey, standing and beginning to put his papers into his briefcase to signal that he had decided that it would probably not be worth his time to try to make me listen to reason, "perhaps you'd like to talk it over and give us a call when you've settled on a price." He snapped the briefcase shut.

"Yes," I said. "Yes. We'd like to do that. Talk it over. I'll—uh—take you back to the mainland—and Albertine and I will—we'll talk it over."

I got up and walked out of the room and out of the hotel and began walking toward the dock. The realtors followed. I stayed in the lead, moving quickly enough to stay ahead of the realtors so that I wouldn't have to talk to them, because I didn't want to have to listen to them appraise my hotel, my island, my life, my folly. I didn't want to hear how little they thought it was worth, and I didn't want to give them the opportunity to convince me that they were right. I didn't say a word to them throughout the trip across the bay, and I mumbled my good-byes when I left them at the town dock.

ON THE WAY back home, when I was about halfway back, I throttled down and chugged along slowly to give myself some time to think. The bay was calm. The pale afternoon light flickering on the surface struck an autumnal note of things drawing to a close, of time running out. I was just beginning to try to sing the chorus to "September Song" when I spotted a rowboat ahead with someone standing in it, waving his arms. When I drew closer, I saw that it was *my* rowboat and that the arm-waver was Lou, the grumpy guy. I pulled the launch alongside.

"Perfect timing!" Lou sang out. "This thing really *does* leak." The water was a couple of inches below the gunwales. I threw Lou a line, and when the rowboat was secure for towing, I extended a hand to him. Clambering aboard the launch, Lou said, "I was sitting there saying to myself, 'Lou, if you get out of this alive, it's time you recognized that most of the sand in the hourglass of life is in the bottom half,' you know what I mean?"

"Yeah," I said, and after that I did not say another thing until the evening, when it was time to read "Have You Ever Wondered Why Microphones Don't Resemble Ears?" the third episode of *Dead Air*.

BECAUSE I am an avid eavesdropper, I have often wondered why microphones are not made to resemble ears. After all, the point of a microphone is not that someone is speaking, but that someone else is, or will be, listening. That is also the danger of microphones.

What we say never gets us into trouble unless it's heard. Shout it at home in your cork-lined room, and you're safe. Tell someone, and you are asking for trouble. Speak it into an open mike, and you're courting disaster. Yet who among us, upon discovering that an idea has popped into our minds, can resist whispering it into an attractive ear or a microphone?

Consider the case of Bob Balducci, who rose to fame as a ventriloquist and ended up as assistant to a dummy. For quite a few years when I was a boy, "Bob Balducci's Breakfast Bunch" was a program everyone knew. It was broadcast from a restaurant where an audience of little old ladies sat at tables eating breakfast. The clatter of cutlery was always in the background. Bob ended his program with the same routine every time, saying, "Well, that brings another gathering of the Breakfast Bunch to a close, but it has been so *wonderful* being here with all of you *lovely* ladies this morning that I think we ought to do it *again* tomorrow . . . don't *you*?"

The audience would call out, "Yes, Bob," and begin cheering and applauding, and then the studio orchestra would strike up the lively Breakfast Bunch theme, and the program would be over.

On the morning that wrote *finis* to his career as host of the Breakfast Bunch, Bob ended the program with his usual routine, and when he said "I think we ought to do it *again* tomorrow . . . don't *you*?" the audience chorused, "Yes, Bob," and the lively Breakfast Bunch theme came up over their applause, but then, thinking that he was off the air, Bob turned to his second banana and alter ego, Baldy the Dummy, and asked, "What were the last words of our dear departed Uncle Don?"

"Gee, Bob," said Baldy. "I haven't thought of Uncle Don in years. I used to listen to him all the time when I was a little splinter. Poor guy."

"I asked you what he said."

"Well, you know, I've heard two versions of the story, Bob. In one, Uncle Don said, 'That ought to satisfy the little bastards,' and in the other he said, 'That ought to keep the little bastards happy till next week,' but in both versions the mike was on. Too bad. That was his best show."

"And his last."

"Yeah."

"But in our case," said Bob with an audible sigh, "there's gonna be a whole new batch of desiccated old bats tomorrow."

The microphone was open.

Like Uncle Don before him, Bob went down. The program went on, though. It was still called "Bob Balducci's Breakfast Bunch," but every show began with the claim that Bob was on vacation. Someone was always filling in for him.

I knew that Bob wasn't on vacation. All I had to do to find him was tune in late at night, and there he was, still on the air—in a way. His new program was called "Baldy's Nightcap." Its star was Baldy the Dummy. Bob had only one line on Baldy's show: "Yeah." Sometimes it was, "Yeah?"

About once a month, at some unpredictable point in the program, Baldy would ask, "Bob?"

"Yeah?"

"Aren't you the guy who insulted those desiccated old bats?"

"Yeah."

"Baldy's Nightcap" had a simple format. Baldy talked. That's all he did. He didn't play music or interview guests. He just talked. As he talked, he seemed to be doing nothing more than letting his thoughts run on, talking to a friend—me. Often he would begin by asking, "Have you ever wondered . . ." and go on to explore some question that he had been wondering about. Sometimes he would employ a prop. I remember his saying one night, "You're probably wondering why I've got this log beside me. Well, you know what? I think it might be one of my relatives," and he went on to reminisce—complain, actually—about growing up as a dummy in Falling Rock Zone, Minnesota. He never offered much detail about his private, off-the-air life. He was wary, I suppose, of suffering Bob's fate. He claimed to live in a cave, but he never said a word about how he spent his days. It was as if he were someone else during the day, or asleep, or in a box. I would lie there, listening, and sometimes I would fall asleep, and wake, and sleep and wake again. It wasn't that Baldy was boring, but he spoke with an infectious weariness that seemed to have begun long before the show came on and seemed as if it would continue long after the show was over.

He always ended the show in the same way, with a look at the miserable side of the news, an item or two from the day's events that seemed to him most vividly to epitomize the pain and vulgarity of everyday life, followed by the words "Good night, boys and girls. Remember what Baldy says: stay in the cave. It's a nasty world out there." Sometimes, he would add, as if to himself, almost inaudibly, "That ought to satisfy the little—" and then the microphone would be switched off abruptly, leaving a wooden silence: dead air.

"BALDY THE DUMMY is still on the air," I remarked later, at the bar, where Lou was again playing bartender. "I tune him in sometimes late at night when I can't sleep."

"Really?" asked Jane. "I don't think I'd want to listen to him late at night in a darkened room. There's something creepy about dummies." She shuddered theatrically. "They make my flesh crawl. I think it's the expression on their little faces, you know—that smile, that creepy smile."

"It puts me in mind of the *risus sardonicus*," said Lou, polishing a glass.

"What the heck is that?" asked Dick.

"It's a bizarre grin that forms on the faces of tetanus victims, brought on by spasms of the facial muscles," said Lou. "Not a pretty sight."

"You don't say," said Dick, pushing his glass across the bar for a refill. Jane reached toward the glass and held her hand over it to indicate that she would rather Dick did not have another.

"Why do they call it the—what was it again?" she asked.

"The *risus sardonicus*," said Lou, "so called because in ancient times there was supposed to be a certain plant that grew in Sardinia, which, when eaten, produced convulsive laughter—sardonic laughter—ending in death."

"Ooh," said Albertine, with a theatrical shudder like Jane's. "That *is* creepy."

"And on that creepy note," said Dick, "I think we'll call it a day." He took Jane's arm and led her toward the door.

To Albertine and me, Lou said, "I'll leave everything in shipshape shape here. You two turn in."

"Thank *you*, Lou," said Albertine. "You're the *perfect* guest."

When we reached the doorway, Lou called to us, in an imitation of the voice that I had used for Baldy the Dummy, "Good night, boys and girls," and when we turned around to wish him good night he twisted his face into a bizarre grin.

IN MY BEDSIDE TABLE, I kept a small radio with an earphone. The battery was nearly dead, and something was wrong with the volume control, which made the sound rise or fall unpredictably when I tried to adjust it, but if the atmospheric conditions were right and if I rotated the radio until I had it aligned so that the signal was at its strongest, I could still pull Baldy in.

"Well, Bob," Baldy said above the static, "it's about time to make another entry in the catalog, isn't it?"

"Yeah," said Bob.

"Gather 'round the radio, boys and girls, 'cause it's time to open Baldy's Catalog of Human Misery." This announcement was followed, as always, by a creaking sound, as if the catalog were contained in an enormous box with rusty hinges. "Yes, indeedy. Every night at this time, we bring our listeners fresh proof that things could be worse, don't we, Bob?"

"Yeah."

"You know how it is, boys and girls—some days you think that things will never go right for you. You begin to think dark thoughts about slipping into eternal night, and you wonder whether anyone would even miss you, am I right?"

"Yeah."

"I wasn't talking to *you*, Bob." He dropped his voice and said, "I was talking to *you*, listener. When those dark thoughts threaten to get the best of you, I am here to bring you comfort! Every night I bring you the story of someone, somewhere, suffering a misery more miserable than yours. Tonight, I want to tell you about a woman who was living with her three children in a housing project somewhere, anywhere, who knows where.

Things were not going well, not at all. In fact, things got to be so bad that, a few nights ago, she got to thinking her dark thoughts about eternal night, and wondering whether anyone would even miss her if she were gone, and whether things would ever be any better for her children than they were for her, and many more things that it is not given to us to know, and in her misery she went up to the roof of her apartment building and she pitched her three small children from the roof, one by one, and then threw herself off after them." Silence, a long silence. Then, "File that under 'Inconsolables,' would you, Bob?"

"Yeah."

"Boys and girls, that's despair, the real thing, the bottom, bad as it gets, not the blues, not the mopes, not that nameless dissatisfaction *you* feel. If you are not all the way down there where that woman was, then take heart! Your little life could be much, much worse. You just roll that rock in front of your cave, and you sleep tight. Tomorrow is another day."

There was a brief silence, but I didn't switch my radio off. I waited. In a moment, Baldy laughed his wooden laugh and added, almost inaudibly, "Well, Bob, that ought to satisfy the little—" and then the microphone was switched off abruptly, and I switched my radio off and lay there in silence, wondering what, exactly, had made that woman so miserable, so desperate, waiting for sleep, hoping for sleep.

September 13
Masters of the Arts

One of the two is almost always a prevailing tendency of every author: it is either not to say some things which certainly should be said, or to say many things which did not need to be said.

Friedrich von Schlegel
Aphorisms from the Lyceum

MORNING CREPT IN like a guilty drunk. I resisted dragging myself out of bed, though I am ordinarily an early riser. I lay under the covers longer than I have in years, brooding. In the numb moments after waking, I felt, for the first time, the burden of our indebtedness as fully as Albertine must have felt it, without the hope that I usually managed to summon to counter the facts. I felt all the weight of it, as I knew she did, and it seemed that if I did drag myself out of bed I would have to spend the day trudging under a double burden: pulling the weight of all the years the hotel had been operating at a loss and pushing the weight of the likelihood that we would never manage to turn it around. Might as well stay in bed. If it hadn't been for Albertine, I would have.

"Are you sleeping in?" she asked.

"No," I said, suddenly ashamed of myself for having wanted to. "I'm getting up."

I got up and began pulling my clothes on quickly, shivering in the cold.

"Do you know what day this is?" I asked.

"Yes," said Al. "I do."

It was the fifteenth anniversary of our purchase of Small's. Only nine years remained on the mortgage, but it was not the mortgage it had been when we first bought the hotel. We had refinanced it so many times for repairs and renovations that the payments had become a burden. I knew that Albertine was worried about making the payment due at the end of the month. I knew because she had told me so.

Dressed, I walked around to her side of the bed and kissed her and said, "Sometime in the night, I became convinced that you're right. We should go."

"Thank you," she said, and after she had said it I realized, from the sinking sensation in my chest, that I had been hoping she would say that she had changed her mind, that she wanted to stay, that she had found some error in the books, that we were doing much better than she had thought, that . . . but none of that was true; all of that was wishful thinking.

I DIDN'T GO down to the kitchen to get a cup of coffee, as I usually do before beginning my day's work on my personal history, because I didn't want to run into Lou. Instead, I went directly to my workroom, turned the computer on, and sat at the keyboard. I didn't slip into the past, as I usually do. Instead, I wrote this:

> Albertine watched Peter pull the bedroom door shut and fuss with the bent latch until he had it closed tight. Then she opened the drawer of her bedside table and took from it *Manhattan* magazine, which she had begun to read in secret because

That didn't feel right, didn't sound right, so I went back to the beginning and tried again:

> I watched him pull the bedroom door shut and fuss with the latch the way he does every morning until he gets the door closed tight, and then when I knew he wouldn't be coming back into the room I opened the drawer of my bedside table—feeling very sneaky and disloyal—and got my copy of *Manhattan* magazine, which I've begun reading in secret because I know that when I read it a smile comes across my face and betrays my feelings

completely. Everything I feel about leaving the hotel is there, written all over my face, when I open that magazine.

Days pass, sometimes a week, during which I do not leave this island. I remember—shortly after we moved here—being shocked to realize for the first time that a whole day had passed without my leaving the island, and there was something splendid about it then, but now, there are times when I feel imprisoned. Manhattan. My heart grows light with the thought of it. It is another place. It will be another life. It will not be this life.

That was as far as I could take it, or as far as I cared to take it. Writing it, even that little bit of it, left me feeling guilty, because I felt that it was probably very close to the truth. I put it away and began making some revisions on the episode of *Dead Air* that I would read in the evening, and in the space of a sigh I was away from all the cares that had made me lie late in bed, brooding. I was no longer the assistant innkeeper at a failing hotel; I wasn't even there, in my workroom, sitting at my computer; I was in the past, my favorite place. Even though the piece of the past that I was exploring was pocked with treachery, shame, and danger, being there, following my former self around, invisible to him and everyone else, I was, if not happy, exactly, at least amused, particularly by the difference between what I saw and understood and what my younger self saw and understood, and by the thought that he would grow up to be me, and would at my age be sitting where I was sitting, amused by his earlier self. After a while, I leaned back and read from the screen, trying the sound of what I had written. I was pleased by it, and I was reminded why I prefer to write about the past. It is a place to go, another place, not this place. It is another life, not this life.

Only after I had turned the computer off and started downstairs did I become depressed by the thought that my childish self would grow up to be assistant innkeeper at a failing hotel, and his wife's jailer.

THAT NIGHT, however, I had my biggest audience so far. It was a Friday night, so we had a few extra people for dinner, beyond the hotel guests, and there were even a few people who in response to Albertine's advertising had come out in their own boats just to hear my reading. I was cheered by this show of support, and I think I did a good job with episode four of *Dead Air,* "Masters of the Arts."

AMONG MY TUTORS when I was a boy were three who almost certainly never thought of me as their pupil. They were a nondescript man who lived around the corner (or, perhaps, across the street, or on the next block), his wife, and a ventriloquist's dummy.

The dummy was Baldy, the host of "Baldy's Nightcap," a late-night show that was nonstop talk, a monologue, a seamless stream of reminiscences, thoughts, and feelings. He was a master of the art of frankness, of revelation, and I wanted to learn the trick of it. The man who lived around the corner, Roger Jerrold, was, I believed, a spy, but he kept it hidden behind a seamless front of conventional behavior. He was a master of the art of concealment, and I wanted to learn the trick of it.

Because the spy business required a lot of travel, Mr. Jerrold was rarely around. His wife was left alone for days and even weeks at a time. She was a pretty brunette with a trim figure, and I thought about her quite a lot, especially on rainy days.

On rainy days when Mr. Jerrold's car was not in the driveway, I would visit the Jerrolds' house, using the excuse that I wanted to play with the Jerrolds' son, Roger Junior, who was younger than I. Often I would play marbles with him indoors, within a ring of string that we laid out on the living room rug. If Mrs. Jerrold was passing when I bent over to take a shot, I could see some distance up her skirt, but the effort required to obtain this view affected my shooting, giving me a handicap that made my games with Junior closer than they would otherwise have been.

When I was in shooting position, I could also see under the living room sofa, and one rainy day I discovered a tape recorder under there. This was a surprise, because almost no one had a tape recorder in those days. They were specialized gear, little used by the general public but widely used, of course, by spies.

Mrs. Jerrold paused as she was passing and said, "That's quite a position you've twisted yourself into."

"I was—ah—looking under the sofa," I said.

"Oh, really? See anything interesting?"

"A tape recorder."

"A tape recorder?" She dropped to the floor and looked under the sofa. "What is *that* doing there?" she wondered aloud.

"Do you think I could try using it?" I asked.

"You can *have* it, for all I care," she said.

"Really?"

"Well, no, I guess not. It's Roger's. But I never see him using it, and it can't be getting much use under there, so I don't see why *you* shouldn't use it. Be my guest."

I slid it out from under the sofa. I opened one of the boxes that were stacked beside it and found a reel of brown recording tape. On a metal plate riveted to the lid of the recorder's case was a diagram showing how to fit the reel of tape onto a hub on the top of the recorder and thread the tape along a pathway from the full reel to an empty one on the other hub. I tried to duplicate what was shown on the plate, and eventually I got the tape threaded in a way that seemed almost right. I found a pair of earphones clipped into the top of the case, put them on, and plugged them in. I shifted the machine to "play," the reels turned, the tape began running, and somewhere along the tape's path the recorder worked the magic of playing sound, but that aspect of the machine—its essence, after all—was to me what technologists call a "black box," a device that we can appreciate for its product without understanding its process, its mystery. Ask a black box, "How do you do that?" and it answers with a silence that seems to say, "I do what I do, and you do not need to know the trick of it."

Through the earphones, I heard Mrs. Jerrold's voice.

"Oh, yes," she said, huskily. "Again. Again."

I listened to enough of the tape to conclude that Mrs. Jerrold had mastered the art of frankness to a degree that even Baldy the Dummy would have envied. More remarkable still was the fact that she had kept this talent of hers so completely hidden from me. She must have learned the art of concealment from her husband.

I wanted that tape. I had no qualms at all about taking it, and in an instant, as if no thought were required at all, I hatched a plan for getting out of the house with it. I said, suddenly, "Hey—I've got to go. I didn't realize how late it was."

I put my jacket on and zipped it up, as if I were in an awful hurry, as if there would be hell to pay if I didn't get home right away, and then, as if I had forgotten my responsibility to pack the tape recorder up and put it away but wouldn't shirk it, since I wasn't that kind of guy, I rewound the tape. When it was fully rewound, I put the empty reel into the box that the recorded reel had been in, closed the tape recorder and pushed it under the sofa, twisted myself into shooting position, and—half hidden under the sofa—shoved the reel of tape inside my jacket. I took it home with me, even though I didn't have a machine to play it on, because I knew that it was chock full of fascinating information, loaded with things that I wanted to learn.

THERE WAS APPLAUSE. It was Friday night, and the crowd—oh, let's call it a crowd even if it was a very small crowd—was in a Friday-night mood. Lou was kept busy behind the bar. He didn't know how to make very many drinks, but he was eager to learn, and he was happy to pay for any drink that his customers weren't satisfied with.

"You know," he said to one of those customers, a short brunette perched on a bar stool, "for me, a cocktail shaker is a kind of black box."

"A black box?" she said, knitting her brows and poking her lower lip out fetchingly.

"Yeah," said Lou. "Like a tape recorder. Like the tape recorder in the story Peter read?"

She looked at him and shrugged. "I guess I missed that part," she said.

"Yeah, I guess so," said Lou. "The point is that I don't really know how the thing works." He held the cocktail shaker up and looked at it as if it were a technologically sophisticated device. "I put in what I think is supposed to go in, shake it up, cross my fingers, and hope that what comes out is what you wanted." He shook the shaker, uncapped it, filled a cocktail glass, and set it in front of the dark-haired woman. "There you go," he said. "Maybe."

She took a taste of the drink and winced. "This was supposed to be a mai-tai," she said.

"Isn't it?" asked Lou.

"I don't think so," she said. "It tastes funny."

"Funny?"

"Funny peculiar."

"I guess my mai-tai isn't your cup of tea. That one's on me. The next one, too, if you'll give me another shot at it. You're not driving, are you?"

"We came by boat."

"Uh-huh. You know, I'm sorry that we don't have any of those little umbrellas. I think a mai-tai is supposed to have a little umbrella in it. I'll get some in for tomorrow night. You come by tomorrow, and I'll give you two umbrellas with every drink."

"I just might take you up on that."

"You know, if you don't have to go home with the guy what brung you—"

"My sister and her husband brought me."

"Then why not stay for the weekend? This is a great place for a weekend getaway, and we've got special rates during the readings."

She looked around, apparently appraising Small's as a place for a weekend getaway, then turned to Lou again and said, "There are going to be *more* readings?"

I decided to call it a night.

IN BED, after we had turned the lights out, found our comfortable positions, and had awaited sleep in silence for a while, Albertine asked me something that I didn't quite catch.

"Hm?" I said.

"Sorry. Were you asleep?"

"No," I said. "To tell you the truth, I was thinking about Mrs. Jerrold."

"Lucky you."

"Hm?"

"You get into bed and you go—away. I can't do that. I can't manage it. It's part of my problem. You use the past, or your version of the past, as a place to go. You use it to get away from here. I have no place to go to get away from here."

"Manhattan," I suggested.

"What?"

"Think about Manhattan."

"Manhattan," she said.

"Just try it."

Again we lay in our separate silences, but after a while Albertine asked, "Was there a Mrs. Jerrold in your life?"

"You're supposed to be thinking about Manhattan," I said.

"Was there a Mrs. Jerrold in your life?" she repeated.

"'In my life,'" I said. "What do you mean by that, exactly? Do you include my mental life, or do you merely mean my material life?"

"In this particular case, I want to know whether there was a Mrs. Jerrold in your material life. It is quite obvious that there was—that there is—a Mrs. Jerrold in your mental life."

"Well," I said, "there were certain ingredients that could be made into Mrs. Jerrold, that I have made into Mrs. Jerrold: a woman who lived across the street, another on the next block, and another around the corner, certain events that occurred to someone else entirely—a man, in fact—and many things that I discovered when I was investigating my memories of all of those people, following where my curiosity led me."

"I see," she said. She rolled over.

"Want to know where she lives now?"

"What?" She rolled back toward me.

She lives just around the corner or across the street or down the block in that part of a boy's mind where he keeps all the girls and women who are the objects of his desires—"

"A boy's mind?"

"Well—my mind."

"So you keep a little place around the corner—"

"Around the corner, across the street, down the block, in that shadowy part of my mind where all those ladies live, spending their days in lingerie, whiling away the hours, waiting for my nocturnal visits."

"And am I there when you go there?"

"Oh, yes, indeed, my darling. You are there in all your ages and stages, even the little you from before I met you, which took some doing, let me tell you."

"And are you there now, in that corner of your mind?"

"No. I'm here, talking to you."

"But couldn't you be talking to me there?"

"You mean—"

"Yeah."

Then she slid to my side of the bed and taught me how sweet life is when dreams come true.

A Case of the Family Illness

ALBERTINE generally spends an hour or so reading in bed after she wakes up, then gets out of bed, pulls her workout wear on, runs seven circuits of the island, lifts her weights, showers, eats a light breakfast (a banana and an English muffin, for example) in the dining room, takes her dishes to the kitchen and discusses the day's menu with Suki, and then carries her second mug of coffee to the reception desk. I gave her enough time to get through all of that and then came down the front stairs to the entrance hall, where I found her behind the reception desk, drinking her second mug of coffee and looking through the reservation book. The phone rang.

"Good morning," she said, hopefully. "Small's Hotel." She listened for a moment, then flipped a page of the reservation book and said, "Yes, I have you down for two cottages for two weeks, beginning— How many what? Jet skis? How many jet skis do we have? Let me check."

She held the phone at arm's length and shouted in my direction, "Peeeter! How many jet skis do we have now?"

"None!" I shouted back.

Into the phone, she said, "I just checked with my assistant, Mrs. Biddle, and I'm happy to be able to report that we don't have any of those damned jet skis. . . . Hmm? No, we have no plans to buy any jet skis in the foreseeable future. In fact, it's one of those over-my-dead-body situations. . . . Ah, I see. . . . Well, of course, how could the little darlings possibly enjoy a vacation without unlimited access to jet skis? Mrs. Biddle . . . Mrs. Biddle . . . I have a suggestion. Perhaps you and your family would be happier at someplace other than Small's Hotel. Oh, I agree. . . .

Of course! Enjoy!" She smiled the smile she smiles when she doesn't want her picture taken and tore a page from the reservation book.

"Al," I said, "I've been thinking about our selling the place, and I just want to ask you something."

"Ask me," she said without looking up from her work.

"Doesn't it bother you that we're going to be selling at a loss?"

"Not at all," she said. "Not at all." She put her pencil down, put her hand on her hip, and looked at me. "The way I see it, Peter, the possibility of our turning a profit on this place vanished years ago. By selling now, we're going to be cutting our losses. Every day we stay, we slide deeper into a hole. I'd like to see us scramble out while we can still get out. Before we disappear. Cut our losses. Cut and run. It's all we can hope for."

"What are we going to live on?"

"We'll get jobs, regular jobs."

"We will?"

"Yes, we will. Maybe."

THE TWO SURVIVING TINKERS showed up in the afternoon to take a look at the roof. Al and I gave them our condolences, and Al gave them each a hug.

"The memorial service will be Wednesday."

"We'll be there," said Al.

"Hey, we're not going to get this job done if we stand around here," said Marty, formerly the middle-sized tinker, now stepping uncomfortably into the shoes of the defunct big tinker. He and his little sidekick shouldered their tools and started off to look at the boiler. As I watched them walk away, I was suddenly struck by the fact that they had somehow made their way to the island without my ferrying them.

"Hey—how did you guys get out here?" I called after them.

"Your bartender brought us—Lou."

"Lou?"

"Yeah—we ran into him on the other side. We weren't going to come out until Monday, but he talked us into taking a look at things today. Oh—you know, you might want to give him a hand. He's down at the dock with quite a load of booze. Wouldn't let us help him. He's a fiend for work, that guy. I never saw anybody who likes his work so much. Except for—" He paused, removed his derby, and held it over his heart.

"—Big Tink." He put his hat back on. "Anyway, I think you might want to give Lou a hand."

I found Lou struggling up the path, trying to pull two of the red wagons, each of them overloaded with cartons.

"Let me take one of those," I said.

"Gladly!"

"You've been shopping."

"Yeah. I took the launch. Al said it was okay."

"If Al says it's okay, it's okay. It didn't sink, I take it."

"I kept it pumped dry, just the way you did when you brought us over the other day."

"Good for you. What are we hauling here? What is all this stuff?"

"I had to get a few things for the bar—"

"Things for the bar?"

"Yeah. Yeah, you were running low—but 'running low' is hardly the way to put it. I mean, you really didn't have any of the top-shelf brands in stock at all, and it doesn't look good to have nothing that *is* good, you know what I'm saying? You were down to Brand X and only the dregs of that."

"Well, things have been slow—"

"You've got to keep up appearances," he said, shaking his head. "Even if you don't move them, you want to make sure you've got a nice display of your cognacs, you know, a nice selection of sherries, your single-malt Scotches—"

"That's what you bought? You—how—? They gave you credit?"

"Huh? Oh. No. No, no, no. Nah, nah. I bought it."

"You paid for this? But what do we owe—?"

"Nothing. Forget it. You know, I enjoy extending a little hospitality, being behind the bar, talking to people, making their drinks. It's fun for me. Forget about it."

AFTER DINNER, in the lounge, Lou stood the entire crowd of eight to a round of drinks from our well-stocked bar, and I read episode five of *Dead Air*, "A Case of the Family Illness."

I SUFFER from a couple of forms of inherited mental illness that have been passed along on both sides of my family for generations.

We get the idea that we can do things that a moment's reflection ought to tell us we cannot, and we are easily sidetracked.

To give you just one example: once, when I was about twelve, I got the idea that I could build a tape recorder. I had come into possession of a recorded tape, but I had no means of playing it and didn't have enough money to buy a tape recorder, so I decided to build one. If this seems preposterous to you, you probably have a good grip on reality and are not related to me.

Not only did I suppose that I could build a tape recorder, but I expected to be able to build it out of common household junk. If that seems unlikely to you, then you have never come across a copy of *Impractical Craftsman* magazine. I think it is safe to say that this magazine has been responsible for more wasted hours of labor in the basement workshops of America than any other single cause.

I walked to the drug store to get the latest issue. It had just arrived, but the stock boy hadn't put it on the rack yet. Men with nothing better to do were lined up at the coffee counter, waiting, staring into their cups with the empty eyes of the desperately addicted. I took a stool at the end of the line and ordered a coffee fizz (a shot of coffee, a shot of cream, a glass full of seltzer). When the stock boy emerged from the stockroom with a bundle of magazines in his hands, the men rose and followed him. So did I.

"All right, all right, stand back," the boy said. He removed the last few dog-eared copies of last month's issue and began, slowly, putting this month's in its place.

The cover offered to show one how to "Build a Photo Enlarger from War Surplus Bomb Sight!"

I wasn't going to be sidetracked by that. I had already tried to go into the photography business, and once was enough. From a company that advertised in *Impractical Craftsman*, I had ordered a Deluxe Developing Kit and E-Z Darkroom Instructions. To give myself something to do while I was enduring the pain of waiting for the kit to arrive, and to recover its cost, I advertised myself as an expert in photographic services. I had a little printing set—actually a Little Giant printing set—from another enthusiasm, another ad. With it, I printed some flyers, and I distributed them throughout the neighborhood.

When the kit and instructions arrived, I set up a basement dark-room (omitted here are details concerning additional costs for materials not supplied in the kit and the expenditure of considerable labor, the need for which was never mentioned or even implied in the advertisement, unless I somehow misunderstood the meaning of "E-Z") and picked up a roll of film from my first customer, Mrs. Jerrold, who lived around the corner (or across the street or down the block).

I'm sure you have already guessed the outcome. I worked on her pictures for an afternoon, and then I gave up. I put the results, such as they were, into an envelope, walked to Mrs. Jerrold's house, and knocked on her back door.

"I have your pictures," I said when she opened it.

"Oh, good!" she said. "I can't wait to see them. There should be some nice shots from our vacation."

"Yeah, there probably were," I said.

"'Were'?"

"Not all of them came out."

"Oh."

"A couple of them came out."

"A couple?"

"And some of them came out partway."

"Oh."

"There was a really good one of you in a bathing suit," I said with genuine enthusiasm.

"'Was'?"

"Yeah. I was trying to get it just perfect, you know, really perfect, but at first it was sort of too light, and then it was still too light, and then it was a little too dark, and then it was black."

"Oh," she said. I could see her disappointment in the furrows that formed on her forehead and the way she pouted her lips. For a moment I thought she might cry. I felt awful.

"It's all my fault," I said.

"Don't be silly," she said, tousling my hair and trying to assume the air of a woman who considers the self-esteem of an adolescent boy who has a crush on her far more important than mementoes of the only family vacation she will take all year. "I'm a *terrible* photographer. *Most* of my pictures don't come out. I'm sure you did the best you could, the best *anybody* could, and besides, *everybody* makes mistakes."

"Yeah," I said.

"How much do I owe you?"

"Oh—no charge."

"I must owe you something."

"No, no. We only charge if the whole roll comes out. That's our policy."

I closed up shop. From then on, I entrusted all my developing-and-printing work to Himmelfarb's photography shop, in the heart of downtown Babbington.

The equipment remained in the basement, but it began a shuffle toward the farthest corner. All the equipment abandoned in the cellar—the gear for my mother's failed projects, my father's failed projects, and my failed projects—shuffled miserably, humiliated, under pressure from the equipment required by our new projects, into the corners, where it accreted in heaps.

There were no plans for a tape recorder in *Impractical Craftsman* or the other do-it-yourself magazines. For a moment I was tempted by the idea of building the enlarger, since I knew that we had a surplus bomb sight in the cellar left over from my father's attempt to build a theodolite and make big money in surveying, but *Cellar Scientist* magazine had plans for a flying-saucer detector, and I decided to build that instead.

AS SOON AS we were under the covers, Albertine said, "The boiler is on its last legs."

"What happened to 'Good night, my darling, I love you a zillion'?" I asked.

"It's the scale."

"Okay, a billion. I can understand that we've got to cut back—"

"The scale in the boiler."

"The tinkers have been saying that for fifteen years."

"And they've been right for fifteen years."

"Will it keep limping along until the place is sold?"

"Who knows? That scale keeps building up, so we're actually putting a lot of our money into heating the scale rather than making steam, and the pressure keeps creeping up because we have to push the steam through these pipes that are being progressively narrowed by scale—"

"High boiler pressure, the silent killer."

"It's like the accumulation of cholesterol plaque in atherosclerosis—"

"So we could suffer a boiler attack."

"Kaboom."

"Aye, yi, yi."

"And the roof really needs to be completely reshingled—"

"Good night, my darling," I said. "I love you a zillion."

Flying Saucers: The Untold Story

When one tells a story, there has to be someone to listen; and if the story runs to any length, it is rare for the storyteller not sometimes to be interrupted by his listener. That is why (if you were wondering) in the story which you are about to read . . . I have introduced a personage who plays as it were the role of listener. I will begin.

Denis Diderot, "This Is Not a Story"

EARLY IN THE MORNING, I ferried our three guests back to the mainland. Dick and Jane sat in the bow with their arms around each other for the whole trip. They had told Albertine, while they were checking out, that their stay at Small's had "really meant something," and they had made a reservation for a week's stay at the end of October, so that they could hear the last of my readings. I was flattered when Albertine told me that, and I wanted to tell Dick and Jane that I was pleased and flattered, but now, I could see, they wanted to be alone. We must give the ends of things their due, even things as familiar as weekends, even the end of a day, or else there is no rhythm to our lives.

"You should be flattered," said Lou, nudging me and whispering.

"What?" I said.

Lou nodded toward Dick and Jane. "They're experiencing the sense of loss that we feel at the end of a piece of life that we can identify as a piece."

"I know what you mean."

"They'll remember their weekend with you, as a piece of life apart from the other pieces."

"'Honey,'" I said in a fair-to-good imitation of Jane's voice, "'remember that weekend we spent at that little hotel with the leaking roof and the moribund boiler? What a dump! What was the name of that place again?'"

Lou laughed as if I had said something funny.

At the dock, when all of us made our good-byes, Lou said, "See you later, buddy," which I took to mean "Good-bye forever, shithead."

LATER IN THE MORNING, Albertine and I waited at the dock for the arrival of one of the realtors who had toured the island a couple of days earlier, Liza, who was bringing a prospective buyer. Liza and her client made the crossing in what looked like a duck blind with an outboard motor on it. The hull was painted olive drab with splotches of black, brown, and beige, in the style of army camouflage. The cabin was thatched with reeds. As the boat approached, I found myself sidling up to our launch, placing a possessive hand on it, and standing a little taller. My heart swelled with pride. I was the owner of the better boat.

The prospective buyer, Mr. Fillmore, was a small man dressed in a mechanic's jumpsuit. To my eye, and I admit that I do not have the trained eye of an experienced realtor, Mr. Fillmore didn't look as if he could raise the cash to buy Small's, but Liza seemed to regard him as a hot prospect. "Mr. Fillmore represents a group that is very interested in acquiring a property like yours," she said when she introduced him, and then, raising herself on her toes, she winked at Albertine and me over Mr. Fillmore's buzz-cut head. I wasn't sure whether she meant the wink to mean that he was a wealthy eccentric or just a poor deluded sucker.

"Thinking of going into the hotel business, are you, Mr. Fillmore?" I asked chummily, as one poor deluded sucker to another.

He glared at me, much the way Spike had glared at Matthew when she had accused him of insulting her mother.

"Mr. Fillmore and his people are thinking of turning the island into a training facility," Liza said brightly.

"Oh?" said Al.

Mr. Fillmore snapped his head in her direction and said, "Do you know that ninety-nine percent of Americans are untrained?"

"I didn't," said Al, "but I guess I could have guessed—"

"We're sitting on a time bomb," said Fillmore, and he cracked his knuckles.

"I see what you mean," I said, lying. "An untrained citizenry—"

Mr. Fillmore ignored me. He began striding off the dock and onto the island, waving his hands and sketching his plans in the air. "This could work," he said. "We drop you here by night. Parachute."

"Parachute," I said. "Of course."

"Your mission: penetrate the redoubt—"

"The redoubt?" I asked.

"The hotel," Liza explained with a smile.

"—and terminate all targeted personnel," said Mr. Fillmore. He stopped and stood with his hands on his hips, looking up at the hotel, where, to judge from the expression on his face, no targeted personnel had been left standing.

"I take it you won't be training people to flip burgers," said Al.

"Or you have your alternate scenario—" Mr. Fillmore went on.

"Can't wait," I said.

"You're chained to the wall of the dungeon below the redoubt—"

"Whoops," I said, frowning and shaking my head. "I'm afraid the old redoubt hasn't got a dungeon."

"That will be taken care of," said Mr. Fillmore confidently.

"Sure," I said. "Of course. Why not?"

"Your mission: escape from the dungeon, and then terminate all targeted personnel."

"Ah! I detect a pattern," I said.

"I want to do a little more recon," said Mr. Fillmore, looking each of us in the eye in turn. "Any problem with that?"

"No, no," said Albertine. "You go right ahead and do all the recon you want."

"Are there any special features you'd like me to point out to Mr. Fillmore?" Liza asked enthusiastically.

"Let's see," I said. "There's the old mine field out in that area somewhere." I swept my hand vaguely in the direction of the center of the island. "But you'll probably find it on your own, an old hand like you."

"Let's move out."

"Oh!" I said, snapping my fingers. "One more thing. Did I mention that the boiler might blow up at any time?"

ALBERTINE and I had the dining room to ourselves that night. After dinner, I built a fire in the lounge, poured the last of the cognac for us, and began reading the sixth episode of *Dead Air,* "Flying Saucers: The Untold Story," to an audience of one.

> DUDLEY BEAKER was a fussy, educated man who lived next door to my maternal grandparents. Encouraged by my mother and tolerated by my father, he took an interest in my development. He never missed an opportunity to correct my course . . .

LOU burst through the door, beaming, pulling mittens from his hands, and said, "What's this? You started without me?"

"Lou!" said Albertine, clearly pleased to see him.

"What are you doing here?" I asked.

"I couldn't stand to miss a single thrilling episode," he said.

"A single—what—do you mean—?" sputtered Al.

"If you've got a room available, I want to sign on for the whole tour."

"Gee, I'll have to check."

"Actually, I'm going to need *two* rooms for the next few days," said Lou. He turned toward the doorway and called, "Honey?"

A woman came into the lounge. She was bundled in an enormous insulated jacket that might have served for an assault on Everest, and she wore a fur hat, but her long and stunning legs were virtually unprotected. "He kidnapped me," she said, laughing.

"Get near the fire," Lou told her. "I'll fix you a hot toddy, or a Tom and Jerry—or how about a hot buttered rum?"

"How about a hot cup of coffee?"

"Good. I don't know how to make any of those other things."

"I'm Elaine," she said. "The impulsive old geezer behind the bar is my father."

"Jeez, I'm sorry," said Lou. "Where are my manners? Elaine—Albertine. Albertine—Elaine. Elaine—Peter. Peter—Elaine."

"We interrupted you," she said to me.

"Oh, that's—" I began.

"No, no," said Lou, flapping his hands. "Go on. Go on."

So I did, beginning again at the beginning.

> DUDLEY BEAKER was a fussy, educated man who lived next door to my maternal grandparents. Encouraged by my mother and tolerated by my father, he took an interest in my development. He

never missed an opportunity to correct my course, and I came to loathe him for that. I kept my loathing to myself, lest he discover it and correct the tendency, but it was bound to come out someday, and, under the influence of flying saucers, it did.

Flying saucers were a craze when I was a boy, but I couldn't make myself believe in them. I tried. I *wanted* to believe in them. I understood that it would be fun to believe in them. I followed the reports of spottings and tried to swallow them, but it wasn't easy. The photographs were especially hard to accept. I kept seeing flying hubcaps, pie pans, and Jell-O molds instead of saucers.

One of the magazines devoted an entire issue to "Flying Saucers: The Untold Story." It began with a summary of saucer sightings from earliest times to the present and ended with plans for a saucer detector. I built a detector, but only for the sake of scientific inquiry. I didn't expect it to detect anything. I was a skeptic and a realist.

When I finished the detector, I was proud of my work, of course, and, full of enthusiasm, I brought it up from the cellar to show it to my parents. I brought the magazine, too, so that they could see how well I had reproduced the detector pictured there, which had been built by professionals who had at their disposal professional-grade tools, a fully equipped workshop, and a staff of assistants.

Dudley Beaker was visiting when I came up from the cellar. He and my parents looked the detector over, and I explained what it was supposed to do. My parents admired it, as parents will. They praised my effort and execution, just as they would have if I had made a painting, written a novel, or cleaned my room.

Mr. Beaker, however, took it upon himself to go further. He had to consider the worthiness of the underlying goal. "I'm beginning to think that the human race will never grow up," he said.

"Huh?" I said.

"People still have a need to *believe* in things."

"Yeah, I guess so," I said.

"They won't accept ideas based on logic and evidence—"

"Like what, Dudley?" asked my mother.

He said, "Oh, quantum physics or evolution, for example, or the dignity of labor—"

"I worked pretty hard on this," I said.

Ignoring me, he continued: "—but quite a lot of them do *believe* in God, and astrology, and flying saucers."

"One of the articles traced saucer sightings back to prehistoric times," I said.

"Stop and think a minute," said Dudley. "If there were sightings in prehistoric times, how could we know about them?"

"Well—"

"Do you know what *prehistoric* means?"

"Yeah," I said, "'before recorded history'—"

"Yes, and—"

"—but *you* know that's not accurate."

"—and—but—what?" he spluttered.

Having made a start, I plunged on, and to my surprise, I discovered as I spoke that I knew more than I realized, that in reading about flying saucers I had actually picked up something that might be true. "It would be accurate to say 'preliterate,'" I said, "but it isn't accurate to say 'prehistoric,' because they recorded history."

"Oh? And how did they do that?" he asked.

"Cave paintings," I said.

"Really?" said my mother. "That's *fascinating*. They kept their history in cave paintings? Why did they paint in caves?"

"Well, they *lived* in caves," I said, guessing. "And caves are a safe place to work, where the painters wouldn't be interrupted by saber-toothed tigers, and other people wouldn't be *criticizing* them all the time."

"Are there flying saucers in these paintings?" asked my father.

"You can judge for yourself," I said. I flipped the magazine open to the cave paintings.

Mr. Beaker took one look, shook his head, chuckled, and said, "You know, flying saucers are presumed to be ships from other worlds, and in a sense this is true, since most of them come from—" He paused and took his pipe from his pocket, and then finished with a sneer in his voice: "—the world of the imagination."

Dudley would have called himself a realist, and he would have been proud to claim the title, but I think that he was a realist only by default, because he was a person who had come to mistrust and even fear his imagination. He had become one of those people who prefer the examined life to the imagined one, who disparage that alternative world where I live so much of the time, the world in which survivors of prisons and concentration camps dwell while they endure their trials because it is a place where they can keep self-respect alive, and thought, and will, and hope. Mr. Beaker had driven me there. When I had looked at the cave paintings earlier I hadn't been able to see *anything* that looked like a flying saucer, but *now* I could, because now, inspired by a desire to annoy Dudley Beaker, I *believed*.

MY LITTLE AUDIENCE was receptive, even appreciative, and my heart was warmed by their attention. We talked for a while. Lou explained to Elaine several times that she didn't have to be concerned about having missed the earlier episodes. Albertine did a hilarious impression of Mr. Fillmore. Elaine laughed radiantly and crossed and recrossed her legs, but when she told us that she worked in public relations there was something about the way she smoothed her skirt and clasped her hands on her knee that made me think that, perhaps, she was not being quite honest. I think we all wanted to stay up late, talking and drinking till dawn, but suddenly we discovered that we were tired, and so, like grown-ups, we went to bed.

I LAY IN THE DARK feeling miserable. I twisted this way. I twisted that way.

"Okay, what is it?" asked Al.

"I'm not happy," I said.

"You'd be happier if you were asleep."

"I've been lying here telling myself that I ought to be happy, that there is no insurmountable reason for me not to be happy. I have told myself that I owe it to *you* to be happy, so that you can be happy—"

"I'd be happy if you were asleep."

"—but everything seems to block the *way* to my happiness, all the mistakes I've made in life—all the disappointments—there they are, heaped upon the road ahead of me like the sand that the surging tide dumps on a shore road in a storm. Shoveling it all away seems much too much for me to do now, so late in life, with so much sand on the road, so much sand in the bottom of the hourglass. I can't get to my future. The sands of error and disappointment block the way."

"Why don't you jot that thought down and go to sleep?"

"That's not quite right," I continued. "It's more like having blundered into a swamp, lost my way. It's hot, steamy. The heat is debilitating, enervating. A swarm of tiny mistakes envelopes my head like a cloud. In constant motion, they hum around me. I flap my hands, wave them away, but there are too many for me to dispel. Disappointments—enormous beetles the size of rats—click and clatter around my feet, biting my ankles and heels with their pincers. I'll never get out of this swamp, never walk in the sun again."

She seemed to be asleep.

I tried to lie still and work on the swamp metaphor. I had the feeling that I was on to something. I began cataloging the mistakes in the maddening swarm, the mistakes—*my* mistakes—that had led me into the swamp. First, and worst, my decision to buy the hotel. It now seemed wrong on all counts. We had wasted years in hard work on endless tasks, and when we added it all up, as Albertine was forced to do every day, it came to nothing. Less than nothing. I had imagined that our work and our profits would buy the hotel for us. I had imagined our growing old here, living in our rooms on the top floor for as long as we continued to run the hotel and then retiring to one of the little cottages at the water's edge as permanent guests. I had supposed that I would go on writing the Larry Peters books, my little stories for boys and girls my age, and they would bring the money we would need. Another mistake: by refusing to introduce blood, gore, mayhem, and misery into the Larry Peters series, I had lost it.

I—I—I! I suddenly realized that I had been using the wrong metaphors, the wrong metaphors entirely, and they had blinded me to the truth. The buzzing swarm, the grains of sand—*wrong*. They didn't describe the problem. Suddenly I *saw* the problem, saw it clearly, as if a gust of wind had cleared the air, blown the buzzing swarm and heaps of sand away. It stood in front of me like a fat man in a narrow hallway. No, no—like a fat man in a tunnel. Yes. A fat man blocking our way out of a cave. Blocking our escape from the dank and dripping cave of our unhappiness, blocking the way to the light, to hope, to a future.

I began to feel better. I wasn't happy, but I felt better. At least I knew who was to blame. The man in the way. Me.

Disturbing the Field

AT MY USUAL EARLY HOUR I sat at the computer to do some work on the passage that I would be reading in the evening, but it was Albertine who wrote:

> Twenty-one years in the hotel business, and what have I got to show for it? Nothing. Nothing at all. Less than nothing, since we're in debt beyond our eyeballs. Once I had hopes for this place, and Peter certainly had his dreams. Together we made our plans and hatched our schemes, but little by little it has all slipped away. Now there's nothing. Nothing but emptiness and exhaustion.
>
> I thought that I would have made this place into something by now. It would be chugging along and it would bring us a reliable income. I thought we would be comfortable now, but we are not comfortable at all. We are both anxious and unhappy, and I am disappointed and angry.
>
> He has a place to go, his past. He can get away from here, and does, for a while every day, but I'm here all the time. It's a prison. It's a nightmare. I am *isolated,* and if I can't sell this hotel I'm stuck here. Stuck here.
>
> Lately, though, I've been thinking about Manhattan. In Manhattan I can get a job. I can get a job, and I'll be in the world. What job can I get? I haven't done anything but run this place, if you don't count the jobs I had as a teenager. I have this idea, that I could teach a course on how to run an inn, a small hotel. Okay, even I laugh at the thought of it, but it's not as ridiculous as it

sounds. I think I would call it "How to Run a Small Hotel" or "How Not to Run a Small Hotel" or "How to Run a Small Hotel into the Ground" or "Do As I Say, Not As I Did." Maybe it could be a continuing education course. It *has* been a continuing education course.

IN THE AFTERNOON, I walked up to Albertine at the desk and said, "Let me take you away from all of this, at least for the afternoon." She protested, pleading work, but I pointed out that with only two guests staying at the hotel, this was the perfect opportunity to refresh ourselves before the hordes arrived for the weekend. I took her by the hand and led her to the dock, and I thought I could feel her spirits lighten as we approached it. I pumped the launch, she started it up, I cast us off, and with Albertine at the wheel we escaped the confines of Small's Island. She was smiling all the way across the bay.

We drove the Small's van to Foggy Cove and spent a couple of hours just walking around. We came upon a little Victorian house undergoing renovation, and we daydreamed a bit about getting enough for the hotel so that we could buy the little house outright. Albertine guessed that our living expenses would be tiny. We could relax.

We ate dinner at the Foggy Cove Inn. They had sent me a coupon for a free meal. It was supposed to be good only during the week of my birthday, but I lied and no one questioned me.

We drove back to Babbington, I pumped the launch nearly dry, and we were back at the hotel in time for me to read episode seven of *Dead Air,* "Disturbing the Field," as advertised.

WHEN I WAS A BOY, there was quite a lot of interest in flying saucers. This was the popular name given to unidentified flying objects that were supposed to be the ships of voyagers from other worlds. Though they were called saucers, they resembled hubcaps. There was also quite a lot of interest in hubcaps at that time. (Since then, interest in flying saucers, inhabitants of other worlds, and hubcaps has declined. Today, it is limited to isolated groups of fanatics. Things change.)

I make no claim to having been immune to these popular enthusiasms, will deny neither the modest collection of hubcaps that

I'd accumulated nor the flying-saucer detector that I built from plans in *Cellar Scientist* magazine.

The detector was a simple device: just a few pieces of wire, a compass needle, a battery, and a bulb. The plans included two diagrams: a "pictorial" and a "schematic." Here is the pictorial, drawn from memory:

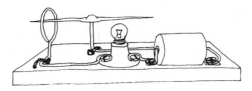

Here is the schematic, also drawn from memory:

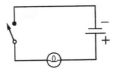

You see the difference. The pictorial depicts the thing as we would see it if it were assembled by a professional using the highest-quality components, but the schematic is a depiction of the essence of the thing; instead of showing the *thing,* it shows the *point* of the thing, its function and meaning, the *ding an sich.* The pictorial is an attempt to represent the object, but the schematic is an attempt to represent the ideal underlying the object. All the electrical projects I built in my boyhood career as a builder of electrical projects included in their instructions both types of diagram: one for the realists and one for the idealists, the dreamers.

Was it the realists or the dreamers who were most expected to expect the detector to work? I'm not sure. I know that I never really expected it to work at all. I tried not to expect *any* of my projects to work; it kept the level of disappointment down.

In order to expect it to work, I would have had to assume that as a flying saucer passed overhead its engine (highly advanced, of course, and employing a source of power unknown on earth) would cause a local disturbance in the magnetic field, which would make a compass needle swing aside from its normal north-south orientation, and when the detector was finished, a remarkable phenomenon occurred: I bought that underlying assumption. I was proud of my work; because I was proud of my work I wanted to feel that it was work worth doing; because I wanted to feel that it was worth doing, I had to accept its conceptual underpinnings; so, I did.

When one accepts something like that, one does not want to be alone with one's beliefs, feeling like a solitary deluded dreamer, so one seeks another who can be persuaded to accept the same beliefs. I turned to Porky White, who ran a clam bar in the older part of town, near the bay.

I climbed onto a stool at the counter and set the detector in front of me.

"Nice work," said Porky. "What is it?"

"It's a flying-saucer detector," I said.

"How does it work?"

"Well, first I have to get it aligned." I rotated the base until the needle was steady within the ring of wire. "There. Now, if a flying saucer passes by, it will disturb the magnetic field—"

I paused. If Porky was going to object, if he was going to refuse to accept the underlying assumption, if he was going to say that my detector rested on a base of preposterous delusions, this was the point at which he would do it.

He folded his arms across his chest and nodded his head and said, "Because of the anti-gravity drive, I suppose."

"Right," I said, without, I think, betraying my relief. "The needle will swing and touch the wire, the current will flow, and the bulb will light."

We both looked at the detector for a while. Nothing happened.

"How do you know it's working?" he asked.

"Well, there are two tests," I explained. I took a magnet from my pocket. "This is the positive test," I said, and I passed the magnet over the detector. The needle swung, and the lamp lit.

"Wow," said Porky.

I put the magnet away. The needle settled down and aligned itself north-to-south, resting in the center of the wire circle, with the lamp unlit.

I said, "This is the negative test."

"Oh. I get it," said Porky. He came around the end of the counter, walked across the room, stuck his head outside and scanned the sky. "Amazing!" he shouted. "Not a saucer in sight!"

LYING IN BED that night, awake, I found that I was *afraid* of moving to Foggy Cove. In my sleepy mind, I heard myself asking myself, "Is that all it will add up to, a little house on a side street in Foggy Cove? You won't have come anywhere from a tract house in Babbington."

"Try to lie still and go to sleep," said Albertine.

"Sorry," I said. "I will try."

"Think about Manhattan."

"What makes you say that?"

"It's what you told me the other night."

"Oh. Yeah. I forgot. Albertine?"

"Mm?"

"Do you keep a diary or anything?"

"I keep the log. You know, my log of what happens here at the hotel. You know that."

"Sure, but I mean something private. Your private thoughts."

"No. Why do you ask?"

"Just wondered," I said. "Good night. I love you."

"I love you," she said.

For a long while I thought about Manhattan.

Kap'n Klam, the Home of Happy Diners, the House of Hopes and Dreams

Have it your way.

The world is ugly,
And the people are sad.
  Wallace Stevens, "Gubbinal"

I TOOK MY COFFEE to my workroom and shut the door. Standing at the window, I reread the letter from Preston and Douglas announcing the cancellation of the Larry Peters series. As I read, I had the oddest sensation that all the characters in the series, with whom I had become so familiar, were in their rooms in the big old Peters family house on Kittiwake Island, packing their bags, getting ready to leave, to go their separate ways, to part from one another forever. I would miss them. At the same time, though, I was disappointed in them. They had let me down. I had imagined that the Larry Peters books would go on forever, and I had expected Larry to provide a comfortable old age for Albertine and me. He was supposed to be our retirement fund.

  I let myself wallow in my misery for a while, and then I went for a long walk, round and round the rim of the island, walking in the shallow water, in my bare feet. The bay was still warm, as warm as summer, though there was a chill in the morning air. By the end of my walk, I had begun to hope again. Maybe the decision to cancel the series wasn't irreversible. Maybe Preston and Douglas were just testing me. At our last meeting, when they had told me that they wanted to see the series "move in a new direction," that they wanted "a touch of evil," I had risen to my feet and said, dramatically, perhaps a touch too dramatically, my voice quaking, my hands shaking, "I remember a day long ago, when I was a child in a high chair gumming a piece of zwieback—"

"Peter," said Preston, "this is neither the time nor the place for an extended reminiscence—"

"Damn it, Preston," I said, striking my fist on the table, "hear me out!"

He shrugged and folded his arms across his chest and, to his credit, heard me out.

"A neighbor, a fussy, educated man named Dudley Beaker, was visiting, and he was talking to my mother, talking about me, without making any attempt to disguise what he was saying because he thought that I was too young to understand, and he told her—I'll never forget it—that childhood is like a moment on a mountaintop in the sun, or maybe he said a moment in the sunshine on a mountaintop, before we descend into the vale of tears, or maybe it was the valley of death. Well, I will not shove the kids who read my books off that mountaintop. The world will do that to them soon enough. It doesn't need *my* help. I won't do it."

I said that, and I meant it. I seem to recall that I pounded my fist on the table a second time.

Douglas got up and came around the table and put a fatherly hand on my shoulder. "You've got your principles, Peter, and we all admire that. What you don't have is much of an audience. The kids are drifting away. If you want them back, you've got to get some action in—"

"You don't mean action, you mean violence. You mean that I've got to start having people beaten up. Battered. Slashed. Hacked. Murdered. You want to see blood. You want to see rape, pillage, horror, and bleeding body parts—"

"Peter, *we* don't want any of that," said Preston. "It's the audience—"

"All *we* want is a series of books that will deliver a sizable audience," said Douglas, "and if it takes a little action—"

"Violence," I said.

"All right, *violence,* damn it! If the kids want violence—"

"—then they'll have to get it from another writer," I said, and I got up and left.

I admit that it must have sounded like a firm, unalterable position at the time, but maybe it wasn't too late to recant. Maybe it wasn't too late for me to capitulate. Maybe it wasn't too late for me to start giving them what they wanted.

I called. I asked for Preston, but I got Douglas. "Sandy," I said, "listen—I was just wondering—is it too late for me to agree to a little murder and mayhem? I've been thinking it over, and I think I've come up with some great ideas for death by amputation, evisceration, immolation, starvation, decapitation, defenestration—in other words, I think I've got some great ideas for capitulation. What I was wondering is, would you be willing to revive the series if I killed somebody in each book?"

"Listen, Peter," he said. "I'm sorry, but it's just not possible to resurrect the series. It's laid to rest, behind us. We're really putting all our efforts into something new here now, night sweats."

"What?"

"The Night Sweats series. Each book puts the readers in a situation of confronting their worst nightmares, but in everyday life."

"Kids?"

"Kids, sure. We've got—let's see—a kid who gets raped by his father, a kid who's enslaved by a retired geezer who lives next door, a kid who ingests the seed pods of alien beings that sprout inside her and grow out of her orifices, stuff like that. Scary stuff. It's showing a *lot* of promise. The focus group response has been *just terrific*. Scares the shit out of the little bastards, but they eat it up, you know what I mean? We've sold the screen rights to two of the books on plot outlines *alone*. It's something that I—that frankly I wish I could have gotten you in on, Peter—but—ah—you made yourself pretty clear about being, let's say, against all that."

"Yeah," I muttered. "I did. I am."

"But the kids *love* it. I mean you could say this is kid-driven. We try the plots out on them and basically they keep saying, 'Gimme more! Scare me more! Make me puke!' It's great!"

"Terrific," I said.

"Hey, got to go," he said. "Good to hear from you. Stay in touch."

"You bet," I said.

I TRIED NOT TO BE GLOOMY during dinner, and I think I succeeded, but by reading time I was exhausted. I felt old, finished. Everything had come to nothing, that was the feeling. There was just nothing. I had nothing, and there was nothing to look forward to. Whatever I had had, or done, or been had slipped away. I had nothing. I was nothing. I began the eighth episode of *Dead Air,* "Kap'n Klam, the Home of Happy Diners, the House of Hopes and Dreams," without much enthusiasm.

THE FIRST INVESTMENT I ever made was in Captain White's Clam Bar, the original of the Kap'n Klam chain of bivalve-based fast-food restaurants that now blanket the globe. (It was, alas, too small an investment to allow me to give my wife, Albertine, the gift she desires more than any luxury: freedom from the hand-wringing anxiety she feels when the bills come in.) That first clam bar had four booths, four tables, and a counter with six stools. There was little to distinguish it from any other clam bar except its proprietor, Porky White. At that time, I was pushing thirteen and Porky was pushing thirty, and the clam bar was not exactly a success, but Porky was tireless in his efforts to make it so.

"Maybe it's the name," he said to me one day, out of the blue, when he was bent over a cup of coffee and we were the only people in the place.

"The name?" I said.

"Yeah," he said morosely. "Maybe we'd get more people if we changed the name."

"You could call it a café," I said. "Captain White's Clam Café."

"It's the 'Captain White's' part I was thinking about," he said. "It's not right."

"Why not?"

"Well, you know, in the morning, I get a coffee-and-buttered-roll crowd here—"

"A crowd?"

"A small crowd. A few guys. And being located where I am here, near the docks, a lot of those guys are baymen, clammies."

"Uh-huh," I said.

"Well, to them, a captain is the skipper of a clam *boat,* not the skipper of a clam *bar.*"

"But you're the captain of this enterprise, so you're entitled to the title."

"You and I may know that," he said, "but they do not agree. It's not that they *say* anything to me about it, but there's something in their looks, and something about the way they stop talking when I come by to pour the coffee, and besides, it's too dull. Captain White's. Blah. You know, it's just So-and-So's Clam Bar. We've got to have a name that stands out, a name like nobody else's. Something distinctive."

"There's probably no other clam bar called So-and-So's."

"Be serious. This is important."

"Okay."

"The Home of Happy Diners."

"Wishful thinking," I said. "You might as well call it The House of Hopes and Dreams."

The clam bar was called The Home of Happy Diners for a week. It did not fill with happy diners. Porky tried The House of Hopes and Dreams. Our hopes and dreams were not fulfilled. He tried Porky's Clam Café, The Golden Clam, The Happy Clam, The Clam Shack, The Half Shell, Distinctive Clams, Porky's Folly, and So-and-So's. None of the name changes attracted a crowd, but they kept Porky busy repainting the sign above the door.

Finally, one afternoon, he said to me, "I have got it. I have really got it. I *know* the name, the right name."

"You do?"

"Yep. It's been in my mind for weeks, but I wasn't sure about it. I had to try those other names first, see how they would work."

"So this was all part of a plan?"

"Sure. Like a field test."

"You didn't let *me* in on it."

"Yeah, well, I am the captain of this enterprise, you know."

"Sure, okay. What's the name?"

"Kap'n Klam's Klam Kar."

"Hm," I said. "Who's Captain Clam?"

"*Kap'n* Klam. You've got to slur it like that. That's the way the clammies say it. And look. Look at this." He wrote the name on a napkin. "See? Those *K*'s? Distinctive."

"Okay, but—"

"But?"

"Who's Kap'n Klam?"

"Nobody. That's the beauty of it. He's not a fake because he's not real."

"Makes sense, but—why 'Kar'?"

"We're going to rework the outside of the place to make it look like a railroad dining car—and then inside we'll—"

"That would be kind of expensive," I said, speaking as an investor in the enterprise.

"I knew you'd say that," he said. "Okay, how about Kap'n Klam's Klams? No kar."

"Why don't you just call it Kap'n Klam?" I said. "You don't need to say 'klam' twice, because what else would Kap'n Klam sell?" There it was. We looked at each other and burst out laughing, because we knew that Kap'n Klam would sell clams, *really* sell clams.

Today, thanks to massive advertising, Kap'n Klam is a household word, but it's not the name that Porky and I use. He calls the outfit The Home of Happy Diners, and I call it The House of Hopes and Dreams.

"MAYBE you should change the name of the hotel," Lou suggested. "Might attract a buyer."

"How about 'Heartbreak Hotel'?" I suggested.

"Ooops," said Lou. He busied himself with polishing a glass.

"Time for bed," said Albertine, and she led me upstairs.

"LET'S OFFER A BONUS," she said when we were in bed, "payable to the individual realtor who sells the place. Maybe it will get them to start bringing more people out here."

"It's only been five days," I said, "and they've already brought one nutcase out to look at it."

She gave me a look. "The realtors like to say that it only takes one person, the right one, but if they're not bringing lots of people out here we're never going to see the right one, the one who is fool enough to actually buy the place."

"Sure," I said. "Why not? Offer a bonus."

I didn't mention the fact that in five days I had learned to look at the hotel with the eyes of a potential buyer. When it first went on the market it looked quite good to me; I thought that I could see the work we had put into it, the money we had poured into it, the years of effort. Now it looked like an old wreck in need of paint—shabby, tired, and weatherbeaten— and I was beginning to feel that no one would be fool enough to buy it.

BALDY SAID, "Time for another entry in the Catalog of Human Misery, don't you think, Bob?"

"Yeah."

"Here's one. You're sitting at the kitchen table waiting for your son to come home for dinner. Got the picture, Bob?"

"Yeah."

"Instead, there is a knock at the door. It's the cops. You know what's coming, don't you, Bob?"

"Yeah."

"You're right. Your son and four of his friends walked into a store—a convenience store, a bodega, a deli, any kind of store will do, right, Bob?

"Yeah."

"Doesn't matter what kind of store—and after they walked in they couldn't think of anything better to do, so they decided to throw a scare into the owner, a person of a different race. Any race will do, as long as it's a different race, right, Bob?"

"Yeah."

"They knew how to scare a shopkeeper, because they'd seen how it's done. They'd seen it on TV, and they'd seen it in the movies. Be a gangster, be a tough, be a killer. Talk the talk. Walk the walk. Exhibit the attitude. They were only acting, just playing a part, but *damn,* they were *good* at it. They were so good at it that the shopkeeper pulled his gun from under the counter and shot your son dead. That's entertainment!"

There was a long pause, and then he said, "Good night, boys and girls. Stay in the cave. It sucks outside, and the rain it raineth every day."

September 18
The Wall of Happy Diners

THIS WAS THE DAY of the funeral of the Big Tinker. The morning was gray, as it ought to be for a funeral. Clouds lay heavy over Babbington across the bay, lowering clouds, the dense livid ones that oppress, that make it seem that the heavens are collapsing on us, slowly, pressing us for an answer. Everything was still, dead. Lou and Elaine rode across the bay with us. Elaine had to catch a train to the city, but Lou had said that he wanted to come to the funeral. The bay was flat, barely rippling. The one catboat that we still had riding at its mooring was not even rocking, just lying there immobile and upright.

At the church, people stood awkwardly outside, in groups, heads down, mumbling. The leaves were turning. In the still air, the autumn leaves drooped from the branches, exhausted, but hanging on.

There were three great surprises at the funeral.

First, there was the Big Tinker's family. They were half a dozen large but handsome people—his wife, his brother, two daughters, and a son—sober, but not sad. When the eldest child, a daughter, gave the eulogy, she smiled throughout it, though she had to keep dabbing at her tears, and she concluded by saying that she spoke for all of them when she said how glad they were that all of us had come, how proud they were that her father had so many friends. While she spoke, she wore her father's derby. The hats had been part of the tinkers' gimmick, a way of putting some ironic distance between themselves and their work, I thought, but in this setting, on this occasion, on the head of his daughter, Big Tink's derby had been cleansed of all its irony. She wore it as a keepsake, a genuine token of her affection for her father.

Second, there were the Big Tinker's paintings. I had had no idea that he painted, and from my conversations with people after the funeral, it seemed that no one outside his family had known it either. He painted the marshes and islands in the bay, a common enough subject for Sunday painters in the area, but he avoided the obvious choice and didn't paint them bathed in sunlight, with the sand and grasses glowing, but in the gray, flat light that is more common here, the everyday gray of Bolotomy Bay, and he succeeded, at least to my eye, in revealing the simple, sturdy, modest beauty of the bay and its shores, a beauty that goes almost unnoticed and hardly seems worth saving. I wished that I could own one of the paintings, but it would have been unseemly to ask if they were for sale, and I couldn't afford one if they were.

Third, the Big Tinker's ashes fit in an urn the size of a bottle of gin.

JUST INSIDE THE DOOR of the Babbington Diner there was a stack of giveaway papers and advertising brochures. We picked up a copy of *House and Home,* a booklet full of real estate ads. The hotel was advertised in it. It would be fair to say that it was featured, since it had been given half a page. There was a handsome photograph, from the front, that made it look like something worth owning. The copy began, "Do you have a dream? Do you dream of running your own luxury hotel?" Albertine read it aloud and burst out laughing. "Do you have nightmares?" she asked. "Do you wake up screaming? Do you worry about leaking plumbing, exploding boilers, and skyrocketing taxes?" I laughed with her, and I didn't ask her what she meant by 'skyrocketing taxes.'"

THERE WERE SIX in my audience for the reading of the ninth episode from *Dead Air,* "The Wall of Happy Diners." Elaine had returned, and she had brought with her a gray and cuddly couple, Alice and Clark, long-time friends of Lou's.

PORKY WHITE and I were friends, despite the difference in our ages. Several times a week I dropped in to see Porky and keep an eye on my investment in his clam bar. Often, the clam bar was empty when I arrived, but Porky was always there, scheming and dreaming, trying to find a way to fill it with happy diners.

"Got a great idea!" he said when I walked in one afternoon. "A great idea!" He came out from behind the counter, grabbed me by the shoulder, and tugged me over to the west wall of the building, saying, "Come here, come here."

We stood in front of the wall, and he asked, "You know what this is?"

"A wall," I said.

"A wall, yes. A wall. A *wall*! And in any other clam bar it would be *just* a wall. But this *isn't* any other clam bar. This is the house of hopes and dreams."

"So this isn't just a wall," I said, extrapolating.

"No, no, no, no, no," he said, shaking his head. "It's the Wall of Happy Diners."

"The Wall of Happy Diners," I said.

"Here's the idea. We're going to keep a camera behind the counter, see?"

"Yeah . . ."

"And we're going to take candid photographs of people eating. Then we'll put them up here, on the Wall of Happy Diners."

"That *is* a great idea," I said. "I'll take the pictures."

"And we can use *your* camera," said Porky.

I launched into the project with gusto. For a week or so, I spent every spare hour at the clam bar, lurking, stalking, spying, and— whenever I saw someone who looked like a happy diner—snapping pictures. I shot a couple of rolls.

When the pictures came back from Himmelfarb's Photography Shop, Porky and I looked through them.

"We'll put the really happy ones in a pile of their own," he said. "Those are the ones I want on the wall."

After the first pass, we had only one unambiguously happy diner. His girlfriend was tickling him. We started through again.

"Is this lady smiling?" Porky asked.

"She could be," I said.

"Yeah, could be. Could be. It's like when people say a baby is smiling and it's really just gas. These aren't happy diners. They're just people with gas."

"Don't get discouraged," I said. "Remember—this is the house of hopes and dreams."

"Yeah, but some dreams are just illusions," he said. He shoved the pictures away.

"Maybe we could hire somebody to—"

"No, no, no," he said at once, reaching over to give me a pat on the shoulder. "We don't need a professional. You're doing a fine job. So, the pictures are a little out of focus—that's okay. It makes them look more natural! It's not the *photographer,* it's—"

"I meant hire somebody to *be* in the pictures."

"What?"

"We could get some nice-looking people to pose. They could be sitting in a booth, eating fried clams. They could be happy diners."

"You mean they could *act* like happy diners."

"Yeah."

"I'm surprised at you. *Really* surprised at you. In fact, I'm shocked. You're talking about faking these pictures."

"Not faking."

"What would you call it?"

"Posing."

"And that's not faking?"

"I guess you're right," I said. "I'll keep taking the candid shots. Eventually we'll fill that wall with happy diners. You'll see."

I asked just about everybody I knew to play the part of a happy diner. Some of them were willing to do it. My friends Raskol and Marvin and Matthew and Spike played a bunch of kids having fun at lunch. I had to buy the lunch, but it was worth it. Mrs. Jerrold, a neighbor of mine, brought her husband and another couple, and the four of them played grown-ups on the town, whooping it up. Porky played the part of someone who didn't know what was going on.

Within a week, the Wall of Happy Diners began to fill with pictures of diners who appeared to be happy. There were Raskol, Marvin, Matthew, and Spike, clowning around, throwing fried clams at one another, and there were Mr. and Mrs. Jerrold leaning together, smiling, feeding each other clam chowder, apparently a happy, loving couple. The pictures made an attractive display. You couldn't tell that they were fakes.

LOU LINED SIX COCKTAIL GLASSES along the bar and filled them from a shaker. "Okay," he said, "now if you don't like this drink I want you please to at least give the *appearance* of enjoying it. My lovely assistant Elaine will be taking some candid shots, and if you seem to be having a good time we're going to put your mug shot up on our Wall of Tipsy Topers." After the third round, we all looked quite merry, and I was not at all surprised when Elaine scampered upstairs, returned with a camera, and began snapping shots. I considered it a tribute.

I WAS READING, already under the quilt, when Albertine came running out of the bathroom naked and shivering, threw herself under the covers and snuggled against me.

"The taxes?" I asked.

"Skyrocketing," she said.

"How rapid a rise is that, technically speaking?"

"Thirty-seven percent."

"*Thirty-seven percent?*"

"Most of it is going into the schools," she said. She paused, and then she added, in a version of Baldy's voice, "It's an investment in Babbington's future, right, Bob?"

"Yeah," I said.

Kap'n Klam's Salad Sandwich

The extent to which our sense of humor can help us to maintain our sanity is the extent to which it moves beyond jokes, beyond wit, beyond laughter itself. It must constitute a frame of mind, a point of view, a deep-going far-reaching attitude to life. . . . A man who can shrug off the insufficiency of his ultimate wisdom, the meaninglessness of his profoundest thoughts, is a man in touch with the very soul of humor.

Harvey Mindess, *Laughter and Liberation*

I SPENT THE DAY going around the hotel touching up the paint where leaks had stained the ceilings and in the thousand little places where the walls had taken a beating, and for quite a while I felt content, almost elated. Painting does that to me. The task is simple. The product of the task is smooth and clean and attractive. During the work the mind is free to wander. When the task is over, or even when a small but significant part of the task is over, the painter is justified in taking a moment to admire the work, and to praise the painter who did it. I generally count as a significant part of the task the obliteration of any one stain, nick, gouge, or smudge, so I spend much of my painting time in self-congratulation, but I feel that I deserve it. On this occasion, however, the mind, free as it was to wander, wandered to some places I would rather not have gone. I found myself thinking about Matthew Barber. I would rather not have been thinking about Matthew, and I hadn't meant to think about Matthew, but other thoughts had led me to him, subterranean thoughts. I had been trying to recall everything I could about the cave we had dug together, once upon a time, when we were boys, a couple of adolescent troglodytes, because I intended to include the cave later in *Dead Air*. In recalling the cave, I found myself "recrawling" the cave, making my way on hands and knees along the corridors that branched from its vestibule. Each of these corridors was the work of a different digger, and each led to a private place, its digger's den. In the course of my recollective crawling, I arrived at Matthew's chamber, his sanctum. Its boy-built door was secured with a boy-built lock. Matthew wasn't inside—I knew that—but his secrets were inside—I knew that, too. I picked the boy-built lock, and I violated his privacy, and I discovered his secrets. I remembered, and I was ashamed. I quit painting for the day.

THE SOUND OF EXUBERANT HAMMERING was coming from the roof. I went outside, walked backwards away from the hotel until I could see figures up there, and called out, "Yo, Tinkers!"

The two surviving tinkers came to the edge of the roof.

"Hey, Peter!" called the little one, waving. "Sorry it took us so long to get around to this." To my surprise, he seemed quite happy in his work, as jolly as he would have been if the Big Tinker had been working beside him.

"That's understandable," I said, "considering the circumstances."

They took their derbies off and held them over their hearts.

"Look," I said, "I never know what to say about death. I'm really sorry about the Big Tinker. I know you'll miss him, and Albertine and I are going to miss him, too, and—and—" and then, to my indescribable surprise, a large form, a third person, wearing a derby, a big tinker, moved to the edge of the roof and called down to me, "Hey there, Peter, how's they hanging?"

"What?" I shaded my eyes with my hand. I bobbed this way and that, trying to get a clearer view. "Who—who—?"

"Not a ghost!" he shouted. "Not even dead yet. It's me, Clark. Call me Cluck. That's what my granddaughter calls me, Grampy Cluck. It comes out *Grumpy* Cluck. Actually, I think Alice taught her that, but when she says it, it sounds so cute I decided it's me, Grumpy Cluck."

"Grumpy Cluck is giving us a hand with the roof," said Middle Tink. "Later he's going to take a look at the boiler."

"He's a wizard with boilers," claimed Little Tink.

Grumpy Cluck shrugged modestly and said, "I'm not making any promises, but I did spend much of my early life in an engine room."

"He was in the navy," said Little Tink.

"Good enough for me," I said. I saluted Grumpy Cluck, in my way, raising two hands with crossed fingers, the official salute of the assistant innkeeper at a small failing hotel who's hoping for the best.

"Look alive, you tinkers!" said Grumpy Cluck. "We're not getting anything done standing around here yakking."

The tinkers came to attention, raised their hammers, shouldered them, spun smartly right face, lost their footing, slipped, slid, waved their arms, bobbled their hammers, lost their derbies, bobbled their derbies, juggled derbies and hammers, teetered on the very edge of the roof, rotated their arms, regained their balance, and gingerly, very gingerly, backed from the edge, wiped their brows, rearranged their derbies, waved, and slowly, carefully, with exaggeratedly measured steps, returned to their work. It was, I think, an act.

THERE WERE NINE at my reading of episode ten of *Dead Air,* "Kap'n Klam's Salad Sandwich," since the tinkers made it off the roof safely and stayed to hear what I had to say, and Suki joined the group, too.

ALL OF THE CONFERENCES that Porky White and I held at his clam bar had the same theme: how to fill the place with happy diners, eating clams with gusto and spending with abandon. In the effort to make that dream come true, Porky changed the name from Captain White's to Kap'n Klam; he and I snapped candid photographs of people who seemed to be smiling as they ate and tacked them up on a Wall of Happy Diners; and he continually tried to invent recipes that would bring clams the wide acceptance that hamburgers enjoyed. The worst of these, I think, was the clam salad sandwich.

"This," he said, putting a plate in front of me, "is going to bring people in. It's going to make this place famous."

"Wow," I said. I lifted an edge of the bread and saw clams and mayonnaise—quite a lot of mayonnaise.

"Looks great, I know," he said, "but the proof of the pudding is in the eating—take a bite."

I took a bite. I chewed.

"Well?" he asked.

I swallowed. "It's—um—chewy," I said.

"Hmm. Is it too chewy?"

"Well—"

"You think I should cook the clams?"

"Maybe," I said, still chewing.

"What about the flavor?"

I took another bite. I chewed. I swallowed. "It's—um—got lots of mayonnaise," I said.

"And a little minced celery! That's the beauty of it, I think. It's simple. Elegant. It's going to be a huge success."

"Could be," I said. "Could be."

Four people walked into the clam bar, and Porky called out to them, "Good afternoon, folks! Take a pew, any pew. It's your lucky day! I've got something special I want you to try, on the house!"

He slid the plate away from me, cut the remains of the clam salad sandwich into bite-size pieces, and brought it over to the booth where the people had seated themselves. "My own invention!" he said. He set the plate in the middle of the table. We all looked at it in silence for a moment. Then Porky announced, "The clam salad sandwich!" The four people looked at one another. "Just sample that," said Porky, "and I'll be back in a minute to take your order."

He hustled me back to the counter, where he got the camera for the Wall of Happy Diners, my camera, on loan to the establishment for an unspecified period.

"Take this," he said, "and when I ask them how they like the sandwich, snap their pictures."

"Okay," I said.

We walked back to the booth. The remains of the clam salad sandwich lay on the plate in the center of the table. Some pieces were gone, some were half-eaten, some were intact. "So, folks," asked Porky, "what do you think?"

I was ready with the camera.

They looked at Porky, and they looked at one another, and then one of them, a man slouching into a corner of the booth, said, "You know, I think I'll *have* one of these clam salad sandwiches." He pointed at it.

"Yes, sir!" said Porky. He pulled his order pad out of his back pocket. "One clam salad sandwich."

"With lettuce and tomato."

"Lettuce and tomato."

"And some sliced onion."

"Sliced onion."

"Oh, and—"

"Yes?"

"Hold the clams."

Together, the group burst out laughing.

"See?" Porky said to me. "They love it! Get that picture."

I snapped it.

"Rush that right down to Himmelfarb's," said Porky. He stuck his hand in his pocket and handed me the money he found there. "And get the rush service. I want that picture on the Wall of Happy Diners as soon as possible."

Today, of course, a new Kap'n Klam restaurant opens somewhere in the world every fifteen minutes, and you'll find a Wall of Happy Diners in every one. Most of the photographs are taken locally, but every wall has some classic photographs from the early days of the chain, including the one that I took of the four people laughing over the original clam salad sandwich, and on the menu board in every Kap'n Klam restaurant from Kankakee to Karachi you will find these listings:

Kap'n Klam's Klam Salad Sandwich
(Try One—It Will Make You Laugh!)

Kap'n Klam's Salad Sandwich
(If You Do Not Kare for Klams)

"IS IT OKAY if I ask a question?" asked Alice.

"Sure," I said. "Questions are encouraged."

"Two questions, really."

"Okay."

"Was there a clam salad sandwich?"

Albertine, Suki, and I burst out laughing.

"No," I said, "but there is now," and Suki produced, from the bar refrigerator, a platter of canape-sized clam salad sandwiches. We all tried them, at least a bite, and I discovered that clam salad was as revolting a concoction as I had imagined it would be.

"Next question?" I said to Alice.

She spread her sandwich open, looked at the mix inside, and grimaced. "Is this one of those things—you know—where you say there are two kinds of people? People who like clams and people who don't?"

"Hmm. I'm not sure that I—"

"So the people who like clams would be the ones who like a laugh," said Lou.

"And the ones who do not 'kare' for clams are the ones with no sense of humor," said Alice.

"You're either a Baldy or a Bob," said Lou. "Is that it?"

"Maybe," I said. "Why not?"

ON THE WAY UPSTAIRS, I noticed all the stains, nicks, gouges, and smudges I'd missed when I was touching up, and with every flaw I noticed, the way up the stairs became harder. Maybe the hotel was beyond patching and touching up, and maybe my life was just as shabby, stained, and leaky as this old hotel—and beyond mending.

"You missed a few spots," said Albertine.

"It's a job for Sisyphus," I said, "but I'll give it another shot tomorrow." Then I had a thought. "Speaking of Sisyphean tasks," I said, "are we—are we paying Grumpy Cluck?"

"What? Who?"

"Clark. 'Call me Cluck,' didn't he tell you that?"

"No."

"His granddaughter calls him Grumpy Cluck, and he's decided that he likes it. Anyway, he's working with the Tinkers—did you know *that*?"

"Oh, yeah," she said, laughing, shrugging. "We're not paying him.

He's paying us, just like any other guest. He's working because—I don't know—he says he likes it."

I lay there for a moment trying to make sense of Grumpy Cluck, but I couldn't. Finally, I asked, "Al? Does that make him a Bob or a Baldy?"

"I am much too tired to think about that," she said. "I'm thinking about Manhattan."

Photographic Proof

The most realistic person is susceptible to the seduction of legends and believes them loyally; ... by a phenomenon of inverted perspective, memory has a tendency to see things growing larger as they move further away, to get them out of proportion, to remove their bases, in short ... nothing is more suspect than evidence.
  Jean Cocteau, "On Guillaume Apollinaire,"
  in *The Difficulty of Being*

I AWOKE feeling much better, even optimistic. I had slept the night through for the first time in weeks. I had no explanation for the change in my emotions, but I wasn't going to poke and probe until I was miserable again. I wasn't in the mood for it. I skipped my coffee and went out for a solitary walk along the shoreline. The morning was bright and crisp, and I felt so renewed, so invigorated, that I broke into a run. I hadn't run far, though, before I came to an abrupt stop, and stood there, bent over, hands on my knees, breathing hard. In the crisp morning air, the memory of a dream had returned to me, and it had staggered me. In the dream, or at least in the memory of the dream, I was someone else, and now it all came rushing back to me, and I knew who I had been.

I ran to the hotel, ran upstairs, grabbed my microcassette recorder and began dictating:

I'm always hungry on the day of a hit. Hungry and horny. Kill, eat, fuck—that's the perfect day, and this promises to be a very good day. A very good day.

I'm standing at the window of my hotel room—a really shitty room in a really shitty hotel—conveniently located across the street from a bank. A small crowd has gathered for the grand opening of this bank, because there hasn't been a bank in this part of town for years. If nobody in the neighborhood's got any fucking money, and nobody in his right mind would lend any money to anybody in the neighborhood, who needs a fucking bank, right?

Well, now they've got a bank, part of the mayor's "enterprise initiative," and in a couple of minutes his honor himself and the president of the bank and half a dozen local politicians are going to stand in front of the bank and take credit for it, and as soon as one of them opens his fucking mouth, I am going to press the button on my remote and fill the air with body parts.

Given the placement of the bomb and the way I've shaped the charge, the deputy mayor is going to be running the city tomorrow, but somewhere in the heap of pieces there will be whatever is left of Theresa Kendall, the darling of the six o'clock news, a beauty, a woman with a lot of talent and a lot of promise. She's the one I'm being paid to kill. The others—the mayor, the bank president, the two kids they've got standing there to show that this is an invest-ment in the future—are just a way of covering my tracks.

My name is Rockwell Kingman. . . .

I played it back. I had intended to transcribe it immediately, but when I heard it I was ashamed of it. I shut the recorder off and put it in my desk drawer.

Rockwell Kingman was a twisted mutation of Rocky King, the square-jawed sidekick of Larry Peters in the defunct series I'd written for so many years. Now, I supposed, following the cancellation of the series he was out of a job, older, and angry. I could see the cover of the book. There would be a photograph of a window of a second-floor office in a seedy building. A card in the window would read:

> Murder While You Wait
> Rockwell Kingman
> (One Flight Up)

The title would be *Murder While You Wait: The Memoirs of a Very Professional Killer*. The author would be Rockwell Kingman himself. "Call me Rockwell. Don't call me Rocky." He might make us some money.

"JEFFREY the realtor called to say that he's bringing some prospects on Sunday," Albertine said, "and he asked me whether we could do anything about the wildlife."

"The wildlife?"

"Actually, he called it the weird life, the weird wildlife. According to Jeffrey, it is definitely going to be a problem for these people, or one of them, anyway."

On the other side of the island, at the farthest remove from the hotel, there was an ecosystem of the bizarre. There were chinchilla rabbits, giant frogs, talking budgies, hamsters, minks, raccoons, parrots, turkeys, chickens, and a colony of feral Siamese cats. The wildlife had been on the island longer than Albertine and I had. Again and again, the previous owners of Small's Island had tried to make the big money by breeding something that would sell, and time and again they had failed. Their abandoned moneymakers had been breeding out there ever since, out on the far western extreme of the island, near the cove where I had my clam farm. The wildlife was not friendly. They were all jealous of the territories they claimed for themselves, and they considered all interlopers targeted personnel. Most of them didn't bother Albertine most of the time, excepting the cats. For fifteen years, she had been waffling between "we've got to get rid of those damned cats" and "I feel so sorry for those poor cats," depending on the weather and the number of cats in heat. I had steadfastly maintained that the cats were the only thing that kept the island from being overrun by chickens.

"What have they got against wildlife?" I asked.

"Nothing at all. Apparently that's the problem."

"I think we've fallen into one of those logical sinkholes that sometimes swallow cars whole."

"It's not the wildlife; it's the need to eliminate the wildlife that's a problem. Not all the wildlife. Jeffrey thinks it would be enough if we just got rid of the cats."

"What have they got against cats?"

"Nothing—"

"And that's the problem?"

"Yeah. Apparently, one of them is a cat fancier, and Jeffrey thinks that she is just not going to want to have to deal with the problem of the cats. Eliminating the cats."

"Oh," I said, since I understood at last. "So we have to find some heartless bastard to get rid of the cats before the cat fancier sees them."

"That's pretty much the idea."

"I'll take care of it."

It sounded like a job for Rockwell Kingman.

THAT NIGHT I read "Photographic Proof," episode eleven of *Dead Air,* to a sizable Friday-night crowd (sizable, that is, for the time of year). We've learned not to expect much business after Labor Day. However, we had a bigger night than we'd had on the corresponding Friday the year before, and I gave myself credit for it.

IN HIS EFFORT to make clams as popular as hamburgers and to fill his clam bar with happy diners, Porky White had posted photographs of smiling patrons, made innovative contributions to clam cuisine, and changed the name of the place eleven times, settling at last on Kap'n Klam. None of Porky's efforts had succeeded, but he had managed to keep his faith. I was beginning to lose mine—not in the clam bar, but in flying saucers. I had been interested in flying saucers for about a year and had allowed my interest to become belief, but the pictures on the Wall of Happy Diners were reawakening the skeptic in me.

When I looked at those pictures—which I had taken—I saw people grimacing, or clowning, or surprised, not happy in the way that Porky wanted his diners to be happy, but Porky didn't seem to see what I saw, and the diners didn't either, not even when they were looking at their own pictures. I remember the Himmelfarb family walking in one evening and going straight to the wall to find their picture, which I had taken a few days earlier.

Mr. Himmelfarb threw his arm around Mrs. Himmelfarb, drew his children in close to him, and said, "That was a great night, wasn't it? What a time we had."

I looked at their picture: in it, they were popeyed and pale, with their mouths full. Then I looked at them, standing there looking at their picture: they were beaming. They gave one another a last hug and shuffled off to a booth to reproduce the happy night they'd had.

Mr. Himmelfarb ran the camera shop in town; if he could be fooled by a photograph—if he, a *professional,* could *allow* himself to be fooled by a photograph—anyone could. Shaken by what I'd learned from the Wall of Happy Diners, I spent hours poring over the photographs of flying saucers in the enthusiasts' magazines that I bought, looking for evidence, looking ultimately for proof. The more I looked, the more I saw shots of hubcaps and pie plates. My face fell, as one's face does when the scales fall from one's eyes.

"Hey," said Porky the next time I showed up for work, "Quit moping. We don't allow moping at Kap'n Klam. This is the Home of Happy Diners, the House of Hopes and Dreams."

"Yeah, but some dreams are just illusions," I said. "Like flying saucers."

"What's this?" he said. "Doubts? A lot of people have *seen* flying saucers, remember."

"A lot of people *say* they've seen them."

"But there are *pictures*," he protested.

"Fakes," I said. I had to keep myself from looking toward the Wall of Happy Diners.

"Fakes?"

"Sure. Give me a saucer from back there." He brought a saucer up from behind the counter. I took it, inverted it, and maneuvered it as if it were flying. "See? A flying saucer."

"Oh, come on," he said.

"Come on, nothing. If I threw this up in the air and took a picture, I could say, 'I saw this saucer flying through the air,' and I wouldn't even be lying."

He took the saucer from me and maneuvered it as I had. "This wouldn't look like a flying saucer," he said. "Not like a real one."

"Give me the camera," I said. "We'll take some pictures—we'll *fake* some pictures—and then you'll have *photographic proof* that flying saucers are just an illusion."

"On the contrary," he said, handing me the camera, "you'll have photographic proof that the pictures *can't* be faked."

We went outside to the parking lot. Porky stood in front of the entrance to the clam bar, and I moved some distance away. "Ready?" he said, and then before I really was ready he tossed the saucer in my direction. I tried to snap a picture of it. It landed in front of me and broke.

"I don't think I got it," I said.

"I'll get some more saucers," Porky offered. "This is fun."

"No, no," I said. "We can't afford it."

"Okay," he said. "Wait a minute."

He returned with a handful of clams. "Try this!" he said, and tossed the clams into the air.

"I got it," I said. "I'm sure I did."

"I'll get you some money," said Porky. "You can take that film to Himmelfarb's right away."

Inside, a couple was standing in front of the Wall of Happy Diners, looking at the pictures.

"Hi," said the man. "Can we get lunch?"

"Yeah, sure," said Porky, at the register.

"Great," said the woman. "It looks like people have a good time here."

There was something in the way she said it, an eager willingness to believe, the hopeful voice of the gullible sucker, that made Porky spin around and stare at her to see if she was kidding. She smiled at him. Porky looked at me. I looked at him. He looked at the Wall of Happy Diners. His face fell, and I knew that the scales were falling from his eyes, that the people he saw pictured there were beginning to look like hubcaps and pie plates. He handed me some money. "Get the rush service," he said. "I want to get a good look at those."

GRUMPY CLUCK turned out to be a great fan of calvados. After a few, he threw his arm across Albertine's shoulders and said, "Jeez, honey, you know, this is a great place. I've never been so relaxed on a vacation in my adult life. You know what I'm saying?"

"That you have never been so relaxed on a vacation in your adult life?"

"You got it. That's it. That's exactly what I'm trying to say. Usually we go to Saint Barth's, Saint Kitts, Saint Croix, Saint This, Saint That—the whole family, the whole frigging family, and the kids are happy, happy as clams—did I tell you my granddaughter calls me Grampy Clark but it comes out Grumpy Cluck?"

"No, but I heard it on the radio."

"You what? Oh, I get it. You heard it on the radio. That's funny. That is. That's funny. What was I saying?"

"Everybody's happy on Saint Barth's."

"Yeah. The kids and the grandkids, and my wife. They shop and they—whatever it is they do—vacation stuff. Me, I got nothing to do. I sit there on the beach, I try to read a book or something, all I do is worry about the shop. God, the time is heavy on my hands. I get on the cell phone, call the shop. Jeez, it's one crisis after another back there, and I'm trying to solve them over the phone. It's fucking frustrating. By the time I come home, I'm a god-damned wreck. I can't wait to get back to work, except that I got to fix all the things that went wrong while I was away. But here, here it's *completely* different. I haven't thought about the shop for one minute, not *one minute* for an entire day and a half. I'm up there on the roof, trying to find those leaks, you know. I go along, see a suspicious spot, I rip up the old shingles, start patching it. That's all I think about—your roof. And because that's all I think about, I don't have anything to worry about. I tell you, it's—it's *paradise*. It's worry-free here. I'm grateful." He took a handkerchief out of his pocket and blew his nose. "I'm really grateful," he said, "for that roof."

Rush Service

And out of what one sees and hears and out
Of what one feels, who could have thought to make
So many selves . . .
    Wallace Stevens, "Esthétique du Mal"

I AWOKE before the alarm went off, got up immediately, pulled some sweat togs on, and went directly to my workroom without any coffee, drawn by the guilty pleasure of working on *Murder While You Wait*. This was a real escape from my life, more effective as an escape than my past had ever been. Rockwell Kingman was nothing like me. I was beginning to spend more and more of my mental time with him, and I was beginning to like him. Already, I felt as if I had known him for years, and of course I must have. Consider this: I had understood his style from the moment when I first saw him standing at the window of that lousy hotel, waiting for the right set of circumstances to detonate his charge. His signature technique was misdirection: he made the target look like one of the innocent bystanders. If he executed a job perfectly, it looked sloppy. The intended death looked accidental, part of the mess left by a guy who couldn't shoot straight, who couldn't kill without overkill. I admired this deviousness. It seemed clever to me. The astonishing fact of his suddenly appearing at that hotel window—full-grown, tough, competent, cynical, bitter, brutal—no longer astonished me at all, because I knew exactly where he had come from, from some dark corner of myself, where he had been waiting for years, confident that the day would come when I would let him out.

"I CALLED LIZA," Albertine said from her spot behind the desk, without looking up from the papers she was working on. When I didn't say anything, she looked up and said, "The realtor who brought Mr. Fillmore out here?"

"I know," I said. "I was just waiting to hear what she had to say."

"Oh. Well, she said that our problem is that this is an island. People don't like the idea of being stuck on an island."

"That bothered Fillmore?" I asked.

"I guess so," she said. She shrugged. I am ashamed to say that I thought she might be lying. I thought that she might be using Fillmore as her dummy to say to me the things she couldn't bring herself to say to me directly—that she hated being stuck on an island and that she wished she had never followed me here. We stood there for a moment looking into each other's eyes, and I couldn't tell whether she was making that kind of disguised declaration or not. I thought of calling Liza to find out for myself. I could invent some pretext. I could say that I was interested in talking to Fillmore about a book I was working on. He would probably have some useful information for *Murder While You Wait* . . . and it was right about there that I began to wonder whether I was going nuts.

"They're not making madmen the way they used to," I said.

WE HAD a fine crowd that night. The day was bright; the sunset was rosy; the night was mild. On days like that, people get the urge to wander, and Small's beckons as an easy getaway. At dinner, the dining room was nearly full. Elaine returned, and for a while Lou was so busy behind the bar that she had to play cocktail waitress. Albertine had to shout over the buzz of voices to introduce my reading of episode twelve of *Dead Air,* "Rush Service."

IF YOU TOOK YOUR PICTURES to be developed and printed at Himmelfarb's Photography Shop on Upper Bolotomy Road, just north of Main Street, in Babbington when I was a boy, you could get regular service or rush service.

Regular service was exactly the same as the service you could get at the drugstore across the street: a man in an unmarked truck came around once a week and picked the film up, and a week later the same man in the same truck brought your pictures back. Ordinarily, regular service was fine. One of its features was the sweet pain of waiting, one of the paradoxes of our emotional life, an ache that is complicated and compounded by its constant companion, anticipation. I would drop my film off at Himmelfarb's and then for an entire day I would feel light, relieved that the film was out of my hands, the responsibility for it off my shoulders. A couple of emotionally neutral days would pass, and then, on or about the fourth day, a tightness would begin to ripple across my back, and by the sixth day, this expectant tension would have me twitching and itching. Sometimes I tried dropping in at Himmelfarb's on the sixth day to see if the pictures had come in early. They never were early; regular service always took a full week.

Not everyone was willing to wait a week. If you were in a hurry, you could pay the "rush" price, a dollar extra, and Mr. Himmelfarb would develop and print your pictures himself, in his darkroom in the back of the shop. You could have them the next day. I had never used the rush service, though I'd spent a considerable amount of my allowance and earnings at Himmelfarb's. For a while I had even been his competitor in the photographic-services business. I had ordered a developing and printing outfit by mail and advertised myself throughout my neighborhood as an adept in the mysteries of the craft. I got one customer, Mrs. Jerrold, an attractive housewife who lived in my neighborhood, but when I tried to develop and print her pictures I discovered that I didn't know what I was doing. After that experiment, I returned to Mr. Himmelfarb for my developing and printing needs. I kept Mrs. Jerrold as a customer because I was attracted to her and eager for any excuse to visit her, and because I was too embarrassed to tell her that I had given up the photographic-services business after a single setback. I picked up her film whenever she called and then took it to Mr. Himmelfarb. When the pictures came back, I took them and their negatives out of their yellow envelope and repackaged them in a small brown paper bag, the sort of thing a kid would use if he were a supplier of photographic services on the neighborhood level. An important reason for my perpetrating this deception was the fact that I got to see all of Mrs. Jerrold's pictures, and her husband took some that could have been called cheesecake. I spent a while looking at those through a magnifying glass; I always suspected that Mr. Himmelfarb did, too.

With an air of self-importance, I tossed my film onto the counter and said, "Rush, please, Mr. Himmelfarb."

"Rush!" said Mr. Himmelfarb. "Must be something important."

I tried to be nonchalant, so that Mr. Himmelfarb would see that I was growing up and beginning to take my place in the world as a young fellow who used rush service whenever it suited him.

"Oh, nothing special."

"Vacation pictures?"

"Nope."

"A new baby in the family?"

"Uh-uh."

He leaned across the counter, looked me in the eye, and winked. Drawing the words out, he asked, "A girlfriend?"

"No," I said. "They're just experiments. I was trying to get some action shots—you know, following the action with the camera, the way the book says." (I wasn't about to tell him that I had taken a picture of a handful of clams that Porky White tossed into the air to settle a dispute about whether airborne objects—saucers, pie plates, clams—would look like flying saucers to the untrained eye. It sounded like a ridiculous experiment even to me.)

"Uh-huh."

"And," I said, under the influence of another wave of self-importance, "There are some more pictures I took at Kap'n Klam."

"For the Wall of Happy Diners," he said.

"Yeah," I said, and, still surfing on self-importance, I added, "and for their advertising, too. I'm doing their advertising."

"Really?"

"Oh, sure. I'm an investor, you know."

"An investor! In what?"

"In Kap'n Klam."

"Oh, I see," he said. Then, with the clear implication that he understood, now, that I was running an errand for Porky, he said, "So this is a rush order for Mr. White."

"Yeah," I said, and I wondered at what point, exactly, I had gone too far, when, exactly, he had stopped believing me.

WHEN I FINISHED, I held my hands up to silence the thundering ovation that was probably impending and said, "I have to ask you to forgive me for two mistakes in there, in that reading. I had intended to make each of these episodes self-contained, and Albertine advertised that they would be, but I realize that a couple of things in this one were not explained; they were just hanging there, and they must have seemed puzzling."

"The Wall of Happy Diners," said a woman at the bar who was holding a drink garnished with a pink paper umbrella.

"Yes," I said, smiling at her. "You've been listening."

She smiled back. Writing has its rewards.

To the room I said, "The Wall of Happy Diners was a wall in Kap'n Klam where Porky posted pictures of people who seemed to be enjoying themselves. I took the pictures, most of them."

"And Kap'n Klam?" asked a beefy fellow with a full beard, black, flecked with gray.

"That was the name of Porky's restaurant," I said, "and that's a long story."

"Porky ran a clam bar near the town dock in Babbington," said Lou. "He was tireless in his efforts to fill the place with happy diners," and he went on to tell the story of the naming of the restaurant. He told it completely, and he told it well.

Local Boy Snaps Shots

Everything we do, we actually do for our own sake. We may appear to be sacrificing ourselves, when we are merely satisfying ourselves.

Denis Diderot

IT IS ALWAYS DIFFICULT to pin down the onset of an idea, but I think that it was this morning, when I surprised Albertine in the kitchen, on her hands and knees, scrubbing the floor, doing a job that we have always paid someone else to do, even in the hotel's leanest early days, and she looked at me and I saw that she was embarrassed to have been caught saving money this way, embarrassed for me, because she hadn't wanted me to see that she thought it necessary, or at least prudent, to save money this way, that I really understood how sad she was, how heavily the weight of everything that was a care to her fell on her, and I think that it was at that moment that inspiration struck. I knew that the ultimate target I wanted Rockwell Kingman to pursue was me.

At the time, I thought that the operations of my mind were being conducted in the pursuit of a goal that was purely—let us not say "merely"—literary, that I had been inspired to use my own situation to construct the final chapter of *Murder While You Wait* and that I would go on to construct the rest of the book to lead up to that chapter. That is what I *thought* I thought, or, to attempt to be perfectly precise about this, that is what I think I would have thought I was thinking if I had thought about what I was thinking at the time. Someone, a man, a desperate man, would come to Kingman in the hope of employing his skill, and in particular his talent for misdirection, to hide a suicide. He wanted to kill himself—or, if Kingman thought it best, to be killed—so that his wife would collect his insurance money.

His business was failing—some business, any business. Make it a small hotel on a small island. . . .

"Look, here's the way it is," he says. He's wringing his hands. "This morning I happened to see my wife—"

"It's an old story," I say. I light a cigarette. I turn my back to the guy and look out the window. I'm not interested.

"No," he says. "That's not the story. Not my story. I surprised her. I saw what she hadn't wanted me to see. I came into the kitchen and there she was, Albertine, my Albertine, my honey-bunchie-wunchie, on her hands and knees, scrubbing the floor, doing a job that we have always paid someone else to do, even in the hotel's lean early days, and she looked at me and I saw that she was embarrassed to be caught saving money this way—embarrassed for *me,* because she hadn't wanted me to see that she thought she had to save money this way—"

I open the window, lean out. I see it's going to be a nice day.

"You see," he says, and I can hear that pleading tone starting to insinuate itself into his voice, "it was at that moment that I really understood how sad she is, how heavily the weight of—of—everything—every care—every worry—how heavily the weight of every worry falls on her, and that all of that is all my fault."

He gets up out of the chair. He walks over to the window. He puts his hand on my shoulder. I hate that. I hate the personal appeal. I shrug him off.

"Sorry," he says. He draws a breath. "It's my fault, and I've got to make amends." He draws another breath, and then he lays out his plan in the measured voice that people always use when they're laying out their plans. "When Albertine and I bought the hotel we also bought a life insurance policy on me, enough to cover the mortgage. Over the years, we've increased the mortgage to finance repairs and maintenance, but whenever we did we increased the insurance too. If I die an accidental death, she will collect enough to pay off her debts and unload the hotel, which she's come to think of as a prison. Then she can add whatever is left to what she's managed to put away in our retirement fund, and she will have—at last—financial security."

He pauses, and I can tell he's considering the hand on the shoulder again, the chummy approach. I spin around and look him in the eye to put the kibosh on that.

He holds his hands out, palms up. He sighs. "Security," he says. "Peace. And I will have provided it. I will be a success."

As I saw it, Kingman would not be interested. He would find the idea bizarre, even perverted. As a killer, he would find the desire for death impossible to understand. It would take Peter weeks to persuade Kingman to accept him as a client. It would involve riveting discussions of the meaning of life and the meaning of death. I anticipated the writing of those scenes with relish.

I SPENT the rest of the morning trapping cats. Lou and Grumpy Cluck helped me. We brought the launch and the rowboat around to the wildlife area, pulled the rowboat up on shore, and laid a catwalk from the bow to the sand. We dotted the walk with food—cat food that Suki had concocted—and set little bowls of it along the shore. We put several large bowls in the rowboat, a movable feast, and then the three of us sat in the launch, drinking coffee—Irish coffee that Lou had concocted—and watched the rowboat fill with cats. When it seemed to be as full as it was likely to get, we began paddling the launch, slowly, gently, quietly. The line on the rowboat tightened, and we drew the boat out behind us toward the open bay. There had been some talk, earlier, about scuttling the rowboat and drowning the cats, but Irish coffee makes a guy verbose and sentimental, and the three of us were soon running on at length about the miracle of life and the joy of living, and scolding what Lou liked to call "the culture of shit" for putting so low a price on life, living, joy, and everything else worthwhile. We towed the rowboat to the largest of the uninhabited islands near us, and we set the cats free there. (In other words, I said to myself without looking back, we marooned the cats there.)

JEFFREY HIMSELF brought the boatload of prospects to the island in the afternoon. They were crisp and efficient. There were a dozen of them, nine men and three women. All of them wore scent of one kind or another, and each one had a notebook with a checklist. From what I could see, no two checklists were identical. It was easy to decide which one would have been upset about the cats—a round pink man with a few strands of white hair combed over his round pink pate, the one wearing the red necktie on which kittens cavorted.

"Very interesting possibilities," was the phrase I heard most. "Very interesting possibilities."

"Would you like to begin at the hotel?" asked Albertine.

"Oh, yes!" said a woman at the head of the group. "That will make a wonderful social center!" She turned toward the others and they laughed awkwardly. The woman flushed and said, "I mean—it might—it could—that is, if we decide—"

"The idea," said Jeffrey, "is to turn the island into a residential community—an *exclusive* residential community."

"Like a gated community?" I asked.

"Yes!" said the round pink man. He swept his arm toward the expanse of bay that separated us from potential interlopers. "The *ultimate* in exclusivity, an island! With a natural *moat* to keep the undesirable element out." When he said the words *undesirable element* he winked at me.

Albertine and I looked at each other.

She said, "Shit," and then she said, slowly, to the round pink man, "While you're looking the place over, bear in mind that the boiler may blow up at any moment and the roof leaks, and you might want to stay out of the area to the west, where there are giant frogs, wild hamsters, chinchilla rabbits, minks, free-ranging chickens, turkeys, talking budgies—and hundreds of rabid feral cats."

"Oh, my goodness," said the round pink man. "That doesn't sound very promising."

THAT NIGHT'S READING was "Local Boy Snaps Shots," the thirteenth episode of *Dead Air*.

THE HEADLINE in the *Babbington Reporter* read, "Saucers Swarm over Babbington, Local Boy Snaps Shots of Mysterious Craft." Below the headline was the picture that I had snapped. Apparently, Porky White's attempt to demonstrate that common objects thrown into the air would *not* resemble flying saucers had been a failure. Judging from the headline, a viewer who was not aware of the circumstances under which the photograph was taken—and that would be every viewer but Porky and me—might assume that the objects in the sky were much larger than clams and, therefore, higher in the sky and farther away than the clams had actually been. Such a viewer might even mistake the clams for flying saucers.

REPORTER

WEAT.
Gray, Damp, Col

Saucers Swarm over Babbington   May

.it"

.c warfare
enough to
.ers in their back
.ir basements, al-
als warn that the
· of shelter is not
·tive as the under-
which should en-
·nts to survive the
·t blast.
·t considered by
·f backyard fall-
·e factor of bore-
·oing to have a
·lving together in
·nderground, un-
· a considerable
·ed on page 14

**Local Boy Snaps Shots
of Mysterious Craft**

BABBINGTON—A swarm of "fly-
ing saucers" visited Babbington today
and went nearly unnoticed. In fact, if
it hadn't been for a photograph
snapped, apparently unwittingly, by
a local boy, Peter Loroy, and broug'
to the REPORTER's attention by (
car Himmelfrab, proprietor
Himmelfarb's Photography Shop
Upper Bolotomy Road, just nortl
Main Street, the home of everytl
photographic for amateur and pr
sional alike) the saucers might l
passed our town without having l
observed at all, which has raise
cern among the popul·
possibi'·
cre·

BABB'
May·
nev·
had
sh·
c

Photo by Petar Leray

Missing Highway Funds

·r when the   might be at his home in Florida,
but telephone calls from the ''''''
''TER were not

When I first saw the picture, I felt the thrill you would expect a boy to feel if the local newspaper published a picture he had taken, but very quickly I began to feel cheated. I hadn't intended to have this picture published in the *Reporter*; I hadn't given permission for it to be published; no one had even *asked* my permission; my name was misspelled; and no one had paid me.

I called Porky.

"Did you see the paper today?" I asked.

"I sure did!" said Porky. "Hold on a minute." Away from the mouthpiece he called out, "Pour some coffee for those guys and apologize for the delay. Make 'em feel good." Into the mouthpiece he said, "Great picture, wasn't it?"

"Do you think I should have him arrested?" I asked.

"Who? What for?"

"Mr. Himmelfarb, for sending the picture to the paper."

"Are you nuts? Himmelfarb did us a favor."

"Really?"

"Sure. Listen to this." He stopped talking, and from the background I heard the sound of animated conversation, clinking china, glasses, laughter, and, some voices raised in dispute. Porky came back on the line. "Amazing, isn't it? The place is packed!"

"Curiosity seekers," I said, the way my father did whenever we were stuck in a traffic jam caused by the rubbernecking curious slowing down to get a good look at an accident.

"Yeah!" said Porky with enthusiasm.

"What a pain."

"Are you kidding?" asked Porky. "I'm not screening people at the door here, you know. All are welcome at Kap'n Klam, including curiosity seekers. You understand?"

"Oh, sure," I said, speaking as an investor in the enterprise, "but," I added, quoting my father, "what is it about these people that makes them think nothing has really happened until they've witnessed it?"

"Just a damn minute there," said Porky. "We are all curiosity seekers, Peter. It's one of the things that make us human. Don't ever disparage curiosity. I think it's the noblest of human traits, if you ask me, and it's honest, not like generosity, for example. You scratch generosity, and very often you'll find self-interest lying underneath it, but curiosity, scratch that, and you're going to find nothing but one-hundred-per-cent curiosity through and through. It's a genuine human trait, unadulterated by other motives. We may be generous to salve a guilty conscience or curry favor, but we want to know because we want to know, and we have a right to know, because we are the only creatures capable of knowing. We *are* life's witnesses. If *we* don't witness a thing, if we don't know about a thing, it is, in a way that I don't have time to explain right now, not real."

"Porky!" called a voice from the background. "I need three clam salad sandwiches!"

"Coming right up!" he shouted, and then asked, "Can you give me a hand?"

"I'll be right there," I said, and a moment later I was on my way, and I was pedaling hard, because I wanted to get down there and see for myself, with my own eyes, what was going on.

BALDY closed his show that night with this: "Is this you, boys and girls? You are a refugee, an orphan, somewhere, anywhere, who knows where. You have been orphaned by tribal warfare, because the people of the other tribe hate your tribe because your tribe is not their tribe. Do you understand that? Everyone who used to sit with you at the family hearth is dead. They were killed by the people of another tribe because the people of the other tribe need to eliminate the people of your tribe so that they can be certain that they are superior to the people of your tribe. Do you understand that? You watched some of the people die. Some died at your home. Some died on the road. Some died in a camp where you learned to understand the limits of international patience with the refugees of tribal warfare. You are alone. Everything you have you can hold in your hands, everything except your memories. Is that you, boys and girls? No? Lucky for you, kids. But be careful, because there is someone out there somewhere, who knows where, who hates you because you belong to the wrong tribe and because we have not grown up enough as a species to stop living in tribes. Do you understand that? Neither do I. Roll the rock in front of the door, my little ones, stay in the cave, and sleep tight."

September 23
Bivalves from Outer Space

HUPPA-THUPPA-WHUP! Huppa-thuppa-whup! Huppa-thuppa-whup! Fizzz. Huppa-thuppa-whup! Huppa-thuppa-whup! . . .

"What fresh hell is this?" asked Albertine as she leaped from bed in the glorious altogether and stood at the window in the pale glow that precedes the dawn. She threw the window open, leaned out into the fresh autumn air, and shouted to the world outside, "What the fuck is it now?"

The world answered, "Huppa-thuppa-whup!" Or, now that I could hear it more clearly through the open window, perhaps it was "Hoopa-thoopa-whoop!" It might have been misunderstood, but it couldn't be missed. It was deafening.

I ran to Albertine's side and leaned out the window to see what was the matter, to ascertain the cause of all this clatter. Offshore, but barely offshore, not more than a few yards offshore, was a barge crowded with ancient mechanical equipment, enormous pistons thrusting, shafts turning, iron gears advancing notch by notch, and every aged piece of the infernal engine complaining every time it did its bit, in a cacophonous chorus of screeching, pounding, hissing, and whining.

"What is it?" she asked me. "What *is* it?"

"A dredge," I said.

We pulled our clothes on and ran downstairs. The sun was still not up, and the dredge was still not up to full steam. We ran to the edge of the water and began shouting, but there wasn't a chance that the operator would hear us over the noise. We began throwing stones. I was trying to land one near enough to the barge to splash the operator, but I think Albertine was trying to hit him. She did. He spun around. It was Dexter Burke.

Albertine—how shall I put this? Albertine threw a fit, a doozie, a temper tantrum, a maniacal display of undirected fury. It was, in its way, a beautiful thing to watch. It drove Dexter to the other side of the dredge, where she couldn't hit him with anything, but it didn't stop the machine.

I dragged her into the hotel. The noise pursued us. It was aggressive, determined, dogged. It was out to get us. It had begun as noise, but it was becoming something stronger, a force that set in motion everything around us. It roiled the water, shook it into waves, shuddered through the sand on which our domain rested, and made the old hotel tremble.

Albertine put through a call, not to Rockwell Kingman, but to the Babbington Department of Public Works. The news was not good. The work would go on for four or five weeks. The plan was to dredge a new channel that would run right alongside Small's Island, and to use the spoil— the sand dredged from the new channel—to create a new island in the bay that would lie between us and Babbington.

"What's the point of making a new island?" Albertine shouted into the mouthpiece. She listened to the answer with a blank expression. She hung up.

"What did they say?" I shouted.

"The Parks Department is going to turn the island into a 'water sports facility'—"

"Well, that's not so—"

"—for 'personal motorized watercraft.'"

"Oh," I said. "Jet skis."

AT THREE O'CLOCK, the noise stopped, just stopped. The entire population of the hotel drifted outside with the dazed and bedazzled look of people emerging from a cave into the bright light of midday. We walked in silence to the water's edge and watched Dexter get into the aluminum skiff he had tied to the dredge, cast off, start the outboard, and head for home. As he headed away, he waved, without looking back. I gave him the finger. Everybody else joined in.

THE QUIET seemed so precious that we broke it only gently for the rest of the day. All our conversations were conducted in whispers, and although I am generally a spirited reader of my own work, my reading of "Bivalves from Outer Space," the fourteenth episode of *Dead Air,* was uncharacteristically subdued.

I WAS ANNOYED when the *Babbington Reporter* ran the photograph that I had taken of Porky White tossing clams into the air outside his clam bar and interpreted it as a photograph of flying saucers on maneuvers. It wasn't true, for one thing, and for another no one from the *Reporter* had even called me to ask for my personal interpretation of the objects in my own photograph.

"I'm going to call them and tell them the truth," I told Porky.

"The truth is a fine thing," he said. "Sometimes it makes a good story."

Then, as if the idea had just occurred to him, he said, "Tell you what, though—why don't you try your story out on the guys at the counter? See what they think of it."

He urged me over to the counter and announced, "Peter's got a theory about those spaceships."

The men stopped talking and looked at me. Slowly, each of them let his expression slip into the tolerant smile that adults turn on a precocious child who's about to serve up a half-baked idea.

"They're not flying saucers," I said. "They're clams."

"Clams!" said one of the men, the clam digger everyone called Mucker.

"Porky threw them into the air," I said, "and I took the picture."

They all looked at the copy of the *Reporter* that lay on the counter in front of them.

"What's going on here?" asked Mucker. He looked back and forth between Porky and me. "Are you testing us? Trying to see if we're gullible enough to fall for a preposterous story like that?"

A grumble rumbled along the line of beefy men.

"Now wait a minute there, boys," said Porky. "Let's think about this rationally. Don't you think it's just the least little bit *odd* that these flying saucers should look so much like clams? Doesn't it seem *awfully strange* that highly advanced beings from another planet in another galaxy would travel around in spaceships shaped like clamshells? It seems strange to me."

"You know," said Mucker, "you're right. It does seem strange."

"Of course," I said. "You see—"

"It makes you wonder how clams got here, don't it?" said Mucker.

"What?" I said.

"I mean," said Mucker, speaking slowly but enthusiastically, in the manner of a molecular biologist addressing an informal gathering of nonscientists, "if clams look so much like these ships from this advanced civilization, how come they're *here,* on *earth?*"

"What are you getting at?" I asked.

"Just consider this," said Mucker. "Suppose clams were *brought* here."

"Brought here?"

"From outer space," said Mucker.

"From outer space?" I said.

"He's right," said Axel Dunne, one of the men who bought clams for the Babbington Clam Company. "Why else would clams look so much like these ships?"

"Wait a minute," I said. "I'm trying to tell you that—"

"Look," said Mucker, with the patience of a teacher of the blind, "clams are one of the oldest living things on earth, am I right?"

"Right," said Porky, and all the clam diggers at the counter echoed him, nodding their heads with the certitude of professionals.

"So," said Mucker, "what that suggests to me is"—and to heighten the effect of the pronouncement he was about to make he paused a moment before continuing—"that these visitors have been here before."

"Come on," I said, occasioning a number of stern looks from the men at the counter and a firm grip on the shoulder from Porky.

"Long, long ago," said Mucker, whose audience now hung on his every word, "they came here—I'm just speculating, now, you understand—these beings came here, and they planted a *crop.*"

"Seed clams," murmured the men at the counter.

"This is all speculation, mind you," said Mucker, holding both hands up to emphasize that he had nothing up his sleeves, "but just follow along here with me for a bit. They plant this crop, these beings, whoever they are, *whatever* they are, and they let it grow.

They let it grow, and they wait." A hush fell over us all. Mucker lit a cigarette. "Now they're back to check up on it. Maybe they're going to do some *weeding*. Maybe they're going to *harvest*. Who knows? Maybe it's only been a couple of *weeks* to them since they planted it. Who knows?"

Confronted with this logic, we all looked at the picture on the front page of the *Reporter* for a while in silence.

"You know," said Axel, finally, as if, for him, the proof had come in at last, "they *do* look like clams."

"That's what I've been trying to tell you," I said, but Porky jabbed me with his elbow, so I shut up.

AFTER THE READING, Lou called out, "Tonight's featured drink is a little invention of my own. I think I'm going to call it the Baldy, after the dummy that Peter's been telling us about—not in tonight's episode, but in a couple of the earlier ones."

He lined glasses up along the bar and filled them.

The Baldy was a fine drink—tart, bitter, and strong. It wasn't appealing at first sip, but it grew on me. I have no idea what was in it. I could guess, but guessing would be like looking at a photograph of blurry objects suspended in the air above Babbington and guessing that they were flying saucers, the mother ships of the family of clam. I might be right, but I'd probably be wrong, and I wouldn't want to mislead you into making a bogus Baldy based on my mistake.

My Grandfather's Cave

Where shall I go, to what cave among the rocks,
To be free of tidings of this gloomy world?
    Anonymous, *Kokinshu 952*
    (translated by Edward G. Seidensticker)

DREDGING did not begin until seven. Albertine had managed to get the Department of Public Works to make Dexter hold off until then. In fact, she learned that there was a town ordinance against beginning work "of a loud or disturbing nature" before seven. On the first day, Dexter had started early on his own initiative. What a hardworking guy.

The inmates of Small's Hotel were up well before seven. We wanted to get ourselves mentally prepared to endure Dexter's work of a loud and disturbing nature before it began. By the time we heard the whine of the outboard on Dexter's skiff, we were lined up on the porch, sitting in rockers, wrapped in blankets, enjoying our coffee and joking about the noise to come. I looked along the line, at everyone sitting there, making light of life, and I thought, *This is the way it should be—minus the noise, of course, and with every rocker full—but this is the way Small's ought to be.* Then the dredge woke up and began complaining. Within a few minutes we'd all been driven inside.

Elaine asked me to take her into town so that she could drop a package off at the office of Rush Service, the package-delivery company. I was a little surprised by this request, since she and Lou had been using the service regularly, calling them for pickups every couple of days. The speedy

Rush Service boat would whip up to our dock, the energetic agent would dash to the hotel, pick up the package, dash back to the boat, and roar off, leaving a lot of wake. He was in a rush, and he wanted it to show. It probably made him feel grown-up.

When Elaine and I were in the middle of the bay, sufficiently far from Dexter's dredge to talk to each other, I asked her, "What does Lou do, exactly?"

"Oh, he's got his fingers in a lot of pies," she said.

"Like Mr. Yummy?" I asked, and regretted it as soon as I'd said it. I think I blushed. She probably thought I was just reddening in the wind, as the captains of launches will do when they're standing at the wheel.

"Mr. Yummy?"

"Sorry," I said. "You weren't here for the first episode—"

"Oh, Mr. Yummy. Dad told me. He's the father of one of your friends."

"In my memoirs he is. In life, he was a quiet man who delivered baked goods, one of the people I knew nothing about. It's amazing what I discover about those people when I start thinking about them. In Mr. Yummy's case, he turns out to be the lonely housewife's friend."

"Oh," she said, laughing, "I see. Well, that's not Dad. He might *like* to be, and in a way—" She stopped and just stared across the bay.

"In a way?" I said.

She turned an impish smile toward me and said, "In a way that he would not want me to say anything about, he *was* 'the lonely housewife's friend,' but I will have absolutely nothing more to say about that."

AFTER DINNER that night, Elaine distributed gifts. Each of us got a small gaily wrapped box, and she commanded us to open them in unison. In each box was a pair of earmuffs with earpieces made of fluffy artificial fur in neon colors. At the moment when I read the opening words of "My Grandfather's Cave," episode fifteen of *Dead Air,* everyone in my audience put the earmuffs on, providing a highly amusing demonstration of the way an idea (good, bad, dumb, or indifferent) can circulate through an isolated population at the speed of thought itself.

WHEN MY PHOTOGRAPH of clams in flight was published in the *Babbington Reporter,* it not only made Kap'n Klam the most popular place in town and brought me quite a few new buyers for the flying-saucer detectors I manufactured in my cellar, but also enabled my grandfather to persuade my grandmother to allow him to dig the cave that he'd been yearning to dig for quite some time.

Cave-digging was a widespread hobby then. People dug them in the hope of surviving fallout, the radioactive dust that an atomic or nuclear bomb would loft into the atmosphere when it detonated, extending its killing power far beyond the point and instant of impact. These caves were called fallout shelters.

We were all afraid then. The likelihood of atomic war was widely advertised, and in school we were taught to expect it. Even my kindly grandfather, whom I still called Guppa though I had reached an age when I embarrassed myself by doing it, had begun to have apocalyptic fears. He wanted to build a fallout shelter, but he knew that my grandmother, Gumma, would have considered his fallout-shelter construction work a nearer and greater threat to her trim back yard than a bomb, so he had little hope of ever persuading her to allow him to build it—until my photograph appeared in the *Reporter*.

On the Saturday morning following the publication of the photograph, while Guppa was putting ketchup on his scrambled eggs, he said, as casually as he could, "After breakfast, Lorna, let's go into the back yard and pick out a spot for the shelter."

"Herb," said Gumma. "Don't be ridiculous."

"Ridiculous!" he said. "Just look at this!" He flipped the *Reporter* to the front page and pointed to the picture. "It's not just the bomb we've got to worry about now—it's these cosmic clams."

"Cosmic clams?"

"That's what they're calling them, cosmic clams. And it says here that there's considerable speculation about an invasion."

"Goodness gracious," said Gumma.

"In light of this intergalactic threat, wouldn't it be all right if I built a shelter?"

Gumma looked at Guppa, and a smile came over her face. "Oh, okay," she said. "Go ahead."

So Guppa dug a hole, and in the hole he constructed a fallout shelter, an artificial cave, to protect us from radioactive dust and cosmic clams. When the shelter was finished, Gumma and Guppa and I lived in it for an entire week, to try it out. It was well equipped—that was Guppa's way. During our stay, he encouraged us to make suggestions about improving the shelter's state of preparedness for enduring a siege. I remember suggesting that he could get by with fewer cans of lima beans, but I told him that otherwise I couldn't find a thing wrong with it, not a single flaw, and that the cesspool cover was a stroke of genius. (Guppa had had the inspired idea of concealing the shelter by disguising its entry hatch as a cesspool cover. A cesspool cover was a common backyard ornament in Babbington, so I suppose the disguise would have worked, but it was never tested. Everyone we knew was aware that the shelter was there and that the cesspool cover was a phony, so Guppa never got to find out how effective a concealment it was. For a while, he thought of attracting people into the back yard so that he could determine whether the average stranger would develop suspicions about the false cover. He planned to lure them into the back yard by selling vegetables from his garden on a pick-your-own basis. When he proposed the test, Gumma said that she didn't want people traipsing all over the yard, so that was that.)

Years passed before I saw the flaw. I was reminiscing, and in my reminiscent ramble I stumbled upon the entrance to Guppa's shelter. While I was standing there in the past, admiring the verisimilitude of the false cover, the thought struck me that a canny refugee, running through Babbington looking for hidden fallout shelters, might have noticed that my grandparents had *two* cesspool covers, and that's when I realized why Guppa had concealed the shelter. The shelter was meant to protect us from people who didn't have shelters of their own. (I'm sorry to have to say this in front of everyone, Guppa, but it's true.) He had hidden his cave from other people, who might need it and want to use it, because he meant to save only the people he had chosen to save, his people, and not the others, whoever they might be, whom he defined only by their otherness, the quality of not being his people. In his nightmares, it wasn't radioactive dust or cosmic clams that threatened us but swarms of city dwellers who would survive the bomb or the invasion and sweep out over our little town, looking for shelter. When I realized this, I thought that I could see, in memory, something I hadn't noticed at all during my stay in the shelter: Guppa with his ear to the entry hatch, listening for the rumble of their footsteps. He must have decided that in their panic they wouldn't notice the two cesspool covers, since panic can keep a person from seeing things that are as plain as the nose on his face.

THE GROUP that lingered in the lounge after the reading couldn't get off the topic of fallout shelters. Apparently, I had revived for them an old debate that had been suspended but never concluded, the question whether or not one would let others into one's fallout shelter beyond the number that it had been designed to accommodate. Forty years ago, people couldn't stop asking one another variations of that question. All versions took the general form of "Would you allow so-and-so into your fallout shelter?" but "so-and-so" could be "someone with an incurable disease who had only a year to live," "a child," "a child with only a year to live," "a pregnant woman," "a woman pregnant with your illegitimate child," and so on. There were also less serious versions of this question in which "so-and-so" became a matinee idol or a voluptuous starlet—at least I think they were less serious. All the variations were revived that evening, and new ones were invented, and the conversation went on long into the night—just as it used to.

I couldn't get a word in edgewise, which was just as well. I had more to say about my grandfather's cave, but it was probably best not said there in the lounge, where atomic anxieties were taking on the rosy glow of remembered pleasures, and I began expecting someone to sigh and claim that those had been the days.

If I had spoken, this is what I would have said:

I BECAME ASHAMED of my grandfather for concealing the shelter. I thought that it was disgraceful. I was shocked and disappointed and puzzled to hear Guppa talk about the urban refugees he expected. They seemed so real and immediate a danger to him that *they* seemed to be the enemy, not the people armed with the intercontinental ballistic missiles. The anticipated refugees were nearer, and so they seemed more real. I was naive and hopeful enough at the time to think that in Guppa's place I would have chosen to save them all. The fact that saving them all would require a back yard considerably larger than Guppa and Gumma's was not material to my thinking. It was the principle that counted, not the practicality. Guppa had never been very practical, so it seemed to me that he could afford to be principled.

Suddenly, as I write those words, the time that I'm recalling seems very long ago. Let me say right now, before I take you back there with me, that when we get there I am going to start something at the family dinner table that will certainly lead to an argument, and that I know it will be my fault. Here's the situation in brief: my father had been in control of my family, including me, for as long as I could remember, and he had intended to rule for life, but when I began approaching thirteen, I initiated a campaign of guerrilla warfare. I was revolting.

Dinners were difficult at that time, most especially difficult for my mother, and it was almost always my fault that they were difficult for her. I brought anger and restlessness to the table; my father brought anger and disappointment; and my mother brought a pack of cigarettes and a bottle of tawny port. Generally, we tried to eat in silence, since we all knew that any conversation was likely to lead to an argument, but one of us did not know how to hold his tongue.

"You know Guppa's fallout shelter?" I said into the silence.

"Uhh," said my father.

"Well, I was wondering—"

A pause. Perhaps my father was wondering too, wondering whether I had something that I really wanted to ask him, in which case it might be the case that I had come back to the realization that he was the boss and that as the boss he was also the living repository of all important information, or whether this claim to wonder was just the bait in a trap.

He took the bait. "Wondering what?"

"You know, whether he really considered, you know, the morality of it."

"What morality is that?"

"Well, you know, Guppa thinks that people are going to come swarming from the city trying to save themselves."

"Sure."

"Well, does he think, you know, that those people are bad some-how for wanting to save themselves?"

"How the hell would I know? Why don't you ask him?"

My mother sighed and said, "Bert—"

"Ella, don't you see that he's not interested in what I think? He's just baiting me."

"No, I'm not," I lied, using the voice of the offended innocent.

"All right, go ahead," he said. "Get to the point."

"Well, I mean, from Guppa's point of view their motives can't be wrong, since they're the same as his own."

"All right."

"Well, I've been thinking about this, and I know that Guppa, like most working people, considers theft of labor a greater crime than theft of property, so—"

"Now, wait a damn minute!"

"What?"

"What in the name of blazes do you know about 'working peo-ple'—or *work*?"

"Well, I—"

"What did you do—watch somebody doing a day's work and now you think you know what makes 'working people' tick?"

"No, I—"

"There's more to work than watching, *you know*. That's your favorite expression, I've noticed, *you know*?"

"Well—"

"That's another one! Well! *Well, you know!* And here's another one: *I've been thinking!* Sometimes you get started with 'well, you know,' and 'I've been thinking,' and I say to myself, 'Oh, Jesus, here we go!'"

Silence fell over the table again. My mother pushed her plate away from her and settled back in her chair. She shook a cigarette from her pack and lit it. She took a long drag, and as she exhaled she poured herself another half glass of tawny port.

I cleared my throat and said, "Well—"

My father gave me a hard look.

"—you know—"

He put his fork down.

"—I've been—"

He reached across the table and picked up my mother's pack of cigarettes.

"—giving this a lot of thought—"

He lit a cigarette and frowned in my direction.

"—and I decided, or I think I decided, that, maybe, the evil of the people fleeing the city must be that they want to use shelters that other people built and prepared—"

"Of course," said my father, blowing smoke.

"—at the expense of great effort and ingenuity."

"Of course, of course."

"But here's the thing: those people never *wanted* a shelter— theirs or anybody else's—until the bomb fell."

"What?" said my mother, startled.

"He means *if,*" said my father, "*if* the bomb fell." He stubbed out his cigarette, though he hadn't finished smoking it. I knew what that meant. He was going to leave the table in a moment, so he would tell me to get to the point, and he would remind me that I had work to do.

"Get to the point, Peter," he said. "You've got the dishes and your homework to do."

"And you've got your beer to drink and the television to watch," I muttered.

"What did you say?"

"Nothing," I said.

"Get started on those dishes."

He got up from the table, got a can of beer from the refrigerator, and went into the living room.

My mother and I eyed each other. I wanted to go on talking—I *usually* wanted to go on talking—but I had caused trouble, and I knew it, and I thought that my mother might not want to hear anything more from me, so I didn't say anything, but she was my mother, so, after a moment of weary silence, she said, "Go ahead, Peter. Tell me what you were getting at."

"I'm not sure what I was getting at, really," I said. "I don't know whether I have a point—but I have a lot of questions."

"Oh," she said, frowning. I think she had hoped that listening would be enough, that she would be able to let *me* talk, with nothing more required of her, but questions implied answers.

I shrugged and said, "I'm not sure that my questions have any answers."

"Oh," she said, smiling. "Well, why don't you go ahead and ask them."

"Okay," I said. "First question: if urban refugees did come swarming into Babbington looking for someone's fallout shelter, wouldn't it be because they had been pushed into it?"

"Pushed into it?"

"You know, because the bomb drove them from the city— pushed them out."

"Oh. I see. Yes, I guess so. You're right." I had the feeling that she had the feeling that we were practicing for a quiz show.

"Okay, second question: they wouldn't necessarily be evil, would they, those people?"

"No. No, they wouldn't." She looked around the room with apparent urgency, and I had the crazy idea that she was looking for a pad so that she could keep score.

"Third question: they could even be *good* people who had been displaced by evil, couldn't they?"

"Yes!" she said, and she jumped up from the table. "Wait a minute, Peter. I want to get a pad from the kitchen and write some of this down."

"Okay." She dashed into the kitchen, where she took from a drawer the pad she used to make her shopping list. She stood there at the kitchen counter for a while, writing rapidly and then came back into the dining room, reading what she'd written as she walked, and settled into her chair, still with her eyes on the pad.

"Okay," she said. "Go ahead."

"Let's see," I said. "Third question—"

"No, no. We had the third question: 'Couldn't they be good people dispossessed by evil?'"

"'Dispossessed'? I said 'displaced.'"

"Oh," she said. She started to erase it.

"But 'dispossessed' is kind of—interesting. Better."

She was surprised and pleased. "It's sadder," she said, "and kind of—"

"Surprising," I said.

"Yes. It *is* surprising."

"That's because it's not what you expect. I mean, people are usually *possessed* by evil, so when you hear *dispossessed,* it sounds like a mistake at first, and then when you think about it, you realize that it isn't a mistake, that it's right, it's true."

"And because it *sounds* like a mistake at first you have to think about it, so it's—well, you know—it's clever, isn't it?"

"I think so."

"'Dispossessed by evil,' she read from her pad. She looked at me suddenly, and she seemed startled. "In fact," she said, "they would be a kind of fallout themselves, wouldn't they—you know, a kind of human dust blown far from home by the fireball of evil?" She looked into the distance.

"Well," I said. "I don't know. That's a little—"

She held her hand up for me to stop.

"I'm sorry," she said. "You really do have to get to work on your homework."

"And the dishes," I said.

"That's all right. I'll do them. I'll let them drain, and you can put them away when your homework is finished."

"Okay," I said. I left for my room, but I made a detour to the bathroom. When I came out, I stuck my head around the corner of the kitchen to thank my mother for doing the dishes, but she wasn't at the sink. She was still in the dining room, but not at the dining room table. She had moved, with her cigarettes and her glass of tawny port, to the little table in the corner where our telephone was.

"Dudley?" she was saying, in a low, husky voice. "It's Ella. Oh, nothing. It's just that, well, you know, I was thinking—about fallout shelters—and—you know—the morality of them. Morality. Well, I'm not sure I have a point, but—you know—I have a lot of questions—"

I went upstairs and did my homework. When I came back down to the kitchen later to put the dishes away I found that they hadn't been done. My mother must have gone to bed and forgotten them. I did them.

Anxiety Pays

> There is no crime in thinking about a crime.
> Jean-Claude Carrière, in an interview on *The South Bank Show*

THOUGHTS OF GUNS filled most of my morning. The day before, while Elaine had been at the Rush Service office (or, as I learned later, pretending to be at the Rush Service office), I had been at Sun and Surf, choosing guns. I had been surprised to finf that they had very few guns on display there. My memory, from decades earlier, when the shop had been called Babbington Sporting Goods, was that there were cases and cases filled with guns. Now there was a single case with guns, and most of the rest of the store was filled with in-line skates and attendant gear designed to minimize the lasting effects of in-line-skating accidents. There was also a line of wet suits and dry suits that would allow the wearer to extend the jet-ski season well beyond the summer. These came in the same range of vibrant colors as the earmuffs that Elaine had given us.

In the gun case, the pickings were slim. I persuaded the clerk, who was much more interested in the other merchandise, to open the case, and I handled every gun they had there. The clerk knew next to nothing about any of them, and when I asked about silencers, he said that he thought silencers were illegal because he had seen that on TV or in a movie. None of the guns in the case was suitable for Rockwell Kingman, it seemed to me, unless he found himself in a really tough spot without any of his pre-ferred weaponry and had to break into a sporting goods store in a little backwater town and make do with whatever he found there among the helmets, knee pads, and jet-ski booties.

I had much better luck at the magazine rack. There, mixed in with magazines for skaters, bikers, hikers, surfers, and jet-ski riders, were quite a few journals for people in the doing-in trade, or aspirants thereto: *Mercenary Monthly, Modern Militiaman, International Assassin, Terrorist Times, Gun Fun, Worldwide Pricing Guide to Pre-Owned Armaments,* and *American Hit Man.* It was the last of these that appealed to me most and would, I thought, appeal to Rockwell Kingman, not only for the pictures of naked women scattered among the pictures of weaponry, but because the emphasis was on the techniques and equipment most useful to the kind of hired killer Rockwell was: skilled, careful, clever, and damned proud of it. Many of the naked women seemed underage, barely women at all, which made me wonder whether Rockwell had tastes of which I was as yet unaware. I'd have to think about that. I bought a copy of *American Hit Man,* and, concealing the contempt that a professional feels for the ignorance of laypeople, I thanked the clerk and made my exit from the store.

I spent all morning going through the magazine, and by noon I had armed Rockwell, furnished his office, chosen his sex objects, and written an ad to run in the classified pages at the back of *American Hit Man.*

Rockwell Kingman
Murder While You Wait
killer@hitman.com

This would be the ad that the character "Peter Leroy" would answer.

IN THE AFTERNOON, Albertine and I walked the perimeter of the island, along the margin, circumambulating our domain. This walk was once a part of every day, a high point of every day. In our early years here, we used the walk to scheme and dream. Later, when our dreams for the place began to seem as improbable as Porky White's for Kap'n Klam, our walks became an escape valve. We would walk and talk and let off steam when we needed to let off steam, and we'd feel better for it, and sometimes we'd even slip back into schemes and dreams. Then the circumambulatory walk began to slip out of the day, and our days have been worse without it.

Walking with Albertine along the western edge of the island, where we were well removed from the dredging, I began to feel the old buoyancy return. I was optimistic about the prospects for *Murder While You Wait*— I'd even begun to think about the movie version and licensing possibilities for a line of active wear and toy weapons—and I thought that the time had come to begin telling Al about it, but she spoke first.

"Fear has become the dominant emotion in my life," she said. "I am afraid of running out of money, completely out of money, of having everything we have taken from us. I am afraid that if we can't find a buyer—a *real* buyer—then we will reach a point where everything is taken from us. Nothing we have done will have amounted to anything."

A dullness came over us, an emptiness. We walked along for a little longer in silence, with our heads down, and then she said, "And I'm afraid that the kids are not going to come to *one* of your readings."

"They're busy," I said. "They—"

"Couldn't they call and ask how it's going, or let us know whether they plan to come? They have telephones." She gave a short, sharp laugh, and said, "I sound like my mother, don't I?"

I stopped her, put my arms around her, held her, told her that I loved her, promised to get her away from the island and take her to another place, another life, raised her chin, kissed her, hugged her again, and pointed out the complete absence of cats in this part of the island. She burst into tears.

"What?" I asked.

"The cats—"

"You want them back."

"Oh, yes, please. They're probably starving over there."

THAT EVENING, in the lounge of an old hotel on a small island artificially infested with feral cats, I read episode sixteen of *Dead Air*, "Anxiety Pays."

IT WAS A TIME when a great many people were anxious about the possibility that otherworldly beings would invade us in fleets of flying saucers. We were already anxious about the possibility that intercontinental ballistic missiles would deliver nuclear warheads to our back yards, so you would have thought we had enough to worry about.

One night, my parents and I watched a television program about flying saucers. We saw blurry snapshots of hubcaps in the sky, scratchy films of fuzzy lights, and we listened to the sketchy, contradictory accounts of the people who had seen the hubcaps and fuzzy lights. The back yards of Babbington were never mentioned, but, even so, the program left my mother wringing her hands. "Peter," she said, "could you make me a flying-saucer detector like that one you've got?"

"Sure," I said, trying not to sound pleased.

My father looked at her over the top of his glasses and asked, "What is all this, Ella?"

"I built a detector from plans in *Cellar Scientist* magazine—" I began.

"I wasn't speaking to you, Peter," said my father. "I was speaking to your mother. Ella, what is all this nonsense?"

"Oh, I don't know," said my mother. She hugged herself as if she were cold, though it was a warm night. "Maybe it's silly to be afraid of something you've never seen—"

"—and never will," said my father. He lifted the can of beer on the table beside him to see if there was anything left in it.

"Maybe not," my mother conceded, "but you could say that about missiles too, couldn't you?"

"That's different," claimed my father.

"It's just that I'd rather know if they're coming," said my mother, softly, with her eyes down. "I'd like some warning. I don't want to be taken by surprise."

That seemed reasonable enough to me. "You can borrow mine for now," I said. I went upstairs, got my detector, and brought it downstairs. My parents were sitting in silence. My father had a fresh beer.

"Where should I put it?" I asked.

"In the bedroom," said my mother.

"I don't want that thing waking me up in the middle of the night," said my father.

"You expect it to go off?" asked my mother.

"No," said my father. "I don't."

"Then you don't have to worry about having it wake you up in the middle of the night. Besides, it only has a little light. I'll put it on my bedside table and sleep with my back to you so that it will wake me but won't wake you."

My father said nothing. He turned his attention to the television set. I went to my parents' bedroom and put the saucer detector on my mother's bedside table. I aligned it properly and made certain that it was stable, and then I switched the bedroom light off and triggered the detector. Its little light filled the room; it would wake my mother.

I left my parents' bedroom, said good night to them, and went upstairs to my own room. I stretched out in bed, but I couldn't sleep. I lay there wondering whether any flying saucers were passing overhead. I got up and went to the window to see. The night was clear, with a fine scattering of stars and a sliver of moon. I stood there, searching the night sky for anomalies, and soon I began to detect movement in the star at the center of my field of vision. I wished that it would move again, so that I could be convinced that I was actually seeing what I thought I was. I got my wish. The star, or whatever it was, moved, or seemed to move, seemed to grow larger, as it would if it were coming toward me. Had it actually moved? Was it really a larger presence in my field of vision than it had been? I turned from the window to find some objective measure and grabbed the first thing I found, a comb. I held it at arm's length, turned sideways, so that the teeth would provide a gauge against which I could measure the increase in apparent size as the star approached, but I couldn't find the star. (Let's be honest about this: I mean that I couldn't find a flying saucer, since that's what I now expected to see.) Where had it gone? I looked this way and that in the night sky, but I couldn't see it. The devious saucerians must be hiding somewhere. Were they hovering above the roof, where I couldn't see them? I leaned out the window, but I still couldn't find the ship.

I tiptoed to the bottom of the stairs, where I could see the door of my parents' bedroom at the far end of the living room. The door was closed, but there was a gap between the floor and the bottom of the door, and I could see that there was no light showing in the gap, and after a while I felt certain that my parents were asleep. If the star that I had seen had been a saucer, it was far away, beyond the range of my detector, and so, in a sense, my detector was useless as a saucer detector in these immediate circumstances, but the presence of the detector and the absence of a warning from it had allowed my mother to sleep, had made her feel secure. I was proud of myself for having given her that security.

"Sleep tight, boys and girls," I whispered in the direction of my parents' room, and crept back up the stairs to my own bed. On the way, I realized that other people would be willing to pay for the security I had given my mother, a night's freedom from anxiety, a good night's sleep, and that I could probably make big money selling saucer detectors.

THERE IS no more effective method of generating apparent anomalies than the hunt for them. I saw movement in the stars because I was looking for movement in the stars. If you doubt the truth of this assertion, try the following experiment tonight when you get into bed: pay close attention to your heartbeat to determine whether anything is going wrong with the old ticker. In a short time, you will begin to detect arrhythmic fluctuations, hesitations, thumps, bumps, and lapses—enough to have you calling your neighborhood cardiologist first thing in the morning.

Is Anybody Out There?

> Despite all my efforts, I was quite unable to get to sleep: an endless succession of . . . unnecessary thoughts dragged one after another persistently and monotonously through my mind.
>
> Ivan S. Turgenev, "Hamlet of the Shchigrovsky District"

AT ABOUT THREE I gave up trying to get to sleep. I slipped out of bed, dressed in the dark, tiptoed to the door, and pulled it silently shut behind me, but before it was fully closed Albertine said, "Be sure you're warm enough."

"I am," I said. "I've got a sweat suit and a sweater on, and two pairs of socks."

"Okay. Come back, though. Don't stay up the whole time."

"Okay."

I stood at the top of the stairs for a moment to see if anyone else was up. The hotel seemed quiet. Everyone else seemed to be asleep. I went downstairs and into the kitchen, where I made a turkey sandwich from the leftovers refrigerator. I took it out onto the porch, and I found Lou sitting there.

"Couldn't sleep?" he asked.

"Couldn't sleep," I said.

"Clam salad sandwich?"

"Turkey," I said.

"Was it anxieties or regrets?"

"Anxieties *and* regrets."

"If it's any consolation to you, by my age the anxieties pretty much disappear."

"No more anxieties?"

"I didn't say that."

"Oh."

"It's more a case of the anxieties being almost entirely overshadowed by the regrets."

"Oh, wonderful," I said. "I can't wait."

We sat there in silence, looking out at the dredge.

"We could sink it," he said.

"Could we?"

"Sure. I've got a friend who was in Korea with me, a very skilled guy, and I could get him out here. Give him a few minutes in the water one night, a night like this, and that thing would be sitting on the bottom in the morning."

I laughed nervously. Lou answered my nervous laugh with Baldy's sardonic one.

"You've got to keep that rock in front of the cave," he said.

"Yeah," I said.

"Even if your cave is an island and your rock is a bay."

"Right."

"Having that dredge out there is like having somebody take a jackhammer to the rock at the mouth of the cave."

"I get it, Lou," I said.

"Want me to give my friend a call?"

"We've got rooms available," I said, which was not quite saying yes, even if it was not quite saying no.

"BEFORE I BEGIN the next reading from *Dead Air*," I said to the group in the lounge after dinner, "I have something more to say about fallout shelters.

"About four years after Guppa had dug his fallout shelter, I arrived at college as a freshman. I hadn't been there more than a couple of days when I was interviewed for the 'man on the street' segment of a local television program. I was walking along, a young man on the street, when an earnest young interviewer stuck a microphone in my face and said, 'Let me ask you a hypothetical question: Let's say that a nuclear attack is under way. Bombs are falling on targets all across America. You run to your fallout shelter, and your neighbor comes running up with his wife and children. They never got around to building a fallout shelter, and now here they are, begging you to let them into yours. What do you do? Do you let them in?'

"Without a moment's hesitation, I said, 'Sure,' and as soon I began to speak, I astonished myself by discovering that I had been preparing my answer for years. 'I'd let them in. In fact, I'd *give* them the damned thing, my gift, and I'd move out. Let me tell you why—'

"I reached for the microphone, and the reporter, startled, handed it to me. (I think he must have detected something in my manner that indicated that I had experience in broadcasting—which I had, on a small, local scale, as you will see if you're here for some of the later episodes of *Dead Air*.) I spoke into it as into an attractive ear.

"'If we creatures, we the people, are so fucked up that we can allow some of us to blow millions of the rest of us from here to forever, then I don't want to be around to pick up the pieces.' A crowd had gathered, and I began speaking to them, shouting now. 'Well, you know, I've been thinking, and I think the evidence is already in. We *are* that fucked up. We have *already* dispatched millions of our fellow creatures for one idiotic reason or another—because we envy them, hate them, fear them—so I'd say we have fully and completely lived up to our potential for fucking up.' I looked right into the camera, dropped my voice, and spoke to anybody who might be watching. 'Add it all up,' I said, almost whispering now, 'and this species probably doesn't deserve to survive. So if we're *going* to blow ourselves up, I'm not going to hide in a cave while we do it. I don't want to miss the show. I want to *watch*!'

"My performance became the lead clip in a feature on disaffected youth. The broadcasters bleeped *fucked up* and *fucking up,* of course, and even *damned,* since those were far, far more reticent times, but even censored I was a hit. As soon as the program was broadcast—in fact, before it was even over—dark-haired, dark-eyed girls began telephoning me to invite me to join them in grieving for the species, and so I spent the first semester of my freshman year in a state of blissful despair, commiserating with brooding beauties, thereby proving that it is a very ill wind indeed that does not blow somebody some good."

Then I read the seventeenth episode of *Dead Air,* "Is Anybody Out There?"

NIGHT AFTER NIGHT, the flying-saucer detector that I'd built to alert me in the event that unearthly creatures invaded my neighborhood had sat on a shelf in my room, detecting nothing, which meant that we were, for the time being, safe. Then, one night, my mother borrowed the detector, hoping that she would sleep more securely with it beside her, detecting nothing.

It worked. She slept. I was the one who couldn't sleep that night, and, in a way, it was the flying-saucer detector that kept me awake, because a succession of schemes for selling saucer detectors dragged through my mind. For distraction from these ideas, I turned "Baldy's Nightcap" on.

"Well, here we are back again," said Baldy. "At least *I'm* back. I *hope* you're back, listener. I *know* I'm back. I am *definitely* back, right, Bob?"

"Yeah."

"Of course it could be that I never left. How would *you* know?"

His question was directed to me; I could tell from the sound of his voice. Baldy had a way of turning aside from the microphone and raising his voice when he directed a question to Bob and of leaning into it and lowering his voice when he was speaking to me. Often I answered him, "Yeah," but tonight I was too occupied with my own thoughts. I felt certain that I could sell my mother a saucer detector, and that sale would get the business started. Maybe she would buy *my* detector, and that would allow me to order the parts for the next one—the next *two*—but if she wasn't willing to buy a used detector, maybe she would advance me the cost of the parts for a new one—for *two* new ones.

"Maybe you never left," said Baldy. "Maybe you've been sitting there in the dark all this time, waiting for me to return. I don't know. How would I know?"

I figured that my grandfather, Guppa, would probably buy a detector for his fallout shelter. That would make the shelter twice as useful, since it would become both a fallout shelter and a flying-saucer shelter. Of course! I could sell a detector to *everyone* with a shelter. If people were going to be hiding in their shelters, they'd want to know whether *anything* was outside—bombs, fallout, desperate refugees, flying saucers.

"Or maybe you went away," said Baldy, wearily. A match was struck, a cigarette lit, a long drag taken, the smoke exhaled. "That's all right. I don't hold it against you. You were gone for a while, that's all right. You're there now, and I'm here, and that's what counts. At least, I *hope* you're there, because if you're not there, then what is the point of my being here?"

Porky would buy one—Porky White, who ran the Kap'n Klam clam bar, the center of saucer speculation in Babbington. The center of saucer speculation *had* to have a saucer detector on the counter. Porky would definitely buy one.

"I'm here because I assume that you are there," said Baldy. "You see the implications of that, don't you? I know you do. Of course you do. Don't be offended by the question—it was just a rhetorical device. I wasn't suggesting that you *wouldn't* see the implications. Not at all, not at all. I always say I've got the most intelligent audience in radio. Don't I always say that, Bob?"

"Yeah."

Leaning very close to the mike, and speaking in a desperate voice that made me take notice, Baldy said, "Without you I'm nothing, you know. I'm just a voice calling into the dark, trying to make myself heard over the static, just a pathetic guy—a dummy, when you get right down to it—sitting in a cave—talking into the dark." After another drag and a long exhalation, he said, "So, don't touch that dial, okay? I beg of you. If you touch that dial, I'm here alone. Don't do it, okay? Don't leave me here alone. We're in this together, you and I. I'm sitting here in my cave, talking, and you're sitting out there in your dark little rooms—your caves, you know, your caves—listening to a dummy in the dark."

It was right about there that I thought of sending a detector to Baldy so that he could use it in the cave to tell him a little something about what was going on outside, so that he would know that I was out here, listening, and so that he would talk about the detector and me and make both of us—me and my detector, a boy and

his invention—famous, and it must have been right about there that
I fell asleep.

IN BED that night, however, I couldn't sleep at all. Rain was falling, and
the roof was leaking. It wasn't leaking any longer in the spot from which
drops fell on my head; now it was leaking in two other places. I could
hear a drip in the corner to my left, near the window on my side of the
bed, and I could hear another drip, or perhaps an echo of the first drip, in
the corner diagonally opposite it. A drop would fall on my left, and a moment later a drop would fall on my right. When one is lying in bed between the extremes of a bipolar drip like that, one's thoughts tend to
arrange themselves in bipolar patterns: call and response, question and
answer, either-or, wet-dry, being and nothingness—to the man who is lying somewhere between drip and drop, all of these are variations on that
theme.

on the one hand, a drip . . .	on the other, a drop . . .
youth	age
fond memories	nagging regrets
eager anticipation	gut-wrenching anxiety
the tendency to stay put	the urge to move on
make it happen	let it be
an island	a piece of the continent, a part of the main
the past	the future
memory	imagination
ventriloquist	dummy

Because I had learned that a little bit of "Baldy's Nightcap" was the
antidote for most kinds of egocentric thinking, I expected it to work for
this man-in-the-middle type, too. I stuck my earphone in my ear and
switched my radio on, but the show was already over, and Baldy was, I
suppose, asleep.

No Worries, No Kidding

ALL OF US were on the porch, lined up in our rockers, waiting for Dexter's dredge to start sucking sand and rending the air. When he started it up, we put our earmuffs on and sat there with our breakfast and our aspirin, watching him, at his mercy, fascinated by his power over us and by the way he operated the dredge in an unpredictable cycle of motion and rest. He would fire the machine up and run it at full steam for a while, then throttle back to a level that allowed us to speak to one another, then bring it back up to full roar. When it was quiet, we took our earmuffs off, and when it was roaring, we put them back on and retreated into ourselves.

He backed off. We took our earmuffs off.

"It reminds me of my digestive system," said Grumpy Cluck. "It sucks up whatever it finds—it rumbles—it farts—it shits out the back."

"Clark!" said Alice. "We're eating."

"Sorry," he said. "What's all of that you've got there?" He pointed to several sheets of hotel stationery that she had covered with figures.

"I've been timing Dexter's cycles."

"Is he taking too many breaks? Maybe he's goldbricking! We can get him fired."

"I don't think so. He doesn't really take any breaks, just slows the machine down, but I think we may have underestimated him. I think he has really figured out how to drive us mad. These unpredictable variations—if he thought that up on his own, he's a kind of evil genius. There is no discernible pattern to the ups and downs of that machine—at least none that I can find—no way to anticipate the changes, no way to—"

The racket rose up and drowned her out, and we put our earmuffs on and ate our breakfast.

When Dexter slowed the machine again, we began drifting our separate ways. Grumpy Cluck announced, "If you're looking for me, I'll be up knocking holes in the roof." Albertine gave him the big eyes and the terrified grimace, and he laughed and squeezed her shoulder and said, "Just kidding, gorgeous. I'm working on the boiler today."

I REMEMBER the rest of the day as a cacophonous competition between Dexter and Grumpy Cluck, with the nod going to Dexter, who put in an hour's overtime, to the surprise and annoyance of all the inmates, with the possible exception of Alice, who found this development "fascinating," and recorded it on her chart. By dinnertime, the island was quiet again, except for the buzz of conversation, and we were all cheered by the thought that Dexter would not be back until Monday. In the evening, I read episode eighteen of *Dead Air,* "No Worries, No Kidding," to a lively Friday audience.

MY MOTHER had begun having trouble sleeping as I approached thirteen. Anxiety hung in the air like a hovering spacecraft or an intercontinental ballistic missile at the crest of its evil arc, and I was no more immune to the ambient anxiety than my mother was. However, one night my mother had borrowed my flying-saucer detector, and, under the influence of its comforting quiescence, she had slept. From the silence of her sleep, I had gotten the idea that I could make big money selling saucer detectors, and that idea had kept me awake most of the night.

The next morning, when I came downstairs for breakfast, I could feel the difference in the mood of the house. Something had relaxed: the system of attractive and repulsive forces that bound the elements of my nuclear family but kept them sufficiently distant to avoid detonation. The forces were still in place, still at work, but they were easy on the job, humming, not whining.

Even my father was humming. He was sitting at the table drinking coffee, smoking a cigarette, and reading a newsmagazine. It had been his habit to drink Strong 'n' Bitter brand coffee, smoke

Rawhide cigarettes, and get his news from *Snap,* a weekly magazine that claimed to deliver "photographic proof," but my mother, in one of the fits of improvement that came over her at the time of fall cleaning, had persuaded him to drink Olde Plantation House coffee, smoke Oriflamme cigarettes, and read *Matters of Moment.* He had been grumbling for a couple of weeks, but now he was humming the Oriflamme jingle.

"How did you sleep?" I asked him.

"Fine. Just fine."

"And Mom? How did she sleep?"

"Fine. Just fine."

"The detector didn't go off, I take it."

"No."

Pause.

"So, she wasn't tossing and turning?"

"What?"

"Mom. She wasn't tossing and turning? She wasn't vexed and tormented by fears of the imminent approach of flying saucers?"

"How would I know? Ask her yourself."

In a moment, I did get to ask her. She came to the breakfast table humming, like my father, the Oriflamme jingle.

"I guess you slept well," I said.

"Oh, I did," she said.

"Would you say that you got a good night's sleep because of the saucer detector?"

"Yes, I think I would."

"Would you say that it was the first good night's sleep you've had in weeks?"

"In I-don't-know-how-long!"

"Would you say that you slept like a log?"

"Like a baby."

"Would you say that you weren't vexed and tormented by fears of the imminent approach of flying saucers?"

"I wasn't even worried about the bomb!"

"No kidding?" I said. This was a surprise.

"No kidding," she said. "No kidding, no worries. I mean, no worries, no kidding."

"So," I said, marshaling my thoughts, "would you say, 'I used to be vexed and tormented by fears of the imminent approach of flying saucers, but thanks to the Magnetomic Flying-Saucer Detector I got the first good night's sleep I've had in weeks—in fact, I slept like a baby!'?"

"Say that again."

"'I used to be vexed and tormented by fears of the imminent approach of flying saucers—*and* the possibility that an intercontinental ballistic missile would deliver a nuclear warhead to my back yard—but thanks to the Magnetomic Flying-Saucer Detector I got the first good night's sleep I've had in weeks—in fact, I slept like a baby!'"

After a moment's reflection, she said, "Yes, I'd say that."

"Would you say it in writing?"

She would, as it turned out, provided that I wrote it out for her. I did, and with the aid of my Little Giant Printing Outfit I printed some flyers. I used what would today be called clip art, which is to say that I held each flyer up to a window in my room and traced the pictorial diagram of the saucer detector from *Cellar Scientist* magazine and the saucer photograph that had appeared in the *Babbington Reporter*. This was not an efficient way of producing flyers, but the results seemed, to me, at that time, well worth the effort. My mother had even given me a slogan:

No worries, no kidding!

GRUMPY CLUCK SAID, "Somebody should invent a detector that gives a readout on that, what you called the mood of the house. If you could invent a gadget like that, you'd make a lot more than you ever did on flying-saucer detectors."

"Oh, Clark," said Alice. "He didn't sell flying-saucer detectors."

"You didn't?" he asked me.

"Not really," I said. "I did build one detector, and I thought about trying to sell them, but part of my inherited mental illness is a tendency to get distracted by the next idea, and I moved on to sex."

"Oh! I see!" he said. "Well, it would still be a useful gadget—not the flying-saucer detector, the mood detector."

"I think it's only men who would need a device like that," said Albertine. "I think women come with mood detectors as part of the basic equipment package."

Elaine and Alice agreed.

"Well *I* could use one," said Clark. "Forty-two years of marriage and I still can't tell when she's happy. If I ask her, 'Are you okay—are you happy?' she says, 'Stop asking me that.'"

"'It makes me unhappy when you ask me if I'm happy,'" I said, quoting Albertine. As soon as I had said it, I wished I hadn't. I glanced at her. She was laughing, but I suspected that my quoting her had made her unhappy.

"Exactly!" said Lou. He extended a hand toward Elaine and said, "I used to look at your mother and she wouldn't seem happy to me, so I'd say, 'I wish you were happy,' and she would get *angry* about it. She'd ask me, 'What have I done? What have I done to make you think I'm not happy?' And she'd say, 'Believe me—if I'm not happy, you'll know it,' and by then I was pretty sure I knew it."

We all laughed at that, and we all knew what we were laughing about. Lou and Elaine exchanged a look, and there was a twinkle in his eye. He winked at her, and she grinned back at him, and then he said, "I bet you *could* make money on a gadget like that, Clark. You'd have to convince people that it worked, and at the same time you'd have to claim that it was meant for entertainment purposes only, but if you sold it through the shopping channels and the horoscope magazines I bet you'd do all right. I bet you would."

THERE HAS BEEN only one goal for my life, only one thing that I have ever wanted to accomplish: to make Albertine happy. There have been side trips, short-term goals, and to-do lists (buy coffee, varnish tables, write memoirs), but if each item had been specified in full the list would have read: buy coffee to make Albertine happy, varnish tables to make Albertine happy, write memoirs to make Albertine happy.

I lay in bed facing the awful conviction that I had failed in the ultimate goal, that all I had done was buy coffee and varnish tables and write my memoirs, but failed to make Albertine happy, and that I was running out of time to accomplish it. That awful draining feeling of time slipping away began to make me panic, to sweat and twitch. Then Albertine stirred, just shifted her position, and my conviction—my belief—that she was unhappy made me interpret her movement as evidence of the anguished dreams of an unhappy woman trapped in a miserable life. My twitching grew worse. I had a need to move my feet. I had to get up, because I simply could not lie still, so I got up, dressed in workout wear for warmth, and went to the lounge, where I stretched out on one of the sofas. I heard a sound, nothing more than one of the thousand nightly sounds an old hotel emits as it slowly collapses, but for a moment it made me think that the other sofas might be occupied, that all the inmates might have been driven from their beds by the twitching ripple of panic across their backs. This struck me as simultaneously absurd and quite likely, and lying there with my feet pressing and releasing against the arm of the sofa, like a cat kneading, I almost laughed.

If Saucers Attack

THE DEMOLITION MAN arrived in the morning. Lou and I went over in the launch to pick him up. We had expected the man and his wife, but we found six people waiting at the town dock. Their luggage was lined up beside them, and beside that was a pile of about a dozen large cartons that I supposed contained the supplies and gear that a demolition man would ordinarily bring along for the elimination of a dredge.

"Hey, hey, hey, it's the Demolition Man," Lou shouted when we neared the dock. By way of acknowledgment, the Demolition Man went into a fighter's crouch and made the motions of throwing a few punches to the midsection. As soon as we were at the dock, Lou leaped ashore and both of them repeated the gesture, the crouch, the punches. "Hey, Peter," he said, "this is my friend Artie, the Demolition Man."

"Hey, Peter," said the Demolition Man, "nice to know you. I got the whole family here, as you can see."

He introduced me to his wife, Nancy, his son and daughter-in-law, Otto and Esther, and his granddaughter, Louise, and her girlfriend, Miranda, and then he said to me, "My buddy Hamlet, here, tells me you've got room for all of us." He gave Lou a nudge, and they exchanged a wink.

"Oh, we've got room, Artie," I assured him.

"Call him the Demolition Man," said Lou. He and Artie went into their fighters' crouches and fired volleys of simulated punches at each other's middles. Artie's son and daughter-in-law rolled their eyes, and his granddaughter and her friend giggled and put their heads together and

exchanged a whispered secret that made them giggle again. It was probably an assessment of the lunacy of adults. The girls wore cropped tops,
which, I noticed, allowed their bellies and their belly buttons and their
belly button rings to show. When I suggested that they would want coats
when we got onto the bay, they smiled winningly and said okay, and I felt
that things were looking up.

ALBERTINE opened a letter, skimmed it, and said, quite loudly, "Oh,
shit. We're being sued."

"Sued?" I asked. "What for?"

"Remember Mrs. Gussman from a couple of years ago?"

"Mrs. Gussman," I said reflectively, as if I couldn't quite manage to
bring her to mind. "I'm not sure that I—"

"Oh, come on. The tight pants? The stiletto heels?"

I furrowed my brow and said "Tight pants—stiletto heels—"

"The widow in heat. The one who asked you to 'fix her plumbing.'
The one who said, and I quote, 'I'd write *my* memoirs if you'd give me
something to remember.'"

"Oh! *That* Mrs. Gussman!"

"That's right, that one." She smiled the smile she smiles when she
does not want her picture taken. "She is suing us because of the mental
anguish she suffered here."

"I did not do a *thing,*" I said, raising my hands, palms out in a gesture
that I've always assumed is a universal indication of complete innocence.
"Nothing at all. I gave her absolutely *nothing* to remember, I swear it—
just the basic guest services."

"Well, maybe you should have given her a little something more, because in her search for some memorable moments to include in her memoirs she has discovered the trauma she suffered while she was here."

"The assistant innkeeper's rejection of her amorous advances?"

"Not quite. According to her lawyer or lawyers, she fell into the habit
of taking long walks on the beach while she was here, at the water's edge."

"She can't call that—"

She held her hand up. "Apparently, on one morning's walk she felt the
ground move beneath her."

"I didn't *do* it. Not my fault."

"She stepped into quicksand."

"Oh. That can happen. It has happened to me. It's an experience rich in metaphorical potential, *valuable* to a memoirist. We should have charged her extra for that."

"And now, whenever she recalls that summer, or Small's Island, or whenever she goes to a beach or sees the sea or draws a bath or drinks a glass of water, even *bottled* water, she gets a sinking feeling."

"A sinking feeling."

"Yes. And it's all our fault."

"This is not a joke."

"This is not a joke. Here's the statement she gave to her lawyer: 'I was sitting on my deck, with my laptop computer in my lap, trying to recollect whether it was my mother, my father, my uncle Toby, my auntie Em, or one of the neighbors who molested me when I was a child, and I had my feet up on the breakfast table, my chair tilted back on its back legs, and then suddenly a sinking feeling came over me, and I realized that I had tipped my chair back too far and I almost fell over, but I caught myself just in time. When I was upright again and sitting there catching my breath and refreshing myself with some bottled water, I realized that the sinking feeling was familiar to me, and in a flash the memory of my stay on Small's Island came rushing back to me and I remembered walking along the water's edge and stepping into a soft spot in the sand—I think it was quicksand—and experiencing the same sinking feeling, and now whenever I'm near sand or water I get the same sinking feeling and it has made my life a living hell.'"

"This confirms one of your convictions," I said.

"Which one is that?"

"That nothing good ever comes in Saturday's mail."

I READ episode nineteen of *Dead Air,* "If Saucers Attack," to a sizable Saturday audience that probably included a few lawyers and several potential litigants.

TODAY, in every Kap'n Klam Family Restaurant from Kenosha to Kinshasa, you will find on the counter, in a glass case, a flying-saucer detector. Let me explain how they came to be there.

Overnight, shortly before my thirteenth birthday, I had become a manufacturer of flying-saucer detectors. I had sold one to my mother, and with the money from that sale I had bought the parts for two more. Flushed with success, I calculated that, at a profit of eighty-nine cents each, if I went through twenty cycles like the first one, doubling the number of detectors I sold in each cycle, my profit on the last cycle would be nearly a million dollars: $933,232.64, to be exact. Of course, I would have to make 1,048,576 detectors in that cycle, but that was a problem that I somehow expected to take care of itself. For now, the important thing was to move the two detectors I had on hand—that is, in stock.

I went to my grandfather, Guppa, for advice. Guppa was the best salesman I knew, a master of the art, and if there was a trick to selling I knew he could teach it to me. He sold Studebakers, and had for years, but it had become a losing game. The Studebaker company seemed to have fallen permanently out of step with public taste, and that made a salesman's job awfully tough.

As Guppa listened to my plan to double the number of detectors in each cycle, he grinned a wry grin and a gleam came to his eye. Put the two together, and even I could tell that he had once made a calculation like this himself. I'm sure that while I explained my plans I had a gleam in my eye, too, but experience hadn't yet given me the wry grin. I kept glancing at him as I laid out my plans, my hopes and dreams, until finally the wry grin stopped me.

"It's not going to work, is it?" I said.

"Oh, I don't know," he said. "It didn't work for me, but it might work for you."

The only real advice he gave me was to believe in what I had to sell and to be myself when I spoke to a prospect. Guppa liked the flyer I had made to advertise the detectors, and before I left he bought a detector himself. I didn't even have to sell it to him. (At least, it felt at the time as if I hadn't had to sell it to him. Thinking back, I realize that I had followed his advice. I believed in what I was selling, because I had reason to believe in it, empirical proof: my own detector had consistently detected an absence of flying saucers when, so far as I knew, no saucers were around; and I had been myself, because with Guppa I couldn't have been anyone else.)

My first *real* prospect, someone not related to me, was Porky White, the mastermind behind the Kap'n Klam chain, my business partner, not in the saucer-detector trade, but in the esculent mollusc trade.

I practiced my sales pitch in front of a mirror, trying to make myself sound like myself, and when I was convinced that I did, I pedaled on down to the clam bar. I took a stool at the counter and set the detector in front of me.

"You know," I said, "it's a funny thing about these detectors. When I built the first one—"

"This is a new one?" he asked.

"Yeah," I said. "When I built the first one, I thought that the purpose of it was to warn people if saucers were attacking, but now I see that the real purpose is to reassure people that saucers *aren't* attacking. Take the case of my mother, for instance—"

"You're selling them, right?"

"How did you know that?"

"It's your manner."

"My manner?"

"Yeah. It's a little different. Hard to say just *how* it's different, but it's different. You're not speaking to me as a friend—"

"I'm not?"

"Oh, you're being *friendly*—too friendly, in fact. Maybe that's it. It's a little studied."

"Studied?"

"You practiced in front of a mirror, right?"

"Yeah."

"That's a good idea, definitely a good idea, but you don't sound like yourself. You sound like a salesman."

"Well, I *am* a salesman, right now anyway."

"In that case, you want to sound like your *other* self, the one who isn't selling anything. Anyway, I'll take one."

"You will?"

"Sure. It will look great on the bar. Good for conversation, too. Might even bring a few people in—curiosity seekers. Lends a little note of uncertainty to the evening. 'Will flying saucers attack while I'm eating?' Hey, I'm on to something. If the saucer detector goes off while you're eating, your meal is on the house."

"Your money back if saucers attack," I said. It just came to me, just like that.

"I CAN'T COUNT the number of times I have calculated money that I haven't earned yet!" said Artie. "You, too, right, Lou?" He pointed at Lou and said to the rest of us, "Of course, my buddy Hamlet usually ends up actually making the money, isn't that right, Lou?"

"Yeah," said Lou. He shrugged as if he were sorry about it, as if he couldn't help it, as if it weren't his fault. "I've got the knack, I guess," he said, and he went back to wiping the bar.

"I wish *I* had it," said Al. "Peter and I used to anticipate the profits from this hotel, but we weren't very good at it. It was supposed to have paid for itself a couple of times over by now. I have all our calculations in cartons down in the basement somewhere, but they're probably sodden lumps."

"That's what becomes of our dreams when they don't work out," I said. "They turn into wet cardboard." I looked down at my drink, a Baldy. How many had I had?

"It's part of the folly of trying to design a life, I guess," said Alice. "We can collect the data from the past, but it's rarely a good predictor of the future."

"Maybe that's why I'm a memoirist," I said. "I roam my past and pick things up because I'm no good at designing a future. I'm like that fucking dredge. My past is spread out all over the whole damned bay, but I suck up what I can find of it—anything—everything—the collapse of a hotel, the failure of a set of dreams. Suck it up. Sand for the dredge. I've got an island to build—an artificial fucking island that I call the past, but it's really just the recovered past, an artificial version of the past."

"How many of those Baldies have you had?" asked Albertine.

"Damned if I know," I said, picking the glass up and examining it as if the answer might be written on it.

Albertine looked at Lou, but he pretended not to have heard her question and said, changing the subject according to the code of bartenders, which requires them not to divulge to the spouse of a customer how many drinks the customer has consumed, "You know, I've been wondering—why don't you have your saucer detector here on display somewhere, or do you?"

"No," I said. "Gone. Long gone."

"But you *did* make one?"

"Sure."

"Let's build another one, then. Put it on the bar. Maybe it will bring in some business."

"Sure," I said. "It would look *great* on the bar."

"Good for conversation, too," said Elaine. "Might even bring in a few curiosity seekers."

"It would lend a note of uncertainty to the evening," suggested Lou.

"Will flying saucers attack while I'm downing this drink?" Artie wondered aloud, looking into his drink.

"Hey, you're on to something," said Nancy.

"If the saucer detector goes off while you're at the bar, your drink is on the house," said Al.

"Your money back if saucers attack," I said. It came back to me, just like that.

"LET'S SEE what interesting things are happening outside the cave, boys and girls. Hand me the paper, will you, Bob?"

"Yeah."

"Say! Here's something! A high-school student was stabbed to death somewhere, anywhere, who-knows-where, doesn't-matter-where. Could have been a boy, could have been a girl. Doesn't matter, but it was a boy. He was stabbed by *another* high-school student. Could have been a boy, could have been a girl. Doesn't matter, but it was a boy. Now, boys and girls, it must take something pretty awful for one of you to stab another of you to death, right? What do you suppose it was? Give up? You give up, don't you, Bob?"

"Yeah."

"Well, according to the police, 'The suspect and the victim began fighting over the way they had looked at each other in the lunchroom.'" Baldy laughed his unnerving laugh and repeated, "'The suspect and the victim began fighting over the way they had *looked* at each other in the lunchroom.'" He laughed some more, and then he began to cough, and when he had recovered he said. "File that under 'Exchanging Glances, Dooby, Dooby, Doo,' and cross-reference it to 'An Educated Electorate Is the Foundation of Jeffersonian Democracy' and also to 'School Days, School Days, Dear Old Golden Rule Days,' will you, Bob?"

"Yeah, yeah, yeah."

"Thanks, Bob. That's our look at the world outside the cave for tonight, boys and girls. You roll that rock in front of the door, and you sleep tight."

Gratitude

LIZA THE REALTOR brought another flock of mixed nuts to the island.
Like the earlier shoppers who had come to kick the tires, these people
were not interested in running a hotel. Their shepherd announced, after
shaking my hand and introducing his followers, "We are seeking a suitable place to welcome the millennium."

"A place for a party?" I asked. The shepherd and his flock responded
with indulgent snickering.

"Not a *party,* but a *celebration.* The *great* celebration, the *final* celebration, when everything will be turned upside down and inside out."

"I celebrate that every evening in the Small's Hotel lounge," I said,
and I indulged in some indulgent snickering of my own.

"But on *that* day, the *great* day, everything that is will cease to be what
it has *been,* and everything that never yet has been will become what it
will be."

"That does sound like a once-in-a-lifetime event," said Al. "Why don't
you look around and see if this is the place for it?"

We watched them walk off. They spent the rest of the day on the island, and they inspected it so thoroughly that Albertine allowed herself to
hope that they might make an offer. "They may be nuts," she said, "but
they went around the island very thoroughly. I think they're interested,
and I suspect that they've got the cash. You know, they're probably one
of those groups that requires the flock to surrender all its worldly goods to
the shepherd."

Toward evening, the entire flock gathered at the dock. Lou had offered
to take them back to shore, and I accepted the offer because if anything

happened on the trip to discourage them I didn't want to be responsible for it. Albertine and I stood in my workroom upstairs, side by side, watching them through our binoculars.

"Can you tell what they're saying?" she asked.

"No, but I think they're engaged in a heated debate of some kind."

"Yeah, it looks that way."

"I was thinking of getting the big ear out."

"Yes, yes. Quick."

The "big ear" is part of my eavesdropper's gear. It's a microphone mounted at the focus of a parabolic reflector, with an amplifier and an earphone. With the big ear pointed at the group on the dock, I was able to hear them quite clearly.

"Well?" asked Albertine. "Are they serious?"

"They're having an argument about whether the millennium closes at midnight on the last day of the year 1999 or at midnight on the last day of the year 2000."

"Oh, that."

"Yeah," I said, snickering indulgently. "But in their case it has particular relevance, because—as that tall one with the tonsure is saying—if the day they are awaiting—the day when what was won't be and what will will—if that day arrives just after midnight on the first day of 2001, then it probably makes sense for them to invest in a new boiler and amortize the expense over the remaining years, but if the day of days is going to arrive at the start of the year 2000, then they should probably just cross their fingers and hope that this boiler will see them through."

"That *is* a practical consideration," said Albertine. "I'm glad to see that they've got their feet on the ground."

"They're going to suspend further consideration of the purchase of the island until there is a consensus of the entire group on the issue," I said.

"Oh," said Albertine, and I believe that she was experiencing a sinking sensation as she said it.

MY AUDIENCE for the reading of the twentieth episode of *Dead Air,* "Gratitude," consisted of the inmates of Small's Hotel (Albertine, Lou, Elaine, Clark and Alice, Artie and Nancy, Otto and Esther, Louise and Miranda), Suki and her boyfriend Daryl, and a quartet of Babbingtonians who stayed on after Sunday dinner.

ONE NIGHT, a couple of months before I turned thirteen, I decided
to believe in flying saucers after seeing five of them and a naked
woman while I was carrying the garbage cans out to the curb,
which I was supposed to have done right after I had finished the
dishes but had postponed for a television show that I wasn't ordinarily allowed to watch. I had fallen asleep in front of the show,
and my father hadn't wakened me until he and my mother were
ready for bed, so I had to drag myself out at an unaccustomed hour.
I carried the cans to the curb, and when I had put the last of them in
place, I looked up and down the street. All the houses were dark but
one, the Jerrolds' house. There, the lights were on in one room on
the second floor. That room, I believed, without giving it a thought,
was Mr. and Mrs. Jerrold's bedroom. I turned toward my own
house and began to walk toward my own bed, when my mind suddenly produced an interpretation of visual details that a moment
earlier had made hardly any impression on me at all but now, figuratively, grabbed me by the shoulder and spun me around. I looked
up at the Jerrolds' house again. Mrs. Jerrold had been standing in
the window, naked. She was gone now, but she *had* been there. I
was sure of it. I believed it.

I wonder how old Mrs. Jerrold was at that time (when nearly
everyone was an insomniac, tossing and turning through night after
night of sweaty anxiety brought on by fear and uncertainty: fear of
spacecraft and the unknown beings that inhabited them and fear of
intercontinental ballistic missiles and the warheads we knew they
carried, and uncertainty over which would do us in first). I suppose
I could figure out how old she was. She was the mother of a boy
who was younger than I, so she probably was younger than my
mother, and my mother was a young mother. She had given birth to
me when she was still a teenager, so she would have been only
thirty-one or so at that time. Mrs. Jerrold may have been thirty.
Perhaps she wasn't yet thirty.

She had a trim figure. I put it that way because that is the way
my father always put it. The Jerrolds had moved into the neighborhood several years after we did. Their house had been there when
we arrived, but someone else was living there. I can't remember
who it was, and because I can't remember who it was I suspect that

it must have been an old couple with no children my age and no interest in children my age. If they *had* had children my age, or if they had been interested in forming a grandparently attachment to a child my age, then I think I would have found my way into their house and life, but I never did, and so I suppose that there was no interest in either direction. They probably died, and then the Jerrolds bought the house.

When I bring Mrs. Jerrold to mind, she is wearing a shirtwaist dress. She can't always have been wearing a shirtwaist dress, of course, but when I see her in anything else, I know that I am imagining it, not remembering it (partly because the something elses tend to be pink nighties and two-piece bathing suits), so I make the effort to push the imagined images aside in favor of the ones I have confidence in, and in those she is always wearing a shirtwaist dress. She has put it on in haste, after daytime sex.

She was trim and leggy, and she was cool. She didn't seem to hurry, and she didn't seem to sweat. She favored barer fashions than the other women on the block. There was always a little more of Mrs. Jerrold available for viewing than there was of the others. She may have been proud; maybe she saw herself as more attractive and sexier than the other young matrons, and so showed off a little. I was grateful.

I turned toward my house again. Above me, above a corner of the house, was a single glowing ring, hovering. In a moment, four other rings emerged from it, as if they had been stacked atop one another. They formed a V, paused a moment, and then rushed away to the east, over the house and out of sight. I looked back at the street. I suppose I expected to see the neighbors, including Mrs. Jerrold, rushing out of their houses in their nightclothes. The light went out upstairs at the Jerrolds'. I wondered whether Mrs. Jerrold would sleep well. Would her sleep be troubled by saucer anxiety? I could help her. I had the solution: from plans that I found in *Cellar Scientist* magazine, I had built a flying-saucer detector that allowed my mother to sleep tight while it stood watch on her bedside table, detecting an absence of menace. If I visited Mrs. Jerrold the next day and told her about the squadron of saucers I had seen, she would be alarmed and she would be anxious, but when I gave her my detector and explained that it would make her nights peaceful, that it would allow her to snuggle into her bed and sleep, she would be grateful to me, and I would be grateful to the saucers, and gratitude is an entirely sufficient basis on which to build a belief.

"HOW OLD would Mrs. Jerrold be now?" asked Louise.

I glanced at Albertine before answering. She smiled; neither of us winked. "Well," I said, "she was about seventeen years older than I am, and I am now thirty days away from fifty, so she would be sixty-seven— around there—sixty-seven or sixty-eight."

"Did you ever think of looking for her—you know like maybe you could find her and go, like, 'I'm Peter Leroy, do you remember me?'" asked Miranda.

"There are two things that keep me from doing that," I said. "First, there is the possibility that I would find out that she is dead. So many of the people who enlivened my past once upon a time are dead now."

"Yeah," said Miranda as if she knew.

"For me, so long as I'm ignorant of the truth, there is the possibility that she is still alive, and I'd rather not have that *possibility* that she is alive collapse into a *certainty* that she is dead."

"I can understand that," said Miranda.

"And the second thing?" asked Louise.

"The second thing," I said with an impish grin, "is that Mrs. Jerrold— Well, you see, Mrs. Jerrold—"

Maybe it was my wry grin that made Miranda say, "You mean you made her up? But I thought these were your *memoirs*."

"They are," I said, "and everything that I include in my memoirs has happened to me."

"I'm getting confused."

"My memoirs are an account of the things that have happened in here" —I pointed to my head—"and in here"—I clasped my hands over my heart—"and out here"—I threw my arms wide to indicate the room, the hotel, the island, the world. "Mrs. Jerrold came from all those places. Did I make her up? Let's say that I *made* her, the way you might make a loaf of bread."

"A loaf of bread?"

"The flour, the water, the yeast, the salt, and so on came straight from my past, but I made dough from them, kneaded, it, made it rise, and baked the loaf."

"Oh, I love it when that happens," said Louise, "that, like, transformation? Making bread? It's beautiful."

"Yeah," said Miranda. "That's good. That's cool. I can understand that. That's really, like, honest."

"Thanks," I said. "Now I have a question for you."

"Yeah?" said Louise.

"Excuse me for asking, but how old are *you*? And shouldn't you be in school? Are you on *vacation* or something?"

Giggles. (I could imagine them, years after this evening, reminiscing: "Remember how we used to laugh at the crazy things he would say, that funny old guy who helped run the hotel when he wasn't making up his 'memoirs'?")

"We're not in school," said Miranda.

"Oh," I said. "I'm sorry. I thought you were—aren't you—like—high-school age?"

Squeals. (That Mr. Leroy! What a wacko!)

"We're out of college—since the spring—and we just, like, spent the summer figuring out what to do next?" said Miranda.

"And my granddad was, like, 'Come with us to this hotel, 'cause my buddy Hamlet says they need help in the kitchen,' so we did, and it was really a lucky break."

"Like fate," said Miranda.

They nodded at each other, and Louise said, "'Cause we've been helping Suki in the kitchen, and now we know we want to learn the restaurant business."

"It's like we *found* ourselves here," said Miranda.

"In one *day*?" I asked.

"Yes!" said Louise.

"And now we have everything, like, planned out? We're going to learn everything from Suki, and then Uncle Lou is going to get us some jobs at other restaurants, so we can, like, compare the way they do things, and then in the spring we're going to get married and open our own place."

"That's good," I said. "That's cool. I can understand that."

A Salesman Calls

I EXPECTED the dredge to be gone when I walked out onto the porch. It wasn't. I think I was relieved, but I was also disappointed, and although I am not quite certain about my being relieved, I am quite certain about my being disappointed. Dexter's skiff was just visible in the distance, and I could hear the hum of its outboard motor. Dexter was on his way, and as he drew nearer I could see that he looked eager to get to work. What had gotten into that guy?

Artie came out onto the porch carrying a cup of coffee. He perched on the railing, drank his coffee, and observed Dexter. There was something about the intense, precise, entirely unemotional way he regarded Dexter that made my palms sweat and my blood run cold. I was going to become an accessory to an act that I couldn't condone, however much I might desire it.

"Look—Artie," I said, "I know that Lou asked you to come out here and—ah—take care of this problem we've got, but I think—well—I may have a problem with the way you're going to take care of the problem."

"Really? What do you want me to do—sink it? Blow it up?"

"I—um—I thought—"

"I know. The Demolition Man. Lou's got a name for everybody, but sometimes they're, let's say, inaccurate."

"You mean you're not—"

"Not what?"

I might have said, "—you're not Rockwell Kingman," but I said, "—you're not going to actually—"

"Actually what?"

"Actually, you know, remove it."

"Remove it myself?"

"Yes. Sink it. Blow it up. Demolish it."

"Nah. My buddy Hamlet, calls me the Demolition Man because I was in underwater demolition in the service and because I've engineered a few corporate takeovers of the buy-and-destroy type—which have made us both some money, by the way."

"Oh," I said. "I see." I must have sounded relieved, because he laughed. "So now I know why he calls you the Demolition Man, but why do you call him Hamlet?"

"Oh—because he's made a career out of wringing his hands over things in a Hamlet kind of way, you know what I mean?"

"Yeah," I said, though I didn't, and I hadn't seen any evidence of Lou's being much of a handwringer, but I was glad to hear him confirm my original impression of Lou as a grumpy guy, since the continued shortage of obvious, external evidence of grumpiness had threatened to force me to modify my belief that he really was a grumpy guy who was hiding his essential grumpiness behind a smile. Hamlet? Well, well.

"Listen," he said, in a no-worries-no-kidding tone. "I'm not going to do anything but make a few phone calls. That's all. I know some people. They know some people. I'll make some requests. I'll ask some questions. I'll call in some favors."

"Okay," I said, and I have to admit that at that moment I was very disappointed. Blowing the damned dredge up seemed a far more certain cure than making a few phone calls.

"Don't worry about it," he said.

"No worries, no kidding," I said.

"What?"

"That's our motto."

I USED TO ENJOY Mondays on the island. The weekend guests would be gone, and everyone who remained—guests, staff, owners—would feel liberated by their departure, enough to be lazy all day, figuring that there were four more before the next weekend arrived. That was in the days before the dredging, of course, and in the days when I still expected the hotel to succeed eventually. Even under the present conditions, however, this Monday was like one of those, and the group that gathered for my

reading of episode twenty-one of *Dead Air,* "A Salesman Calls," was so
relaxed that Artie and Clark fell asleep.

ONE SATURDAY MORNING thirty-seven years ago, I went to
the Jerrolds' house in the hope of selling one of the flying-saucer
detectors I had made. Mrs. Jerrold's husband was often away; I
suspected that he was a spy. I hoped that fear of flying saucers
might be keeping Mrs. Jerrold awake, as it had kept my mother
awake, and that she might buy a flying-saucer detector to relieve
her anxiety, as my mother had.

Junior Jerrold was in the side yard, sitting in the sun, eating a
cruller. He had an entire box of crullers beside him. The Jerrolds
were, like my family and most of the families in Babbington, patrons of Yummy Good Baked Goods, which were delivered by a
man whom the children of the town called Mr. Yummy. I paused,
hoping that Junior might offer me one of their crullers. He didn't.
After a while, I asked for one. "Ask Mr. Yummy," he said. "He'll
give you one, but you have to eat it outside, because of the sugar."
The crullers were covered with powdered sugar, and so was Junior.
I could see the wisdom of eating the crullers outside.

I went to the back door. The house was quiet. No one was in the
kitchen. Mr. Yummy's tray of baked goods was on the counter, at
the end of the counter, on the corner, set there at an angle, so that
the corners of the tray projected over the edges of the counter.
There was something odd about this, odd enough that I felt that
looking through the screen door, noticing the empty kitchen and the
abandoned tray, felt like something that I shouldn't do. Visible
above the low rim of the tray were loaves of bread and boxes of
doughnuts, crullers, cupcakes, and cookies, including my favorite, a
glazed cruller twisted into a pretzel shape.

I heard a laugh, from upstairs, Mrs. Jerrold's laugh, then light
and rapid footsteps, and then Mrs. Jerrold spun around the corner of
the living room, laughing, singing. She was wearing a shirtwaist
dress. It had buttons up the front, but only a few of the buttons were
buttoned. It had a belt of the same fabric as the dress, but the belt
wasn't buckled or tied. It hung from its loops, the ends dangling at

the sides of the dress. Mrs. Jerrold was barefoot. I had never seen her barefoot before.

When she saw me standing at the door, she cried "Peter! What are you doing here?" Her hand fluttered to the neck of her dress.

"Well," I said, a little rattled, but moving right into my sales pitch, "I was wondering if you have trouble sleeping at night."

"What?" she said. She came to the door.

"My mother was having trouble sleeping," I explained.

"But what makes you think that I do?"

"Oh," I said, "well—" The only answer that came to me quickly was the truth, that I had seen her standing in her window the night before, naked, so I said nothing.

"You haven't been peeking through the windows, have you?" she asked.

My mouth fell open. I stood there, sweating.

"I'm only kidding," she said. She was in a very good mood, playful. She pushed the door open, put her hand on my shoulder, brought it up to my ear, and gave my ear a tug, pulling me into the kitchen and, an instant later, pulling me against her, hugging me to her chest, against her breasts. I felt embarrassed and awkward, and delighted.

"Oh, my God," she said suddenly. "What am I doing?" She released me, pushed me from her, held me at arm's length, laughed nervously, and said, "What are you doing here? Did you want to use the tape recorder?"

This seemed like the easiest way out, so I said, "If it's okay."

There were footsteps on the stairs, heavy footsteps.

"It's fine," she said, hurriedly, pushing me back out the door. "It's okay, but—"

"I guess you're busy," I said.

She raised her eyebrows and gave me a helpless look. "Yes," she said.

"Shall I come back later?" I had seen door-to-door salesmen say this on television, when the lady of the house was trying to push them away.

"Yes," she said. "Later. Come back later."

"This afternoon?"

"Yes. This afternoon."

"Okay," I said. I went down the porch steps, around the corner of the house, and into the side yard, where Junior was scratching in the dirt.

"Is Mr. Yummy finished?" he asked.

"Almost," I said, without giving a thought to what, exactly, that might mean.

WHEN I CAME TO BED, Albertine was reading, quite openly, the latest issue of *Manhattan* magazine. "Listen to this," she said. "It's my horoscope: 'For years now, you've felt like you were riding on a roller coaster through an emotional nightmare on stormy seas. One day you're up, next day you're down. One day everything you touch turns to gold, next day you're overwhelmed by literally myriads of kinds of tumultuous developments in your business and personal life. Due to the damage that these stormy experiences have done to your head, your heart, and your pocketbook, your emotions have been strained to the limit, and beyond that even. But cheer up! Soon your ship will come in . . .' and so on," she said, and she tossed the magazine aside. "Who reads this junk? Who *writes* this junk?"

"What do you mean?" I asked. "That sounds uncannily accurate to me. It's as if they knew you."

"Are you kidding?" she said. "If my ship comes in, it's sure to be sinking." She waited for me to laugh, and when I didn't she started tickling me and said, "Just kidding, Peter. That was supposed to be a joke."

"Ha," I said.

She climbed onto me and said, "I thought your reading was wonderful, and I think the whole book is wonderful and I hope you noticed that I did not fall asleep, not even for a second."

"Just kidding?"

"No kidding."

"You are completely useless as a critic."

"Why?"

"Because you love me." I waited for her to agree, and when she didn't I asked, "Don't you?"

Her answer was a silent but convincing yes. If she was kidding, I didn't care.

Later, when she was asleep and I was still awake, I watched her sleeping, apparently untroubled, free of anxiety, secure, and I made a silent promise that I would find a way to keep her feeling that way—some way, any way, whatever it took. No worries. No kidding.

October 1
No Sale

HAVING IMAGINED Rockwell Kingman, I seemed to be stuck with him, and he was becoming annoying. He wouldn't dance to my tune. "I am not in the business of assisted suicide," he said. He took me by the arm and urged me toward the door.

"What's the matter?" I asked with a condescending sneer. "Scruples?"

He laughed a humorless laugh and said, "Scruples? Are you kidding me? I will kill women, children, cripples, your mother, or my mother, on contract or for the sake of deception. I have no scruples—but I do have a well-developed sense of self. I know who I am, and I know what I do, and I know why I do it. Let me tell you something." He yanked me back into the room, pushed me into a chair, and began to lecture me. "Perhaps you've heard people justify the violent acts that they commit on the grounds that we are really just animals underneath our civilized exterior, and violent death, kill or be killed, is a fact of everyday life in the animal world—kill, eat, fuck—the pattern of life and death in the animal world, therefore the pattern of life and death in our world. Well, let me tell you what I think about that argument. We are *elevated* animals, blessed, or cursed, with the ability to distinguish right from wrong. We *know* good from evil. We have our appetites, we have our hungers, we have our animal urges, but we know how to control them, and if we do *not* control them it is because we *choose* not to control them, and so a killer who chooses to kill—a killer like me—is *not* simply being a slave to his animal nature. He is—and I say this with pride because I have made the choice, I have chosen to kill—he is *evil*. That's what I am. Evil. I am an evil motherfucker. I have no scruples—they don't even enter the picture—but *I know who I am,* and I know what I am, and I know what I will do and what I won't do, and I won't kill *you*. It's not what I do. In fact, it runs against the *grain* of what I do. In my business, every killing starts with a triangle, a stable base: you've got the killer, the client, and the target. Among them there is a business relationship, and there is also a kind of social contract. Two are aware of the relationship: the killer is aware of it, of course, and the client has to be aware of it, too. The client has to participate in the choice to kill. The *victim,* on the other hand, has to be *unaware* of the contract. How can the victim be a victim if the victim is aware, if the victim has also made the choice? It's a perversion of the whole setup. I mean, if you get right down to it, your *wife* would really be my client, since she's the one who's supposed to benefit from the killing, but she isn't going to know she's the client, and if I do my job the way I do my job, which is to say excellently well, she'll *never* know it. You're trying to take something away from me, do you realize that?"

I shrugged.

"My *audience,*" he said. "The only audience I've got for my work, besides myself, is the client. You're asking me to give that up. If the work were successful, if I did it right—and if I did it I *would* do it right—you would never know it and she would never know it. Neither of you won't know how good a job I had done. Nor would anyone else. Where are the rewards in that? Do you think I'm only in this for the money?"

He opened the door and shoved me into the hall. "Let me just plant a thought in your mind," I said. "I am the captain of a launch that leaks." I grinned and winked, and he slammed the door in my face. I was getting to him. I was sure of it.

I COMPILED my monthly letter to our sons. This has been my custom since they went away to school, some twenty years ago. Back then, I sent them a postcard or letter every day. I still write every day, but I now mail my letters only monthly, since asking someone to pay attention to you every day is asking a lot. Included was everything you have read here, reader, and more, since I didn't begin preparing this for you until the tenth of the month and because I had things to say to them that would not have interested you, and because I had some things to say about you that I intended only for them.

ALBERTINE paid the month's bills, but she couldn't afford to pay them all. "I have two stacks here," she said. "These I'm going to pay, and those

I'm not going to pay. I just can't believe the way it mounts up. It's not just the mortgage. It's the thousand little things that break every month and have to be fixed or replaced. This is a losing battle, and we're losing it a little faster every day."

I looked through the stack of bills that were going to go unpaid.

"You have to pay this one," I said. "It's my life insurance premium."

"It goes up every year," she said, "and now that Edward and Daniel are on their own, what's the point? Why not let it lapse?"

"Because everyone needs life insurance," I said lamely.

"I'm the beneficiary," she said, "and I'm not paying the premium."

She tore the bill in half and dropped it into the wastebasket.

I SPENT the rest of the day doing the hundred little chores that consume an assistant innkeeper's day at a failing hotel, chores that leave no visible sign of their having been done, but which if left undone scream, "Look at me, look at me! Fix me, clean me, mend me!" In the evening, I read the twenty-second episode of *Dead Air,* "No Sale."

IN THE HOPE that there might be a market for the flying-saucer detectors that I was building in my cellar, I had begun canvassing my neighborhood, door-to-door. I had started at the Jerrolds', but Mrs. Jerrold had been busy choosing baked goods from the Yummy Good delivery man, so I went next door, to the Breeds'.

There was a throng of children in the Breeds' yard, as there always was. It was difficult at times to say just how many of the children who swarmed around the Breeds' house were actually part of the family and which were only there to play. Mr. Breed was the only person I knew, at that time, who had given his house a name; he called it "The Breeding Ground." He had carved the name into a wooden plaque that he hung beside the front door.

I had never managed to sell *anything* to the Breeds—not the *Babbington Reporter,* not raffle tickets, not even the *Babbington Cub Reporter,* the neighborhood newspaper that I published for three weeks one summer. Because I had found that there was no real news in my neighborhood, I had reported the things I overheard while I was standing around, minding my own business. Before my father shut it down, the *Cub Reporter* was so popular that many people came directly to my house to get a copy hot off my Little Giant press—but not the Breeds. They borrowed a copy, read it, and returned it with coffee stains. Nevertheless, I knocked at their door.

Inside, a dog began to bark, a child began to cry, and Mrs. Breed began to call out, "Just a minute! Wait a minute! Just a gee-dee minute!" In a little less than a minute, she parted the soiled curtains that hung inside the kitchen door. When she saw me, she opened the door at once and said, "Peter! My favorite informant. Come on in and tell me what's going on outside this kitchen."

I allowed myself to be pulled into the kitchen, which stank. Most of the Breed children were boys, and boys have a well-known tendency to miss the toilet when they urinate, so the house smelled of piss most of the time, but this may not have been the exclusive fault of the boys; the Breeds may have had a few cats that I never saw because they were hiding under the sofa all day long, away from the little Breeds' feet, until at night it was finally safe, and then the cats would come out and mark their space. Maybe.

"Did you start publishing again?" she asked.

"No. My father said, 'Everything that comes off that Little Giant printing press from now on has to be subjected to my scrutiny.'"

"I guess that shut you up."

"Not quite," I said, brightly, since I could recognize an opening when I saw one. "He said I could print these flyers." I handed her one of my flyers for the saucer detectors. "This is what I'm selling now. They can help you sleep if you're worrying about saucers and missiles."

"Ha!" she said, balancing a tot on her hip while she read the flyer. "Trouble sleeping? Are you kidding? By the time the day is over, I can hardly hold my head up. I get into bed and I go into a coma. You could burn this house *down,* and I wouldn't wake up. Saucers could land, bombs could go off—I wouldn't know anything about it. In the morning I'd say, 'It looks like a bomb hit this place! Funny it didn't wake me up.' As it is, one morning a year I say, 'Hey, I'm pregnant! Funny it didn't wake me up.'"

"What?" I said.

"Oh, nothing. Never mind."

"You can get pregnant while you're asleep?"

"Never you mind," she said. "Why don't you go sell one of your detectors to Mrs. Jerrold? I'll bet she's in the market for one."

"I tried, but she's busy."

Mrs. Breed looked out the window over her kitchen sink, toward the Jerrolds' house.

"Ah, yes," she said, more to herself than to me, "I see she's getting a delivery from Mr. Yummy. That can take a while." The baby, without any particular fuss, threw up on her shoulder.

"I guess I'll go try the Learys," I said. Mrs. Breed said nothing. She continued to move the mop around the floor while singing, softly, the Yummy Good Baked Goods jingle.

Who's that knockin' at my back door?
It's the Yummy Good man with goodies galore!
Let me in, let me in, let me in, I implore!
You've never had goodies so *good* before!

ESTHER SAID, "I loved that bit about 'I'm pregnant and it didn't even wake me up.'"

"Uh-oh," said Otto, "I think the conversation is going to take one of those anti-male turns."

It might have, except that Clark, who may have had one too many, gave it an anti-isolationist turn instead.

"Jeez, I miss door-to-door salesmen," he claimed. "It used to be kind of exciting when somebody would ring the doorbell, and you'd go there and it was somebody you didn't know. Now you'd call the cops, you see somebody you don't know going around the neighborhood. You'd press the panic button on your alarm system. It's the fucking fortress mentality. The bomb-shelter mentality. We've all retreated into our little houses and our little neighborhoods, and we only open the door to people we know and the rest of you can go fuck yourselves, but not in my back yard. I've got my door locked, and I do not choose to know anybody I don't already know, thank you. Who's that knockin' at my back door, somebody I don't know, somebody not like me? Bringing me news of the world that lies beyond my little corner of it? No, thank you. Slam! Not interested.

That's why there aren't any door-to-door salesmen anymore. No intrusions allowed. No interlopers. We don't want the outside world worming its way into the isolated little nest we made for ourselves, you know what I mean? That's what you've done here, isn't it, Peter? Tried to do? Isolate yourself? Cut yourself off from the world? Does it work? Have you succeeded in keeping the world away?"

"No," I said, and things might have gotten very gloomy indeed if Louise hadn't struck up a boogie-woogie introduction to Miranda's lively and hilarious improvised version of the Yummy Good Baked Goods jingle.

Who's that knockin' at my back door?

It's the Yummy Good man with goodies galore!
Let me in, let me in, let me in, I implore!
You've never had goodies so <u>good</u> before!

LOOK!
Here comes
something
YUMMY!

LOOK! Isn't that the Yummy Good man
knockin' at YOUR back door?

Yummy Good Baked Goods Company, a Division of Balducci Enterprises, Inc.

Driving a Bargain

I STOOD AT THE WINDOW of my workroom, looking down into the courtyard behind the hotel. It faces southeast, so it catches the sun in the morning, preserving an isolated bit of summer well into fall. Louise and Miranda were out there, taking a break from their kitchen work, sunning themselves, naked. Because they were so gorgeous, so delightful to look at, and because they were, let us say, carrying on a dalliance, I could not keep my eyes off them. I mean that, reader. They were so attractive that every time I turned away from the window and told myself to get back to work I would find my thoughts drawn back to the window, and a moment later I would find *myself* drawn back to the window, back to the beautiful view. After this had happened several times, I decided that my debt to you, my obligation to record all the significant events that occurred during my reading of *Dead Air,* required me to stand at the window and watch the girls, that watching was, if we were to be perfectly accurate about it, work.

Miranda was slowly rubbing sunscreen onto Louise's breasts when Albertine crept up behind me, put her arm around my waist, and looked over my shoulder. "Oh," she said, when she saw what I saw. "Keeping an eye on the guests, I see."

"Right," I said. "I feel a responsibility to observe and record any goings-on that I happen accidentally to notice, even if it does make me feel a little like an old goat."

Albertine and I stood there together, watching. Miranda completed her attentions to Louise's breasts and began rubbing the lotion down along Louise's belly. When she slipped her hand between Louise's thighs, Albertine slipped her hand between mine, and when Miranda began licking Louise's lips, Albertine pulled me to the floor.

Later, when we were dressing, Albertine tiptoed to the window and whispered, "Thanks, girls."

"Did you come up here just for that?" I asked hopefully.

"No," she said. "I brought three pieces of news."

"Yes?"

"First, listen to the silence."

"Oh, my God," I said. "I never noticed."

"I guess your attention was focused elsewhere."

"What happened?"

"Dexter came out to the barge in his little skiff, got on board, and chugged away, just like that."

"The Demolition Man—"

"Well, maybe not, because the second piece of news is that Hurricane Phil is moving up the coast and is expected to strike here tonight or early tomorrow morning."

"It's late in the season—"

"I tried to explain that to Hurricane Phil, but he just wouldn't listen."

"We'd better go into our routine—get the candles out, fill the tubs with water—"

"Item number three," she said. "There is no water."

THE CISTERN was empty. There had to be a leak somewhere. It would have to be fixed, but that would have to wait until the storm had passed. Half of the inmates spent the day on the island with Albertine and me, battening the hatches, while the other half went to Babbington with Lou and bought supplies, including all the bottled water they could get. In the odd twilight and preternatural calm that precedes a storm, I read "Driving a Bargain," the twenty-third episode of *Dead Air,* and in the pauses we could hear the wild cats roaming the island, anxious and confused, seeking shelter, caterwauling.

AMONG THE LIKELY PROSPECTS for a flying-saucer detector in my neighborhood was Mr. Leary. Mr. Leary was retired, and, as my father liked to say, he was making a career out of it. When he was still working, he had been tall, slim, and nervous, but upon retiring he went to bed for an entire week, and when he emerged from his house he had metamorphosed into a short, bald man with a paunch who wore suspenders and cardigan sweaters, chuckled more or less constantly, issued epigrams about the absurdities of life, and preferred the company of what he called little nippers to the company of adults, whom he called damned fools. I figured he was good for a sale—a pushover, in fact.

I walked around to the back of the Learys' house, and I was on my way to the back door when I heard Mr. Leary whistling in the garage. I found him there, surrounded by wood shavings, whittling away at something.

"Hi, Mr. Leary," I said.

He looked up. "Say there, nipper," he said with a chuckle, "what brings you all the way over to this side of the street?"

I knew that there was no point in beating around the bush with Mr. Leary. If you did, you were likely to fall into a conversation, and if you got into a conversation with him, you would learn a great deal about linoleum flooring, his business before he had retired. I had found that, as far as I was concerned, when it came to linoleum a little learning went a long way, so I got right to the point. I held the saucer detector out in front of me and said, "I came to see if you wanted to buy a flying-saucer detector."

"A flying-saucer detector?"

"Yes, sir. They relieve your anxieties. Before my mother got hers she had trouble sleeping because she was tormented by worries about flying saucers and thermonuclear warheads."

"Flying saucers *and* thermonuclear warheads?" he said, chuckling and shaking his head at the thought that life should have become so absurd overnight.

"A lot of people are worried about them."

He took the detector from me and looked it over from all the angles. "Do I get a discount for buying the demonstrator?" he asked.

"The demonstrator?"

"What I'm holding in my hands here. You take this one around to show to people, to demonstrate how the thing works, right?"

"Oh. Yeah. I see. The demonstrator."

"Your grandfather gave me a discount when I bought my Studebaker."

"You bought a demonstrator?"

"Sure. I'm driving a bargain." He chuckled and shook his head to indicate that he was about to issue an epigram on one of the absurdities of life. "Some people throw their money away," he said, and then he just went on shaking his head.

"But?" I said.

"Huh?"

"Aren't you going to say 'but' and go on?"

"Go on?"

"Maybe—'but a wise man drives a bargain'?"

"Hey," he chuckled. "That's pretty good. For a nipper you've got a good head on your shoulders. Tell you what—I'll *take* the demonstrator."

"It's not really a demonstrator," I said. "It's new. I just finished it this morning, and I haven't really demonstrated it to anybody. I've just been showing it to people."

"I'd call that demonstrating," he said.

"What do you figure the demonstrator's worth?" I asked.

"Well—how about—half price?"

I had set my price by simply doubling what the parts of a detector cost me, right down to the lengths of wire and nails. Half price would wipe out all of my profit.

Mr. Leary reached into his back pocket and pulled out his wallet. "What do you say?" he asked, with his wallet still closed. There was a twinkle in his eye, and I recognized it for what it was: the old man was going to cheat me, and he was going to enjoy it. He was *already* enjoying it. "Half price for the demonstrator?"

"You know," I said, taking the demonstrator from him, "a lot of people are willing to sell themselves cheap."

"But?" he asked, and when he chuckled I saw that the chuckle had become involuntary, that he was stuck with it forevermore.

"But only a fool would sell at cost," I said, and, chuckling and shaking my head, I turned and left, chuckling involuntarily at the astonishing discovery that what people said was true: there really is no fool like an old fool.

LYING IN BED, waiting for the storm to strike, I was struck again by the astonishing discovery that there really is no fool like an old fool, and by the more astonishing discovery that I had become one—not so much because I was willing to sell without making a profit, but because I had bought something that I couldn't even sell at a loss. How had this happened? After all the hours I had spent in my workroom examining my life, how had I ended up as the fool in the story? I had meant to become something else. I think I had meant to become a happy man. I know I had meant to make Albertine a happy woman, had meant to make us a happy couple, but I had staked our happiness on this hotel on this island. For me, living here alone with her, apart from a world that displeased me, was enough to make me a happy man, but her becoming a happy woman depended on our making a success of the hotel, and for her living apart from the world was not a happy state, just an unwelcome consequence of the location of the hotel. I had trapped her here, and now I had no way to get her out. I couldn't even imagine anyone who would buy this damned hotel from us, at whatever price, because I could think of only one person in the world fool enough to buy it, and he was already living in it.

The Mysteries of Mrs. Jerrold's Bedroom

THE WORST of the hurricane struck us in the night. The winds roared, the shutters banged, the doors shook in their frames. Employing the same calm and confident tone that I employed whenever I had to ferry guests across the bay in the leaking launch, I reassured the inmates, explaining that the hotel had survived a hundred years of hurricanes, and I trotted out old photographs and clippings as visual proof of its venerable status as a safe haven in a storm. Lou made everyone a Baldy, and we took to our beds to ride the hurricane out. I lay awake in my bed, of course, trying to calm myself by reminding myself that everything I had said about the staunch and stalwart old hotel was so, that I wasn't making it up, but I heard every groan that the old place made when the wind beat against it, every creak and drip, and for a while I thought there was a good chance that it was too old and tired to hold itself together, that it might be ripped from around us, snatched away like covers from a bed, leaving us exposed and shivering.

In the first light, I let myself out into the storm and began perambulating the grounds to see how bad the damage was so far. In the past, I would have seen the damage in terms of work, the work that I would have to do to repair it, but now I saw it all in terms of money, and that made me feel desperate. Had it been only a matter of work, I would have felt that I could provide it, that even now I could have found the vigor to do what had to be done (and I will confess that there was a time when I looked at repairs with a kind of pleasure, a time when I enjoyed the work, was proud of my ability to do it, usually did it pretty well if I stayed within the range of my abilities, and felt that the time I put into it was time well spent), but repairs had never really been a matter of work alone, because I could never manage to do all the work alone. They had always meant money, too, and money was another matter. I couldn't make money appear. Once I had been able to, but I seemed to have lost the knack.

"Peter?" It was Albertine, calling to me from the front entrance. I ran to her.

"Come upstairs. I've got to show you something, something very, very funny."

"Funny?" I said. "There's something funny happening here?"

"Funny peculiar."

We went upstairs and walked along the hall until Albertine stopped and put her hand on the doorknob of one of the guest rooms. "Alice and Clark asked to change their room this morning."

"Water damage?"

"No. Alice said she was ready for a new challenge." I knitted my brows to indicate that I didn't have the faintest idea what she was talking about, and she flung the door open. I stepped into a room I had never seen before. It was completely redecorated—no, completely renovated.

"It's—it's—" I said.

"A little fussy for my taste, but—what the hell, it's a miracle!"

"How did she do this? How did she get the supplies? The tools?"

"Remember all those cartons that Artie brought with him?"

"Demolition equipment, I thought. Explosives. Torpedoes."

"Wallpaper, ceramic tile, doorknobs."

I walked around the room, touching everything to make sure that it was real. "This is really weird," I said. "Very peculiar." I tried the closet door. I had invested many hours in trying to make that door hang straight and open easily, but I had never succeeded. Alice had.

"This is very odd," I said, "like a prisoner digging through the walls, working silently, at night. Very, very odd. But she does good work."

THE WIND was still roaring in the evening, the tide was still high, the basement was completely flooded, the cabins were partly submerged, and our island was only a fraction of its usual size, but the fire was crackling in the lounge, and we survivors were rosy with self-congratulation when I read "The Mysteries of Mrs. Jerrold's Bedroom," episode twenty-four of *Dead Air*.

AS A BOY, I sometimes worked as a door-to-door salesman. I sold the *Babbington Reporter*, raffle tickets, the *Babbington Cub Reporter*—a neighborhood newspaper that I published myself—and, for a couple of months in the fall before I turned thirteen, flying-saucer detectors.

Of all the potential buyers of flying-saucer detectors in my neighborhood, Mrs. Jerrold was the most attractive. She had been my first call. She had been busy with another door-to-door salesman when I called, but my grandfather had taught me that persistence is the rock on which a salesman builds success, so after I had made a couple of other calls I returned to Mrs. Jerrold's house and knocked at the back door.

Mrs. Jerrold came waltzing to it. "Hi, Peter," she said dreamily. "What's up?"

"I'm selling flying-saucer detectors," I said.

"Mmm," she said, abstractedly.

"I was here before, remember?"

She smiled languorously, stretched, giggled, tousled my hair, and said, "I remember."

"My mother has one of these detectors," I said, "and she finds that it really helps her sleep."

"Does your mother have trouble sleeping?"

"Not now, but she used to. She used to worry about flying saucers and intercontinental ballistic missiles, but now, thanks to the Magnetomic Flying-Saucer Detector, she has no worries. 'No worries, no kidding,' that's our slogan. Here's her testimonial." I handed Mrs. Jerrold a flyer.

She read it, smiled, and said, "Okay, I'll take one." I would have been delighted by this easy sale if she had spoken to me in the tone of a passionate woman who would have preferred the comforts of the flying-saucer-detector salesman to the comforts of the flying-saucer detector he was selling, but she didn't. She used the tone of a suburban housewife amused by a little boy from the neighborhood and one of his little follies.

"My mother had me install hers on her bedside table," I said. "Having it right beside her while she sleeps gives her the maximum relief from anxiety."

"Mmm," said Mrs. Jerrold, taking a strand of my forelock in her fingers and tugging it, pulling me toward her. "Do you think I should have mine installed beside the bed, too?"

"Probably."

"Go on upstairs and set it up then."

"Sure," I said, trying to sound as if it didn't make any difference to me.

I walked upstairs and into the Jerrolds' bedroom. The bed was rumpled. I touched the sheets. They were warm. There were two bedside tables, one on either side of the bed, and I didn't know which side of the bed Mrs. Jerrold slept on, so I began looking for clues. I slid the drawer of one bedside table open and found a pipe, a scattering of bits of tobacco, a pack of playing cards with a photograph of a naked woman on the back of each one, and a box of condoms. In the other I found hairpins, a brush and comb, and a sachet. I decided that this one was hers. I put the detector down, aligned it quickly, and then began looking into the drawers of the dresser beside the bedside table. My recollection of what happened next is a little fuzzy. I remember handling her stockings and underwear, sweating, breathing in irregular gulps, and trembling to the rhythm of my throbbing heart; then, I think, I may have fainted, because the next thing I recall is lying on the bed, on Mrs. Jerrold's side, with my hand in my pants.

"How's it going?" she called from the stairs.

"Not aligned yet," I said, leaping up.

"Okay. Let me know when you're ready."

Since I wasn't ready for her, and wouldn't be without a moment to calm myself, I allowed my curiosity to turn me to the closet. I put my hand on the knob and twisted it. It did not move, didn't even budge. This was not a familiar experience: more than merely odd, it was completely wrong, not at all the way a doorknob ought to behave. I touched it again, drew a breath, and gave it another twist, tentatively, and it resisted me again. I stood there with my hand on the knob, wondering whether I should try harder, holding my breath, and in the stillness of the moment I heard a sound from under the bed, a humming sound. I let go of the doorknob, got down on my hands and knees, and looked under the bed. There was the Jerrolds' tape recorder, and it was running.

"Peter? Are you ready for me yet?"

"Yeah!" I said. "I'm ready. Come on up."

She came up the stairs and into the bedroom, paused a moment in the doorway and ran her eyes around the room, then came to my side, and we stood there, side by side beside the bed, looking down at my little gadget, which rested there doing nothing, as it was supposed to when there was no danger.

"Cute," she said, and as she said it she put her arm across my shoulders. "Very cute."

"THERE IS ACTUALLY a drink called a hurricane," said Lou, filling a line of glasses along the bar, "but I tried it and I didn't like it, so this is my version of it, the Hurricane Lou."

When everyone had a Hurricane Lou, I raised my glass and said, "Here's to Alice, whose room holds as many mysteries as Mrs. Jerrold's."

We drank, and then Alice said, "Okay, what was really going on in Mrs. Jerrold's bedroom?"

"For thirty-some-odd years now," I said, "I have wondered. First, was anyone in Mrs. Jerrold's clothes closet? Maybe not. Maybe the door was just stuck. But I don't think so. I think that there may have been a man there."

"It must have been Mr. Jerrold, spying on Mrs. Jerrold," said Otto.

"But it might have been Mr. Yummy, waiting for Mrs. Jerrold to return to him," said Esther. "Maybe you interrupted them, Peter, by returning to the house to sell your flying-saucer detectors. What about Mr. Yummy's tray of baked goods? Was it still on the counter in the kitchen?"

"I don't know," I said. "I don't have a mental picture of it. Maybe I expected it still to be on the counter, and so I didn't notice it, or maybe it was gone. Maybe you're right, though; maybe my knocking had taken Mrs. Jerrold away from him. Perhaps I'd spoiled things for them a little, interrupted them. If so, maybe she sent me up to the room to—make mischief—you know—to make him scramble into the closet and hide."

"In that case, she was kind of playing with you, wasn't she?" asked Louise.

"Maybe," I said reluctantly.

"I think it was Mr. Jerrold in the closet, spying," said Otto.

"Then why would he also have the tape recorder running under the bed?" asked Elaine.

Otto shrugged and said, "I guess he wanted a recording for proof, so it wouldn't just be his word about what he'd heard from the closet."

"What if it *was* Mr. Jerrold in the closet," said Miranda, "but he wasn't spying? Like what if he had stayed home from work to screw around with his wife?"

"Could be!" said Lou. "Playing hooky for some nooky! Put in a couple of hours rekindling old feelings. Maybe so, maybe so."

"Then maybe I spoiled things by returning with my stupid little gadget," I said, occasioning some laughter at the expense of a boy and his stupid little gadget. "Really. If Mr. Jerrold-as-lover was up there, waiting for Mrs. Jerrold, wanting her, he must have been frustrated and annoyed by my being there."

"And in that case why did she send you upstairs?" asked Albertine.

"To punish her husband for what he'd done to her," said Alice without a moment's hesitation.

"What had he done to her?" asked Clark.

"He had made her a lonely and unhappy woman," said Alice.

"How do you know that?" asked Clark.

"Because she was looking for love from a bakery man and a little boy."

"Oops," I said.

"Well," said Alice. "Sorry, but I think it's true."

Was it? I don't know. I don't know, but I wonder. I still wonder.

Testing, Testing

It's a true sign of prudence not to want wisdom which extends beyond your share as an ordinary mortal, to be willing to overlook
things along with the rest of the world or to wear your illusions with
a good grace. People say this is really a sign of folly, and I'm not
setting out to deny it—so long as they'll admit on their side that this
is the way to play the comedy of life.

    Folly, in Erasmus of Rotterdam's *Praise of Folly*

WHEN I WENT DOWN to the dock to pump the launch dry, I found that
someone was already there. From a distance, he looked like a hood from
my school days. (If you were not around during my school days, reader,
you may not know that hoods were bad boys, or boys who wanted to be
mistaken for bad boys. They were a school generation ahead of my
school generation; the style was already fading by the time I reached high
school. Hoods wore black jeans and white T-shirts. They kept their cigarettes—no filters, natch—rolled in one sleeve of the T-shirt, exposing
more of their lean but muscular arms. They greased their hair and combed
it so that the sides swept back to meet in a shape called a DA, a duck's
ass. Some hoods drove hot rods, and some rode motorcycles. Some
hoods had tattoos. Rockwell Kingman would have been a hood.) This
guy was stripped to the waist in the brisk sunlight that had followed the
storm. He was wearing black jeans, leaning over the side of the launch,
arranging the hose that *I* usually used to pump the bilge. He seemed to

know just how to do it—even to know just how I did it—but he looked as
if he should have been working on a hot rod instead of the launch.

"Hello there," I said. "What's up?"

"Hey! Mr. Leroy!" he said, raising himself out of the bent-over position he'd been in, and wiping his hands on a rag. "How's it goin'?"

I said, "Well—ah—it's going okay, I guess, for the day after a hurricane. The hotel wasn't washed into the bay, which I'm counting as a
Good Thing, and—do I—do I know you?"

"No, no, no. We ain't met. I'm Tony T." He extended a big mitt and
shook my hand with vigor, smiling all the while.

"What—ah—Tony—what are you up to here?"

"Tony-Tee," he said. "It's gotta be the whole thing, Tony T."

"Tony T," I said, "let me ask you something."

"Shoot."

"What the fuck are you up to here?"

"I'm—ah—I'm just pumpin' out the bilge. You got a little leak problem here on this launch."

"Yeah," I said. "We've had that little leak problem ever since I bought
the damned thing. I think I was snookered."

"Hey, listen. We all make mistakes—and all boats leak. But we're
gonna slow it down to the point where you don't even notice it."

"We are?"

"Hey—I am. Don't worry about it, Boss, I'll take care of it."

"'Boss'?"

I looked at him, and I thought about questioning boss-and-employee as
a description of the nature of our relationship. Specifically, I thought
about asking him how much he was expecting me to pay him, but he went
back to his work with such relish that I decided for the moment to accept
boss as an honorific and the work as a gift.

"We're gonna be usin' this one exclusively for freight," he said.
"We're bringin' in another boat for the customers."

"We are?"

"Yeah. I'll be making a run every hour on the hour. Every half hour on
weekends. And on a as-needed basis. That's what Lou said."

"Ahhh, Lou," I said, and *boss* slid a little further toward metaphor, at
least as it applied to me. I stretched, looked up, and saw the dredge coming our way.

"Oh, shit," I said.

Tony T looked up. "Hey!" he said. "It's about time! That's a guy I hired in town, Dexter somebody."

"Dexter Burke."

"Yeah. Lou told me to hire him. He calls him Dexter Jerk. If you say it right, the guy don't even notice."

"You're both working for Lou?"

"Not me. I'm just here for a vacation—"

"Of course," I said. "Of course. You're pumping the launch to keep your mind off business, right?"

"Yeah. Lou told me about it."

"But Dexter is working for Lou?"

"Yeah. He's carryin' a tank of water on that god-awful shitbox he's drivin', and he's gettin' a crew together to build—is it a sister?"

"A cistern."

"You got it. And he's gonna use the dredge to suck your cellar dry, and—" He broke off suddenly, threw his arm around my neck in a head-lock and rubbed his knuckles on my head, playfully. "Looka dere, looka dere, looka dere! Oooh-baby-baby! Look at what he's towin' behind that dredge. That's my baby."

She had been, once upon a time, *my* baby. She was a 1938 Chris-Craft triple-cockpit barrel-back mahogany runabout with seats for six—but maybe my baby wasn't the baby he meant when he said "That's my baby," because perched on the mahogany, sunning herself, striking a bathing-beauty pose, was a hood's girlfriend, very much like the bad girls of my high-school days—sexy, sassy, and cynical—except that she was, like Tony T, about sixty years old.

THAT EVENING, I read "Testing, Testing," episode twenty-five of *Dead Air,* to an audience of thirty-four—Albertine, Suki, Lou, Elaine, Clark and Alice, Artie and Nancy, Otto and Esther, Louise and Miranda, Tony T and Cutie, and twenty daytrippers.

AMONG MRS. JERROLD'S many attractive qualities was the fact that she owned a tape recorder. Actually, it was her husband's re-corder, but he was rarely around. When he was away, I used to visit if I could find any excuse at all for doing so, since I didn't like to think that Mrs. Jerrold, the little Jerrold boy, and the tape recorder were there all by themselves, alone and lonely. On one visit, while setting up a flying-saucer detector in the bedroom that Mr. and Mrs. Jerrold shared, I had discovered that the items in the second drawer of Mrs. Jerrold's dresser included a set of red underwear, and I had also discovered that the tape recorder was under the connubial bed, running.

When Mrs. Jerrold came upstairs to inspect the installation of the flying-saucer detector, a kind of madness came over me, the way it sometimes does when a boy is nearly thirteen, and before I realized what I was doing I found myself beginning to ask her to model the red underwear for me. "Mrs. Jerrold," I was saying, "could I ask a favor of you? Do you suppose that—"

"What, Peter?" she asked.

"Do you suppose," I said, getting a grip on myself, "that I could use the tape recorder?"

"Sure," she said. "It's in the hall closet."

"No, it's not," I said.

"What?"

"It's under the bed."

"Under the *bed*?" She got down on her hands and knees. I got down beside her. Her shirtwaist dress, buttoned carelessly or inattentively, fell open at the neck, and I could see the swelling curves of her breasts above the top of her brassiere, which was white, not red. "Oh, my God," she said. "It's *going*!"

"Somebody must have left it on," I said.

"Get it *out* of there, will you?"

I crawled under the bed and tugged the tape recorder by its cord until it was out in the open.

"Jesus!" she said. "Shut it off, okay?"

I shut it off, and I unplugged it.

"How did you know it was there?" she asked.

"What?"

"How did you know it was under the bed?"

"Oh. You mean, how did I know it was under the bed?"

"That's what I mean."

"I—well—the detector."

"The detector?"

"Yeah. I was having trouble getting it aligned, so I—ah—started looking around for the—uh—the source of the interference, and—what do you know—there was the recorder. The detector detected it."

She looked at me without speaking for a moment, and then said, "Let's take the damn thing downstairs."

I carried the recorder, and she carried the lid, the microphone, and the headphones.

"Set it up on the coffee table, Peter," she said. "I want to hear what's on that tape."

I set it up, and as I did, I realized that I too wanted to hear what was on that tape.

"Let me have the headphones," she said. I passed them to her, and she put them on. "Let me hear it," she said. I ran the tape back a bit and then shifted to play. The tape ran, and Mrs. Jerrold listened. "It's you and me," she said in the loud voice of a person wearing headphones. "Go back more." I shifted to rewind, let the tape run for a while, and then shifted back to play. Her eyes grew wide. She put her hands over the earpieces, as if some of the sound might leak out. Her jaw dropped. "Stop it!" she said. "Stop it!" She yanked the earphones off as if they hurt her. "Peter, can you erase this?" she asked.

"Probably," I said, "but I don't know how. I could record over it, though."

"What does that mean?"

"If I record something new on the part of the tape that has a recording on it now, then the new stuff will replace the old stuff."

"No one can hear what's there now?"

"No. All they would hear is what I record."

"Will you do something for me?"

"Sure."

"Go all the way back to the beginning of that tape and fill it up with—anything, so that no one can hear what's on there now. Can you do that?"

"Uh-huh."

"Thanks." She gave my shoulder a squeeze, and she went into the kitchen.

I rewound the tape, put the headphones on, shifted the machine into gear, picked up the microphone, held the microphone in front of my mouth, and said the words that I'd heard everyone with a microphone in his hand say: "Testing, testing," and I said it again and again, but I had the recorder set to play, and while I said "testing" I was listening to Mrs. Jerrold engaged in vigorous, passionate, loud, and apparently quite enjoyable sex with the man who delivered baked goods, the man we kids called Mr. Yummy.

AFTER THE READING, and after some discussion of the reading, I made my way to the bar, where I ordered a drink from Lou. When he handed it to me, I leaned across the bar and said, "We have to talk."

"No, we don't, Peter," he said. "Go and talk to the people who want to talk about *Dead Air*. You don't have to say anything to me."

"But I feel that I owe you—"

"Nothing," he said. "You have no obligation to the person who gives you a gift. None. None at all."

"Well, thank you, but—"

"Enough."

"But why—what are you—what are you up to?"

"I'm having a good time here, and you do not need to know the trick of it. This is making me happy. Don't spoil it."

"Okay," I said, raising my glass to him, "I won't."

IN BED, I snuggled up to Albertine and said, "Things seem to be looking up, don't you think?"

She turned toward me and ran her fingers over my face and said, "Oh, Peter, you're such a dreamer."

"I am? I mean, I am, but what does that—?"

"We had a nice little crowd this evening, and Lou is having fun bringing his friends here and Alice is probably renovating another guest room right this minute, but that doesn't mean that things are looking up."

"It doesn't?"

"It's just a little blip in the graph."

"Mm."

"But despite the blip the trend is the same. Costs are rising. Income is falling. We have been making up the difference by borrowing. We cannot borrow any more. Our ship has not come in. We can't borrow any more time to wait for it to come in."

"Yeah."

"I'm sorry," she said. "I wish it were different. I wish it were the way you want it to be."

"Yeah."

"Go to sleep," she said.

"And dream?"

"And dream."

Filling Time

I'VE SAID IT BEFORE: imagination can be a curse. Do you think that the unexamined life is not worth living? Consider this: the closer you look at the life you've led, the more likely you are to find the mistakes you made, the ones you wanted to forget, the nasty little gritty bits that settled to the bottom of your life and would have stayed there if you hadn't stirred them up yourself, examining, examining, examining. I have long thought that the *unimagined* life is not worth living, that what might be and what might have been surround what merely is with luminous layers of nacre that make life a multiple experience, enriched by its possibilities. Consider this, though: the further the imagination rambles, the more likely it is to step into quicksand, and if you have ever stepped into quicksand you know that the memory of the experience returns again and again, at the slightest provocation, for the rest of your life, bringing with it a sickening, sinking feeling, like the feeling that came over me when I sat at my computer and Albertine wrote:

> Peter is halfway through the reading of *Dead Air,* just twenty-five days away from the end, and I feel more and more sorry for him with every reading, every passing day. He's going to turn fifty with all his dreams lying in pieces at his feet—my dreams, too— and he's convinced that it's all his fault. I know he's convinced of that, because I know that he thinks *everything* that goes wrong is his fault. Bad enough that he has to blame himself for his own shattered dreams, but mine, too? And I can't find any way to convince him that I don't blame him. I can't even summon the strength to find a way. I am just too exhausted by too much work

and too much disappointment, too much time spent measuring what is against what I hoped would be.

How can a few small problems add up to such a mass, such a mess? I feel so vulnerable, unable to make any progress, not even able to keep up any longer, losing ground every day. Everything could fall apart at any time—after all, a day will come, someday, when this hotel just falls to the ground—why not today? I am seeing the essential fragility of everything, which we allow the routines of daily life to obscure most of the time. (I suppose I should be grateful that my situation has given me this insight into life. Thanks, God.) Now and then, when things go wrong, we see that the state of things-going-right is an aberration, that bad luck is normal luck, good fortune is the oddity, and in the long run things go very, very wrong.

Lost. Beaten. Defeated. What a terrible feeling. I can never succeed at this. There will be no peace until it is over. I want another life.

THE HEADLINE over the lead story in the morning's *Babbington Reporter* read "Mayor Indicted in Dredging Scam."

"Did you arrange this?" I asked Lou.

"Talk to Artie," said Lou. "He does all my arranging."

"Artie?" I said to Artie, holding the paper out toward him.

"Yeah?"

"Did you arrange this?"

"I made some phone calls."

"Did you—did you set him up?"

"People set themselves up, Peter. We've all got dirty hands. It's just a question of who notices."

I READ "Filling Time," the twenty-sixth episode of *Dead Air,* to a good crowd, but as I looked out over their faces I couldn't help seeing them as agents of destruction, people who were going to make messes and break things and cost us money.

THERE I WAS, sitting in Mrs. Jerrold's living room wearing headphones, listening to a tape recording of her coupling with the man who made deliveries for the Yummy Good Baked Goods Company.

To conceal from Mrs. Jerrold the fact that I was listening to her approaching orgasm, I pretended that I was recording, not listening, and in the service of that pretense I repeated, relentlessly, "testing, testing," until Mrs. Jerrold leaned around the door frame from the kitchen and called out, "Peter!"

"What?"

"Say something else!"

"Huh?"

"I can't stand it anymore. If I hear you say 'testing' once more, I'll scream."

"Oh—um—okay," I said. On the tape, she had already begun screaming.

I looked at the microphone. What to say? Nothing came to mind, nothing, that is, except "testing." I looked toward the kitchen. Mrs. Jerrold wasn't watching, at least. I looked around the living room for inspiration and found none.

"Testing," I whispered into the microphone, as softly as I could. I glanced, warily, guiltily, in the direction of the kitchen. Mrs. Jerrold leaned slowly around the door frame, just until her left eye showed.

"Sorry," I said.

She leaned a little farther around the door frame, enough so that I could see that she was smiling. "Want some help?" she asked.

"Okay," I said, and, hastily, I stopped the recorder, so that she wouldn't see that I'd been playing, not recording.

She came into the living room and sat, in a single smooth motion, folding her legs under her, on the sofa beside me, facing the recorder, which I'd set up on the coffee table. I shifted it to record, and the reels began to turn. Mrs. Jerrold leaned toward me to speak into the microphone, and since I was holding the microphone she put her hand on mine to turn the microphone toward her. Then, without a moment's hesitation, she slipped into a character, she became the announcer who opened the radio program that my mother always tuned to on the kitchen radio in the mornings, the program that greeted me when I came downstairs for breakfast: "Good morning, everybody, and welcome to Bob Balducci's Breakfast Bunch! We've got a great show for you this morning. I'm sure you're going to enjoy it. Bob's off on vacation this week—lucky guy—but sitting in for him is one of your favorite radio personalities—Peter Leroy." Then she did an amazing thing. She made crowd noises by breathing into the microphone and changing the shape of her mouth. While she did this, I looked closely at her, since this behavior was so odd, and I knew, from the way she shifted her eyes in my direction and grinned, that there was nothing wrong with my looking so closely, because she knew that she was doing a mysterious and magical thing. She was *performing,* and one is always invited to watch a performance. I took the opportunity to notice and record the fullness of her lips, the luscious frosting of the lipstick that she wore, the tip of her tongue when it tapped her teeth or licked her lips, and, with the quickest flick of my eyes, the bulge of her breasts beneath her shirtwaist dress.

Then, suddenly, I found myself looking at the microphone again. She had turned it back toward me. She was still holding my hand. She was looking at me expectantly. She wanted me to say something. A remarkable thing happened to me: because she had established the context of a radio program, I experienced the broadcasting professional's reluctance to allow more than the briefest moment of "dead air," time during which the station is broadcasting no music, no commercial message, no official announcements, no chatter, nothing but static. I didn't actually know that this was something that people in radio worried about, but I had intuited it from my experience as a radio listener, from the fact that I rarely *heard* dead air when I listened to a program, and from the fact that if an empty moment *was* allowed to pass, the announcer or host or whatever would return to the air after the lapse, embarrassed, with a comical reference to the silence we had heard, a reference that suggested that this gap was a mistake, and so, to avoid embarrassing us, I rushed right into the breech with, "Hello, there, everybody, and welcome to another meeting of the Breakfast Bunch. How about a big hand for my lovely assistant?" Mrs. Jerrold made crowd noises, and, invisible to the listening audience, she and I exchanged the collegial grin of two performers filling time.

BALDY THE DUMMY ended his program that night with a story that began with a question, his favorite kind of question.

"Have you ever wondered what evil looks like, boys and girls?"

He waited a moment, gave his listening audience a moment of dead air, so that we could answer, "Yeah."

"How about you, Bob, have you ever wondered what evil looks like?"

"Yeah."

"A red devil with horns and a tail? A serpent? A black cat? A nasty-smelling man with broken teeth? How about a five-year-old girl with an adorable smile? Yow! Scary! Right, Bob?"

"Yeah."

"You bet! You see one of those cute little girls and you might as well be looking at the heart of darkness itself! That's what happened to the woman in this news clipping I've got here, Bob. She was sitting there in her apartment having dinner with her cute little five-year-old daughter, and she looked at that cute little girl, and she kind of squinted a little to get a better look at her, sitting there drinking her milk, and she looked at her real close, and all of a sudden, what did she see? Not the little girl she usually saw, but a demon! A milk-drinking, bright-eyed, smiley-faced de-mon! Yow! She saw the devil in that child! Gotta do something! Gotta rid the world of this demon child! So she wrapped the little demon in gar-bage bags—wrapped the little milk-drinking, bright-eyed, smiley-faced, five-year-old demon in garbage bags—and taped her up with duct tape and threw her into a dumpster. Quick thinking, eh, Bob?"

"Yeah."

"The little girl's body wasn't found for a couple of days. I bet the de-mon was all out of her by then, don't you, Bob?"

"Yeah."

"Now you know what evil looks like, boys and girls. Now you know what evil looks like. File that under 'This Bag Is Not a Toy,' okay, Bob?"

"Yeah."

October 6
Enough Is Enough

There are ancient and modern poems which breathe, in their entirety
and in every detail, the divine breath of irony. In such poems there
lives a real transcendental buffoonery.

Friedrich von Schlegel, *Aphorisms from the Lyceum*

ANOTHER OF THE REALTORS, Lana, brought a group of potential
buyers to the island. They came in their own boat, one of those long,
powerful speedboats modeled on offshore racers, the kind that my friend
Mark Dorset, the unaffiliated psychosociologist, calls a penis boat. They
were well tanned, fit, brisk, and efficient, and they seemed annoyed. I
was so depressed and pessimistic that I could hardly say anything to them,
certainly couldn't manage to seem enthusiastic about their plans, didn't
even inquire about their plans, in fact, just shook their hands and mumbled at my shoes. Albertine, however, managed to smile and be vivacious
and, it seemed to me, even flirted with the tanned and square-jawed
spokesguy.

"So what do you guys have in mind for the place?" she asked. It
seemed to me that she canted her hip provocatively when she asked and
that while she was waiting for his answer she swayed to some song that
only she could hear.

"Let me just say that we—and you understand that there are more of us
than those of us you see here—we're just the tip of the iceberg, the tip of
the consortium, you could say—we were very disturbed by this whole
dredging fiasco."

"We were pretty fucking pissed off about it out here, too," I said.

"It *was* annoying," said Albertine, smiling at the spokesguy. Did she wink, too?

"We were assured that the project was in full compliance with all local regulations and that Mayor Asshole could deliver the approval of the town council and the general population."

"Oh?" said Albertine. She knit her brows.

"Completely. Absolutely. There was no wrongdoing on our part. No monies were proffered." He winked at Albertine and added, "None that could be traced to us." The group of tanned guys behind him chuckled conspiratorially.

"Pretty clever," said Albertine.

"But now we're screwed. There's no way that new island is going to get built, so we're interested in yours."

"You mean you're—"

"We're going to build a world-class water sports facility—"

"For personal motorized recreational watercraft?" asked Albertine.

"Right!" said the spokesguy, thrilled that Albertine should know the lingo. "And maybe we'll build it here." He looked around him, assessing the island by world-class standards, and he looked skeptical. "Frankly, we considered Small's Island some time ago, but we rejected it because of its distance from the mainland, its small size, and its inappropriate shape. We figured we could enlarge it and we could reconfigure it, but we couldn't very well move it, could we?" The guys behind him chuckled at the absurdity of life. "Easier to build a new one from scratch—we *thought*." He clenched his jaw and pounded his fist in his hand. "And it would have been perfect if the whole thing hadn't blown up in our faces." He made the motions of wringing someone's neck. "If we hadn't been victimized by the perfidy of politicians." He finished throttling the invisible effigy and let it fall to the dock, then suddenly he relaxed and said, "But hey, it's water down the slide, as we say." The guys chuckled in acknowledgment of the fact that they had to admit that this was indeed what they said.

"Let me ask you something," said Albertine.

"What's that?"

"How many jet skis would you have?"

"Oh, a couple of hundred, easily."

"Oh, swell," said Albertine, apparently giddy at the prospect. "Cool. What fun." Somehow she managed to give the impression that she was chewing gum.

THE TIP OF THE CONSORTIUM stayed for my reading, and they insisted that Lana stay with them, so I had an audience of twenty for my reading of "Enough Is Enough," the twenty-seventh episode of *Dead Air*.

MRS. JERROLD AND I were sitting side by side on her sofa, making a recording. We were imitating a morning radio program called "Bob Balducci's Breakfast Bunch." I played the part of a guest host sitting in for Bob, who was on permanent vacation, and she played the part of my lovely assistant.

"Hello there, everybody," I said, "and welcome to another meeting of the Breakfast Bunch. How about a big hand for my lovely assistant, Mrs. Jerrold."

Mrs. Jerrold made the noises of a crowd applauding and cheering herself.

"Thank you, thank you," I said. "As my lovely assistant, Mrs. Jerrold, has already told you, Bob can't be here today—"

Mrs. Jerrold made noises of disappointment.

"—but we've got a lot planned for you, and we think we're going to have a wonderful show, don't we—um—Mrs. Jerrold?"

"Well, Peter—"

"Call me Larry, Mrs. Jerrold."

"Larry?"

"That's my radio name."

"It is?"

"Sure."

"Well, Larry—"

"*Say,* folks," I said, "this is embarrassing, but the truth is—*I don't know my lovely assistant's first name!* Let's find out what it is, shall we?"

I held the microphone toward her.

"Betty," she said, like a shy girl.

"Betty!" I said. "That's a wonderful name, isn't it, folks?"

Mrs. Jerrold made the noises of an appreciative crowd, the kind of crowd that really gets a kick out of the name Betty.

"Reminds me of a cousin of mine."

"Betty?"

"Yes, indeed. Did I ever tell you that story?"

"No."

"I never told you that story?"

What on earth was I talking about? What story? I didn't know any stories about a cousin named Betty, but because I was talking to fill the air and the time, without giving much thought to what I was actually *saying* to fill the air and the time, I'd committed myself to telling a story. What story was I going to tell? It would be interesting to find out. "Oh, she was a lovely girl, Betty, lovely. Not as lovely as *you,* Betty, of course. Isn't she lovely, folks?"

Crowd noises of agreement from Mrs. Jerrold.

"Yes, well, let's see, I was going to tell you about my cousin Betty, wasn't I? You see, Betty wanted to get onto the radio in the worst way . . . and if there was a worst way to do something, Betty was sure to find it." As I spoke, I became aware of a remarkable phenomenon, a change that was occurring within me as I talked, I was speaking less and less as myself and more and more as Larry Peters, the boy hero of a series of books to which I was addicted. As Larry, I spoke easily, glibly, because, in a sense that I hadn't yet explored, speaking wasn't as risky if someone else was speaking. I could say anything—whatever came into my mind. "Isn't that right, Betty?" I said.

"Wait a minute," she said. "I'm not Betty."

"I thought you told us your name was Betty."

"It is, but—"

"You're getting a little confused, Betty."

"I mean that I'm not the Betty you're telling the story about."

"Oh, no, of course not. That's my cousin Betty, a lovely girl, but not as lovely as you."

"You said that."

"Isn't she lovely, folks?"

"You're starting to sound like a broken record, Peter. Larry."

"A broken record! What do you think, folks, do I sound like a broken record?"

"Yes!"

"Sorry," I said, to Mrs. Jerrold, not to the microphone, and as Peter Leroy, not as Larry Peters, "I don't know what else to say."

"Take some time and think about it."

"But you have to keep talking when you're on the radio. You can't stop to think."

"Who says so?"

"Nobody. It's just something that I noticed. They never leave any spaces."

She thought about that for a moment. "Maybe you're right," she said. "But you can be different. You can be the one who leaves spaces. The one who takes time to think."

I looked at her, closely, and I took some time to think, enough time so that she reddened, gave my cheek a little slap, turned aside, and said, "That's enough thinking, I think."

THE RECEPTION WAS rowdy. The tip of the consortium was plastered. They kept shouting "Mosh! Mosh!" and trying to persuade Lana to get up onto the bar and jump onto their outstretched hands, and when she refused they tried Albertine, and when she refused they tried Cutie, and when Tony T threatened to rearrange their faces, they feigned terror and began shouting "Encore!" in my direction.

"Okay," I said. "How about this—I have omitted from *Dead Air* quite a few of the details of my obsession with Mrs. Jerrold—the way I stole snapshots of her now and then when she entrusted her film to me for developing and printing, the nightly masturbation with her in mind, and so on. These are my memoirs, after all, and in them I present myself not as I was but as I might have been. The simple truth is that I wished I could spend rainy afternoons with Mrs. Jerrold, in Mr. and Mrs. Jerrold's bed, as Mr. Yummy, the bakery delivery man, sometimes did, and I have often asked myself, in the years since then, what would have happened if I had simply asked her. Suppose, just suppose, that on that afternoon—when Mrs. Jerrold said, "That's enough thinking, I think," I had told her what I

was thinking, exactly what I was thinking. Ready?   No manuscript, no
notes, just thirty-seven years of dreams. Here goes."

I CAUGHT HER HAND and said, "I was just wondering—"
    She raised an eyebrow inquiringly. "Yes?" she asked.
    "What does Mr. Jerrold do?"
    "What?"
    "What does Mr. Jerrold do?"
    "That's what you were wondering?"
    Was she being evasive? She seemed to be.
    "I don't mean to you—"
    "What?"
    "I just mean—what does he do—at work?"
    "Oh," she said. She wiped her hands on her skirt and looked at
me, hard. "What did you *think* I thought you meant?" she asked.
    "Um—well, I thought you thought—"
    "Peter," she said, slowly, "have you and your parents had a talk
about—" She paused.
    "What?" I asked.
    "About—you know—what you're asking me about?"
    "Yes," I admitted, with my eyes down. "I guess I let my imagi-
nation run away with me."
    "Peter!"
    "What?"
    "What do you mean by that?" She put her hand under my chin
and tilted my head upward until I was looking into her eyes.
    I said, "Well, see, I got the idea that Mr. Jerrold—" I was about
to say that I had gotten the idea that Mr. Jerrold was a spy, but a
look of panic came across her face and she put her finger to my lips
to stop me from speaking.
    She whispered, "You haven't said anything to Junior about
what you—imagined—have you?"
    "Oh, no," I assured her. "No."
    "Good," she said, and I could see that she was relieved. "What
does Roger do?" she said with a sigh. "Let's just say that he doesn't
do anything unusual." She winked.

I winked back and said, "I guess that's the way he wants it to look."

"What?"

"He doesn't want to give himself away."

She raised both eyebrows. "That's a funny way of putting it," she said.

"I mean he wants to look as if he does the same thing everybody else does, nothing unusual."

"You're right," she said, knitting her brows. "I think you're exactly right. He's worried that he won't seem to be—"

"Ordinary," I suggested.

"I was going to say normal, but I guess ordinary is close enough."

"Well, he's doing a great job. Most people would think that he was ordinary—or normal. I don't think most people would put two and two together, you know what I mean?"

She brought her hand to her brow and shook her head. "Peter," she asked, "how did we get onto this subject? What made you ask about all this?"

"It was—um—the tape recorder," I admitted.

"The tape recorder? Oh, my God! You listened to that tape?"

"I did," I confessed.

She put her hand on my shoulder. "Look, Peter," she said, "I have to ask you to forget what you heard and never—"

"Oh, I would never," I said. I wanted to say I would never betray her and that I would never betray Mr. Jerrold, either, since revealing that he was a spy would cause her pain, but it sounded melodramatic in my mind's ear, so I just repeated, "Never," and then added, "but—"

"But?" she said.

"Could I ask a favor?"

"Anything," she said, "so long as you keep that tape a secret between us. What's the favor?"

"I want to do with you what Mr. Yummy does with you."

"What? *What?*"

"Don't be upset. I don't mean to upset you."

"Oh, my God."

"I—ah—I think about you a lot, Betty. Lots of times, at night, when I'm in my bed, I—"

"I get the picture. You don't have to go into the details."

"It's the details that I'm interested in," I said.

I held my hands out to her as if she were a girl my age, and she, with a self-conscious laugh and a self-conscious sense of indulging a neighborhood boy with a passion for her, put her hands in mine.

"Betty," I said, "kiss me."

She opened her mouth as if she were going to object, then stopped, hesitated, leaned forward, and kissed me. It was an informed kiss, and I gave myself up to learning from it, and among the things I learned, or thought I learned, was that she would not, perhaps could not, allow herself to initiate anything, but that she was willing—maybe even eager—to give in to the pleading of a boy who needed her, but she wasn't going to seduce that boy. The boy would have to seduce her, as well as he could.

"Betty," I said, "let's go upstairs." It was the best I could do in the seduction-of-a-woman-more-than-twice-my-age line, but the best I could do turned out to be good enough, and when I stood and took her by the hand, she stood and followed me.

In bed, everything went beautifully. We maintained the fiction that I was the initiator in all things, but it was really she who took the lead, and we both knew it though neither of us acknowledged it. I was a little shaky and overeager, but she was composed and patient. She was a little large for me, and I was a little small for her, but passion saved me from embarrassment, and novelty saved her from disappointment. In fact, she sounded far more pleased in person than she had on tape, so I've always considered the afternoon a success.

"ALAS," I said, "I didn't do that. For one thing, I had my suspicions that Mr. Jerrold might be hiding in the bedroom closet, and since I also had my suspicions that he might be a spy, there was no good reason not to suspect that he might be packing a rod, and for another I would never have had the nerve, and for another—well, at any rate, I never did that, but maybe I should have tried. Maybe there was no one in the bedroom closet. Maybe, if I had asked politely, Mrs. Jerrold would have said yes. If I had asked, and she had said yes, and we had spent the rest of the afternoon in her bed, would I have been happy about it? Probably. Would she? I don't know. Would I have been happy about it a day later? A week later? Would she have been happy about it a week later? Would I still be happy about it now? Would she? Was it a mistake not to ask her? I wonder. I have often wondered."

AL TRIED TO CONVINCE the tip of the consortium to take rooms and spend the night, but they wouldn't be convinced, and they carried Lana, who was unconscious, down to their penis boat, with all the inmates following, like worshipers of a dead goddess. They roared off into the night, their wake washing over our feet, and Al said, "You know what I wish I had now?"

"What?" I asked.

"A torpedo," she said.

October 7
Artificial Insinuation

ROCKWELL KINGMAN was steamed. He was having a very bad day. He had missed a target. That was not a good thing. It was the kind of thing that could ruin a career. He sat on a park bench across from the scene of his disgrace watching the police pick up the pieces. He had killed a second-echelon member of a third-rate crime family, his two bodyguards, and three passersby, but they were the wrong passersby. He had missed the object of the hit, the abusive and philandering husband of the head of a mail-order cosmetics firm. He sat there, eating a tuna salad sandwich and cursing his luck. What a waste of great camouflage. For a long while, he thought about giving it another shot. Second attempts lay very far outside his book of unwritten rules for the conduct of Rockwell Kingman. It was his conviction that things went wrong on second tries. Something got into the works—sloppiness, hastiness, pride, anxiety— something that guaranteed failure, and with a second failure a guy could get caught. "No," he said to himself. "Don't do that. Do what you do." So he went to the home of his client, driving a car identical to her husband's, and he apologized to her, and when she wasn't looking he killed her with three deliberately clumsy blows to the head, using the first heavy object that came to hand, a candy dish. Then he simulated a clumsy attempt to simulate a robbery gone bad, an amateur's attempt at camouflage, took some jewelry from the bedroom, and left. On the way to the car, he stepped into a newly seeded spot beside the driveway, leaving a nice imprint of the heel of a right shoe identical in every way to the right shoe of the pair he had observed the husband buying two days earlier. He drove to the parking lot beside the husband's office and placed one of his client's "stolen" earrings under the driver's seat. Then he drove away, leaving no one behind who knew that he had botched a job.

He sat in his office tracing figures in the dust on his desk and drinking from a bottle of dark rum that he kept in the bottom right-hand drawer. The late afternoon sun threw the slanting shadows of his venetian blinds across the trophies of a long and brilliant career: a crystal statuette from the Societé Internationale des Tueurs, the award of merit from Kalashnikov Arms, a picture of him with his arm across the shoulders of old man Kalishnikov himself, other photographs, taken during the shooting of *Blown to Bits* and *Shot to Hell,* for both of which he had served as murder consultant—and suddenly he threw the rum bottle against the wall beside the picture of old man Kalashnikov.

It was that little guy, Leroy! That's why things had gone wrong. He'd thrown a monkey wrench in the works somehow, with his idiotic suicide plan. It was all his fault. He had misunderstood everything, and Kingman hated being misunderstood. It had rattled him, that was it. The little twerp seemed to have no understanding of his principles whatsoever. He adjusted the venetian blinds so that he wouldn't lose the slanted shadows in the last of the light. Suddenly inspired, he sat at his desk, rolled a sheet of paper into his old Underwood, and typed:

```
There's a certain slant of light, October
afternoons, that sends the shadows of the slats
of my venetian blinds across the wall of my dusty
office in such a way that they start out thin and
parallel and separate on the left but end up
broad and bent and overlapping on the right, like
lives driven together by the dark hand of fate.
Whenever I see those shadows slanted like that, I
start thinking, and when I start thinking I start
to feel a need to explain myself. On this
particular afternoon the need was particularly
strong, because I had been offered a job that
called into question all my assumptions about
who I was and what I did and why I did it. I had
just completed a couple of assignments
successfully--one involving a car bomb, the other
a simulated robbery--and in the pause that every
worker takes after a job well done I found myself
```

thinking about this other job. The owner of a
failing hotel wanted me to kill him and make it
look like an accident, so that his wife would
collect his insurance. Greater love hath no man,
I guess, but I explained the triangular nature of
the contract killing (see Appendix A) and threw
the bastard out. Now, however, under the
influence of the slanting shadows of my venetian
blinds, I began to think about the job I had been
offered, and although at first I was actually
repulsed by it and I was glad that I had refused
it, when I began to think about it, I began to
ask myself how I _would_ have gone about it if I
had taken it on, and almost against my will I
began to hatch a plot. I knew that the target—
let's call him Larry—sometimes captained a
leaking launch, a fine vehicle for an accidental
death to hide a suicide, but I am not in the
business of assisted suicide. I had another
idea. I would be the client. He would be the
victim. To complete the triangle, all I needed
was a killer. I threw a few things into my
battered leather valise and headed for a small
hotel on a small island.

"LANA CALLED," Albertine said, "and she thinks that we just might
hook the water-sports consortium if we lower the asking price."

"How much?"

"She doesn't know, and she wouldn't guess, but she said there is only
one way to increase our chances of selling, and that is to lower the price."

"Okay, what do you think?"

"Ten percent?"

"That seems like a lot."

"Five percent?"

"One?"

"Okay, that ought to do it."

OTTO AND ESTHER checked out, and they apologized for doing so, although they had already stayed longer than they should have, and they
promised to return for the last reading, or the last couple of readings if

they could arrange it. On the return trip, Tony T brought a new guest to the hotel, though. He was a small man, wiry, with darting eyes and a Spanish accent. He said that he had been passing through Babbington on his way to the Phantoms, the string of islands that stretches eastward from Montauk Point, and stopped for lunch at the Babbington diner. At the cash register, one of our flyers had caught his eye and he decided that Small's Hotel might be as good a place as any to get away from it all for a couple of weeks, and "besides, it's way closer than the Phantoms." Albertine wrote the copy for those flyers. I think that she had intended to whip up a little more enthusiasm in the getaway-seeking community than this little fellow displayed. He signed the register Manuel Pedrera, but he told us to call him Ray, and we assured him that we would.

"Is there nude sunbathing?" Ray asked, jingling the key to his room.

I looked him up and down and said, "No."

ON MONDAY NIGHTS, we don't get much of a dinner-and-drinks crowd, and on this Monday night we didn't get any dinner-and-drinks crowd at all. Elaine was off-island for a couple of days, so with Otto and Esther gone, I had only Albertine, Suki, Lou, Clark, Alice, Artie, Nancy, Louise, Miranda, Tony T, Cutie, and Ray Pedrera as audience for my reading of "Artificial Insinuation," episode twenty-eight of *Dead Air*.

MRS. JERROLD was in the cellar, doing the wash. She had left me alone in her living room to obliterate a tape recording of an exchange between her and a bakery delivery man known as Mr. Yummy. It went like this:

> MRS. JERROLD: We only have a minute before Junior comes looking for me.
> MR. YUMMY: I gave the little fellow some of our new twisted crullers to keep him busy. They're quite popular with the young folks. They're twisted into the shape of a pretzel, and—
> MRS. JERROLD: Twisted? I like my crullers straight, if you know what I mean.
> MR. YUMMY: Why you little cream puff! How about this? Do you like this?

MRS. JERROLD: Mmm, mmm, mm. Yes, yes. That's my
      kind of cruller.
MR. YUMMY: Want a free sample?
MRS. JERROLD: Oh, yes! Give it to me!
MR. YUMMY: Open wide.
MRS. JERROLD: Oh, yummy, yum-mmm-mmm-mm . . .

The recording gave me an idea, an idea born of jealousy and
envy. First the jealousy: I didn't want Mrs. Jerrold to be with Mr.
Yummy (or, to be technical about it, to have been with Mr.
Yummy). If that had been my only motive, I would merely have
done what Mrs. Jerrold had asked me to do and obliterated the
record of their having discussed their preferences in crullers, but
there was more to it than that. There was envy: I wanted to be in
Mr. Yummy's place.

I rewound the tape a bit and played it again. When I heard Mrs.
Jerrold say ". . . Junior comes looking for me," I stopped the tape,
shifted to record, and said, "I gave the little guy a whole box of
those new twisted crullers with the sugar glaze. They're my favorites, because they're puffy and sugary and kind of chewy. They
ought to keep the kid out of our hair for a while."

I rewound, shifted to play, and listened. I heard Mrs. Jerrold,
and then myself, and then Mrs. Jerrold, coming back abruptly, a little overrun by what I had recorded, but still, apparently responding
to me, ". . . I like my crullers straight, if you know what I mean."

The illusion wasn't perfect, but it was good enough to inspire
me to continue the work until I had gone through the entire conversation, replacing Mr. Yummy's voice with mine, insinuating myself
into the exchange that they had had. When I had finished and I
played the whole tape, I was able, if I suspended my disbelief sufficiently and employed the aural equivalent of letting my eyes drift
out of focus, to imagine that this was a recording of Mrs. Jerrold
and me, made upstairs, in her bedroom, during an impassioned discussion of baked goods. However, each subsequent listening made
me more aware of its small but annoying imperfections. For one
thing, my voice lacked the teasing self-assurance that I had heard in
Mr. Yummy's. I re-recorded some sections, trying to imitate that

tone, but all I could manage was a boyish eagerness, so I decided to settle for that. There was also another: the ambience was wrong. I could hear the living room in my parts and the bedroom in Mrs. Jerrold's. Mine were surrounded by echoing space and silence, Mrs. Jerrold's enclosed within a smaller, padded space and layered over by the swishing of bodies moving on sheets. I decided to carry the machine upstairs, get into Mrs. Jerrold's bed, and go through the whole process again.

At the top of the stairs, something made me pause. I stood there, holding the heavy recorder, looking into the bedroom, waiting. A band of sunlight lay across the bed. For a long moment, nothing happened. Then the smallest bit of a shadow fell within the band of sunlight. I began backing up. After a couple of steps, there was a sound, clear and loud, from the cellar, the sound of a washing machine door closing, followed by the sound of footsteps on the cellar stairs. When I reached the entry hall, Mrs. Jerrold reached the kitchen. She leaned around the kitchen door frame, holding a basket of laundry in both hands, the way I was holding the recorder.

"What are you doing, Peter?" she asked.

"I was going to put the recorder back where I found it," I said.

"Oh, you don't have to—"

"Okay," I said, setting the recorder down on the floor. "I guess I'll head for home then."

"ISN'T IT FUNNY the way we don't sound like ourselves when we hear ourselves on a tape recorder—not to ourselves, I mean?" asked Nancy.

"It *is* funny," I said. "I close my eyes now, and I can hear myself through those earphones, and the voice I hear coming from the tape doesn't sound like me."

"Which is to say that it didn't sound like you as you wanted to sound," said Lou.

"I thought it was just that we're used to hearing ourselves through the bones and tissues of our heads, but that other people hear us through thin air," said Alice.

"It's that, yes," said Lou, "but both metaphorically and literally. This is a well-known phenomenon. It's a desire to have a distinctive style of utterance that is one's own and is a part of the persona that you project to the world. We shape that voice according to what we hear in our heads, so that it matches the person we *are* in our heads, but then we hear that voice on a tape recorder and our first reaction is 'Oh, no! That doesn't sound like me!' But what that reaction really *means* is, 'Oh, no! That is not the voice of the person I want to be! People are not perceiving me as I would like to be perceived.' This is why people in the broadcasting business often develop a 'voice,' a voice for when they're on the air, and it's got the timbre, the emphasis, the rhythm that they hear in their heads, because they *work* on it, *relentlessly*—"

He looked around. We were all listening to him intently, fascinated, not only because what he was saying made good sense, but because his voice had begun to take on the authoritative tone of a news broadcaster, as if he were demonstrating his argument as he made it.

"Geez, I'm running on and on," he said, reverting to the voice we knew. "If Elaine were here, she would've shut me up by now."

I LAY IN BED wondering about the mysterious Manuel "Ray" Pedrera, asking myself, "Is this guy for real?" My thoughts ran something like this:

Manuel. Manwell. Man. Well. Ray. Rey. King. Pedrera. Stone. Rock. Man, well, king, rock. Rock, well, king, man. Rockwell Kingman. He's here.

I decided that I was in another of those either-or situations: either Rockwell Kingman had come here to Small's Island, or I was leaving it, slipping away into some region of my mind from which I might never return.

October 8
Bedroom Suits

"DO YOU KNOW ANYTHING about this 'Manuel Pedrera'?" I asked Albertine.

"Nothing much," she said. "He's a cute little guy, though."

"I think he's a phony of some kind," I said. "Doesn't he seem a little shady to you?"

"Not particularly—"

"I don't think he's even Spanish. I mean, *I* speak better Spanish than he does. Maybe we should have run a background check on him or something or called the cops to see if he's a fugitive—instead of just giving him a room, just like that."

"We didn't *give* him a room. He's a paying guest. To quote the immortal Porky White, 'I'm not screening people at the door here, Peter.' This is a hotel. We're in the business of providing overnight accommodations for paying guests."

"Yeah, but he could be—a—deadbeat dad—or—a—a *hired killer* for all we know. Maybe he's stalking somebody who's here at the hotel."

"Come on, Peter. Slip out of your imagination and into the real world for a minute. He is just a cute little man—who is on a vacation alone— and while he's away he wants to be someone else, you know? For a couple of weeks he wants to leave his everyday life behind—maybe it's a life full of worry, or sadness, or maybe it's just a thin little life, not enough to feed the soul—and he wants to be away from that life for a while—and to be away from the little man who lives that life, and instead be—Manuel Pedrera."

"Contract killer."

"Get real," she said, laughing, and I laughed too, not because I thought that I had said anything funny, but because her laughter is infectious and irresistible.

When our laughter had subsided, she said, still with a laugher's twinkle in her eye, "By the way—the washing machine that used to be the last of our working washing machines decided—sometime in the night, early in the morning, I don't know when—to join the other washing machines in the suicide pact they've got going down there—who knows what mortal thoughts come to those machines at night down there in the damp and dark."

THAT EVENING, I read episode twenty-nine of *Dead Air,* "Bedroom Suits," to an audience that was not, even though water was still being rationed and we had no working washing machines, noticeably more odoriferous than any of the audiences for any of my previous readings.

THAT NIGHT, I lay in my bed trying to recall and comprehend everything I had seen in the Jerrolds' bedroom, remember every piece of furniture in their matching set, every smell, every sound, every private object. It was tiring work, so after a while I turned my radio on to distract me from it. For the previous Christmas, my parents had given me an Emerson clock radio. Before the Emerson arrived, I had had a radio but no clock. Having a clock was, I felt, a badge of entry into the world of adult time.

Whoever designed this clock radio must not have fully accepted the concept of a clock radio as a single unified device, because it was more a "clock-and-radio" than a "clockradio." The radio was housed in a plastic rectangular solid about the size of a shoe box, while the clock was housed in a plastic hexagonal solid—an extrusion of a hexagon—that was grafted onto the left end of the radio housing. The whole functioned as a single device, but the clock looked like a clock and the radio looked like a radio, as if they had been fused by accident during a fire at the factory.

This clock radio had been styled to the point of exhaustion. Consider the knobs. They were decapitated cones (if we think of the narrow end of the cone as the head, as we in our relentless anthropomorphization of the world and all of its bits and pieces do).

For the sake of style, they were mounted so that they tapered inward. Around the inward-tapering edge of each knob were radial indentations, shallow splines, which might have been there to give the knob-turner a better grip if curving the tips of the fingers inward to conform to the inward taper of the conical knob was the way the knob-turner was likely to turn the knob; in my experience, that was not how the knob-turner was likely to turn the knobs, so the indentations made no sense to me. (A couple of years later, however, I came to understand the meaning of the knurling on these knobs, and when I did I felt up-to-date and savvy. The knurling was there, I decided, as a vestigial reference to an earlier time in the evolution of radio receivers, a time when knobs were linked to big, clumsy devices inside the radio's case, making them hard to turn and so actually needing knurling so that the knob-turner could gain a better purchase for the knob-turning task. The reference was nostalgic, ironic, and witty. Maybe. Maybe not.)

The tuning knob was on the right, the volume knob on the left. Behind the tuning knob was a small window, a sixty-degree section of a circle. Behind the window was a milky-white plastic disk with golden numerals imprinted on it that indicated the frequencies on the AM band.

I roamed up and down the dial, but at last I turned, as I usually did late at night, to the station that broadcast "Baldy's Nightcap," a program that consisted entirely of a rambling dialogue between the host, a dummy named Baldy, and his assistant, a voice in the background called Bob. In the course of his ramble, Baldy would read his sponsors' commercial messages as if he had come upon them by accident, just discovered them on his desk. He had no national sponsors, no soft drinks or cigarettes or deodorants, just local businesses. One was a store called Rooms for Rent, where people could rent furniture. Even I understood the impermanence and uncertainty that this implied. Listening to Baldy read their ad, I could imagine living in a rented apartment reading a library book in the light from a rented lamp, and then nodding toward sleep in a rented bed.

"'Get yourself on down to the showroom at Rooms for Rent and pick out the bedroom suit of your dreams,' he read, but then he stopped, crumpled the paper loudly and dramatically and shouted into the microphone, "'Bedroom suit'? Who the hell *writes* this stuff? Who *are* these people? Let me tell you something, listener, if they weren't paying me to read this crap, I wouldn't do it. I've got my pride. Well, I *used* to have my pride, didn't I, Bob?"

"Yeah."

"Now I'm only in it for the money, right?"

"Yeah."

"We've sunk about as low as we can go, haven't we, Bob?"

"Yeah."

He purred into the microphone, "Here's an idea, boys and girls. Maybe you'd be willing to do old Baldy a favor. Hmm? Go take a look at those bedroom 'suits' at Rooms for Rent and tell those ignorant bastards that Baldy says they are bedroom *suites, suites, suites!*" For a moment, there was dead air; then: "Now we'll find out whether anybody's listening, won't we, Bob?"

"Yeah."

The next night, Baldy came on at the regular time, and nothing was changed. Apparently, no one had telephoned the station to complain, not even the people who ran Rooms for Rent. Reasoning from that remarkable lack of response, and employing an adolescent's egocentric logic, I concluded that I must have been the only one who had heard him. For a moment, I was elated, but a moment later, I felt the enormous weight of the role fate had dealt me: I was Baldy's only listener.

WHEN I FINISHED READING, I remained standing in my reading spot beside the fire, and I said, "If I may be permitted to say something slightly sentimental—a great sin in our cynical times—I would like to thank all of you for being here and listening to me, and saving me from suffering Baldy's fate—"

"You don't really think you were his only listener, do you?" asked Lou, calling from the bar.

"I—well, no, probably not, but—"

"Most people just don't bother to respond to an appeal like that," Lou suggested.

"I'm sure you're right," I said, "but I really only wanted to say—"

"There were probably *thousands* of people listening."

"Probably—"

"*Tens* of thousands."

"Hey, Hamlet, my old buddy," called Artie, "shut up."

"Geez! You're right," said Lou, smacking himself on the forehead. "I don't know what got into me. Sorry. Go on, Peter."

"All I wanted to say was that, as grateful as I am to all of you for listening to me, I have found that an audience of one is all the audience anyone needs—" I turned toward Albertine. "—if she's the right one."

"Oh! That's wonderful!" said Alice.

"You see that, Lou?" said Artie. "You almost spoiled a beautiful moment there."

"Yeah," said Lou.

Butts of the Joke

To take one of the most commonplace examples in life, what is there so delightful in the sight of a man falling on the ice or in the street, or stumbling at the end of a pavement, that the countenance of his brother . . . should contract in such an intemperate manner, and the muscles of his face should suddenly leap into life like a timepiece at midday or a clockwork toy? . . . The man who trips would be the last to laugh at his own fall, unless he happened to be a philosopher, one who had acquired by habit a power of rapid self-division and thus of assisting as a disinterested spectator at the phenomena of his own ego. But such cases are rare.

    Charles Baudelaire, "On the Essence of Laughter"

ALBERTINE WAS STILL IN BED when I returned to the bedroom after writing. She had the covers pulled up to her chin, and she was lying on her back staring at the ceiling. I ran my fingers along her cheek, then sat on the edge of the bed and leaned my elbows on my knees. For a while, neither of us said anything, then she said, "There are mornings now when I don't want to get up."

"It's so cold," I said, and by saying it I intended to put the blame on something neither of us could control, but as soon as I spoke I realized that she might think that I was referring to the moribund boiler, growing feebler by the day, and that she might consider the reference a complaint about her hotel-management skills, so I added, "This is the coldest fall we've had in years."

"Oh, it's not the cold," she said. "I mean, yes, it's cold, and you know that I don't like getting out of bed on cold mornings, but it's really fear. I guess I'm reluctant to get up and find out what new messes the day will bring. I'm afraid that things will go wrong, that people will be after me, making demands on me, screwing life up for me."

I wished that I could say something to change her mind about that, but I couldn't think of anything convincing. "You're probably right," I said at last, and for some reason she laughed at that. She got out of bed, pulled her workout clothes on, and went for her run.

IN THE LAUNDRY ROOM—though it might be more accurate to call it a "laundry nook," since it is a corner of a corner of the cellar, a dark, dolorous place that some employees, back when we used to have some employees, refused to visit on the grounds that it was "spooky"—Lou, Clark, Artie, and Tony T stood watching me and kibitzing while I tried to find out what was wrong with the last of the washers. I noted the absence of Manuel Pedrera from this bunch of guys and assumed that, if I was right about his true identity, he was inspecting the launch and plotting some crafty sabotage or, if I was wrong about his true identity, he was pestering the women with offers of massages.

As soon as I began examining the washer, I felt the chill down the spine that one feels in the presence of death, but with everyone watching I didn't want to look like a shirker, so I went through the motions of dismantling the housing and inspecting the machinery.

A point comes in jobs like trying to resuscitate a dead washer when the worker begins to curse not only the work but also the fates that have put him in the miserable position of having to do the work. When I reached that point, Clark said, "I gotta get back up on the roof," Lou said, "Gotta take inventory," Tony T said, "Gotta find the gas leak in the launch," and Artie flipped his phone open and said, "I gotta find you somebody who knows what he's doin'."

Tony T brought the washer repairman over in the launch, not the runabout, because he reasoned, wisely, that a washer repairman was likely to be greasy, if not on the way over then certainly on the way back. The repairman was short, wide, and moronic. He looked at each of us from below heavy eyebrows as if he were sizing up the likelihood that we might have designs on a piece of raw meat that he had hidden in his back pocket to snack on later. I showed him to the laundry nook, and when he saw the line of silent washers he grunted, then he snorted, and then he blew his nose on his sleeve, which I interpreted as the professional washing-machine-repairman's way of indicating that he would prefer to be left alone with the machines. So, I left him to his work and went back to mine, painting, patching, and plastering my way from one end of the hotel to the other. The repairman spent some time making things go thump and bump in the cellar, and then he came upstairs and found me.

"Gonna come to this," he said. He held in front of me a computer that had been beefed up and dressed in armor to withstand the abuse of washing-machine repairmen. On its screen was an estimate for the repairs. The total came to the price of a good dinner for two at the hotel, with cocktails, wine, dessert, tax, tip, a night's lodging, a moonlight sail, champagne breakfast in bed, and a couple of souvenir Small's Hotel T-shirts.

"Holy shit!" I said, if I remember correctly.

Lou, Clark, Artie, and Tony T materialized silently and immediately, as if they had been loitering around the corner until the repairman appeared with his estimate. They jostled one another for position until each of them had had a view of the screen, and then they put their heads together for a quick conference. "How much to fix them all?" asked Lou.

The repairman gurgled and looked at the screen of his computer, as if he were hoping that the answer might appear there without his having to do anything to prompt it. The rest of us looked at the screen in the same manner. When nothing appeared, the repairman grumbled some more and returned to the cellar. We waited at the top of the stairs. We heard thumping and banging, and more thumping and banging, until he had thumped and banged each of the eight machines, and then the repairman came to the top of the stairs, held his computer out toward us, and said, "Gonna come to this," as, I suppose, he had been taught to do in a customer-relations seminar. My four benefactors went into conference again, and while they conferred I tried to think of some way to thank them for the generous gesture they were about to make. I had just about settled on the idea that some sort of special dinner, on the house, would be appropriate and would still leave the house far ahead of the game, when Lou said, "Why don't you do two of them," and I decided that a round of drinks would probably do just fine, maybe just a round of beers.

The repairman turned and disappeared down the stairs into the dark, and in a moment there came forth from the cellar the anguished screams of washers undergoing organ transplants without benefit of anesthesia. It was enough to make strong men turn to drink.

"How about a beer on me?" I suggested, and we retired to the bar to await the outcome of the operation. Lou had hardly finished drawing five pints when, suddenly, it was over. No more than ten minutes had passed, but the washer repairman stood in the doorway with his armored computer, printing a bill. He tore it off and handed it to Lou.

"There is a three-year warranty on the parts," he announced.

"Which cost eight dollars," Lou said, examining the bill.

MY READING of "Butts of the Joke," the thirtieth episode of *Dead Air,* was interrupted after the first paragraph, as you will see.

> WHENEVER, during the nights of my adolescence, my own thoughts became too much for me, I turned to "Baldy's Nightcap" for relief from them. Baldy's incessant talk usually set my thoughts aside, and thereby relaxed me, but sometimes Baldy himself set me thinking. Sometimes I would wonder, in the idle, unfocused way of a boy on the edge of sleep, where he got all his ideas, and in a similarly idle and unfocused way I came to the conclusion that he did it in exactly the same idle, unfocused way as I allowed my thoughts to wander in my head at night—that all of his earlier life, every moment up to the present moment, was material for the next utterance. I never wondered *why* he did what he did, only *how* he did it, until Baldy brought the question up himself. . . .

"HOLD IT! HOLD IT!" called Lou. "Sorry, Peter, but we just can't hear you back here at the bar—not over that racket."

We had all been trying to ignore the scraping, grinding sounds that were coming from the two washers that had been repaired and were currently at work washing clothes, but the noise had seemed to increase as soon as I had begun reading, and I couldn't manage to read over it.

"Be right back," said Al, and she ran downstairs to shut the machines off. She came back with a handful of shredded cloth, which she held out for all to inspect. "The good news," she claimed, "is that everything seems *really clean.*"

Once the groans and laughter had died down, there seemed no reason not to continue where I had left off, so I did.

"You wonder why I do this, don't you?" Baldy said one night. "And why I go on doing it, why I'm here every night when you tune in. Well, let me ask you something: why are you *there* every night, tuning me in? I'll tell you why: we are all actors in a bad joke, isn't that right, Bob?"

"Yeah."

"'Yeah'? What do you mean, 'Yeah'? You don't have any idea what I'm talking about, right, Bob?"

"Yeah."

"Damn straight. That's what we are: actors in a bad joke." He took a drag on his cigarette and let the smoke out into the microphone. "Actors in a bad joke," he repeated. "And most people—not *you,* listener, but *most* people—don't even get the joke!" He laughed his wooden laugh. "Well, I've got exciting news for you: here's somebody who gets the joke." He rustled a sheet of paper. "He writes to me. He's just a kid, 'nearly thirteen,' he says, which means that he is *twelve.* He sends me a flyer, a printed flyer, printed it himself, I bet, on one of those Little Giant printing presses, and it's got illustrations added by hand. Here's how it starts: 'Have you ever wondered whether a flying saucer or atomic warhead might be headed in your direction?'"

I sat up in bed. My heart began to pound. He was reading the flyer that I had sent him.

"Where does he get a style like that? Huh? No beating around the bush, just *wham*—right to the point. And that 'Have you ever wondered,' that's good, that direct personal address. I use that, don't I, Bob?"

"Yeah."

"I think he got it from me. That's pretty *flattering,* when you think about it. It's a little trick of mine, addressing the listener personally, as if I were speaking to one person out there." He leaned into the microphone and said, "You," and I knew he meant me.

"This kid—his name is Peter—he's selling flying-saucer detectors. Probably makes them in his basement."

How did he know that? I wondered.

"He's even got a *slogan*! You want to know what it is? Of course you do. It's 'No worries, no kidding.' We could use some of that here—a lack of worry—right, Bob?"

"Yeah."

"Maybe I ought to order a detector for us. Maybe I'll do that. I think I *will* do that. I'll get one of these, and we'll be *safe* here." He began laughing his wooden laugh. "*Sure* we will!" he said. "No worries! No kidding! What a joke. You get it, don't you, Bob?"

"Yeah."

"Yeah. You and I get it, and this twelve-year-old kid gets it, but here's something I *don't* get: why do we bother going along with the gag? Why do we bother reading our lines? Why do we bother doing *anything*? Why draw that next breath, why take the next step, why say the next word—why not just *sign off*?" He drew on the cigarette again, exhaled, and then said, in a measured voice, breathing into the microphone, "Let's try it, shall we? Come closer. Lean in here, toward me. Here's what we'll do—when I stop talking, you stop breathing. I won't talk. You won't breathe. We will experience the power of refusal, the restful silence of dead air."

Then he stopped talking, and there was silence, or the closest thing to silence that we get on a radio, a hissing vastness, but it wasn't restful: it was disturbing, like the insistent rustle of apprehension that fills our heads when we close our eyes on sleepless nights.

After a long while, Baldy asked, "Are you still there?" I smiled in the dark, amused by both of us, and whispered, "Yes."

Baldy's theme music began coming up behind his voice. "We lost the game," he said. "You drew a breath, and I spoke. Life got the best of us. The joke's on us." Then the music overwhelmed him and the show was over.

AFTER I'D HAD A BALDY and slipped into a confessional mood, I said, "I have to admit that I have never understood what Baldy meant when he said that I got the joke. In fact, to be completely honest about it, I don't think I even know what the joke is. When Baldy said that, I thought that—well, I was flattered—I thought that I must have gotten pretty sophisticated without even noticing it, if I understood things—understood life—the way Baldy did, even if I didn't understand quite how I was supposed to understand it. It was a joke, I got that. The idea that life is a joke. Okay. But I didn't get what he meant by the idea that I *got* the joke, and over the years I have wondered sometimes if Baldy wasn't just—you know—filling time, saying whatever came into his head, without—"

"Oh, I don't think so," said Lou. "I think that what he meant—what he *might* have meant—when he said that you seemed to get the joke, because of the flyer you sent him, the way you had this little flying-saucer-detector scam going—no offense, but it was a kind of swindle, wasn't it?"

"Well," I said, "I don't think I would call it a swindle."

"Then maybe we could say it was a kind of practical joke, since you didn't really believe that the gadgets had any value, did you?"

"I wasn't sure, but—"

"—but you suspected that you were taking advantage of the people you sold them to."

"I guess so. Yes."

"So what Baldy thought you understood was that there is always a butt to a joke. Joke implies butt of joke. There are no harmless jokes. Every joke is made at someone's expense. The object of the joke—the butt—might be someone near or someone distant, but there is always someone, somewhere who ends up with 'KICK ME' pinned on the seat of his pants, always somebody who's getting kicked so that somebody else can laugh."

He was red-faced when he finished, and the room was silent. He looked around at us, then picked up a glass and began polishing it vigorously and said with a shrug, "Anyway, that might be what he meant."

Up the On-Ramp to the Road to Riches

THIS WAS A BUSY DAY for all of us. After writing, I spent most of the day at the dock, repairing and patching and reinforcing, and chatting with Tony T, who was working on the launch, trying to find the source of a gas leak that might have been useful to someone who wanted to fake an accidental death so that his wife could collect on his insurance policies, if his wife had not allowed his insurance policies to lapse. Albertine, in addition to all her other duties, spent nearly an hour on the phone trying to get the washing-machine repair service to send a different washing-machine repairman to repair the damage done by yesterday's washing-machine repairman, but trying to do it without actually saying that he seemed to be incompetent, because she didn't want to be the cause of the poor guy's losing the only job he could get, even if it was a job he couldn't do. Elaine returned with piles of documents for Lou to review, and the two of them spent the day closeted in the library, reviewing the documents and making decisions and, I suppose, money. Cutie, who had taken to wearing a Small's Hotel T-shirt, pearls, and very pink pumps as her indoor outfit, energetically pursued what had become her preoccupation: the development of a complete line of Small's Hotel paraphernalia, reaching far beyond T-shirts to include luggage, swimwear, prepared foods, and a radio-controlled model of the triple-cockpit runabout that was used to shuttle guests to and from the hotel, now by Tony T, formerly by me. Nancy was her collaborator in this effort, but she concentrated on marketing, rather than design; she was laying out a mockup of a catalog and creating a Small's Hotel Web site, where she had already begun to advertise the items that Cutie had envisioned, even though they were only visions, not the sort of goods that the Federal Communications Commission or whatever government agency surfed the Web with an eye out for offshore scams would consider tangible enough to qualify as legitimate. Alice spent most of the day in her room, of course, redecorating it. Artie, master of arrangements, spent the day moving briskly from one project to the next, phone in one hand, walkie-talkie in the other, overseeing the construction of the new cistern and the redistribution of the stillborn island to the bottom of the bay, where it belonged, a job that kept Dexter Burke and his dredge—make that Lou's dredge—occupied at a good distance from our island. Nancy had apprenticed herself to Albertine and was learning the hotel business by clucking over the books while Albertine was occupied with the washing-machine repair service. Clark nailed shingles to the roof and fiddled with the boiler, singing all the while. Suki cooked. Louise and Miranda peeled, chopped, sliced, and diced. And in the afternoon Manuel Pedrera hunkered down beside me on the dock and asked me to teach him to write.

"What?" I said.

"I want to write my memoirs—"

"I know."

"What?"

"Well—I mean—who doesn't?"

"Oh. I see. I wouldn't know about that. I don't read much. Never seem to have the time. That's why I think I need some instruction, if you see what I mean. I've always prided myself on doing good work, so I want to do this well, too, and—"

"Look," I said, "I think you should know that I have no insurance."

"Insurance? You mean like libel insurance?"

"No, I mean life insurance."

"Interesting," he said, and then, to his credit, he modified it with, "I guess."

I handed him my hammer and a handful of nails. "Writing a memoir," I said, "is a lot like repairing a dilapidated dock. Get into the water and I'll explain what I mean."

"What? Into the water?"

"If you want to write a memoir, you need memorable experiences— and this is going to be one of them. Into the water."

He let himself into the water and spent some time cursing in what sounded to me like a phony Spanish accent.

I said, "You see that the pilings—the uprights—are not in very good condition, right?"

"Right."

"And you see that there are crosspieces that tie the pilings together so that the weak ones are strengthened by association with the strong ones?"

"Yeah."

"Our problem is that some of the crosspieces that ought to be there are there, but some are missing, and some are rotten, and some are just dangling there, connected to nothing."

"Yeah."

"You're going to pry those useless old pieces off and replace them with these nice solid timbers I've got here." I handed him one.

"Are you sure this has instructional value?" he asked, shivering.

"Far more than the recommended daily allotment," I said.

FOR MY READING of "Up the On-Ramp to the Road to Riches," episode thirty-one of *Dead Air,* Manuel—that is, Ray—sat virtually at my elbow, and he took notes.

I EXPECTED my flying-saucer-detector business to get a boost from the publicity it got from Baldy the Dummy, but Baldy's plug had no detectable effect at all. I seemed to have been the only one to hear it. My parents hadn't, none of my friends had, not even Porky White, in whose clam bar speculation about flying saucers was the favored topic of conversation.

I was particularly disappointed that Porky hadn't heard the free publicity, because the clam bar was the source of most of my sales. One of my detectors sat there day after day detecting nothing and bringing me customers who wanted one just like it to sit on a table at home detecting nothing. I was pleased that this sales technique should work, but I was also amazed that people should want this gadget when they had never seen it do what it was advertised to do—detect a flying saucer. They bought detectors entirely on the strength of their *not* detecting any flying saucers. They were buying something that did nothing *because they had seen with their own eyes that it did nothing.*

"How stupid can they be?" I asked Porky.

"I'm not sure," he said, "but I've got an idea, and I think that idea is giving me an idea about how to make more money on each detector."

"Great!" I said, "because to tell you the truth there really isn't much profit in them."

"You're kidding."

"No."

"Peter, how stupid can you be?"

"What?"

"Hey, I don't want to make you mad at me, but why would you keep making the things if you're not making money on them?"

"Oh, I'm making a little money on them," I said, "and it's kind of fun to make them, although it's a little less fun each time—"

"Just like making clam fritters," he muttered.

"—and I can't ever stop making them because there's always an order coming in, and when an order comes in I know that some-body's waiting for a detector, so I figure I'm obligated, and I've got to make another detector."

"Yeah, there's always somebody walking in the door wanting another damned order of clam fritters, too."

"Is this what they mean by the rat race?"

"I guess so," he said. We both stood there for a moment in si-lence, wondering how we had gotten into the rat race. Then Porky sighed and shook himself like a wet dog and said, "Look, right now you're selling each detector for twice the price of the parts, right?"

"Right."

"Okay, so your cut is exactly equal to the cost of the materials, since you're not charging anything for your labor."

"Should I start charging for my labor?"

"No, too much trouble. What you should do is use fancier mate-rials that cost more. Then when you double the cost of the materi-als, your cut will come to more."

This seemed brilliant to me. "What a great idea!" I said. "I'll make a fancy one right away, and you can have it here to show on the counter, right beside the basic model."

In a couple of days, I brought Porky the deluxe model. It was identical to the original in every way, except for the materials. The base was mahogany, the uprights that held the wire were maple, the shaft that held the needle was walnut, and the warning lamp was red.

"Nice," said Porky. "Very nice."

It was a great success. It outsold the basic model two-to-one. Many people who had already bought basic models wished that they'd bought deluxe models, so Porky and I hashed out a trade-in policy. We took the basic models back at half their original price and applied that toward the purchase of a deluxe model.

"We could sell these again," said Porky, looking one of the originals over. "They're like new."

"What should we charge?" I asked.

"The same as usual."

"But they're used," I said.

"Nah, they're not used. None of them has ever gone off, has it?"

"Well, no."

"So, you couldn't really say they're used. They've been tested."

"Tested."

"Rigorously tested."

I put a little sticker on each trade-in that said TESTED, and re-sold them at the original price, which made me a hundred-percent profit. It didn't take a genius to see that the way to get onto the road to big bucks was to push the new models into the purchase stream and sell the trade-ins again and again. I figured I was on the way.

BALDY THE DUMMY said, "Let's try this, boys and girls: sit up in bed for a minute, okay?"

"Yeah," said Bob.

"Not you, Bob. I'm talking to my vast unseen listening audience, out there in the dark. Are you sitting up, boys and girls?"

"Yeah," I whispered, not loudly enough to wake Albertine.

"Now close your eyes and hold your hands out in front of you, with your palms up, as if you were holding a couple of melons and trying to decide which one is heavier. Got it?"

"Yeah."

"But instead of a melon, in your left hand you've got your life. Feel the heft of it?"

"Yeah."

"In your right hand, we're going to put somebody else's life, and you are going to be the person living that life, and in that life you are just thinking about what to make for dinner when a cop shows up at the door and says, 'I got news for you. No need to set so many places at the table, because your eight-year-old girl—'

"And you say, 'Are you sure you mean my little girl, the one I put my hopes in, the one who eats far more pizza than is good for her—'

"And the cop says, 'Yes, that one, that one was just killed by a shot to the forehead from one of her little eight-year-old friends while they were watching a bootleg videotape of the movie *Shot to Hell* and playing with a small pistol so that they could act out their favorite scenes.'

"Her last words were, 'Go ahead and shoot me—I won't die.'"

A few seconds of dead air, then, "Now, boys and girls, weigh the life in your left hand against the one in your right. If yours is as bad as that, you can get into Baldy's Catalog of Human Misery! You deserve an entry *all your own* in Baldy's catalog. Apply now! No waiting!" He drew on his cigarette. "But if it ain't that bad," he said in a lower tone, "then it ain't that bad, so roll the rock in front of the cave and pull the covers over your head and tuck yourself into a little ball and sleep well. Rest assured that things could be very much worse."

Beyond the Firelight Lies Endless Darkness

WHILE CIRCUMAMBULATING the island in the morning, I came upon Ray Pedrera. He was standing with his hands in his pockets, looking at the wavelets lapping at his feet. To my eye, he looked uninspired.

"Morning," I said, as I approached. This is my favorite greeting in the morning, nothing more than an announcement that I am aware of the presence of another human being at a time when I am also aware that the light of the sun has returned. Then, in an uncharacteristic gesture of matutinal camaraderie, I asked, "How's it going?"

"Not well," he said.

"How come?"

"I spent the whole night discovering that I have nothing to say."

"That's one of the reasons I try to sleep at night and write in the morning," I said.

He kicked at the sand.

"You can't have explored your past very thoroughly in one night," I suggested.

"That's all it took," he said. "Nothing exciting has ever happened to me. I haven't done anything, and I haven't amounted to anything. I'm nothing. Nobody."

"Look," I said. "If you're going to write an honest memoir, I think you're going to have to drop the mask."

He looked at me as if he were puzzled.

"Correct me if I'm wrong, but I suspect that there is more to you than the little man I see standing here in front of me."

"You do?"

"Yes, I do. I think you are a master of the art of concealment. And I think you know what I'm talking about."

"Huh?"

Shaking my head in admiration, I said, "You never let it rest for a minute, do you? Never let your guard down. How long did it take you to erect this seamless front of conventional behavior?"

"Thirty-nine years," he grumbled.

"Well it's a hell of a piece of work," I said, and I paused for a moment before adding, "but I'm not interested in 'Manuel Pedrera.'"

"Neither am I," he said, and he kicked at the sand again.

I poked his chest and said, "I want to know who you're hiding in there. Work on that."

I TRIED TO RECORD my reading of episode thirty-two of *Dead Air,* "Beyond the Firelight Lies Endless Darkness," but I failed. I owned four tape recorders of various degrees of sophistication, but I couldn't get one of them to make a decent recording. Even my little microcassette recorder seized up halfway through the episode. These failures brought on a feeling of creeping incompetence that might have led to depression if I hadn't steered it in the direction of fury. After I kicked the microcassette recorder around the room for a while I took it to the cellar and threw it into the firebox of the boiler, which made me feel better. Not good, but better.

I had been trying to record my reading because Albertine and I had been invited to the opening of a new bed-and-breakfast in Babbington, and I had painted the evening for her as a romantic getaway, with Tony T as our chauffeur on land and sea, free drinks and snacks, a nice dinner somewhere, and a few hours without cares.

I passed Grumpy Cluck on the cellar stairs. He was on the way down to have another go at the boiler. He asked me what was up, and I told him.

"Use Lou's," he said.

"Lou's?"

"Sure. He's got a tape recorder. I'm sure he'll let you use it."

I found Lou in the bar, where he was supervising the installation of a dozen new spigots for draft beers from microbreweries. When I explained my problem and asked to use his tape recorder, he seemed rattled, and I ascribed his reaction to his embarrassment for me, my having to ask him a favor when I had been accepting his gifts for weeks now.

"Of course," he said. "Just—ah—just give me a little time to get things cleared up—and—get the recorder set up. Give me half an hour, okay?"

In forty-five minutes, I knocked at his door, and he let me in. His tape recorder was a magnificent piece of equipment, digital, good enough for studio use, with a sensitive microphone mounted on a stand. I was surprised that he should have such a piece of equipment, and my surprise must have shown, because Lou seemed to feel that he had to explain.

"Inspirational speeches," he said. "I've got a lot of little businesses—"

"'Fingers in a lot of pies,' Elaine said."

"Yeah. I've kind of lost interest in keeping an eye on them, personally, but I've got a team that puts together seminars for employees, and—"

"You don't have to justify it to me," I said. "If I could afford a gadget like this, I'd buy one, too."

"Anyway," he said. "You're welcome to use it."

We carried everything down to the lounge, and I recorded episode thirty-two for replay that evening.

NATURALLY, the people who ate their clam fritters within the low-anxiety zone surrounding the flying-saucer detector at Kap'n Klam, secure in the knowledge that there were no saucers in the immediate vicinity, wanted detectors of their own for home use.

The orders that came in from Kap'n Klam kept me busy, and they began to put a little money in my pocket, but the detectors didn't bring me the calm that they brought to my customers. I developed a restless urge to devise and build the ultimate detector, a curse that kept me awake for a good portion of every night.

I developed a high-sensitivity model, the result of extensive research and development in my research-and-development department down in my basement, where I worked on the "folding table," which was not a table that folded but the table where my mother folded the wash, which activity brought my research and development to a halt now and then. The only difference between the high-sensitivity model and the basic model was that the tolerances were tighter. Essentially, my detectors consisted of three parts: a switch, a power supply, and a warning lamp. On all models, the switch was a compass needle swinging within a circle of wire, but on the high-sensitivity model the circle of wire was considerably smaller than on the basic model, so that a smaller disruption of the magnetic field would light the detector's lamp. I called this model the Magnetomic Distant Early Warning Saucer-and-Warhead Detector, and I tried charging three times the basic price for it, reasoning that the customers would recognize the value of the performance increase and be willing to pay for it. I was wrong. Sales were sluggish, and I didn't understand why.

"It's because it's pretty much the same as the other two models you've got—the standard and the deluxe," said Porky.

"But it's a lot more sensitive," I said.

"Doesn't matter. It looks the same."

"But the circle of wire is much tighter, and—"

"Only you notice that. If you're going to introduce a new model, you've got to have tail fins—dual headlights—push-button transmission—you know what I mean?"

"Yeah," I said. I did know what he meant, but I couldn't imagine what the flying-saucer-detector equivalent of tail fins, dual headlights, or a push-button transmission might be.

At that moment, a bayman named Danko walked in, carrying a deluxe detector.

"Here," he said, pushing the detector at me. "Take the damn thing back. It don't work."

"It don't?" I said.

"No, it don't. You said it would help me sleep, but it's got me awake all night."

"How come, Dank?" asked Porky.

"I'm up watching it all the time," he said.

Porky and I looked at each other.

"Well, *somebody's* got to watch it," said Danko. "Got to give the alarm if them saucer creatures decide to make a visit in the night while everybody else is asleep. That dim little lamp won't wake nobody up, that's for *damn* sure."

"You're right," I said. "I'll make you one that wakes you up, so you can sleep."

The problem was, as I saw it, simple. Danko needed an audible alarm. So, I tried a simple solution, wiring a doorbell in place of the lamp, and it was not a success, because the doorbell needed more power than the single battery I was using. So I replaced the battery with a doorbell transformer and plugged the whole contraption into a wall socket. Then it worked, after a fashion. When I deflected the compass needle with a horseshoe magnet, simulating a saucer fly-by, a spark arced across the space and completed the circuit. The magnets in the bell drew the clapper toward them, and it struck the bell dome once. Then the jolt of the spark sent the needle swinging backward, and contact was broken. If I kept the horseshoe magnet in position, the process would be repeated again and again, but not rapidly enough to make the bell ring. Instead, it went clank, pause, clank, pause, clank, and so on. It might wake someone up, a light sleeper, but it wasn't likely to, and it wasn't something that lent it-self to convincing demonstrations. People who saw the doorbell were going to expect it to ring, not clank.

I sought the advice of my grandfather, who could draw on a life-time of experience in the construction of impractical gadgets.

"You need a relay," he said.

Of course! I didn't know what a relay was, and that fact alone was enough to make me sure that I needed one, since my work with saucer detectors and my friend Spike's suggestion that she was probably the daughter of Mr. Yummy, the man who delivered baked goods door-to-door, had taught me that most of what I need-ed to know to make my way through life lay beyond the range of what I understood, out there in the endless darkness beyond the flickering light of the fire at the mouth of the cave.

WHILE THE RECORDING was playing at Small's, Albertine and I were touring "Summerset," which the owners called a bed-and-breakfast, em-ploying the obvious irony of deliberate understatement. We tried to keep our mouths from hanging open, but it wasn't easy. They had spared no expense or effort in the remodeling, from William Morris wallpapers to imported tiles, and for their cheapest room ("The Poet's Garret" up in the attic) they were asking three times what we were asking for our largest cottage, but they probably provided a nice breakfast with that, judging from the hors d'oeuvres.

The event was actually a fund-raiser, with an auction, to raise money for the Babbington Shelter for Battered Women. Albertine had donated a dollhouse—at least that was the way it was listed in the program. Actually, it was a miniature of Small's Hotel. She had built it years ago, when we still had hopes for the place, but she had modified it considerably for the auction. The paint was peeling, the shutters were askew, a chubby, grumpy-looking man sat on the roof replacing shingles, steam hissed from the cellar windows at unpredictable intervals, and in a room on the top floor a tiny memoirist sat at a computer, tearing his hair. The whole thing had a farcical appeal, everyone chuckled about it, and it went for a good price.

101 Fascinating Electronics Projects

Don Fernando asked the captive to tell them the story of his life. . . .
The captive replied . . . "pay attention and you shall hear a true tale
which possibly cannot be matched by those fictitious ones that are
composed with such cunning craftsmanship."
Miguel de Cervantes, *Don Quixote*

WE HAD the busiest Saturday we had had in a very long time, and if I
had not come to believe that every new guest was more money lost, I
would have thought that we were making progress, but I had come around
to that point of view. I understood our situation as Albertine understood
it. I believed what she believed for the simple and sufficient reason that I
saw the truth in it. I believed in the truth of our failure here, past, present,
and future, but I had a little extra belief that, I thought and think, she did
not, a bonus belief: I believed that it was all my fault. I had reached the
point where the present seemed to be entirely the product of my past mistakes, large, medium, and small, right down to the level of a careless word
spoken at a party after one drink too many. Even the new guests who
would be arriving that afternoon, two more guests to put us a little further
in the red, were almost certainly my fault, since they were probably coming to hear my readings. My fault. My fault.

THE WASHING-MACHINE REPAIRMAN returned: the same washing-
machine repairman. Albertine and I stood in the entrance to the hotel
watching him make his way up the path, trying to read in his walk and

posture something that would tell us whether he had been told that we had tried to have him replaced.

"What do you think?" she asked.

"Can't tell," I said.

We stood there, watching and waiting, while he drew nearer, walking with his head down. When he was about twenty yards away, he stopped, set his toolbox down, and knelt on one knee to tie his shoelace. He looked up at us and we tried to read the look in his eyes.

"Well?" she asked.

"Hard to say," I said. "It's as if nothing that might be going on in his mind shows on his face."

"Oh yeah?" she said. "I would say that what you see there is the look of a man who is going to wreck something and enjoy doing it. I think he's scary, very scary. Let's lock the door and pretend we're not here."

"He's seen us," I said.

"Maybe he'll think it was just an illusion, a trick of the light. He'll bang on the door for a while, and then he'll give up and ask Tony T to take him back across the bay and he'll never come out here and bother us again for the rest of our lives. He won't even mind. It will make a good story for his friends back at the Sons of the Visigoths lodge."

"Look," I said. "Maybe I'm reading too much into this, but the look in his eyes is—well—I think, in his own way, he's pleading."

She looked at me incredulously.

"Everything is at stake for him here," I said. "His pride, his professionalism, his job, his family, maybe. Let's give him one more chance."

She laughed, "Ha!" and said, "Okay," shaking her head as she said it to show me that she thought we were making a mistake.

We sent him to the cellar, and there ensued ten minutes of crashing and banging, followed by a strong smell of smoke. Al and I went downstairs and stuck our heads around the corner of the laundry nook.

"What the hell is going on in there?" Al shouted.

He said, as nearly as we could make out, "Murhgah."

"Is something burning?" she asked.

"Murhgah," he said.

"Well that's a relief," she said, and she went back upstairs muttering "Murhgah."

He came upstairs half an hour later, and the first thing he said was, "Your fault."

I was on the point of saying, "I know, I know, and I'm sorry, profoundly sorry," but Al snapped, "What the hell are you talking about?"

In answer, he held out a handful of viscous black glop. "Sand," he said. "Lint. Salt air." Then he grinned, slowly and added in a chiding tone, "Cheap detergent." He squeezed the glop and some of it extruded between his fingers. "Gums up the works." He wiped his hands on a rag, to little effect, and picked up his computer. Almost immediately, it printed a new bill.

"What's this?" asked Albertine.

"Bill."

"Why gimme bill?" she asked.

"Unrelated problem," he claimed. "Your fault."

He tucked his computer under his arm, picked up his toolbox, and started for the door.

"Could I just ask you something?" I said. He looked at me. "Do you have a wife—children—you know, a family?"

"Ya kiddin'?" he asked.

Albertine and I watched him walk toward the dock. There was a jolly quality to his walk, a lightness, that made me think he might launch his bulk into the air and click his heels.

When Albertine tried to use the washers, neither of them would fill with water. I think that Albertine might have gone right over the edge if her apprentice, Nancy, hadn't worked up a schedule for Lou, Clark, and Tony T to make runs to the coin-operated laundry in Babbington.

THE TWO NEW GUESTS were a couple. They took the smallest of the cottages, and for my reading of episode thirty-three of *Dead Air,* "101 Fascinating Electronics Projects," they sat right up front, displacing Manuel Pedrera. She was a small blond woman, about my age, whom I will call Effie. There were silver threads among the gold of her hair, but the impression still was of gold, and if it was plated it was a good job, subtly done. Her boyfriend, if it is right to call a man my age a boyfriend, was the person whom I have called in *Dead Air,* and throughout my memoirs, Matthew Barber.

I HAVE BEEN CHASING MONEY ever since I was a kid, and I still am, trying to squeeze a living out of an old hotel and fifty years of reminiscences. In my fondest dreams of the future I imagine myself doing only what is priceless or worthless, but for now, here I am, doing what I do, doing what I can.

The flying-saucer detectors on which I once hung hopes of making big money (and which I also allowed people to believe would alert them to incoming warheads from ICBMs) used a compass needle to detect disturbances in the earth's magnetic field caused by the saucers' mysterious drive mechanism—or somehow or other caused by a warhead, in a manner that I didn't even bother trying to understand, since I had no real conviction that the detector was worth a tinker's damn when it came to detecting warheads. The needle acted as both sensor and switch, swinging within a circle of wire to complete a circuit that lit a warning lamp if a saucer came within range. One of my customers suggested that the detector should have an audible alarm, and my grandfather—an expert in the construction of gadgets of the saucer-detector type—informed me that to include a bell I would have to include a relay, which I could buy at an electrical-gadget supply house called Two Regular Joes. However, I was reluctant to go to the shop and buy a relay, because I knew that if I went there I would have to stand in front of a clerk and display my complete ignorance of what a relay was and how it worked. (There was also another reason. I feared that the clerk would try to take control of my project. He would explain to me what a relay was and how to hook it up to my detector, and end up redesigning my saucer detector for me on the flimsy grounds that he knew what he was doing. This fear of losing control of a project may be the reason for a famous characteristic of men: when traveling, we will not ask directions. We prefer to blunder along until we find our way on our own, if we ever do. Setting aside for the moment the plausible likelihood that our craving for adventure and novelty makes us prefer not knowing where we're going, let me suggest that we do not want to ask directions because we do not want to surrender the leadership of the journey to someone else, and certainly not to a stranger, some hayseed leaning against a rail fence, scratching his balls and chewing on a stem of grass, whose only qualification is that he knows how to get from here to there. By refusing to ask directions, we are saying, in effect, "This is *my* trip, thank you, and I'm going *my way,* even if I'm lost.") Fortunately, the Two Regular Joes published a catalog with a picture and description of every nifty gadget they sold. There wasn't much useful information in the descriptions of the relays, but I found a kit that could produce 101 fascinating electronics projects, with a photograph of the kit that showed all the parts spread out as if they had exploded from the box. Among them was a relay, so I ordered the kit right away—to get the relay, of course, but also because one of the 101 projects was an electric eye, something I had long thought that I probably needed.

When the kit arrived, I discovered to my surprise and delight that the electric eye was one of the projects that used the relay, so that was the first one I made. It worked. I didn't understand quite *how* it worked, but it worked. A photocell detected light (somehow or other), and bafflingly complex circuitry sent the news (somehow or other) to an electromagnet in the relay, which pulled the metal armatures of a switch within the relay to complete a circuit that would activate anything I plugged into the electrical socket wired to it. If I plugged a doorbell transformer into the socket and wired the transformer directly to a doorbell (that is, without another intervening switch, such as a doorbell button) the doorbell would ring when light was detected, and that was exactly what I needed, whether I understood how it worked or not. I added one of my basic saucer detectors at the front end of the process, and the Magnetomic Electronic Five-Stage Distant Early Warning Saucer-and-Warhead Detector was born. [At this point, I displayed the diagram that appears at the top of the next page.]

Here is a pictorial diagram of the stages in the process. The flying saucer's drive mechanism emitted electromagnetic radiation (magnetism), which switched the detector on and lit its lamp, which emitted electromagnetic radiation (light), which switched the electric eye on, activating a circuit that made the electromagnet close the relay, which sent power to the doorbell, which rang.

FIVE-STAGE DELUXE MAGNETOMIC FLYING-SAUCER DETECTOR

**PICTORIAL DIAGRAM
(NOT DRAWN TO SCALE)**

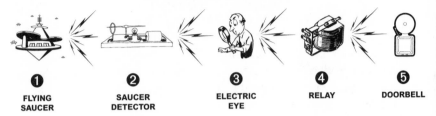

| ❶ | ❷ | ❸ | ❹ | ❺ |
| FLYING SAUCER | SAUCER DETECTOR | ELECTRIC EYE | RELAY | DOORBELL |

A schematic diagram of the stages in the process of detecting a saucer and raising the alarm, as I *understood* it, would have looked like this [I displayed the diagram below], with the black boxes representing stages in the process where I understood *what* happened but not *how* it happened.

**SCHEMATIC DIAGRAM OF BUILDER'S UNDERSTANDING OF
FIVE-STAGE DELUXE MAGNETOMIC FLYING-SAUCER DETECTOR**

I could see that this was not the most efficient way of achieving the desired result, but it was *one* way, and it was a way with a bonus: the resulting saucer detector was complicated, and it *looked* complicated, since it obviously had many more parts—make that components, or, better yet, component parts—than the basic model, including one entire 101 Fascinating Electronics Projects kit, and since I sold my detectors for twice the price of the component parts, I could sell this one for big bucks.

AFTER THE READING, I stood Matthew and Effie to a round of drinks. (To be completely honest about it, I ordered drinks from Lou with the expectation that I would never have to pay for them.) After we toasted each other and old times and clinked our glasses, Matthew said, "It is really remarkable that you should have read that particular story, with the electric eye—"

"Well, it's one of my themes," I said modestly.

"Mine, too," he said. He put his arm around Effie's shoulders and hugged her to him. "Lately anyway, ever since—well—" He paused for effect and waited until he was quite sure that everyone in my audience was listening to him, and then he said, giving Effie another squeeze as he did it, "ever since I began telling people the story of my death."

It was a hell of an opening. Who wouldn't want to hear the story that it promised? The inmates began gathering around us, and I asked Matthew to tell us the story. "It must be an extraordinary tale," I said generously.

"And one well worth hearing," guessed Albertine.

"I'd be glad to tell it to you," said Matthew. "I'm afraid that my story won't be as polished or artful as yours, but if you want to hear it I'd like to tell it to you anyway."

Lou and the others responded with a chorus of curiosity. "Okay," he said, setting his drink on the bar. "I promise you that what I'm going to tell you is true. You're not going to believe it. I know that. Not even Effie believes it, although for my sake she tries to take an attitude of suspended disbelief. Nobody believes it but me."

As he said this, we all settled ourselves in our places and a deep silence fell. Matthew began speaking in a calm voice—no, a controlled voice.

"THE STORY BEGINS on a cold winter's night in Charlestown—part of Boston—where I was running along a dark street, breathing hard. I had been in a fight, which isn't like me—Peter can certainly tell you—and I wouldn't have thought that getting into a fight, a fight between adults, two grown men, was anything at all like me, but I think that I had actually tried to kill a cab driver. I hadn't tried too hard, but there was a moment when I—" He shook his head, apparently disgusted by the memory. "Anyway—there I was running, and running, and I kept on running until I reached the Charlestown Bridge—the bridge to the North End of Boston—where I stopped, thinking that I'd catch my breath, and I kept—*pulling* at the air, trying to suck it into my lungs, but it didn't seem to penetrate me, didn't seem to do me any good.

"I was leaning against the bridge, gasping, trying to get my breath, and I started—*berating* myself. There I was, wheezing, hardly able to breathe, and at the same time I was talking to myself, telling myself, 'You're out of shape. You shouldn't have let this happen to you, you jerk.' Actually, I said 'you asshole.' I put my hands on my knees and tried to breathe. I felt nauseated, and I heard myself talking to myself, as if there were two of me, and one of me had been passing by and saw the other one, bent over, with his hands on his knees, and started saying, 'Catch your breath. Catch your breath. And then you've got to get out of here.' But I was the person saying this.

"I stood up straight and waited until I was sure I wouldn't fall down, and then I tried to run again, but I hadn't gone far before I felt a numbness in my left armpit, and in my left elbow, and down my forearm, and in my little finger, and I heard myself saying, out loud, 'Heart attack This is a heart attack. I'm having a heart attack.'

"Then I answered myself—the other me did. Out loud. Out loud, I said, 'It's just a pinched nerve.'

"'A pinched nerve?' I said—out loud, mind you. 'You think that's all it is?' Fortunately—I mean fortunately for my reputation—all of this was happening on a winter night and the streets were quiet, virtually deserted. It was late, and Boston is not a late-night town.

"'A pinched nerve,' the other me said. 'I wouldn't give it another thought.'

"'That is fucking stupid,' I told him. 'In a few minutes I could be lying on the sidewalk, dead.'

"I turned toward Causeway Street. He asked, 'Where are we going?'

"'Charlesbank Hospital,' I said. I was really getting annoyed with this guy—and he was me.

"'Don't be ridiculous,' he said. 'You're going to embarrass yourself. You're going to get everyone excited about a heart attack, when all you've got is a case of bad nachos and too many margaritas.'

"'Shut up,' I said, and I began walking, slowly, toward Charlesbank Hospital. I began contemplating my mortality.

"'What are you doing now,' he asked me, very sarcastically—contemptuously, I would say—'contemplating your mortality?'

"'Maybe,' I said, 'maybe.'

"'And well you might,' he said, 'walking along these streets this late at night.' I wasn't going to give him the satisfaction of laughing, even though I thought that was pretty funny. 'That was a joke,' he said. 'Where's your sense of humor?'

"'This is no laughing matter,' I said. 'I'm confronting death, and I feel—I feel—'

"And he said, 'Cheated.' I could have killed him. 'Am I right?' he asked. He was taunting me. 'I am,' he said. 'I know I am. You didn't get what you wanted out of life.'

"I wasn't going to give him the satisfaction of answering that, but the truth is that he was exactly right, and what I felt cheated out of was Effie."

He looked at her, she nodded, and he said, parenthetically, "We were not together at that time, and if you had asked me I would have said that it was an impossibility for us ever to be together, but that's another story," and he went back to the story of his death.

"The two of us walked along in silence—and that's exactly the way it felt, that the two of us were walking along—and we finally came to a narrow street that I knew led to the emergency entrance at Charlesbank. It was a short street, but I was so tired that it seemed long, longer than I could manage. A taxi came my way, leaving the hospital, turning out of the circle at the emergency entrance, and I thought *maybe I could just flag it down and go home to bed.*

"The other me said, 'Let's get that cab.'

"'No,' I said, and I began walking toward the entrance. Each step seemed harder than the last. I had never felt so tired in my life. When I reached the edge of the building I saw some steps that led to a side door, and I thought of stopping and sitting there, but I thought that if I did stop there I would not get up. I would die there, on those steps, so I made myself keep on going, even though I was just barely shuffling along, mechanically, with my head down, and I felt so cold and heavy, as if I were covered with wet snow.

"'I'm going to get that cab,' he said, and his voice was coming from behind me now, and I thought *he didn't stay with me—he's going home.*

"I found myself at the doors, a pair of doors, flat glass doors, closed, with no handles or doorknobs, and I was confused. I couldn't figure out how I could get through them, and I thought *maybe he'll help me,* and I turned around to call out to him, but when I turned around I felt dizzy and I knew I was going to pass out, and as I fell, backward toward the doors, I saw him get into the cab—I saw *myself* get into the cab—and then I fell backward toward the doors, and I expected to fall against them, but they slid open, sideways, and I thought, *electric eye,* and now the insane part begins—unless you think it's *all* been insane—because I am convinced that I am *still* falling toward those doors, that these are my last thoughts, and that *this,*" he said, looking around at all of us and smiling wickedly, "is the story of my death."

The Persistence of Memory

BRIGHT AND EARLY, Tony T brought two realtors and a chubby couple in identical nylon suits of the type that used to be called jogging suits, and may still be called jogging suits for all I know, but are now more frequently worn by fat people at their leisure, shopping in malls, strolling the streets of quaint seaside towns, or sitting in front of slot machines, so should probably more properly be called shopping suits or strolling suits or sitting suits, or perhaps just leisure suits.

"Mr. and Mrs. . . . ."

Reader, I am embarrassed to say that I can't remember the name of these people. Was it Widebottom? Littlewit? Vulgarhorde? Packagetour? Something like that. I'll call them Mr. and Mrs. Highroller.

"Mr. and Mrs. Highroller—"

"Arnold and Bobbi!" said Mrs. Highroller.

"Arnold and Bobbi are looking for a very special spot," explained realtor number one.

"Look no further," I said jocularly.

"Well, actually, the Highrollers have some very special needs," said realtor number two.

"Of course," said Albertine sweetly. "Anyone looking for a very special spot must have very special needs."

"We want to build a casino," said Arnold.

"A casino," said Albertine.

"Oh? What's your tribe?" I asked.

"We're not sure," said Bobbi. "Arnold is looking into that."

"Where there's a will there's a way," he said. He gave me a wink, and I had the feeling that if I had been standing near enough to him he would have given me a nudge too.

"He's quite certain that he can turn up some Indian blood some-wheres," said Bobbi.

"If necessary, I'll get a transfusion," said Arnold. He winked again, and he began shuffling my way with nudging in his eyes.

"But if we don't find that we're actually Indians per se, then we're quite confident that we can find some and bring them into the venture."

"Strictly as figureheads, you understand," said Arnold, "or I guess I should say totem poles." He sidled up to me and aimed an elbow at my ribs, but, drawing on the uncanny ability of my people to see the nudge-that-follows-the-joke-that-is-not-funny coming, I dodged it.

"I think that there's more to it than that," said Albertine. "I think those casinos have to be on tribal land."

"Hey, all of this was tribal land once upon a time, wasn't it?" asked Arnold.

I said, "Well, I guess it was, now that I think about it."

"You must have some evidence of Indians here somewhere."

"Actually, we do," I said. "Shell mounds. Heaps of clamshells at spots where the Indians used to hold feasts."

"There you go!" said Bobbi. "This is tribal land."

"Do you think we'd have any trouble building a causeway out here?" asked Arnold. "It's kind of inconvenient as it is, you know, being an is-land and all."

"A causeway?" said Albertine, twisting her mouth into an adorable smirk. "I'm sure it's just a matter of slipping the mayor a little wampum." She winked at Arnold and dealt him a nudge too swift to dodge.

I TRIED to persuade Matthew and Effie to stay for my thirty-fourth read-ing from *Dead Air,* "The Persistence of Memory," because it was one of two episodes—the other being number forty-nine, "Shame on Me"—that I would have wanted Matthew, especially, to hear, but he said that he had no idea how much time he had before he fell across the threshold of the hospital entrance and died, and he wanted to cram as many experiences into his last moments as he could, even if those experiences were figments of his imagination, so they checked out and said goodbye, perhaps forever, and Tony T ferried them across the bay.

MANY YEARS AGO, I became a master builder of "electric eyes," gadgets that could detect the presence or absence of light. I made them from a kit, 101 Fascinating Electronics Projects, and I incorporated them in an advanced type of flying-saucer detector that also included a relay and an electric doorbell. I squeezed all the bits and pieces onto the pegboard rectangle that came with the electronics projects kit so that the whole thing looked neat and complete, as if it were everything a flying-saucer detector ought to be, everything a flying-saucer detector *could* be, and perhaps it was, since I found that I had no interest in trying to improve the design further. I was willing to keep turning them out whenever someone wanted to buy one, but I grew tired of building the same project all the time, while the hundred others that the kit promised were waiting to be tried.

With every kit that I ordered I received a manual with full instructions for assembling all 101 projects. They were handsomely printed, with each project presented in a schematic diagram and in a series of step-by-step "pictorials," drawings of the work as it was supposed to progress as the builder performed it. Throwing the manuals away seemed wasteful, so I stacked them on a shelf as they accumulated, and I sometimes read one of them in bed at night, as I might have read a story. As I read, I experienced the identification that one sometimes feels with the protagonist in a story: I identified with the unnamed someone who was assembling the projects depicted in the step-by-step drawings. Because of the way the manual was arranged, starting with the simplest project and moving through ninety-nine others to the most difficult, this unseen someone—a teenage boy, I imagined, not too much older than I—seemed to travel a road that I wanted to travel. He seemed to become, thanks to 101 fascinating electronics projects, the capable and sure-handed fellow I hoped to become.

I wanted to follow in his footsteps, to go somewhere I hadn't been, make something I hadn't made, but I found that most of the projects already bored me. Given the nature of the kit, the fact that each of the projects was built on the same pegboard base, with the same basic components in the same relative positions, all 101 projects looked very much alike, so there wasn't much reason to choose one of them over another in that respect. Since they all functioned differently, the choice would be made on the basis of function, not form, but the manuals never made any mention of what it was like for the mystery builder to use the things that he had built. Previously, when I read through the manuals, I had imagined building each project; now I imagined owning and using each one. I grew tired of most of them quickly, but of one of them I did not grow tired, and that was the one I built.

When I summoned my friends Raskol, Marvin, Matthew, and Spike to see what I'd made, I said, "Wait till you see what I made," full of builder's pride. They came to my house at once, and when I said, "It's in the cellar—come on down," they followed where they were led. They were my pals.

I indicated the completed project on my workbench. "What do you think?" I asked.

"Is it another saucer detector?" asked Spike.

"No, no, no," I said, chuckling indulgently.

"It looks like a saucer detector," said Raskol.

"True," I said, enjoying myself enormously.

"Well, since it *looks* so much like a saucer detector, I think you shouldn't have used that tone of supercilious indulgence when you told Spike that it wasn't what you must have known it would appear to her to be," said Marvin.

"Oh," I said. "Well, I just—"

"You just brought us down here to demonstrate that you know something we don't," Spike suggested.

"No. No. I—"

"You're just showing off the fact that you can tell a saucer detector from whatever this is. The whole point of getting us down here is to rub our noses in the fact that even though it looks like the same bunch of electrical gadgets to us, to your eye, the eye of an initiate in the arcana of electronics, it is something altogether different," said Matthew.

"No, really," I said. "I only wanted to—"

"You only wanted to play big shot," said Marvin, "to show us that you're an adept, while we're the rubes, gawking at the mysteries in the sideshow of life."

"Hayseeds," said Spike.

"Bumpkins," said Raskol.

"Ignoramuses," said Matthew, and the four of them turned and started for the door with their heads down, apparently wounded to the depths of their souls, wounded beyond repair.

"B—but don't you want to know what it is?" I asked. I may have moaned.

Slowly, they turned. Slowly, they smiled.

"Of *course* we do," said Raskol. "What the hell is it?"

"It's a transmitter!" I said. "We can broadcast with it. We can be on the radio, and—and—" Shame and gratitude overwhelmed me. "I'm sorry," I said.

"Forget it," said Matthew, but I never did.

"YOU THINK you still owe him an apology?" asked Artie. "Matthew, I mean."

"Yes, I think so," I said. "Him and the others, for insulting them, taking advantage of their ingnorance, taking advantage of our friendship—"

"You're a sensitive guy, Boss," said Tony T.

"A little too sensitive for your own good, I think," said Artie. "I think he owes *us* an apology now, getting all of us to listen to that bullshit about the story of his death last night."

"Artie," said Nancy.

"Sorry, folks," said Artie, "but if it *looks* like bullshit, and it *smells* like bullshit—"

"I'm with Artie," said Grumpy Cluck. "I was a little ticked off—*more* than a little ticked off—to be told that I'm nothing but a bit player in some guy's last wet dream."

"Oh, Clark," said Alice.

"That's what he was saying to us, wasn't it? That he's having this dream about the little blonde, Effie, and we're just there for—"

"Verisimilitude," said Albertine.

"Gesundheit," said Tony T.

"I, like, didn't want to say anything at the time?" said Louise, "But when you just said that about rubes and hayseeds and bumpkins? I'm like, 'That's how I felt last night!'"

"You think he was just putting us on," I suggested, and because the expression suddenly seemed as antique as my interest in flying saucers, I added, "having some fun at our expense—the rubes."

"The butts of the joke," said Lou, before turning the blender on and inserting a pause into the conversation.

"I believe him," Ray said, after Cutie's daiquiri had been blended. This brought on loud noises of disagreement from Cluck, Artie, and Tony T, but Ray stuck to his guns like a true professional. "I don't mean that I believe what he said—I'm not *that* nuts. I mean that I believe that he was telling us what he believes is the truth."

"You mean *he's* that nuts," said Miranda.

"Yeah," said Ray, unwilling now to take the idea any further. "It could be, maybe."

"Don't you think it's more likely that he just meant all of that figuratively?" asked Elaine.

"Yes, I do," said Alice. "That's exactly what I think."

"Of course," said Nancy. "I think that he *did* have a heart attack, he *did* collapse there at the entrance to the hospital, he *did* trip the electric eye as he fell, and the doors *did* open—but he didn't die."

"He had surgery," said Alice. "A bypass or angioplasty—"

Lou, Cluck, Artie, and Tony T all raised their hands as members of the me-too club.

"—and he lay there in bed in the hospital trying to remember how he got there, and what he remembered was the story he told us."

"So it *is* the story of his death, because it's about realizing that time is running out," said Elaine, "for all of us."

"We're all falling toward those doors, you mean," said Cutie.

"Yes," said Nancy. "We're all at death's door, on our way through it sooner or later."

"So, carpe diem, boys and girls," said Albertine.

"I'll drink to that," I said, and I did.

Thank You for Letting Me into Your Home

VERY EARLY in the morning, I was at my computer working on *Murder While You Wait.* I was working on a scene in which Rockwell Kingman killed the owner of a dry-cleaning establishment who had noticed blood on his clothing, and the point of the scene was supposed to be that in the course of committing this murder Kingman began losing his grip on himself, that the cool professionalism he had employed to separate himself from the truth about himself was dissolving, and he was beginning to recognize that he enjoyed killing. I wasn't yet sure how he was going to react to this bit of self-discovery, what he would think of himself when he finally got a good look at himself.

As I wrote, I insinuated myself into the mind of Rockwell Kingman, as I would have done with any other character. I visualized the scene as he would see it, entered the moment as Kingman, did what he would do, thought what he would think, and felt what he would feel, and that turned out to be an emotional rush so strong, so exhilarating, thrilling, and ecstatic that I shoved myself back from the keyboard and out of the character of Rockwell Kingman and sat there, breathing hard, sweating, shaking. Sitting back, keeping a safe distance between myself and Rockwell Kingman, I read what I had written, and I found it so repugnant—not only the words but the person who had written them, me, and the corner of my mind where a Rockwell Kingman could be born and raised—that I felt a shame as physical as nausea. I went to the window, opened it, and stood in the cold air. I was sweating. I was shaking.

When I had myself under control again, I went back to the computer and read what was on the screen. It was disgusting, but it wasn't badly written. It had the rough verve that the scene demanded. There really wouldn't be any sense in throwing it away. All I really had to do was find some framing irony for it, some way of indicating to the reader that although I could write this gory stuff pretty well I had no taste for it and was doing it only for the money.

I was sitting there wondering how to achieve that effect when there came a hesitant rap-tap-tapping at my workroom door. I got up and opened it. Manuel Pedrera was standing there. He was violating the sanctity of our private space, and my first impulse was to point out to him that Albertine had most certainly made it clear that guests were not to enter our quarters, or indeed to ascend to the third level at all, without an invitation. She told everyone, and I'm sure she had made no exception in his case. I would have told him that, and I would have asked him to leave immediately, if he hadn't had such a hangdog look. The poor guy had obviously come in need of my help. I couldn't turn him away. To tell the truth, I was flattered.

"Ray!" I said, betraying nothing, I think, of the *crise de l'âme* that I had just endured. "You're a little out of bounds here without an invitation, but come on in."

"I was hoping you could help me," he said.

"Sit down," I said. He took the chair I indicated, an oak armchair facing my desk, and I left the computer to sit across from him, but the effect wasn't quite right, so I got up and adjusted the venetian blinds. Ordinarily I keep the slats slanted upward in the morning, so that the light of the rising sun doesn't reflect from the computer monitor, but I tilted them the other way, so that strong shadows fell in stripes across the desk.

"That's better," I said. I resumed my seat, clasped my hands, and leaned on the desk. "How's the memoir coming?" I asked earnestly.

"It's not," he said. "I've still got nothing. I just can't seem to come up with anything at all."

"Really? Have you looked inside the outside? Have you sought the inner man? Have you knocked on your noggin and asked who's hiding in there?"

"I tried."

"Hmm. Let's try something else then, just to get some ideas going."

"Okay."

"Close your eyes."

"Right."

"Can you picture yourself in a dry-cleaning establishment?"

"Yeah."

"Are you behind the counter or in front of it?"

"In front."

"Okay, so you're a customer, not the cleaner."

"I guess so."

"So you won't be writing *Out, Out, Damn'd Spot: The Memoirs of a Dry Cleaner.*"

"Guess not."

"Do you have some garments with you to be cleaned?"

"I—um—yeah, I do. A couple of flannel shirts, and a pair of pants."

"Okay. Let me be the cleaner for a minute. 'You can have these by—oops, what's this? I see you've got some stains here.'"

"Stains? What stains?"

"'See? On this shirt, and on the pants leg here. What is that? It looks like blood.'"

"It can't be blood."

"'I've been in this business for more than twenty years, and it sure looks like blood to me.'"

"It's probably tomato juice."

"'Okay, okay. Mister, I don't want any trouble. We'll call it tomato juice. Better yet, I never saw any stains at all, okay?'"

"Good. Yeah. That's fine."

I leaned back in my chair and fixed Ray with the steely gaze of the professional memoirist. "Ray," I said, "why were you trying to hide those stains?"

"I wasn't."

"Why are you now trying to hide the fact that you were trying to hide those stains?"

"I'm not."

"Ray, I was there. I heard the man behind the counter—a man with more than twenty years in the business—identify those stains as blood."

"I—I don't know how they got there."

"Let me ask you something, Ray."

"Yeah?"

"Have you considered the possibility—I'm just tossing out ideas here—do you think it's possible that you are—or let's say that you were—or that you have been—a contract killer?"

"What?"

"A freelance assassin."

"Huh?"

"A hit man."

"Me?"

"Isn't it possible, or couldn't it *be* possible, that you have been trying to run away from your past, trying to forget it?"

"I don't think so."

"Ah! But how would you know, Ray, since you've forgotten, or made yourself forget, repressed the memory of everything you'd rather not remember, like those stains on your flannel shirt and your pants."

"That's a point."

"Work on that, Ray."

"Okay," he said. "Thanks."

PIANO MOVERS, sent by Steinway at Albertine's request, came and took her piano away. They left her a check for what it was worth to Steinway, which was about a quarter of what a Steinway representative had told her they would sell it for after they had refurbished it, or about sixty-five percent of what we had paid for it, representing an immeasurably minuscule fraction of the pleasure it had given Albertine to play it or had given me to hear her play it, but approximately equal to the cost of a couple of new washing machines and one month's mortgage payment. By late afternoon, Tony T had brought the new machines on the launch, he and Dexter Burke had removed the carcasses of the eight deceased machines, and the two jolly tinkers, with the assistance of Grumpy Cluck, had installed the new ones so that they were nearly level and hardly leaking. With the machines came Loretta Pearl, who registered as a guest, went to her room and unpacked, and descended the stairs as Director of Maintenance for Small's Hotel, equipped with a personal digital assistant—a computer in the form of a clipboard—and the firm conviction that if it was kept well oiled no machine need ever die.

"Friend of Lou's?" asked Albertine.

"Why, yes," said Loretta.

"Escaping the cares of business?"

"Giving it a try," she said. "After my husband died, I had to step in and run his advertising business myself. It has now been—well, let's just say a long time—and the responsibilities are exhausting. I haven't had a vacation in years. That is, I haven't *enjoyed* a vacation in years. I've tried to get away—"

"But the business keeps crying out to you."

"Yes. You've heard this before."

"We have a few friends of Lou's here."

"Well, he's quite persuasive about the therapeutic value of the place. Now where are your warranties?"

"That's a question I often ask myself," said Albertine.

MY READING of the thirty-fifth episode of *Dead Air,* "Thank You for Letting Me into Your Home," was preceded by the first dinner that Louise and Miranda had prepared entirely on their own, designing the menu to complement the simplest of the dishes on it: bay scallops quickly sautéed in olive oil, drizzled lightly with lemon juice, and sprinkled with pepper—one of my favorites.

A COUPLE OF WEEKS before my thirteenth birthday, I built a radio transmitter from a kit. When I brought my friends Raskol, Spike, Marvin, and Matthew down to my basement to see it, they were impressed. For one thing—I'll be frank about this—when they looked at the transmitter sitting there on my workbench, I think they found that they had to admire my ability as an assembler of electronics kits. I know I did. For another, I think they were awed by the power of the machine, by the very idea that through the agency of this device I might insinuate myself—or at least my voice—into the homes of my friends and neighbors. I know I was.

"You mean, with this you can broadcast to a regular radio?" Spike asked.

"Yes!" I said. "You can talk into this microphone, and anybody can tune you in."

Spike picked up the microphone, gingerly.

"Hello?" she said. "Anyone listening?"

"It's not on," I said. "But if it were on, people would hear you all over the neighborhood."

"Wow."

"Is that legal?" asked Matthew.

"Legal?" I asked right back.

"Isn't it an invasion of privacy, going into somebody's house without being asked?"

"I wouldn't actually be going into their houses—"

"Your voice would, and if they didn't want to listen to you, you'd be invading their privacy."

"I guess I would," I said, "but people decide that they're willing to have their privacy invaded when they buy a radio, right?"

"Sure they do," said Raskol. "They wouldn't buy a radio if it wasn't okay with them to have somebody's voice come out of it."

"It's like a deal you make when you buy a radio," said Marvin. "You agree to let the people on the radio into your house."

"Of course," I said. "Of course. That's why some of the announcers say 'Thank you for letting us into your home' at the end of the show. '*Letting us into your home,*' get it? If you're on the radio, people let you in."

"Sure," said Spike, giving Matthew a punch, "When you turn the radio on, it's like saying, 'Hi. How you doin'? Come in. Come on in.'"

Matthew frowned. "I don't know," he said. "Don't you need a license or something for this?"

A pall fell over the group. A license. If operating a radio broadcasting transmitter required a license, then we all were immediately convinced, without any need for discussion, that we could never do it. We couldn't get a license. We were kids.

"The booklet says you don't," I said, weakly.

"Really?" said Spike, brightening.

"Yeah, but—"

Their faces fell.

"—you're not supposed to broadcast too far. It says here, 'With regard to this type of device, regulations issued by the Federal Communications Commission (FCC) provide that, as long as you keep its working range below 250 feet at the low frequency end of the broadcast band, you do not need a license—'"

"But?" said Spike.

"What do you mean, 'But?'"

"You had that tone again."

"Tone?"

"It's like holding your breath. It comes right before 'but.'"

"'—but there are significant penalties for exceeding that range with an unlicensed transmitter,'" I read reluctantly.

"So," she said, "what's the range?"

"I don't know. I haven't tried it."

"You haven't tried it?"

"No."

"Why not?"

Why not. Perhaps you know, reader, the reason I hadn't tried it. The potential for failure was greater than the potential for success. The transmitter could either work or not work. If it worked, people might actually reach out toward their radios, grasp the tuning knob, and turn to my spot on the dial to see what I had to say, or they might ignore me. If they tuned me in, they might find that I had something to say, or they might find empty prattle and long intervals of dead air. Every success brought a new possibility of failure. I had thought this through.

"I don't know," I said.

"Come on, let's try it," said Raskol, who had apparently not given a moment's thought to the relative likelihood of success or failure, and in a moment I had the transmitter up and running, and I was standing at my workbench, speaking into the microphone, saying, "Testing, testing," and Marvin, Spike, Matthew, and Raskol were roaming the neighborhood, knocking on doors and asking my neighbors to let them into their homes to listen to me on the radio.

ALBERTINE sat at her vanity, looking through a photograph album. I looked over her shoulder. A depression was coming over us. I could feel it, not only in myself, but in her, too. She was trying to find some good shots of the island in the summer that she could send to a realtor who wanted to send them to a potential buyer, in Maine. It was a long shot, the realtor had admitted. She suspected that he was just an armchair shopper, intrigued by the fantasy of running a small hotel on an island in a place where there was summer. The photographs were depressing us because so many of them had been taken in the lounge, with Albertine at the piano and happy guests, flushed with booze, mangling the lyrics to their favorite songs, and because we looked so good in them. There we were, over a succession of summers that had had their ups and downs, but in every one of them we had been younger than we were at the moment, and, if the photographs were accurate, we had been happier and slimmer and healthier, and we had had nice tans, too.

"We look so happy," I said.

"Yes," she said.

"Everybody does. I guess it's partly because this kind of photograph is supposed to commemorate a happy occasion, and one feels good and looks good on those occasions. Or fakes it. But I wonder—I wonder—"

"Whether we could ever approximate those two people again."

"Yes," I said. "Why is it that we were able to be happy then and can't seem to be happy now?"

"We weren't flat broke then."

I leaned closer to one of the pictures. In it, Albertine was smiling, glowing. She was playing, and a group around the piano was singing. I couldn't recall the occasion for all this juice and joy. It was almost certainly someone else's occasion, a guest's, a birthday dinner at Small's followed by drinks in the lounge, but in our early days out here Albertine often used to claim that a stranger's occasion like that was, remarkably, coincidental with an occasion of our own, so the verve she was putting into her playing in the picture I was looking at might have been in celebration of the anniversary of the third night we spent in bed together, which I remembered perfectly well without the benefit of photography.

"I guess that was it," I said.

ON THE EDGE OF SLEEP, I remembered something about Mr. Himmelfarb that I had forgotten to use in "Photographic Proof." I turned toward Albertine and raised myself on one elbow so that I could see her face. She seemed to be asleep. I wouldn't be able to tell her until the morning, when I would have forgotten it again. If I tried to write it down I was sure to wake her. Even uncapping my pen usually woke her up. I lowered myself again and sighed.

"What is it?" she asked.

"I thought you were asleep," I said.

"On the edge."

"I remembered something about Mr. Himmelfarb—"

"Mmm."

"He used to mix up the pictures sometimes, on purpose. Every now and then he would slip a picture of a mysterious stranger into a package of snapshots—a beautful woman or a handsome man—the sort of thing that could cause a sensation in a suburban household."

"My heart races at the thought," she said.

The Relay System

She heard him. He said the most melancholy things, but she noticed that directly he had said them he always seemed more cheerful than usual. All this phrase-making was a game, she thought, for if she had said half what he said, she would have blown her brains out by now.

 Virginia Woolf, *To the Lighthouse*

I SAT AT MY COMPUTER, staring at the screen and writing nothing. I spent an hour that way, and then I turned the thing off and went to the kitchen for some coffee. The other early risers were in the lounge, but I avoided them. I took my coat from the closet under the stairs and let myself out the front door quietly. I walked to the dock with my mug of coffee, sat myself down, and tried to get started on a good stretch of uninterrupted brooding, but the coffee was delicious that morning—Miranda's work, I think—and the rising sun was gilding the windows of Babbington across the bay, so for a while I had some difficulty working myself into a blue mood, but by castigating myself for being a person so shallow that he could be cheered by good coffee and the morning sun I had just begun to make some headway toward self-loathing when Albertine plunked herself down beside me.

"Feeling suicidal?" she asked.

"Not yet, but I'm working on it."

"The coffee's good."

"You're right. It is. Between that and the golden light of the dawn, it's hard to work up a good funk—but—"

She had brought her hand up to her face. She seemed to be on the point of tears.

"What's the matter?" I asked.

She shook her head and waved me off for a moment, then blinked hard and said, "A news story Lou read to us on the porch—a twelve-year-old girl who killed herself—shot herself in the head—and her body was found by her little boyfriend—and I—" She looked away. "—I don't understand it. There is a cult of misery that—goes far beyond the blues—somehow kids fall prey to it—and I just don't understand it." She sighed, but what came from her wasn't simply a sigh. There was a catch at the end of it that would have been a sob if she hadn't kept a grip on herself. I put my arm around her. "It's a nasty world out there," I said.

"Yeah," she sighed, and then she asked, "What's your problem?"

"Compared to that? Nothing."

"Come on."

"Nothing, really."

"Out with the bad air," she said, in the singsong of a lifesaving instructor teaching an outmoded method of artificial respiration.

"Well, aside from the fact that I now feel tremendously guilty for feeling that I have any problems at all, my problem is that I seem to have lost the story of my life."

"You mean like losing the thread?"

"No, I mean like losing a contest. When I began writing it, I thought it was a success story. Well, maybe success isn't quite the right word, since it suggests striving and struggling, succeeding against the odds, and I thought of my personal history as a story of good fortune—or dumb luck. When you and I moved here and I started writing, it was a time when I felt very lucky, singularly fortunate. I had you. I had my little kingdom. I had money coming in from my Larry Peters stories. I had my own story to tell. I lacked for nothing."

I stopped, and I sat there, staring.

"And now?" she asked after a while.

"Now, I look across the bay at Babbington, at my past, and all my feelings about it have changed. It's not an escape for me anymore. Now it's the place where things began to go wrong, somehow, in some way that I haven't figured out. It's where I began to become the man I am, a dreamer, an escapist, and a loser, and my younger self—well, I've spent a lot of time with him, back there, while he has his little adventures, and I used to like him—I wished sometimes that I could make contact with him—but my attitude toward him has changed, and now I blame him for becoming me, the man who bought this fool's paradise, and—"

Suddenly I was exhausted. I just stopped talking.

"And?" she said.

"And I feel that it's all my fault, and that it has always been my fault, the fault of every one of me, every age and stage of me down the years, adding mistakes on mistakes—and now I've gotten us into the mess we're in and I can't find a way to fix it. I try. I have tried, and I do try. I try to think of ways to bring some money in. Every idea starts out full of promise, but then the more I think about it the less promising it becomes, and in a few minutes all its promise is gone, and in a minute more it has become another failure. I've even tried to—well, never mind."

"What?"

"Oh, I tried writing—" I shook my head and expelled a bitter laugh. "—the confessions of a hit man. The memoirs of a professional killer."

She leaned against me and kissed me, and then she said, "A world in which little girls shoot themselves does not need the memoirs of a professional killer."

"It could make some money," I said. "Maybe. But probably not, because I have a hard time keeping myself from undercutting the story and the character. I try to be evil but the irony keeps creeping in. The story's becoming a bloody farce, and the character is a despicable clown. I can't stand him. I—"

"Get rid of him," she said. "I don't want to meet him."

"Actually," I said, "it's kind of funny. His name is—"

She stuck her fingers in her ears and said, "I don't want to know his name, and I don't want to hear anything more about him."

"Okay," I said. We sat in silence for a while, and then I asked, "Got any other ideas?"

"I thought you'd never ask," she said. "The truth is I followed you down here to make a suggestion."

"Yeah?"

"I think that if you tried you could sell the hotel—"

"Me? So far the realtors haven't even been able to coax people who seem to me to be certifiably insane to make an offer on the place. How can I—"

"—to Lou."

"To Lou?"

"To Lou."

"Of course. Lou will buy the hotel. All will be well. It's such an obvious solution—why didn't we think of it before?"

"Because 'panic can keep a person from seeing things that are as plain as the nose on his face,'" she said.

FOR MY THIRTY-SIXTH READING from *Dead Air,* "The Relay System," I was in a very good mood, a little high on hope.

THE SIGNAL from the broadcasting set that I built from a kit about thirty-seven years ago, thus launching my brief career in the radio business, didn't reach very far. My mother could pick it up loud and strong in the kitchen, where the receiver was about fifteen feet from the transmitter in my bedroom. People in neighboring houses and in a few of the houses across the street could hear me well enough to understand most of what I was saying, and people in a ring of houses beyond that could detect my signal as a presence on the dial where there would otherwise have been a void, although this presence was a negative kind of presence, an absence of static rather than the presence of a program. In all, I reached a potential audience of about twenty households, which was going to make it hard to sell advertising.

My most likely prospect for advertising was Porky White, who ran the Kap'n Klam clam bar near the docks. He was an enthusiast and a dreamer. So was I. We had an unspoken agreement between us to be gentle with each other's schemes, so I felt sure that I could count on his support. However, most of the town of Babbington lay between my broadcasting station and his clam bar, so there wasn't a chance that my signal would reach him. To overcome that obstacle,

I put the transmitter in a box and took it to the clam bar, where I set it up in a booth, and by way of demonstration broadcast the word *testing* to a radio on the counter.

"That's great," he said, and in his voice I could hear the enthusiasm I'd hoped to hear. "When are you going on the air? I'll cater the grand opening—all the clam fritters you want. But I tell you what—every now and then, could you just kind of pause, interrupt whatever you're saying, and kind of smack your lips and say how delicious the clam fritters are that you're having at the grand opening, which came from Kap'n Klam? That would be a big help to us, because when people hear you saying that right over the radio, I bet they're going to get a pretty irresistible urge to have some clam fritters, and I mean immediately. I'll tune you in on the radio in the restaurant here, and—hey—I'll even be a sponsor. What are your advertising rates?"

I was strongly tempted to take the money and run, but Porky and I had been friends for a long time, and I felt that I owed him the truth, so I said, "I can't broadcast very far. The signal's kind of weak, and anyway the FCC won't let me go past 250 feet."

"So what?" he said, now completely besotted by enthusiasm. "You could come and set up here. We could put you in the kitchen, and tune you in on the radio in the dining room."

"But that's not broadcasting," I said. "I might as well just sit here and talk to the people directly."

"I wouldn't say that," said Porky. "I think there's a fundamental difference between listening to someone directly and listening to someone's voice transmitted to a radio, even if it's only over a distance of 250 feet, but I see what you mean. It wouldn't be much fun. It wouldn't be like really being on the radio."

"No."

"There's got to be a way. Tell me about this transmitter. "

"Well, let's see. I made it from a kit—"

"Uh-oh, wait a minute. Not the whole story. I know you want to tell me the *whole* story, but now's not the time."

"Okay."

"Don't take offense, it's just that I know you would tell me the complete history of this transmitter, and how radio works, and what your favorite radio programs are—"

"Okay," I said. "I see what you mean."

"Sorry, but—"

"That's all right. Let's see. It's got a dial that lets you pick the frequency you're going to broadcast on."

"Uh-huh."

"It's got a microphone, so that what you say gets broadcast."

"There's your answer," said Porky.

"Really?" I said. "Where?"

"You can broadcast anything the microphone hears, right?"

"Yes."

"So if I had a radio a block away from you, and next to it I had a transmitter with the microphone on—"

"You could send the signal to the next block!"

"Where somebody else—"

"—with a radio and a transmitter—"

"—could send it to the next block—"

"That *is* a great idea," I said, and I meant it, since practicality was never a requirement in the house of hopes and dreams.

BALDY THE DUMMY'S closing story that night was the one that Albertine had read, about the twelve-year-old girl who killed herself with a single gunshot to the head. When I recognized the story, I pulled my earphone from my ear and held it between Albertine and me so that we both could listen.

"Her body was found by her little boyfriend," Baldy was saying. "Most of the right side of her face was gone. Gone. Can you picture that, Bob?"

"Yeah."

"There is a cult of misery out there, isn't there, Bob?"

"Yeah."

"That's what you were saying," I whispered to Al. "A cult of misery."

"Shh."

"That's what it is," said Baldy, "a cult of misery, and somehow kids fall prey to it—but not my boys and girls, not my boys and girls—I don't think she could have been one of our listeners, do you, Bob?"

"Yeah."

"You do? You think so?"

"Yeah."

"You're not suggesting that it's my fault, are you, Bob?"

"Yeah."

"It can't be, Bob. It *can't* be my fault. *You* don't think it's my fault, do you, boys and girls?" There was a silence, and then a weary, shaken Baldy stammered, "You—you do? I—I don't understand you, boys and girls. I try to tell you that your little lives could be much, much worse than they are. I try to cheer you up. I don't *want* you to be miserable, boys and girls. Don't let it happen to you. Please don't let it happen to you. Stay in the cave, and be happy. *Try* to be happy. *Please* be happy. Baldy's counting on you. I always meant to cheer you up. Honest. When Baldy says 'Stay in the cave' and 'It's a nasty world out there,' he doesn't mean it's so nasty that," but his time was up, and his theme music drowned him out.

Act Now! Offer Limited!

If the secret history of books could be written, and the author's private thoughts and meanings noted down alongside of his story, how many insipid volumes would become interesting, and dull tales excite the reader!
William Makepeace Thackeray, *Pendennis*

THIS IS THE STORY of the death of Rockwell Kingman. Like every success story, it begins with a need. In this case, the need was money. That need had driven me into the dark recesses of my mind, where I turned down a littered alley, stepped through an unmarked door, and walked up a flight of broken stairs to the dingy office of Murder While You Wait. I was ashamed of that excursion now. Kingman had become an embarrassment—more than an embarrassment. The mere fact of his existence as a figment of my imagination was a shameful offense against everything I stood for—or, at least, an offense against everything that I wanted to believe I stood for—or, at the very least, an offense against everything that I wanted to stand for and wanted everyone else to believe I stood for, foremost among them my darling Albertine, who had been so repulsed by the idea of the existence of a Rockwell Kingman in my mind that she had banished him without even meeting him. What a relief. I was grateful to her, because I wanted to get rid of the bastard, too. I didn't care where he went or what he did. I just didn't want him around me anymore. I didn't want anyone to know that he had come from me, that he was my idea, my issue, my spawn. I suppose that I could have pushed him back into whatever corner of my mind he had sprung from, and I suppose that if I had been strong and vigilant enough I could have kept him there, but he would still be there, blowing something up every now and then to remind me that he was there, waiting, ready, pacing his dingy office, chain-smoking, with a sign pinned to his back that said RENT ME. No, that wouldn't do. He would have to go. He really would have to go, but—

But?

But he still represented a chance to make some money, and even if I could manage to sell the hotel to Lou we were going to need money. When our debts had been paid, there wouldn't be much remaining from the proceeds of the sale, and we would have to have an income in Manhattan. There it was, the same damned need that had led me to Rockwell Kingman: money. Suddenly, inspiration struck. Inspiration is one of the black boxes of the human mind, the precise workings of which are still unknown, but I suspect that the process goes something like this: two ideas grow individually to such a size that each of them begins to shudder with the great energy in it, and if they move near enough to each other, the energy arcs between them in a jolt of electromagnetic radiation sufficient to light the I've-got-it lamp in the conscious mind of the person to whom all of this is happening, and to make him shout "Eureka!" or something similar in his own tongue.

"What a great scam," I muttered. I had found a way. I could make money and still travel the high road. Well, not quite. I could make money and still appear to be traveling the high road. Close enough.

I went to the kitchen for some coffee, hoping that I would find Ray waiting for me. He was.

"I think I've got something," he said.

"Really?"

"Maybe."

"In that case, pour yourself some coffee, and let's get to work."

We took our coffee upstairs to my workroom. I sat at my computer, and, putting myself at some personal risk, said, "Shoot," and typed while Ray read from the piece of paper in his hand: "I took a couple of shirts and a pair of pants to the dry cleaners to get them cleaned, and the dry cleaner said, 'Hey, these are bloodstains here.' I couldn't believe it. He said he would try to get them out, but I killed him anyway."

When he finished, I said, "Powerful stuff, Ray. Let me read it back to you." I read what I had on the screen: "'There is grandeur in the smallest lives; I'm convinced of that. There is something to be learned from even the smallest and most banal occurrences of everyday life; I'm convinced of that, too. Consider the encounter that led to the writing of this book. I had taken a couple of shirts'—and so forth, and so on, just as you said, up to—'He said he would try to get the stains out, and I said thanks and left. On the way home, I became troubled by the thought that I had left him with a mistaken idea of me, because the bloodstains that he supposed he had seen were really just some spots of tomato juice that I'd spilled on myself. After considering all the angles and implications'—actually, maybe we'll put in a few paragraphs about the angles and implications next time through—'I decided to let him persist in his error. It allowed him to believe in his professional competence, and, measured against the dubious standards of our time, it made me more glamorous and more graceful—or at least less clumsy—than I actually was.'"

Ray sat for a moment, mentally comparing what I had read with what he had written. Then he said, "You left out the part where I kill the guy."

I chuckled indulgently and said, "There are enough killers in the world, Ray."

"But won't I be remembering—?"

"Oh, yes. You'll explore all those memories, Ray—in your rough drafts. Everything. All those hideous urges and heinous acts that have made your past so colorful."

"Swell."

"But then we will excise them in the revision process, because, to tell you the truth, Ray, they do you no credit."

"Yeah," he said, shamefaced, letting his head droop.

"Don't worry," I said, with the reassuring steadiness of a seasoned captain of a leaking launch. "When I get through with your memoirs, we'll have the killer in you hidden behind a seamless facade of conventional behavior. No one will ever know the evil that lurks within the heart of Manuel Pedrera."

"Whoa, thanks, man," he said with a sigh.

"Don't thank me, Ray," I said. "Pay me."

I extended a hand toward my laser printer, from which a flyer for my new business, Memoirs While You Wait, would have emerged on cue if the delinquent accounts department at Babbington Light and Power had not at that precise moment suspended our electrical service.

WE DINED BY CANDLELIGHT that evening, and by candlelight I read episode thirty-seven of *Dead Air,* "Act Now! Offer Limited!"

MY BROADCASTING NETWORK was the jewel of the set of enterprises that I ran before I became a teenager. Like many another business success story, mine began with a flash of insight and an invention born of necessity. With the radio transmitter that I had built from a kit, I had gone on the air as WPLR, but the transmitter's range was too limited for a boy with my ambitions. Thus the necessity: a longer reach. Porky White had come up with the invention: the idea of linking transmitters like a string of pearls to extend the range of WPLR.

"That could work," I said to Porky. "That could actually work."

A little time spent with a map of Babbington and a compass showed me that if it was going to work, if I was going to make a necklace of transmission that would reach from my bedroom to Kap'n Klam, I would need 106 transmitters. This was daunting, and a lad with less gumption or more sense might have abandoned the effort then and there. Fortunately, however, my mother had just signed on as a Beauty Gal for Beauty Gal Cosmetics, and her experience showed me that assembling a string of 106 transmitters was not only possible but a cinch, if one went about it in the right way. Part of my mother's job as a Beauty Gal was selling cosmetics door-to-door, but another part, the more lucrative part, was selling the idea of selling cosmetics door-to-door. Every time she recruited another Beauty Gal she got a bonus, and from then on a portion of the income of each of "her" Beauty Gals came to her. It didn't take a genius to see that she should forget about selling the cosmetics and sell the occupation instead, since that was the road to the big money, so I set out on a similar path to riches in the radio game.

I knew that I could never build 106 transmitters on my own

(well, by "never" I mean "not in less than fifty-three weeks") so I got out my Little Giant Printing Outfit and printed some flyers based on an ad in *Impractical Craftsman Magazine* that offered a happy life raising giant frogs:

The Future Is in Radio!
Learn Radio Broadcasting in Your Spare Time!
Make Big Money as a Network Affiliate of WPLR!
Act Now! Offer Limited to 106 Applicants!

I recruited 106 of my schoolmates in a couple of weeks, ordered their kits for them at a premium, negotiated a volume discount from the supply house where I bought the kits, charged the affiliates for showing them how to assemble transmitters from the kits, and—when they had finished their work—gave them certificates authorizing them to solicit advertising, with a portion of the revenue to come to the parent station—that is, to me. (Actually, "gave" is not correct; I charged them a licensing fee.) Circle by circle, my affiliates extended my range.

If my success seems to have come too easily, let me assure you that I am sparing you tedious accounts of 106 struggles, 106 setbacks, 106 foolish mistakes, and 106 puzzling malfunctions. I'll let the ordeal of feedback stand for all of them. The instructions in the assembly manual had the young broadcaster find a "blank spot" on the dial, a frequency where no other station was broadcasting. I had found a good, clear spot that I was using, so I told my affiliates to use the same frequency. The result, when all 106 sets were turned on, was a hideous wail rising from radios all over Babbington. It brought my father running upstairs to see what I was up to.

"What the hell is that?" he inquired.

"Feedback," I said with enthusiasm. "I've read about it, but this is the first time I ever heard it! You see, the microphone is picking up what's coming in over this radio and the transmitter is broadcasting it, but what's coming in over this radio is what the transmitter's broadcasting, so it broadcasts it again, and it goes around and around, and that's feedback! Amazing, huh?"

"Shut it off!" he said, and, reluctantly, I did.

Although quite a few of the affiliates liked the effect enough to want to continue it, I knew that it was likely to cost us listeners. After some blind mental fumbling, serendipity brought me the solution: each affiliate station had to find its own "blank spot" on the dial; that is, no station could broadcast at the same frequency as another. This rule, and the short range of each station, eliminated the feedback, but it meant that WPLR was all over the place. Not only was the station physically located in 107 houses, counting my own, but it was at 107 different spots on the dial, depending on where you, the listener, were located. We were everywhere, but if you didn't happen to tune us in on the right frequency for the little corner of Babbington where you happened to be, we were, for you, at that place and time, nowhere. This circumstance made it difficult to establish the kind of loyal listenership that might have made me a powerhouse in the broadcasting business.

I HAD HOPED to begin putting my salesmanship to work on Lou that night, but he stood behind the bar in unwonted silence, looking for all the world like a grumpy guy. My instincts told me that the direct approach wasn't going to work; I was going to have to be subtle.

"The lounge looks really cozy by candlelight, doesn't it?" I began.

"Yeah," he said.

"Maybe we should just forget about electricity and forget about the boiler, and revert to candles and cozy fires in the fireplaces," I said.

"Not very practical," he said.

"Cozy, though."

"Mm."

"Say, Lou, pardon my asking, but is something bothering you?"

He looked at me, considering whether to answer or not. Finally, he leaned an elbow on the bar and said, "All my life I've tried to cheer people up—most of my life, anyway—for years—I've tried to cheer people up, but—"

He stopped and stood there for a long while staring into the candlelit room.

"But?" I asked after a decent interval.

"Never mind," he said, in a manner that convinced me that my first impression of him had been correct: he was a grumpy guy.

A Technical Question

You slip between the sheets, you turn out the light, you close your
eyes. Now is the time when dream-women, too quickly undressed,
crowd in around you.
    Georges Perec, *A Man Asleep*

WE WERE STILL POWERLESS by mid-morning, when Ms. Fletcher-
Hackford's seventh-grade English class from the Babbington Central Upper Middle School arrived. Their visit had been planned some time ago,
and I had forgotten all about it, which meant, of course, that I had forgotten to prepare anything for it. The eager kids constructed a colorful display of fiber-filled coats in a heap at the back of the entrance hall and then
created a colorful display of limber body parts on the furniture, rugs,
floors, and along the bar in the lounge. They flung themselves about in
such a way that the pieces of them seemed not necessarily still to be attached to the kids who had brought them. Louise and Miranda arrived
bearing platters of tiny sandwiches and pitchers of colorful juices, and under the influence of this stimulus the body parts reassembled themselves,
snapping back into position with remarkable rapidity, as if they were attached by elastic bands, and the kids became whole kids again, quick, ag-
ile, hungry kids, who emptied the platters and pitchers before I could say,
"Welcome to Small's Hotel." Then, satisfied for the moment, they resumed their places, flung their arms and legs every which way as they had
before, and turned their attention to Ms. Fletcher-Hackford, who introduced me by reminding her charges how fascinating it was going to be to

get the straight poop on memoir writing from "a living author," and then I stepped forward, the author, live and unprepared.

"While I was thinking about what I might say to you today," I lied, "I came to the conclusion that what matters most is not what I think I might want to teach you, but what you think you would like to learn from me, so what I've decided to do is read to you an episode from the installment of my memoirs that I'm working on now, just to give you an idea of what I'm up to, and then go right into the question-and-answer period. Okay?"

The responses to my "Okay?"—which I had intended as a merely rhetorical question, since I was going to go right ahead and do what I wanted to do whether they thought it was okay or not—were highly individual, ranging from a solemn murmur of endorsement to a ripping imitation of a fart, which seemed to me a comforting indication that, however much the times might have changed, humor, at least at the seventh-grade level, remained an essentially immutable cultural constant.

A girl sitting on a sofa directly in front of me answered only with a smile, but a knowing smile, a smile that made me decide that she had seen through me. It said something along the lines of "Why, you old fraud. You haven't prepared any sort of lecture or seminar at all, have you? You're just going to wing it and hope for the best." I winked at her, so that if she actually *had* intended her smile to say something along those lines she might join me as a co-conspirator in my fraud, and she winked back. She was tall and slender, with dark hair and budding breasts, and I'm sure she must have been Ms. Fletcher-Hackford's star pupil. She was a child, of course, probably twelve, but she was a desirable child, and I was elated by her wink, as buoyed and hopeful as I would have been if the wink had come from an eligible and available woman.

The inmates slipped quietly into the back of the room, and I began reading episode thirty-eight of *Dead Air,* "A Technical Question." As I read, I played to the entire house, as a good reader should, but whenever I came to one of the bits that I thought most effective—not the punch lines, but the throwaway phrases that make the punch lines work and carry the import of the piece, the subtle bits—I turned my eyes to that pretty pupil sitting on the sofa and for a moment slipped out of character, by which I mean that I slipped out of the character of the benign old man reading his reminiscences and into the closest approximation I could manage without practice of the dream lover of a pubescent virgin, the experienced man, a writer (every girl's dream), who could initiate her into the delights of love and help her write her memoirs—even at the same time, if you count providing those all-important initial sexual experiences as part of the writing process—everything a young girl could want in one package, a little worn around the edges but, after all, still living.

WHEN I WAS A BOY, I was for a while the head of a broadcasting network that stretched from one end of my home town to the other. It consisted of 107 small radio transmitters built from kits. Mine was the parent station, WPLR; the other 106 were repeater stations that extended my transmitter's range like a string of pearls. We created the network to circumvent a Federal Communications Commission rule that restricted the range of an unlicensed AM transmitter to 250 feet, and it worked, but in the back of my mind there lurked the suspicion that what I and my 106 cohorts were doing was illegal. Every time we went on the air I grew a little more paranoid.

I guess it began to show, because my friend Spike asked me, "What the heck is the matter with you, Peter? You've started exhibiting signs of worry—wringing your hands, biting your nails, pulling your hair."

"I guess I am worried," I admitted. "With all those transmitters out there, I keep thinking that somebody's going to hear us."

"That," said my friend Matthew, "is the idea."

"You know what I mean," I said. "Not just somebody, but—somebody from the FCC."

"But we're not breaking the law," said my friend Raskol. "None of our transmitters broadcasts more than 250 feet."

"Yeah," I said, "technically, that's true, but when I imagine myself working for the FCC—"

"Oh, brother," said my friend Marvin. "Here we go."

"There I am," I continued, "working for the FCC, and we've got a fleet of trucks with antennas on them. We cruise around trying to pick up signals from illegal transmitters."

"Trucks with antennas?" said Raskol.

"I've seen them in movies—one movie anyway. Some fascist goons were after a group of underground satirists—"

"What the hell are you talking about?" asked Spike.

"These people were trying to undermine an oppressive and gloomy government by making fun of it, so they had to go underground—keep out of sight."

"Oh."

"Anyway, the fascist goons had a truck and they drove around the city, with a goon in the back of the truck, with earphones on, listening to a radio, and on the roof of the truck was a circular antenna with a handle that the goon could turn to figure out what direction the signal was coming from. The goon was listening for the signal from the satirists' transmitter, and he would call out, 'Kapitan! Id's gedding veaker!' or 'Id's gedding stronker!' and the driver would go screeching off in a new direction, and when they found the hiding place they broke in and blew everything up. So, when I imagine myself working for the FCC, I picture myself in a truck with one of those antennas, driving around everywhere, listening through earphones, searching for illegal transmitters. First I discover a transmitter with a range of 249 feet, so I say to the other FCC guys in the truck, 'It's okay, boys. Leave it alone. Why don't we go get some coffee?' Then after we have our coffee we go back to work and this time I find a transmitter with a range of 251 feet, so I say, 'Okay, boys, we're goin' in and shut it down!' and we do. Then we take our lunch break, and after that we go out on the road again, and this time I find a transmitter with a range of 249 feet, which is okay—"

"And you say, 'It's okay, boys. Leave it alone,'" said Marvin.

"Right. But then I find another one with a range of 249 feet that's broadcasting the same thing, which makes me say, 'Hmm,' and then I find another one like that, broadcasting the same thing, which makes my mouth twist into one of those grins that Spike grins when she's asking somebody if he wants a fat lip, and then when I find *another* transmitter broadcasting the same thing at a range of 249 feet, I say to my fellow FCC workers, 'Hey, boys, we've got a kind of a technical question here,' and we go get some coffee and slices of pie and talk it over and come to a decision."

"What decision?" asked Spike.

"We decide that some kid is trying to use a technicality to get around the law, so we call for reinforcements, and in a couple of minutes we've traced the signals back to the original transmitter. I call out, 'That's it, boys! That's the ringleader. Let's get him!' and in seconds a squad of enforcers wheels up to my house, pounds up the front steps to the stoop, breaks through the front door with a fire ax, stomps up the stairs to my room, blasts my transmitter with machine-gun fire, and drags me away to the hoosegow."

Spike couldn't help herself. She pulled the curtain aside an inch or so and looked out the window to see if there were any FCC trucks cruising around. "We've got to go underground," she said.

I HAD A WONDERFUL TIME reading to this group. They were shy about responding at first, but when I began hamming it up a little more than usual they began to realize that they could laugh, that they weren't required to suffer through this live literary experience with the fake reverence that they were expected to bring to the dreary "selections" in their literature anthologies, pressed and preserved there like dead moths. When I finished, they applauded, they whistled, they stamped their feet. I was tempted to read another episode, but before I could make the mistake of giving in to that temptation, Ms. Fletcher-Hackford announced that I would take their questions.

Most of what they asked was what I would have expected, but there were some questions that I had never been asked by an adult audience. One of those was, "Where are those friends of yours now?"

"Well," I said, "first, you have to understand that the people in my memoirs are not always exactly as they were in my life. Sometimes I combine people, because I couldn't ever write about everyone I knew, and because sometimes they just seem to drift together over time, at least within my memory, and sometimes I invent people, if there seems to be a blank spot in my life that should have had someone in it. With that in mind, let's see where they are now. The boy I called Marvin died in Vietnam. The boy I called Raskol started out as my imaginary friend, but I've added to him characteristics of many of my friends over the years, so he has become a kind of scrapbook, a repository of friendship. If he were based on a single person, he would be running a boat yard in Babbington now, *still* running it as he has for—hmm—quite a few years. The boy I called Matthew was here just a few days ago, with a woman he's been in love with for a long time, a wonderful woman who has been combatting social injustice, legally, long enough to have become exhausted at last by the massive indifference of human beings to the sufferings of their fellow creatures. She has thrown in the towel and decided to live the rest of her years for herself. Matthew was ill for a while. I guess he had a heart attack, and is now very aware of his mortality, so he's concentrating on the time left to him, and what he can make of it. That leaves Spike, or the girl I called Spike. She had quite a life." At his point, I might have said, "She dropped out of college, got pretty heavily into drugs for a while, worked for a telephone sex service, then started her own, made a success of it, raised two daughters entirely on her own, went back to college, became a teacher, and is standing at the back of the room right now," but I did not. All I said was, "She disappeared from my life for quite a while, but we made contact again, and now I see her from time to time."

"How old were you in that story?"

The question surprised me. "Didn't I say?" I asked. I glanced at the first paragraph. "Funny," I said. "I usually mention my age in these episodes, but I left it out of this one. I was twelve, almost thirteen."

Exclamations greeted that news. I wasn't sure whether the kids found it hard to believe that I had once been twelve or were just pleased to have the little Peter of my memoirs be the same age as they were.

"Do you ever wish that you were twelve again?" asked the enchanting schoolgirl on the sofa.

Before I quite realized what I was doing, I smiled at her meaningfully and said, "I'm wishing that right now."

Laughter exploded from the back of the room. All the adults were amused by me and embarrassed for me, including me.

"It was a great time of life," I said, trying to camouflage what I had actually meant. The girl on the sofa smiled up at me, a smile with nothing much in it, and I was struck with the full realization of what I had been doing—flirting with a twelve-year-old girl, trying to seduce a child—and by the great gulf that lay between me and this girl—the whole story of my life between nearly-thirteen and nearly-fifty—a gulf that the man of good will could not bridge, must not bridge, must not even entertain the thought of bridging. "It is a great time of life, boys and girls," I said in the manner of Baldy the Dummy, with a dummy's creepy grin. "Enjoy it."

I HAD TO ENDURE a great deal of kidding for the rest of the day and evening, and when Albertine and I got into bed that night I said, sheepishly, "Sorry."

She wiggled over my way and snuggled me and said, "Peter—don't you think I have any fantasies?"

"I—well—I—"

"I, too, lead a rich inner life," she whispered.

"Of course," I said. "Sure. I never doubted it."

"It is something for which no apologies are necessary."

CAN YOU CONTROL your dreams, reader? I can't. I think that some people have that talent, but I don't. Long ago, I used to try, now and then, to will myself to dream about a certain something that would make the night pleasant, but it never worked, so I gave it up. Now I let my dreams drift unbidden from whatever corner of my mind happens to have come to a boil. Sometimes I get lucky.

Before I fell asleep, I made sure that Spike's star pupil was comfortably settled at that old hotel of the mind where the man of good will keeps his lusts to himself, and later, when I was asleep, I visited her there. I can't say what dream she was having, or whether she had the talent to will her dreams, but I hope that if she did dream she had the same dream that I, in the person of my twelve-year-old self, had. I will not give you the details of what he licked and flicked and tickled, the slurps and slips and squirts, the giggles and wiggles, and what went where. Suffice it to say that everything slipped into place and the three of us—she, my younger self, and I—enjoyed it all, though I was not quite there, was everywhere, but, as is proper for a man of good will in such cases, nowhere. Do you see what I mean when I say that the unimagined life is not worth living? Had I done anything wrong, reader? Well, since none of us was any the worse for any of it, and since thinking of a crime is not a crime, that is at most a technical question.

The Hole and the Hill

Are you in earnest? Begin this very minute!
Boldness has genius, power, and magic in it.
    Johann Wolfgang von Goethe
    Faust (translated by John Anster)

AN EARNEST YOUNG COUPLE, Theodore ("Don't call me Ted") and Carolina ("With an *a*"), friends of friends of Lou's, arrived in the morning with a couple of small gasoline generators to provide electricity for the island temporarily, and as soon as they had those up and running they began surveying the island to produce an "energy-independence proposal." By cocktail time they had it written and printed and distributed to all interested parties, which operation tied up my printer and kept me from distributing the flyers for Memoirs While You Wait. Theodore and Carolina proposed that we make a huge investment in a network, a "power grid," that would combine wind, solar, and tidal generators to provide us something for almost nothing, which sounded to me like the sort of deal that my grandfather taught me was usually too good to be true. Since they were friends of friends of Lou's, I didn't want to tell them that it sounded too good to be true—particularly since their estimates for the maintenance costs of the system seemed to have completely overlooked the fact that most things break, and that here on Small's Island most things break twice as often—or to tell them that I couldn't begin to imagine how we could ever come up with the huge initial investment, so I said that I would take it under advisement. They gave Lou a copy of the plans, too, and although he thanked them for their work he didn't have much else to say. I couldn't help noticing that Lou had started exhibiting signs of worry—wringing his hands, biting his nails, pulling his hair—and frankly I was worried about him, not only as a potential purchaser of my albatross, but as a fellow creature.

The rest of my fellow creatures on the island got right back to work as soon as we had power again. Albertine called a couple of lawyers who specialized in tax grievances, because the town had raised our taxes again while we weren't looking, and she began looking for a new insurer, because our insurance costs had gone up as the value of the hotel had gone down, a correlation that struck Albertine as ass-backwards. Suki, Louise, and Miranda were launching Small's Affairs, a catering and party-planning service that looked very good on paper, thanks to the promotional efforts that Nancy and Elaine had made. I was beginning to think that I might have been wrong about Elaine; maybe she actually was in public relations. She certainly seemed to have connections. She managed to get a feature on Small's Affairs on "Gilligan's Wake Up with People Magazine," a morning television show. The footage showed the trio arriving at a bayside party in a 1938 Chris-Craft runabout, each of them holding a platter of hors d'oeuvres. Tony T played the part of chauffeur in the piece and clearly enjoyed doing it. In his spare time, he had actually managed to find and repair the gas leak in the launch. He would never manage to stop the hull from leaking, but he'd taken a shine to the old tub, and he was doing a fair business with short excursions on the bay, which he sandwiched in between his hourly runs to the island in the (sigh) triple-cockpit barrel-back mahogany runabout. He had begun to talk about a water-taxi business, linking the towns along the bay, using a dozen or so vintage runabouts that would require a great deal of maintenance and keep him, happily, very busy. Cutie was working out the manufacturing arrangements for reproductions of Albertine's miniature of Small's Hotel, with battery-powered annoyances and miniature inmates to be sold separately. Alice had four rooms remodeled and had begun working on a cottage. Clark was driving her a little nuts by replacing the shingles on the roof of the cottage while she worked inside, despite my having pointed out to him that the cottage roof didn't leak very much at all. Loretta made sure that all our supplies arrived just in time, and she had begun looking into the possibility of a group health-care plan. Artie was on the phone more than ever. He always gave the impression that something big was in the works, but that he wasn't at liberty to talk about it yet. You would have thought that the cellular telephone had been invented for him, personally, at his request. Manuel Pedrera spent most of each day sitting in his room, writing *The Confessions of Manuel Pedrera,* his life story.

FOR MY READING of "The Hole and the Hill," episode thirty-nine of *Dead Air,* I had quite a sizable audience. The Friday turnout for dinner and drinks was very good, and we acquired seven new resident guests in the afternoon: my old friend Mark Dorset; both of his ex-wives, Margot and Martha Glynn; their daughters, Martha and Margot, each daughter named for her aunt; and the daughters' husbands, our sons, Edward and Daniel.

WITH MY FRIENDS Raskol, Marvin, Spike, and Matthew, I operated a radio network quite a few years ago, when we were all about thirteen. Our worries about the Regulations Enforcement Squad of the Federal Communications Commission drove us underground. When we put our heads together and thought about the best location for an underground radio station, we reached a consensus quite quickly: a cave. Unfortunately, we lived on the south shore of Long Island, which is essentially a large sandbar. There were no caves.

"Why do we have to live in a crummy place where there aren't any caves?" asked Spike.

"Couldn't we make a cave?" I asked, and as soon as I heard myself saying it, I wished I hadn't. I realized that it sounded like the sort of thing I would say, the sort of thing I would want to do, and I regretted having spoken my mind so quickly, without subtlety, without any of the cunning gambits of persuasion that might have rallied my friends to the cause of cave-building.

"Making a cave," said Matthew, "typically requires several thousand years, during which the geological conditions have to be just right. You need limestone and dripping water—"

Spike gave him a poke.

"Ohhh," said Matthew. "Now I see what you mean, Peter. You mean couldn't we dig a shallow hole in the ground that we can just about crawl into and just about all fit into at once, where we can get sand in our hair, and sand in our shoes, and sand in our sandwiches, and—"

"Great idea," said Raskol.

"You said it," said Marvin.

"I'm in," said Spike.

"Okay, okay, me, too," said Matthew.

So, we began, boldly, and without a plan. First, we dug a hole. I cannot recall the digging of the hole clearly, because whenever I try, my memory of my father's digging a new cesspool overlaps my memory of the digging of the cave, like the overlapping signals of two radio stations that are close together on the dial.

My father hadn't had much trouble rallying his friends to the cause of cesspool-digging. No cunning gambits were required, because our old cesspool had been overflowing for several days, creating a broad and malodorous puddle, the elimination of which must have offered a powerful incentive. They began digging on a Saturday morning, dug a hole that seemed enormous to me, lined it with cement blocks, capped it, and still had time for one last beer before the sun set.

From those men, I learned that a hole-digger has a highly developed sense of economy of labor. Almost from the start of their work, the men asked my father, often, with increasing frequency as the day wore on, "Is it deep enough yet?"

Marvin, Spike, Matthew, and Raskol and I kept asking one another the same question.

Leaning on his shovel, Raskol asked, "Is it deep enough yet?"

"Your head is still sticking up above the ground," said Marvin. "We wouldn't be able to stand up in there."

"So, do we have to stand up in the thing?"

"That's a good question," said Spike. "Maybe we don't have to stand up."

"Sure we do," said Marvin.

"We could sit down."

"We wouldn't all fit if we sat down," said Marvin. "It's not wide enough."

"We could kneel," said Spike.

"Kneel? Are you kidding? I'm not kneeling," said Marvin.

"We've got to be able to stand up. Anything else is humiliating, degrading. We'll be huddled in a cave, bent and dirty. No, thank you. I won't be bowed. I kneel to no one. I want to stand tall. A man's cave is his castle."

"Do you think the cavemen stood up in their caves?" asked Spike. "I don't. Whenever you see pictures of them, they're all kind of bent over."

"Yeah, their knuckles drag on the ground," said Raskol.

"They probably got that way because they couldn't stand up in the caves," said Marvin.

"I think that it will be a sorry state of affairs if after thousands of years of evolution we can't stand up to our full height in a cave of our own making," said Matthew.

"'A cave of our own making,'" said Marvin. "That's an interesting way to put it. I mean, we call this a cave, but when you get right down to it, it's a hole—let's face it—and can we say that we've *made* a hole? Or should we say that, in making a *hill*"—he indicated the pile of dirt beside him—"we left a hole behind?"

"I see what you mean," I said. "A hole is the *absence* of something, and a hill is the *presence* of something, so—"

"Yeah," said Spike, "but in this case the hole is the motive for the work. We're *digging a hole,* not *building a hill.*"

"True," I said, "but the hill *looks* more like the motive. It *shows.* To most people, the hill is a hill but the hole is just—what's left behind after making the hill—the not-hill—the anti-hill," and to my surprise I found that when I said "most people," I meant "me."

I HELD MY HANDS UP to forestall the applause that would probably otherwise have drowned me out and said, "You may be asking yourself, 'What on earth made those kids think that they could dig a cave?' To answer that question, we have with us tonight the author of *You're Not Playing Hard Enough: How Childhood Became an Occupation,* a study of work and play as they have been defined and differentiated in our society, and our collective attitudes toward both: my friend, one of my oldest friends, practically decrepit, the unaffiliated researcher and amateur psychosociologist Mark Dorset."

Mark, who is nearly always ready to speak on nearly any subject, rose to the occasion and came to the front of the room.

"First, let me say that I didn't meet Peter until we were in high school, so I don't know anything about this cave-digging escapade at first hand. However, Peter and I are of an age, and based on my own experience I think I can safely say that most of the kids I hung around with when I was a boy, and by extension most of the kids in my generation, grew up to become adults who told their offspring—and any other sprout who came within range—that they were very hardworking when they were young. I know I did."

Whoops and catcalls came from Edward and Martha and Daniel and Margot and Louise and Miranda.

"In my experience, that wasn't really true. If you had been around to observe us, you would have concluded that we were not a particularly hardworking bunch at all. I contend that it is the nature of kids' work that has changed, and that today's young people actually work much harder at the work society has assigned them.

"Now, I would argue, *consuming* has become the proper work of most kids. Entire industries depend on them. If you are willing to accept that as true, then I think you will have to agree that today's young folks work hard at what they are expected to do. I never see them shunning this work. There are no slackers or shirkers among the kiddie consumers.

"Now, childhood seems to be not so much a period of life as one manner of living life among many from which one might choose, with no assumption that a fuller, richer period will follow it, a period for which childhood will then be seen to have been only preparation. At that time, all of childhood was an apprenticeship. Now, children sit somewhere on the ladder of consumption, and that is the main purpose of their being children. This is one reason why we are willing to allow people to extend childhood beyond the years formerly allotted to it. It's not a period of one's life or a stage of development; it's a job."

Mark was not speaking from notes—that is, there were no notes in evidence—but I think he had slipped into the performance he'd prepared for the publicity tour for *You're Not Playing Hard Enough.*

"Formerly," he continued, "childhood was not a job, though it is true that children at that time did more work than young people do now, work of the type that adults did. In part, that was simply because there was more of that kind of work to be done. Fewer things were prepared by others for us to consume. We occupied a low rung on the ladder of preparation. Prepared foods were not so widely available then as they are now, so we were pressed into kitchen service at a peeling-and-stirring level. There were fewer packaged entertainments, so we were forced to amuse ourselves. I think that I agree with those of my coevals who claim that this was good for us in the long run, since it taught us to rely on our own wits, rather than the wits of others, but anyone who has had to listen to one dumb joke told repeatedly by an inept twelve-year-old comedian will testify that it is preferable to listen to a series of dumb jokes told one after another by a mediocre television comedian, provided that each joke is told only once.

"However, our attitude toward the work we were made to do was much the same as the attitude I've witnessed in children ever since. It can be summed up in the whine that goes, more or less, 'Aw, gee, do I gotta?'

"However, again, when there was something we *wanted* to do, something we *chose* to do, then, I submit, there was never a more industrious generation of kids, ever. We had the energy of youth on our side, of course, but we also had a poorly developed sense of the impossible, which was still part of the zeitgeist then. That allowed us to labor away at projects that attracted us, so that what we were doing was never work. It was play, despite all the effort that went into it and all the time that we expended on it. It was hard play, but still play.

"If we *chose* to, if it seemed like *fun,* we could move mountains—small ones. More importantly, for Peter's story, we could *make* mountains, or to phrase that backwards, which is even more important for Peter's story, we could make holes."

Hardly Working

> The artist, even if he has been relegated to the position of a buffoon,
> tries to assume—even at the price of an apparent, momentary abne-
> gation of the self—an ambiguous stance, to place himself on a
> shaky seesaw, to transform the loss into a later gain.
>
> Norman Manea, *On Clowns: The Dictator and the Artist*

WITH THE GENERATORS supplying the power, I was able to get
Memoirs While You Wait off the ground. I printed a stack of flyers on
my Little Giant LG-6000 laser printer and wrote an advertisement for the
classified sections of popular magazines that I thought were likely to
reach the segments of the population most likely to yield clients: magazines intended for the aged but still compos mentis and magazines
intended for egotists of all ages.

Then I placed the flyer and the advertisement on the keyboard in front
of me and sat there for a while, reading them, imagining people responding to them, and imagining what the work of ghostwriting other people's
memoirs would be like, as a way of deciding whether I really wanted to
do it.

I found—somewhat to my surprise—that I could imagine myself being
happy as a professional aide-mémoire. For one thing, I could see that
there would be a certain satisfaction at the textual level, simply making
the words work, but I could also see that most of the pleasure would come
from insinuating myself into the lives of others. In the written versions of

the lives of my clients, I would be everywhere and nowhere, a ghost, a wispy bit of ectoplasm, but ghosts materialize sometimes, and I would find a way to show myself here and there in the words of the work, to anagrammatize myself beyond a simple *retype role,* appearing in the background, in a bar scene, as a *leery toper,* even popping up as a skittish lapdog *or leery pet,* or, if it came to that, I could *try* to *rope* an *eel,* but such tricks are a little crude and obvious, I think. I'd want something subtler, something that would not only do the trick but satisfy the trickster. I would make myself a man of convenience, a not-at-all mysterious man who would drift through all the memoirs I aided, that handy man who turns a corner in a narrative, collides with the narrator, nudges the story in the direction it ought to take, then disappears into the crowd. I would become that unknown man: what's-his-name, no-man, nobody, everybody, anybody. In aiding and abetting the writing of other lives, I could find a way to relieve my obsession with my own, a way to step aside from myself for a while, to absent myself from myself, and a way to make some money.

"I could enjoy this," I said aloud, to try the sound of it and see whether Albertine would believe it. Was I trying to talk myself into it? Perhaps. Would the work become tedious, sooner or later? Probably, but I could postpone that, possibly for a very long time, by focusing on the craft of it, and executing it well enough to allow myself to be proud of the craftsmanship. If I did those two things—turned in a creditable job and insinuated myself into the life that I was supposed to be writing so that every one of the books I ghosted became mine—then I could make something more of this memoir business than just ghosting or hackwork or making a living. In fact, it would hardly be working at all.

Little by little, the satisfied clients would amplify my advertising through word of mouth, and that would bring more clients, and they would bring more clients, and almost before I knew it I would have become the mogul of memoirs, with a staff of writers and a personal assistant. I already had one client, Ray. That was Step One. Now I needed the next client—no, the next two clients. If I got two clients in the next step, I'd have a growing business on my hands—and if I could get four clients in the next step, and if I went through twenty steps like that, doubling the number of clients in each step, I'd have—let's see—1,048,576 clients. Wow. We'd be rich. Where would I find all the writers? I told myself not to worry about that now—I would cope with it somehow when the time came. For now, the important thing was to move on to Step Two and find the next two clients.

THAT NIGHT, I read episode forty of *Dead Air,* "Hardly Working."

A SIMPLE HOLE in the ground would have served to hide our radio transmitter from the Federal Communications Commission, and that's what Raskol, Marvin, Spike, Matthew, and I began with—a hole in the shape of a cube about four feet on each edge. We roofed it over but left an opening in the roof so that we could get in and out. When we were in the hole, we were more or less invisible to the outside world, unlikely to be found by the FCC, but as soon as we were all inside we saw that this hole in the ground was only a rough sketch of what we wanted.

"Well, we're underground," I said.

"Just barely," said Marvin.

"You know what's wrong with this hole?" asked Raskol, and he answered himself at once: "It's not enough of a hole."

"It isn't even half a hole," said Matthew.

"We should have an entrance, a tunnel that leads into this room," said Marvin.

"Yeah," said Spike, "and we've got to make this part bigger, so we can move around, sit down, get comfortable."

"Yeah," said Raskol, "and we should make a room off this one that's even more secret than this, so if somebody finds the place and gets into this room, he won't even know that there's another room, an inner sanctum."

"Yeah," said Matthew, "and then we should make a room for each of us, even more secret than that, so that if we just want to be alone with our thoughts we can have some privacy."

They all looked at me, waiting.

"What?" I said.

"And?" said Matthew.

"What do you mean?" I asked.

"Didn't you notice that we had a pattern going? You're supposed to say 'Yeah, and—"

"Yeah," I said, "but—"

"*But?* But what?"

"If we do all of that, people are going to notice."

"Who? The FCC?"

"Maybe. We've got to cover our tracks. We've got to find a way to dispose of the dirt, or hide it, and we've got to make sure that each day's work gets roofed in and concealed before nightfall, and we've got to hide the entrance, and we've got to start approaching the place from different directions, so that people can't follow us, and we should have a password, and the entrance has to be hidden really well, and there should be a trick lock of some kind, and maybe we should stop talking to one another when we're in school, so that people don't know we're working together on this, and we ought to have a back entrance, so that if we're discovered we can escape, like prairie dogs, squirrels, moles, basically, I think, all of the burrowing animals—"

"Hold it!" said Spike. "I've only got one life to give to this. We'll dig the cave, and you take care of all the rest of that."

So I got the job I wanted: I worked on concealment, camouflage. At first, I was surprised to discover how much it resembled cleaning up. I tried carrying the dirt away as it came out of the hole, but when I discovered how hard it is to control a wheelbarrow, with the damned thing wanting always to twist on its single wheel, I gave that idea up.

If I wasn't going to take the dirt away, I'd have to find a way to hide it. I removed a layer of leaves and topsoil from a large area, and I dumped the excavated sand there as it came from the hole. When the work below ground drew to an end for the day, my busiest and most challenging time began. Quickly, I shaped the sand from the hole into a pleasing hill and covered it with topsoil and leaves. I added some plants and some of the trash of the woods— twigs, fallen acorns, and the like. What I was doing didn't feel like work. I wished I had more of it, and I urged my comrades to dig faster, to send me more sand to hide. When they climbed out of the hole at the end of the day, there was no evidence of anything I had done. I had camouflaged the hole and I had camouflaged my efforts to camouflage the hole. I worked at least as hard as they, but it seemed to them that I was hardly working, and—now—I would agree with them. It wasn't work. It was hard play.

AFTER THE READING, I delivered an advertisement for myself. "I've been in the memoir racket for as long as I can remember," I said, "since I begin counting from my first memory, the moment when I arrived at my maternal grandparents', a newborn in my mother's arms. Over the years I have developed techniques that I am now making available to the public at a reasonable price. I've printed some flyers describing my services. Please take one. All inquiries will be treated in the strictest confidence."

October 20

The Art of Obvious Subtlety

[A] television producer once made a drawing of a horse for me and said, "You and I know this is a horse. But here is what is necessary to get it over to a large audience." Above the drawing he wrote, "This is a horse," and made an arrow from the words to the horse.
    Larry Rivers, *What Did I Do?*

"The curse of the perfect artist had fallen upon me. I had been too subtle, I had been too true."
    Wilks, the actor, impersonating the German nihilist philosopher Professor de Worms, in G. K. Chesterton's *The Man Who Was Thursday*

I BEGAN THE DAY in my cave, at my computer, working on the forty-first episode of *Dead Air,* but when I took a break to get a second cup of coffee from the kitchen, I found Albertine on her hands and knees scrubbing the floor again, and when I got back to my workroom and took my place at the computer, she began writing in her diary:

Peter is full of optimism about making big money writing other people's memoirs, and I wish I could join him in his hopefulness. He is such a little boy at times. I love him for it, and I think it's really one of his admirable qualities. Most days, I think he actually wakes up thinking that things are going to get better. At least he wakes up with the feeling that they *might* get better. He has—or I

suppose I should say he had—the sunny disposition of a happy
child, and he has a mind that sees every angle, and wants to know
what's around the corner of every angle, and the kindness that I see
in him every day I rarely if ever see in anyone else at any time. I
love him for those qualities, but those qualities have made him feel
like a failure because the culture has rejected them. That sunniness
he used to have, for instance—it made him perfect for writing
those Larry Peters books, and that would have been the ideal
employment for him if only the whole miserable culture hadn't
decided to just let go and fall to the bottom rung, where the popu-
lace lies there, fat, bloated, open-mouthed, stupid, ignorant as sea
slugs and proud of it, bottom-feeders, trash fish, scavengers,
leaving him dangling as far up the ladder as he'd managed to
scramble with no one to read what he was writing, maybe even
with no one who *could* read what he was writing. Consider this,
from the morning's news: the applicants for teaching jobs at a New
York school were given the statewide exam that their *students*
would be required to pass—and most of the applicants failed it.
It's the death of the culture, the literate culture, and Peter is dying
with it. I wish I could help him, but I can't see past my own
troubles to a solution for his. When I get out of bed, I can't see
beyond what is. We are utterly broke, at the bottom of a pit. I hide
from him the truth about how bad things really are, but I know that
he peeks at the books and I suspect that he knows. We have a
hundred dollars in the checking account, the van payment is past
due, I can't make the payment on the mortgage, and there is barely
enough to buy groceries for the next week. I'm going to have to
break into our anniversary jug—the old gin bottle where we save
pocket change toward or anniversary dinner each year—for the
groceries. He doesn't quite see all this. He sees that the hotel is
nearly full, and that money is coming in from the guests we have,
and he sees the good dinner business on the weekends, and the bar
crowd, and he sees all the amateur repairs and maintenance we're
getting from the friends of Lou, but he just doesn't seem to notice
the thousand little things that break and have to be replaced, the
bills and more bills that suck the money out of my hand before I
get to decide where it ought to go. A length of gutter, a piece of

flashing, a valve, a washer, a strip of carpet, a broken tile, a missing brick, and the money is gone. It doesn't even show, but it's gone. The only way out is out. I know he loves this place, and I know how hard it is for him to surrender his dreams about it. I think that's why he's putting off approaching Lou about buying it, waiting for the right moment, and waiting, and waiting, and hoping—I suspect—that some bit of Leroy luck will make it unnecessary that the right moment should ever come. He's a dreamer. I wish I were.

JUST BEFORE I began reading "The Art of Obvious Subtlety," episode forty-one of *Dead Air,* a guest arrived from out of the past. He slipped into the back of the room—as well as a big man with a face familiar to millions can slip into a room—and settled himself into a wing chair. He gave me a wave, and I returned it, and then I read.

WHEN I WAS A BOY, about thirty-seven years ago, I dug a cave in my parents' back yard with my friends Raskol, Marvin, Spike, and Matthew. This cave was our hideout, a place to be safe from anyone who might be out to get us. We divided the labor in a way that seemed fair to me. While they worked underground, enlarging the lair, I worked above ground, concealing it, and concealing their work, and even concealing my own.

On the roof of the underground structure that was growing beneath me, I began to remake the landscape of the back yard into what it ought to have been. I didn't realize how dissatisfied I had been with the yard until I stepped back from my work after a day or two and saw how much I had deviated from, and improved upon, the original. What had been a flat and uninteresting bit of Long Island had taken the form, in miniature, of an imaginary bit of the Adirondacks. The contours I had made gave the landscape the gift of vistas, and the scrubby trees I had transplanted assumed by association with hills and vistas a grander stature than they had ever had on their own. Sometimes, after an afternoon's efforts, I would stretch out on the ground, bringing my eye down to a mole's level, so that the effect would be exaggerated, and in that position I could imagine my molehills as mountains. Unfortunately, I was often discovered in this position by my comrades, with the result that they began to think of me, unfairly and inaccurately, as a layabout, a shirker.

I complained about this sad circumstance to my friend, confidant, and business partner Porky White, proprietor of the Kap'n Klam clam bar. "I don't get it, Porky," I said. "I work as hard as they do. I work harder than they do. I mean, I have to hide all the dirt they bring out of the hole, and I do it. By the time they climb out of that hole, tired, dirty, and pleased with themselves, they can't even tell where the dirt went. What do they think I'm doing with it, eating it?"

Porky chuckled and shook his head with that look he wore whenever he was about to ask me when I would ever learn and said, "They don't even seem to notice how much work you've done, right?"

"Yes! Yes! That's exactly right. At first, I thought they were just pretending not to notice. Then I began to think that they were flattering me, that they were exaggerating my success by pretending they didn't notice. Then I saw the truth: they really *don't* see what I've done, they don't appreciate it, and they don't think I've been working very hard. Why? Why is that?"

"Because you've done the work too well," he said at once. "I think you've done an extraordinary thing, done your job so well, performed your magic so smoothly that the sleight of hand is entirely imperceptible. When will you ever learn?"

"I knew you were going to say that," I said.

"You've been too sly, Peter. Or maybe I should say that you've been applying your skills to the deception of the wrong audience."

"I don't follow you."

"You're doing all this work of hiding the hole and the sand from the hole, right?"

"Right."

"And you are trying to hide it from some potential interloper, an unknown someone who might come along and discover the fort."

"The cave."

"The cave. Sorry. You've done a great job—I'm sure you have—but you have no audience for your work. There is no one who can appreciate it. The interloper certainly can't, because if you've done the job as well as it ought to be done, as well as you hope you've done it, the interloper will never see it!"

"Of course." I said. "That's the whole point. I don't see what you're getting at."

"All along," he said, "you've had another audience—Raskol, Marvin, Spike, and Matthew—and you *want* them to appreciate your work."

"Sure. That's—"

"If you want them to appreciate it, you've got to make them *see* it, and sometimes people just can't see what's right in front of them." He pointed to the flying-saucer detector on the counter. "Look," he said. "Look at this. Most people can't tell that this is a flying-saucer detector. Basically, it looks like those transmitters you build—or like a regular radio without its cabinet. It's got the bell and the compass thing, but otherwise it could be a radio. If we didn't have the sign on it, 'Magnetomic Electronic Five-Stage Distant Early Warning Saucer-and-Warhead Detector,' nobody would know what it was."

"So I put all that effort into work that they couldn't even see," I said, since I saw at last.

"Right. If you want them to see it, hang a sign on it."

"When will I ever learn?" I asked.

"Quite possibly never," said Porky.

AFTER THE APPLAUSE had died down, I extended my hand toward the big old man at the back of the room and said, "Ladies and gentlemen, it gives me great pleasure to introduce to you the reclusive genius behind the worldwide Kap'n Klam chain of bivalve-based family restaurants: Kap'n Klam himself, Porky White!"

Porky got to his feet, with some difficulty, it seemed to me, and he waved a sheet of paper that he was clutching. "I meant to be here much earlier in the series," he said to me, "but I just got caught up in this whole fiasco of the vegetarian clam we're introducing, and it just—well, you probably haven't given much thought to how hard it is to *make* a vegetarian clam. It's the kind of thing you start working on full of optimism and then before you know it six months of your life have gone by like a billboard on a highway, and you say to yourself, 'How did I ever get into this?' But I think we've got it licked now." He dropped his voice and looked over his shoulder, as if he were checking for industrial spies, then turned back toward the room and said, in a confidential tone, "Basically, for the bodies we're using a rubbery, chewy, slippery kind of Chinese mushroom—elephant ear—and for the bellies, the guts, a little ball of mashed eggplant—but there's a lot more to it than that, as I'm sure you can imagine. Anyway, Peter, I did intend to get here earlier, but I'm glad you faxed me this memoir flyer to remind me." He waved the sheet at me. "Sign me up!"

"Really?"

"Sure. I've been thinking of writing my memoirs for a long time now, but it's just one of those things that I never get around to. There's always a vegetarian clam or something getting in the way."

I MADE A START on *Kap'n Klam: The Memoirs of Porky White, Non-pareil American Restaurateur, Entrepreneur, and Raconteur, As Told to Peter Leroy* that very night. I only had two episodes, but writing them felt like making a start on a new life. The first was about the architecture of the Kap'n Klam huts that are now perched on transparent bases from Kennebunkport to Kursk:

> My young friend Peter Leroy, to whom I am indebted for so many of the clever ideas that have made Kap'n Klam the success it is today, had inadvertently caused a local sensation in Babbington when he photographed some clams that I tossed into the air. The *Babbington Reporter* published the picture as a photograph of flying saucers, and since the name of my clam bar showed prominently, people flocked there out of curiosity. I decided to capitalize on the fact that people seemed fascinated by the near resemblance of the putative spaceships to clamshells. I began sketching, and I came up with the first rough version of the "hovercraft clam" restaurant that you see replicated all over the globe today. Basically, each Kap'n Klam restaurant is housed in a giant fiberglass clamshell—the top shell is the roof, and the bottom the base, with a gap all around for the shell-to-shell windows—but the bottom shell perches on a glass cylinder, as if the clam ship has just arrived at its

site after an intergalactic expedition. It seems that virtually every time we open a new restaurant, some guy comes lurching out of a gin mill half crocked, gets in his car and starts driving down the road, sees one of our restaurants looming ahead, and figures aliens have landed. There are a couple of standard reactions. Some of these people call the cops, the FBI, and the Marines, and others drive in and try to make contact. This happens often enough that I've got a clipping file of "eyewitness" accounts. They are much alike, so I will let one represent them all:

I was driving along Route 14 on the evening of Friday, June 12, when suddenly I saw a huge alien spaceship up ahead, on the side of the road. It looked like two saucers, one on the bottom and then one upside down, on the top. You know, I honestly didn't realize until then that that was why they call them flying saucers? I approached the ship very cautiously, since I knew from movies and TV that aliens possess superior weapons technology and are capable of turning a person into a heap of smoking ashes before he can say "Welcome, Creatures!" I walked all around the ship, and I could see that the saucers were not like the kind of saucer we use here on earth. For one thing, they were not flat on the bottom, to keep them from tipping and rocking on the table. They were rounded over their whole surface, and kind of clam-shaped. I've thought about this a lot since that night, and I've come to the conclusion that the planet they came from must have a more equalized kind of gravity than ours, if you know what I mean, so that it's easier to get things to balance. You can see that if you have that kind of gravity, then you wouldn't need to have flat bottoms for things, so I think that explains it.

I stood there for a moment, trying to think. More than anything else, I wanted to make contact with the superior beings who had flown this ship to earth and landed in what I now noticed was a parking lot right there on Route 14 because I figured that with their superior intelligence and spirituality they could probably help me get on top of some of the things that were making a mess of my life and help me find a point to it all and get me directed onto the right path to a rich and meanigful future. I knew that the risks might be great, but I also knew that I had been given an opportunity that no other human might have. I felt that for the good of human-kind I had to enter that ship. I determined that the entrance was in the front, a rectangular arrangement consisting of pairs of smooth, hard, transparent panels. Inside, I could see that there were dozens of aliens disguised as human beings. I stepped toward the entrance, and the doors opened automati-cally. *Elecric eye,* I thought. I was able to pass among the aliens without being detected because the aliens mistook me for one of them—I mean an alien disguised as a human be-ing. I even sampled some of their alien food, and let me tell you it was *delicious.*

Actually, the first flush of interest in flying saucers had worn off long before we opened our first hovering restaurant, so I think we can take credit for launching the flying-saucer revival. Of course, a lot of people accused us of planting these stories. To tell you the truth, we did.

The second episode was an attempt to get some of Porky's wit and wis-dom into the book.

If there's one thing I pride myself on, it's my ability to turn ad-versity to advantage. I've had to do this again and again. You take the very nature of the commodity I'm selling—clams. A lot of peo-ple don't like clams. One of the things they don't like is the fact that when you eat a clam you're eating pretty much everything. You know what I mean—guts, digestive tract, the contents of the digestive tract, reproductive organs—pretty much everything. With a chicken, most people just eat the muscle tissue, some skin, maybe a little liver, but even the liver makes some of them feel a little funny. So you see, from the very start I was wrestling with this problem of how to get people to overcome their squeamishness about eating the little guys whole. Well, I had one of my famous brainstorms. That's what I call them. They start with kind of a period of dark mental turbulence, when I seem to sense a change coming on, a shift in my intellectual wind, if you know what I mean. Call it confusion, if you like, but, as I said, I prefer to call it a period of dark mental turbulence. Then some small stimulus—maybe just a passing remark from my young friend Peter Leroy, who has a singular knack for saying the right thing at the right time—will cause a little spark in my brain, and out of that dark mental turbulence, whammo! A bolt of lightning! Not a bolt out of the blue, as some people say—people who probably haven't ever really experienced this particular kind of inspired idea—but a bolt out of the mind, out of this roiling kind of cloudy thinking that's been going on in my mind for some time. And that's just how it happened that I came up with the idea for the famous "guts" campaign. You've seen the ads, I'm sure. "Have you got the *guts* to eat a clam?" That was the first. Personally, I think the best was "If you've got the guts, *we've* got the guts," kind of a clever twist on an ad for beer that was running at that time, but the lawsuit on that one cost us plenty.

Playing to the House

The worms had done their work in covert, subterranean fashion. . . .
No sign of this insidious labor showed on the surface.
    Georges Perec, *Life: A User's Manual*

THE LAST GROUP of potential buyers for the hotel arrived early in the morning. (I call them the last group of potential buyers because two days later I persuaded Lou to buy the place.) Their arrival was preceded by the sudden death of a great number of fish. Albertine and I went down to the dock to await the arrival of the launch and found the surface of the water covered with fish, belly up, gill to gill as far as the eye could see. This happens sometimes. It has been blamed on red tide, on lightning, and on ecological imbalance. Babbingtonians have always blamed it on despair.

The launch parted the fish bodies and chugged to the dock. The group began to disembark. They were a motley crew, men and women from many walks of life, various levels of society, at least three races, and half a dozen creeds, but they were all Babbingtonians, and I have no doubt that each of them, if asked about the dead fish on the surface of Bolotomy Bay, would have said, "Sometimes they just get disenchanted with the life of a fish and they up and die."

"Albertine," they said, and then, "Peter," one by one, with a handshake for each of us, by way of greeting.

"Ralph," we said (or Denise or Nathan and so forth), by way of acknowledgment.

"Heard the place was for sale," said Ralph, who seemed to have been elected spokesbabbingtonian.

"That it is," I said.

"Well, we'd like to take a look at it, if we wouldn't be in the way."

"Not at all," I said. "Not at all."

"What do you have in mind for it?" asked Albertine.

"Well," said Ralph, and he turned toward the group as if to see whether they would approve of his telling us what they had in their collective mind. They looked at their shoes, which gesture in Babbington often means "Don't matter all that much to me, I guess."

"Things are changing," said Ralph. "Over in town." He looked back across the bay toward Babbington so that I would know which town he meant. "It's not the place we grew up in."

"Things do change," I said.

"But do they have to? *Muss ess sein?* That's what we asked ourselves, one night, just a few of us. And we said, 'No!' This was after some discussion, you understand. We came to the conclusion that all it takes is a determined bunch of like-minded people who are willing to invest some sweat and money, and by golly we can arrest our headlong rush to chaos and turn back the hands of time."

"Which bar were you in when you came to this conclusion?" asked Albertine.

"Let's see—I think it was—"

"Never mind," I said. "I think I see what you have in mind. Olde Babbington. A quiet place, a place where life moves slowly, where people take the time to stop and talk to one another, where the elm trees arch over Main Street, where—"

"Where you can't go right on a red light," said Ralph, pounding his fist in his hand emphatically.

"Yeah!" chorused the other olde Babbingtonians.

"Folks," I said, "you're welcome to look the place over, but take some advice from somebody who has been obsessed with the past almost from birth: you can remember, but you can't return."

I should have left it there. It was all that had to be said, but of the two prevailing tendencies of every author—either not to say things that should be said or to say many things that do not need to be said—mine is the latter, so I added, "On the level of existence at which we live our lives, time is a one-way street."

"We won't have any of those, either," muttered Ralph.

They roamed the island, but the spirit was out of them, and they left after a while, chugged back to Babbington with the dead fish bobbing in their wake.

THE FISH had begun to smell by the time I read episode forty-two of *Dead Air,* "Playing to the House." The odor hadn't penetrated the hotel yet, but I knew from experience that it would the next day.

WHILE my boyhood chums Raskol, Marvin, Spike, and Matthew dug a cave to make a hideout from which I would be able to broadcast without being discovered by agents of the Federal Communications Commission, I worked on camouflage. I did my work so well that my friends couldn't see how well I'd done it. Because the hand of man was nowhere evident, they began to suspect that the hand of man—my hand, to be specific—had never been applied to it, to suspect, in short, that I was shirking my duties.

So, I set out to make my work obvious. One evening, I left my shovel leaning against one of the spindly trees I had transplanted: a telltale sign of digging, if an interloper should ever come along to see it. I devoted about twenty minutes to getting the shovel into just the right position, choosing the right tree, dashing back and forth between the site and the spot where the five of us usually stood at the end of the day to admire our work so that I could judge the effect from my comrades' point of view. I changed trees, changed shovels, changed the angle of the shovel against the tree—all of this to make the shovel more or less noticeable, until I got it exactly right. Then, when I thought I had made it obvious enough to be noticed but not so obvious that it looked staged, I nudged it a little in the direction of the obvious.

As the five of us were walking away from the site, we turned, as we always did, to give the day's labor the admiring glance one gives to one's own work, and Raskol spotted the shovel at once.

"Uh-oh," he said. "Something's wrong."

"What?" I asked, as if I didn't know.

"Don't you see it?"

"No," I lied.

"Me neither," said Spike.

"Come on," said Raskol. "Look harder."

"It looks great to me," said Marvin. "If I didn't know there was a cave under there, I'd *never* know it, if you know what I mean."

"You're right," said Spike. "It's *amazing*. Before now, I never really noticed what a great job you've been doing, Peter."

"Maybe you just never saw it in the right light before," I said.

"Maybe not," she said, "but now that I look at it, it's amazing. Everything is sort of—just the way it ought to be—you know what I mean?"

"Yeah," said Marvin. "It's—I don't know how to put it—"

"I know!" said Spike. "It's the spot you try to find for a picnic."

"Yes!" said Matthew. "You've got it. It's that spot in the woods that my mother's always looking for. It's got everything: that nice little mound or hummock, the fallen log, where you could sit down and enjoy the view, that rock there, where you could put your feet up if you were sitting on the log, the little clump of birches—*everything*."

"It's great!" said Marvin. "Perfect!"

"Wait a minute!" said Raskol. "Don't you see? Don't you see what's wrong?"

"No," said Marvin.

"I don't either," said Matthew.

"*Look,*" said Raskol. "Look at *this*." He begin striding toward the shovel, but Matthew, Marvin, and Spike still didn't see what he was headed for. He walked to the shovel, turned back toward us, and folded his arms. *Still* they didn't see it. He picked the shovel up and waved it over his head.

"Oh," said Matthew. "That."

"So what?" said Spike. "He forgot a shovel. A little mistake. That doesn't mean anything. You've got to look at the great job he did, not at the one little mistake."

The others agreed with her, even Raskol. After he handed the shovel to me he said, "They're right. It was just a tiny mistake, and other than that it's perfect."

I knew, of course, that for that audience of four the shovel itself had been the perfect touch, the one little mistake that had made them see the great job I'd done. However, standing there with them, looking back at the camouflage, I was disappointed with myself for not having seen before the *real* flaw, the flaw that I saw so clearly now.

"It needs a stump," I said.

I was already beginning to see the scene with a stump in it. It would hide the entrance. We would tilt the stump back and crawl in under it. If the putative interloper ever came along, he would never guess that under that picturesque stump lay an underground broadcasting studio, and I was beginning to wonder what was keeping that interloper. Would he never come along and, by failing to notice it, applaud my work?

IN BED, Albertine asked, "Do you know where the word *camouflage* comes from, my sweet?"

I said, "No, *ma petite.* I confess that I do not, but I imagine that you are going to tell me that it comes from the name of one of your countrymen, a Capitaine Camouffe who dressed in leafy green and woodsy brown so that he could hide in the trees and bushes when Napoleon was looking for volunteers to lead the Russian campaign."

"How did you know?"

"Just guessed."

"But seriously, *mon petit pierrot,* it is a strange word, I think, probably derived from *camouflet,* which is an underground explosion—"

"Really? You're not kidding?"

"No."

"Underground?"

"Yes, and it gets better. A *camouflet* is an underground explosion not visible on the surface—"

"Perfect!"

"But wait, there's more. The use of *camouflet* for an underground explosion not visible on the surface is figurative. It literally means a puff of smoke intentionally blown in someone's face as a practical joke."

"This happens so often in France that they needed a word for it?"

"Apparently."

"Amazing."

Refinements and Improvements

He whose penetration extends to remote consequences, and who, whenever he applies his attention to any design, discovers new prospects of advantage, and possibilities of improvement . . . will superadd one contrivance to another . . . multiply complications, and refine niceties, till he is entangled in his own scheme.
Samuel Johnson, *Rambler* 134

'Tis with a poet, as with a man who designs to build. . . . He alters his mind as the work proceeds, and will have this or that convenience more, of which he had not thought when he began. So it has happened to me; I have built a house, where I intended but a lodge.
John Dryden, "Preface to the Fables"

ONE STEP FORWARD, one step back. With two clients for Memoirs While You Wait, I spent hours planning how to deal with the crush of new clients that was clearly on its way, or would be on its way just as soon as Manuel and Porky did their word-of-mouth work. I made a list of ways to recruit writers, figured out the appropriate markup on the work of those writers, laid out organizational charts for MWYW ("mew yew"), Incorporated, at various stages of its growth, calculated the growth in revenues, and the growth in profits. I made a tentative list of sidelines and marketing gimmicks—pens, leather-bound notebooks, mouse pads, clothing ("Memwear, the Duds Mnemosyne Dons"), that sort of thing. I calculated the likely response to an initial public offering, and I counted the years, months, weeks, and working days until Albertine and I could retire in comfort to Florida. I was so absorbed in this work that the hours flew by unnoticed, and I only turned from the screen when I heard a knock at the door.

It was Manuel.

"I'm sorry for interrupting you," he said, "and for violating the sanctity of the third floor, but I have something to say to you in private, so I was hoping you wouldn't mind talking to me here for a few minutes."

"Come on in," I said.

"No, that's okay. This'll only take a minute, and I—well—Tony T is warming up the runabout—"

"You're leaving?"

"Yeah—I—look—ah—you know—I called a friend of mine on the phone and I read him some of my memoirs, and he listened to what I'd written—you know, he's a friend of mine, so he's got to listen, right— but—ah—when I finished I said, 'What do you think?' and—ah—for a little bit he didn't say nothin'—then he said, 'Well, Ray, it's—ah—it's okay, but where's the action, man?' and I got to thinking about that you know, so—"

He stopped talking. He shrugged. He grimaced. He shrugged again.

"So?" I prompted him.

"So I took out that stuff about the dignity of small lives and that kind of stuff—"

"You mean 'that kind of crap.'"

"Aw, no, no—I didn't say—"

"Go on, go on."

"Well, I got rid of that—stuff—and I went back to some of those hideous urges I had—you know, the stuff we were going to suppress?—and I put all of that back in and now it's got a kind of—it's got a kind of *edge* to it, you know?"

"Yeah."

"The action—it—it kind of gets me *pumped,* you know?"

"Yeah."

"So I guess I'm gonna, like, follow my own path, you know what I'm saying?"

"I do, Manuel. I do."

He thrust his hand at me, and I shook it. "Come on," I said. "I'll walk you to the dock."

At the dock, over the rumble of the runabout's engine, I said, "Manuel, let me give you one last piece of advice. You don't have to take it."

"Okay."

"If you're going to keep all those hideous urges in, don't use your real name. That is, assuming that Manuel Pedrera *is* your real name."

"Huh?"

"Never mind. Just think about a pseudonym, something like—oh, I don't know—Rock—Rock something—Rockwell Kingman. Put it in quotation marks so that everyone will know it's a pseudonym. Think about it. It could add an air of mystery to the whole production. *'Who is "Rockwell Kingman"?'* That kind of thing."

"Yeah. Yeah. You're right. Thanks."

"*De nada.* But—ah—you could, if you don't mind, when you get around to it—just write me a brief testimonial to use in my advertising."

"Hey, no problem."

"Thanks, Manuel—or should I say 'Rockwell'? And good luck."

He got into the runabout, and Tony T pulled smartly away from the dock. I stood watching Rockwell Kingman make his exit from my life, and I remained on the dock, watching, despite the ripe odor of rotting fish, until they were out of sight, and even after that I remained on the dock for a while, because I thought that there was at least a slight possibility that the boat might blow up.

My audience for "Refinements and Improvements," episode forty-three of *Dead Air,* consisted of the remaining inmates—Lou, Elaine, Clark and Alice, Artie and Nancy, Louise and Miranda, Tony T and Cutie, Loretta, Theodore and Carolina, Mark, Margot, Martha, Martha and Edward, Margot and Daniel, and five lingering dinner guests.

I THOUGHT THAT MY CAREER as a camouflage artist was humming along just fine until the afternoon when I realized that the surface I had so carefully crafted to hide the cave my friends were digging lacked a stump.

I got to work on that right away. When there is no stump handy and a stump is needed, the solution is obvious: create one. I cannot tell a lie: I axed a tree. Then, with a hand saw, I cut the stump off as close to the ground as I could. It took a long time, it was boring work, and it gave me blisters. My plan was to make the stump the entrance to the cave, so I had to build a trap door and mount the stump on it. Building materials were easy to obtain in those days, if scraps would do, because so many houses were being built for the rapidly rising postwar population. In the evenings, when the carpenters, electricians, and plumbers had gone for the day, we would roam among the scraps like rats, scavenging anything that was useless to them but useful to us (and like my boyhood self, I roam the scrap heap of the past now, salvaging memories and impressions to use here). From the scraps we harvested, I was able to construct a lid for the opening, build a framework to support it at the end of the entrance tunnel, cover the lid with tar paper, and cover the tar paper with leaves, attached with the black goop that sat in black buckets at every building site. I screwed the stump to the lid with lag bolts from the underside, and *voilà*.

When my comrades saw the lid, they were so impressed by it and so eager to be able to use it to go in and out of the cave, that they decided the cave had assumed its final shape.

The digging was finished. What we had at that point, it occurs to me now, was a form without content. The excavationary team had removed the content, which a glacier had deposited long ago, leaving the form, and now we were going to fill that form with new content, ourselves and our stuff. We did this each in his own way. Marvin turned his area into what he called a contemplatorium; Matthew turned his into a sanctum, where he kept secrets not even we were permitted to see; Spike created a research library of contraband publications of a sexual nature; Raskol turned his into a cache for things he had "found"; and I turned mine into an underground center for the detection and transmission of electromagnetic signals from local and extraterrestrial intelligences, equipped with radio transmitter, radio receiver, and flying-saucer detector.

Although the digging was finished, the cave itself would never be quite finished. We continued to add comforts and make refinements. A periscope, built from plans in *The Boys' Book of Homemade Spy Gear* and concealed with leaves attached with the aforementioned black goop, allowed us to keep an eye out for the

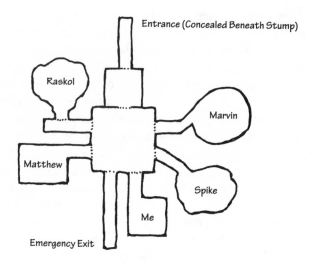

Entrance (Concealed Beneath Stump)

Raskol

Marvin

Matthew

Spike

Me

Emergency Exit

hypothetical interloper. A mirror, in an ornate frame, obtained from a source that I no longer remember, concealed a hollow behind it where we kept the most revealing of the nudist magazines in Spike's collection and a few new-car catalogs. We ran an extension cord—a heavy-duty model intended for use by professionals in the construction trades that we found snaking across the unfinished floor of an unfinished house, apparently abandoned—from an outlet in my cellar through a narrow trench the length of the back yard to the cave to bring power to the transmitter. We ran an antenna wire from the broadcasting studio through a similar trench to the trunk of a cherry tree not far away, up the trunk of the tree and along the sturdiest of the branches to the top of the tree, and from there along the tops of nearby trees until we ran out of wire. This work, which I describe so easily in a single sentence, was actually the hard part. It was the part where Spike fell from the tree and broke her arm, for one thing.

Every day, I thought of a refinement or improvement for the surface that concealed the cave and all its secrets. I adjusted the contours of the little hills I had created, rearranged twigs, scattered acorns just so, even shifted the leaf cover to try to make it look equally convincing from all angles. I transplanted grasses and wildflowers from other parts of the woods, and I installed a plush carpet of rich green moss on the northern slope of the largest hill. This became the centerpiece of my design, the spot that anyone with an eye for nature who had been wandering through my back yard and happened upon the camouflage would have chosen for a picnic.

WHEN I FINISHED, I said, "I would like to say a little something about getting caught up in one's own work, something I sometimes call the art of self-deception. I think it's something that I've always aspired to—or, to consider it from another point of view, possibly the point of view of my long-suffering wife, have fallen victim to. The camouflage of the cave was only one of many examples I could cite, but I'm not sure that in 'Refinements and Improvements' I've managed to convey how obsessive I was about the work I did. I worked on camouflaging that cave *all the time*. If I wasn't actually out there in the back yard reshaping a mound or changing the inclination of a transplanted birch sapling, I was *thinking* about doing so, or I was in the library, browsing through books and magazines for photographs of woodland scenes in the Adirondacks and Appalachians. No matter how much I did, I could never escape the feeling that I'd left something undone, and that feeling kept me going, pursuing some eternally elusive horizon of perfection, like the hiker who comes upon a lovely spot for a picnic and immediately has the uneasy feeling that just over the next little hill is a *better* spot, and so pushes on and never gets to settle down and eat his lunch. I was determined that if the FCC inspectors came around, looking for the source of the signal they'd picked up on their receiving sets in their unmarked vans with the circular antennas on the roof, they would find in my back yard *nothing but* the ideal picnic spot, that they would abandon their search, settle down, and eat their lunch, but the real truth was that I wished I could complete the job and then somehow forget it, forget it so completely that when one day *I* happened to be rambling in that corner of my own back yard I would see it as if for the first time, recognize it as the ideal picnic spot but not as my own work, abandon my rambling, settle down, and eat my lunch."

Funny Peculiar

A stranger with whom we have been exchanging—quite pleas-
antly—our impressions, which we might suppose to be similar to
his, of the passers-by, whom we have agreed in regarding as vulgar,
reveals suddenly the pathological abyss that divides him from us by
adding carelessly, as he runs his hand over his pocket: "What a pity,
I haven't got my revolver here; I could have picked off the lot!"
    Marcel Proust
    In Search of Lost Time: Within a Budding Grove

DICK AND JANE returned, as they had said they would, and Albertine
gave them their old room, as she had said she would, but it wasn't the
same as it had been when they left it, because during their absence Alice
had redecorated it in art deco style and then a leak in the corner had
stained the wallpaper in a pattern closer to art nouveau. When Albertine,
responding to a flatness in their oohs and ahhs, said that she was afraid
that they were disappointed to find it changed, they demurred, professing
to find it throughly charming, just a little surprising, so much different
from what they had remembered.

At cocktail time, Jane had one too many, and when Albertine said, in
all innocence, "It's good to have you back on our little island," Jane began to discourse on the manifold ills of the world beyond the bay. She
began, as I recall, by waving her glass approximately in the direction of
Babbington and saying, "Beyond this lovely little island lies the land of
shit triumphant."

"Here, here," said Artie.

"Jane," said Dick, raising both eyebrows.

"Oh, it's true, Dickie," she said. "It's true. It's all lost now. The shit-heads have won." She paused, thought for a moment, and said, "Oozie Holtz has won." She took a swallow of her drink and repeated, emphatically, "Oozie Holtz has won."

"What's that?" asked Artie.

"That," said Dick, "is Jane's bête noire."

"Oozie Holtz was a girl I knew in high school," said Jane. "She was very stupid, and she was very ignorant, and she was very crude. She oozed. She was covered with makeup, and when she began to sweat, she would ooze. Not a pretty picture. Believe me. She couldn't understand jokes, that was one of the things about her. She had no sense of humor. She would listen to a joke, but she had no way of telling when it was over because she just couldn't follow it. We would have to tell her when to laugh. And we'd have to tell her what was a joke and what wasn't. We'd say, 'It's a joke, Oozie—laugh,' or we'd say, 'It's not funny, Oozie—stop laughing.' So, now, here's what has happened: the world has been entirely remade to accommodate Oozie Holtz. Oozie Holtz and her ilk. Her oozie ilk."

"She's talking about television," said Dick. "She tried watching television, and she discovered that she didn't like it."

"It's immaterial whether I liked it," said Jane, "because it's not meant for me. It's meant for Oozie Holtz. Allow me to place before you for your consideration one single example," she said, aware now that she had the attention of everyone in the lounge, and turning on her stool to face the larger group. "Setting aside the shitcoms and the news and the afternoon exhibitionists, let's just look at the monologues on the late-night shows, the talk shows." She held her hands in the air, above her head, as if she were the victim of a holdup. "The host comes out and tells 'jokes.'" She wiggled the first two fingers on each hand to indicate quotation marks and let her arms fall. "The jokes aren't particularly funny, but they're supposed to *be* jokes, so you're supposed to laugh. This is a concept of humor on the Oozie Holtz level. When the host gets to the punch line, he pauses a moment, then he rises up on the balls of his feet, and he raises his eyebrows, and sometimes he even holds up his hands with his fingers spread—all this is so that Oozie knows the punch line is coming. Then he *shouts* the punch line, and in case Oozie *still* doesn't get it, the camera pans across the audience so that she can see that everybody—most of them guys, did I say that?—everybody is laughing, and whistling, and pumping the air with clenched fists even though I strongly suspect that not a single fucking one of those imbecilic assholes has got the faintest idea what the hell he's laughing at, and when he gets home, he's going to remember that he didn't get the jokes in the monologue, and he's going to feel stupid and embarrassed and you know what he's going to do then? He's going to hide his embarrassment by beating the shit out of his wife or his girlfriend or his daughter, that's what he's going to do—unless, before he ever gets back home, somebody does the world a favor and slits his fucking throat from ear to ear—"

"Say good night, Jane," said Dick, offering her his arm.

Slowly, with dignity, she drained her drink, slid from her stool, nodded to her audience, and, with Dick's assistance, made her way to the door and up the stairs.

"Has it occurred to you that we're running an asylum here?" I whispered to Albertine.

THE READING of episode forty-four of *Dead Air,* "Funny Peculiar," was delayed beyond the usual time, at the request of Lou and Elaine, who repaired to Lou's room for nearly an hour to take care of some urgent business involving one of Lou's fingers and pies. When I did begin the reading, I had a sizable audience for a Wednesday, but the audience did not include include Jane, who was upstairs, sleeping off that one or two Baldies too many.

WHEN I WAS A BOY, not yet a teenager, I found myself engaged in several projects that seemed to ask more and more of me—improvements, embellishments, and enlargements that kept me very busy for a boy of my age at that time. I built a flying-saucer detector on a whim and became the exclusive supplier of flying-saucer detectors in all of Babbington, my home town. I built a radio transmitter that grew into a network. I set out to camouflage an artificial cave and wound up transforming a corner of my back yard into a sylvan paradise, the ideal picnic spot.

One afternoon, after school, I walked out to the area where the hidden cave was and found my mother and two neighbors, Mrs. Jerrold and Mrs. Kilmer, sitting there on a checkered tablecloth that they had spread out on the attractive ground. They were pouring coffee from a Howzitno Hot-or-Cold vacuum jug and passing a tray of crumb cake and crullers from the Yummy Good Baked Goods Company.

"Peter!" said my mother. "You've discovered our hideaway! Come and have a cruller."

The crullers she offered were the glazed kind, my favorite, but I held back. I was afraid that if I passed the secret opening to the cave while they were watching me I would do something to betray it. I put my hands in my pockets and scuffed my feet on the ground, in the manner of a shy adolescent in the presence of adult women.

"Join us, Peter," said Mrs. Jerrold. She was wearing a shirtwaist dress, and she had her legs folded under her in such a way that her dress was pulled up a bit. I would have liked to join the group, sit near Mrs. Jerrold, lean across her in reaching for a cruller, and so on.

"Isn't this a perfect spot?" asked Mrs. Kilmer. "I mean, just look at it! It's got everything—that nice stump, the fallen log for sitting on, the wildflowers, this cute little mound—"

"Yeah, I know," I said.

"It's a little piece of paradise right in our own back yard!" she declared. "Well, *your* back yard, Ella."

"I never knew it was here," my mother said. "I came out to see what you were working on back here, Peter, and I discovered this."

"You know," said Mrs. Jerrold, "sitting here, I feel as if I'm— well, it's as if I've been *released*—released from the ties that bind me to the everyday world—the world of laundry and dinner and dishes, and the thousand little cares of life, all the nagging little worries, the ones that make wrinkles. They vanish—poof! Here I feel *young* again, lighthearted and happy. It makes me want to sing! Don't you feel that way?"

"It *is* pretty," said my mother.

"Anyone want another piece of crumb cake?" asked Mrs. Kilmer, cutting a piece for herself.

"Just look around, Peter," said Mrs. Jerrold. She put her hand on the back of my head so that she could turn me like a ventriloquist's dummy and make me see the scene as she did. "Isn't it just perfect?"

I looked around as she turned my head, and I couldn't see anything wrong with it. Mrs. Jerrold was right: it was perfect. As soon as I found myself about to agree with her, I realized that perfection was its flaw! Surely an interloper, looking for a hidden cave, would notice the grotesque unblemished perfection of this spot? Though emotions warred within me—pride in the perfection of the place, disappointment in myself for having omitted the flaws that would have made it better camouflage, fear that its impossible perfection would give it away—I felt that I had to test its verisimilitude, so I looked around, shuddered, and said, "Is it just me, or is there something funny about this place?"

"Funny?" asked Mrs. Jerrold. She turned to look around at the scene. Her skirt rode up along her legs another fraction of an inch.

"Funny peculiar," I said.

They demurred, professing to see nothing at all odd about it.

"There's something *artificial* about it," I suggested. "Look around you. The gentle contour of this little hillock that we've settled ourselves on, the angle of that fallen log, that cluster of wildflowers over there, the proportions of that stump. The hand of nature is not as sure as this, not this steady."

They all looked around, and they wrinkled their brows, and I thought that I could see them beginning to feel uneasy in the place and trying to decide what it was, exactly, that made them feel so.

"Where are the *weeds*?" I asked. "Where's the ragweed, the milkweed, the skunk cabbage?"

"Oh, Peter, you're a funny guy," said Mrs. Jerrold. She touched my hand.

"Funny?" I said.

"Funny peculiar," she said.

BALDY THE DUMMY was miserable throughout his program that night. His wisecracking style was gone. He didn't even tease Bob as he ordinarily did. He was bitter and snappish. When he got to the end of the show and turned to the news, the Catalog of Human Misery, I had to turn the volume up to hear him. The quality of the sound of the broadcast changed, as if Baldy had retreated to some distant recess of the cave and spoke to us from there. In a wheezing, rasping voice, he began. "I was reading the newspaper today, boys and girls, and I came upon a story that it pains me to have to relate to you. It pains me, doesn't it, Bob?"

"Yeah."

"A man made a cave, boys and girls. I don't mean that literally, of course—no one could make a cave. That requires thousands of years, tens of thousands of years, maybe millions of years, and the geological conditions have to be just right. But metaphorically speaking, he made a cave. Literally, what he did was dig a hole."

He sighed.

"This man, this monster, dug a hole in his yard, first a deep shaft, and then, at the bottom of the shaft, a larger hole, and inside the hole he built a room. A little room, boys and girls, just big enough for a monster and a little girl. He took some pains with this room. He put a mattress in it, to make the floor soft, softer than dirt, and he made wooden walls, and he had some kind of system for ventilation. Baldy isn't too sure about how this ventilation system worked, because the newspaper article was silent on that subject. Never mind about it. It is one of those things you do not need to know the workings of, boys and girls. There are things we need to know, and there are things we do not need to know, and there are many things we would rather not need to know, right, Bob?"

"Yeah."

"But this is something you have to know, boys and girls, what Baldy is telling you now."

He lit a cigarette.

"The monster made a cave, and he hid it from any prying eyes. It was right there in his yard, his suburban yard, but nobody walking by would have seen it."

He took a drag, exhaled into the microphone.

"Now we get to the hard part, don't we, Bob?"

"Yeah," said Bob.

"He perverted the concept of the cave, didn't he, Bob?"

"Yeah."

"Boys and girls, he got a little girl, some little girl who lived nearby, some neighbor girl, to come into his cave. Maybe—Baldy can't be sure about this, boys and girls, because the article is silent on this point, too—but maybe he told her that she would be safe in the cave. Maybe."

Another drag, another long exhalation.

"Beware the neighbor who invites you into his cave, boys and girls."
A pause.

"When this monster got the little girl into his cave, he locked her up in there. He kept her there, in that little room under the ground, hidden under his lawn. And then, from time to time, he—visited her—he visited her there. He—he visited her."

A silence, a sigh, then, "That's not what I mean, is it, Bob?"

"No," said Bob.

"I meant to say—that—he—*fucked* her—*fucked* her—again—and again—that monster forced the little girl's legs apart and forced his prick into her little cunt—and forced his prick into her little mouth—and forced his prick into her little asshole—and he made her hurt and bleed and cry and want to die—and if you ever see him, boys and girls, you would do the world a favor if you slit the fucker's throat from ear to ear."

Another sigh, and then, "*That's* what I meant to say, wasn't it, Bob?"

"Yeah."

"Good night, boys and girls. Stay out of your neighbor's cave."

Project Number 102: Electronic Eavesdropper

The storm in the soul of Augusto ended in a terrible calm: he had resolved to kill himself. . . . But before carrying out his plan it occurred to him, like a drowning sailor who grasps at a straw, to come and talk it over with me, the author of this whole story.

Miguel de Unamuno, *Mist*

THUNDERING WINDS pummeled the hotel all night, drafts blowing through the windows and under the doors, but by morning, everything was still, and a heavy fog filled the unmoving air. The inmates shuffled listlessly through their morning rituals, exhausted by the pounding wind, baffled by the fog. Lou had become so glum that Elaine was worried about him. I could see her worry. It showed in her expression when she looked at him from a distance, the way her brow furrowed and her lips pursed, and it showed in the deliberate way she teased him and joked with him when she was beside him, trying to cheer him up.

"Hey," he said, after a while, "cut it out, will you?" He tousled her hair and chucked her chin and said, "I know what you're up to, and it's not going to work. There are times when a person cannot be cheered up, and for me this is one of those times." He looked out toward the bay, but the day was so foggy that the water wasn't visible from the porch. "I'm going to go for a walk in the fog to be alone with my thoughts," he announced.

"And when you come back, will you be happier?" asked Elaine.

"Maybe," said Lou, "and maybe not."

"But you will come back?" she said, as if it were a joke.

Lou didn't answer that, just gave her a dismissive look, as if he considered her a silly girl for asking such a question, but there was something in the heaviness of his step that I recognized, something that made me think he might have given the same answer: "Maybe, and maybe not."

He put a coat on and let himself out the front door into the fog. Elaine looked as if she were considering following him, for his own protection, but I touched her shoulder to get her attention, and when she looked at me I put my finger to my lips, winked, and pointed to myself. She smiled and nodded her thanks. I waited a reasonable interval and then took my coat from the closet and went in search of Lou.

I could just make him out in the fog, as a bulky darkness in the grayness, moving slowly and silently. I had expected him to walk the perimeter of the island, but instead he took the path to the dock, and when he got there he walked to the very end and sat with his legs dangling over the edge, just as I do when I want to be alone with my thoughts. I held back for a while, watching him, looking for some sign of his intentions. Was he going to pitch himself into the water, or was he just going to sit and think? After a while, I decided that he probably wasn't going to pitch himself into the water, and I also decided that if there ever was going to be a time when I might sell Small's Island to him, this was it. I walked the length of the dock, sat down beside him, and, looking out into the fog, not at him, asked, "Feeling suicidal?"

"Yeah," he said, looking out into the fog, not at me.

"Do you have a method in mind?"

"Gunshot. Quick and messy. How about you?"

"Drowning. At least, I used to think of drowning. We had a leaky launch, before Tony T got through with it. A dark night, a foggy night. A leaking launch. The captain runs out of gas in the middle of the bay and sinks slowly into the cold gray water. An accident. It would have been taken for an accident, and Albertine would have collected the insurance money, but now I don't have any life insurance anymore, so it would be pointless. It would just look like a mistake, just another mistake, one more mistake in a long line of mistakes, a futile gesture of an insignificant man. Might as well leave it all up to time and fate."

He looked at me, shook his head, and snorted. "Did you come out here to cheer me up?" he asked.

"I'm not sure," I said. "What's the matter? What's bothering you?"

"Did you happen to listen to Baldy the Dummy last night?"

"Yes. It was—sad—and horrible. That's what has you so upset?"

"Yeah," he said. "That. Because it was the last straw. And because it has brought me to the realization that with very few exceptions I hate the world and everyone in it." Pause. "All of that—" he said, flinging his arm outward to indicate all of that, everything out beyond us in the fog. "I hate it. I want out."

We sat there for a while in silence. I was trying to think of the right words with which to begin to broach the subject of his buying the hotel as a way out of the world he had come to hate, as a cave in which to hide from it. The broaching would have to be subtle, it seemed to me, and I couldn't quite think of the right opening; in fact, all I could think of was reasons for not buying the place, and as the reasons mounted I succeeded in convincing myself that Lou never would buy it, that no one would.

When he said, after a while, "You know, you've got a great life here," I didn't hear the wistful longing in it. I thought he was joking.

"Yeah," I said, with a sneer, befogged by the thought of the thousand things wrong with Small's. "A great life. You bet."

"I detect sarcasm," he said.

"It's just that life here has become a nightmare—"

"Are you kidding?" he asked, almost shouting. "A nightmare?" He pushed his face close to mine. "You're not kidding, are you? Of course not—you can't see it. You can't see how good it is because you're right on top of it. Look." He put his hand on the back of my head and turned me like a ventriloquist's dummy, so that I looked out across the bay, and then he turned my head around, with a firm, insistent grip, forcing me to twist around, to shift my position on the dock, to turn around until I had swept the entire panorama of the island, the hotel, and come back to the bay again. I couldn't actually see anything, because of the fog, but I got the point. "Life is a cruel joke, Peter," he said, "and there isn't any way to go through it without getting your hands dirty. Every pleasure you experience comes at the expense of someone else, so the only happy people are the ones who ignore the suffering and misery they cause—the secret to happiness is self-deception. All of us, when we go out after some pleasure, know, somewhere, deep in our minds or deep in our hearts, that we're going to be taking this pleasure at the expense of someone else. But out here, you're as close to harmless as you can get. Here a guy could be almost inoffensive, almost benign, almost nothing, and I think that has become my ideal—to pass through this world the rest of my days as *not* a presence, as a hole, not a hill, to be nothing. I think I could do it here. I could come close to it here."

"All this could be yours," I said.

"Okay," he said. "I'll take it."

"Of course, the roof leaks—"

"Yeah," he said, chuckling, as if the leaking roof were one of the most endearing qualities of Small's Hotel, something we should have been touting in our flyer.

"—and no exterminator could ever get rid of the weird wildlife out there—" I gesticulated in the direction of the far side of the island, where the cats were wailing and the frogs were croaking.

"True," he said, still chuckling.

"—the boiler is about to give up the ghost—"

"Peter."

"—any day now the town will announce the first annual Tour de Small's 24-Hour Jet-Ski Race—"

"Really?"

"Probably not—I made that up."

"Too bad. The Demolition Man would have enjoyed the challenge."

"There's no talking you out of this, is there?"

"I've already tried. Believe me. Listen, I know everything that's wrong with it. I've been here for almost fifty days now. I love it. All the rest of them, too. They love it here, you know? They love the tinkering and banging around on the roof—they love this place because of all the things that are wrong with it, the little worries that push their big worries way out into the fog somewhere. This is going to be our place to get away from the world, our asylum."

"I think you should know that a woman is threatening to sue us because every time she recalls Small's Hotel she gets a sinking feeling."

He snorted. "Ah, don't worry about that," he said. "If the Demolition Man can't get rid of her, I'll settle with her. Maybe I'll invite her out to talk it over. Maybe that's all she wants. You know, most people just want somebody to pay attention to them—just like me, and just like you, when you get right down to it. We make our little noises, and we'd like to think that there's somebody listening to us, somebody who wants to listen to us, wants to listen to us enough to go to the trouble of tuning in."

ALBERTINE sat on a stool at the bar for my reading of episode forty-five of *Dead Air,* "Project Number 102: Electronic Eavesdropper." She was drinking champagne and beaming, glowing with the relief that had come with the news that in a few days she would be free.

ABOUT 13,320 DAYS AGO, I installed a piece of sophisticated spy equipment in the bedroom of an attractive housewife who lived nearby—across the street, around the corner, down the block—I'm no longer sure. In the weeks before that day, I had been a busy boy: I had built flying-saucer detectors, electric eyes, and radio transmitters; I had helped dig a cave; and I had single-handedly camouflaged the site of the cave with an artful imitation of an idyllic little piece of the Adirondacks. The deception was so successful that one afternoon I found my mother hosting a picnic on my camouflage. One of her guests was the attractive housewife from across the street, around the corner, or down the block—Mrs. Jerrold, Betty. I had reason to believe that Betty was cuckolding her husband with Mr. Yummy, a man who delivered baked goods, and I was jealous. I didn't mind her cheating on Mr. Jerrold, but I was hurt by her having chosen Mr. Yummy instead of me.

In the manner of all jealous suitors, I wanted to know the worst, and my friend and business associate Porky White had given me an idea for a way to learn the worst, a way to eavesdrop on Mrs. Jerrold. He had pointed out that most people weren't likely to recognize the difference between one of my deluxe flying-saucer detectors and one of my radio transmitters. If that was so, and I agreed with him that it was, then a person could be deceived into thinking that a radio transmitter was a deluxe flying-saucer detector and only a deluxe flying-saucer detector, with no talents as a transmitter at all. If, for example, I were to assemble a transmitter, take it over to Mrs. Jerrold, and pass it off as the latest in flying-saucer detectors, I could install it in her bedroom in place of the flying-saucer detector that I had installed there a few weeks earlier. Then, in secret, hiding in my cave, I could tune in to the Mrs. Jerrold show and savor the worst, like the pain of a rotten tooth.

Assembling the false detector was simple, thanks to the 101 Fascinating Electronics Projects kit. The idea behind the kit was that a young electronics enthusiast first mounted all the components on a piece of pegboard and then wired the components together on the underside of the pegboard. The enthusiast could change the project from, say, Number 56, Rain Detector, to Number 23, Lie Detector, by unsoldering the connections that had enabled the components to detect rain and resoldering them in a way that enabled them to detect lies. When the wiring was finished, the young technologist attached the piece of pegboard to a base, a black metal box, as if the pegboard were the top of the box, so that none of the wiring showed. This arrangement spared the novice solderer the embarrassment of having the evidence of his ineptitude on display, and because the wiring was hidden one finished, fully assembled project looked just like another. The electronic eavesdropper that I was making would look like a Magnetomic Electronic Five-Stage Distant Early Warning Saucer-and-Warhead Detector, since all the differences lay underneath, hidden within the kit's black box, camouflaged by the unvarying arrangement of the components visible on the top.

When it was finished, I took it across the street and knocked at Mrs. Jerrold's back door.

"Hi, Peter," she said. "Junior's not here. Roger took him roller skating."

"I noticed that the car was gone," I said. "I brought you the latest flying-saucer detector."

"Pretty fancy," she said. "It looks like a whole radio you've got there."

"A radio?" I said. "Does it look like a radio?"

"Well, it's got those dials and knobs and—"

"Oh, those. Those are for adjusting the range and the—ah—sensitivity—and—this one—the volume—because you get an audible alarm with this model, not just that little light that you've got on the detector you have."

"So you think I should trade mine in?"

"I would recommend it," I said.

"I don't know—"

"Tell you what I'll do," I said. "I need some people who would be willing to participate in field tests of this new model. I'd be willing to install it free of charge if you would try it out and give me a testimonial."

"Sounds like a pretty good deal."

"It's a once-in-a-lifetime opportunity," I said.

She tousled my hair and said, "You're a cute kid, Peter. Okay. Sign me up for the free trial."

"I can install it right now if you want," I said.

"Okay," she said.

She led me through the living room and up the stairs. When we reached her bedroom, she threw herself backwards onto the bed, put her hands behind her head, and smiled at me in a way that made me realize that she knew nearly everything I was thinking, and that she *thought* she knew *everything* I was thinking, but she did not, because just at that moment I was thinking that because I had camouflaged myself so thoroughly as an ordinary adolescent boy with the usual set of dreams and desires she couldn't see that I was a spy.

"LOU," I said to Lou, at the bar, where he was pouring free drinks for everyone, "I want to tell you a story."

"Isn't that what you've been doing?" he asked.

"All my life," I said, "but this is a story with a message."

"Okay, go ahead."

"Once I owned a clam boat, a handsome boat, but it was sinking."

"Uh-huh."

"You heard that part about sinking?"

"Yeah."

"Well, after a summer of trying to make enough money clamming to pay my college expenses, I sold the boat to three milkmen who wanted to get out of the milk racket and into the clam racket."

Lou said nothing. He went about his bartender's duties, and he accepted the congratulations of the tipsy topers. When he worked his way back to my part of the bar, I said, "I sold them a sinking ship, Lou. You see what I'm getting at?"

"Yeah, I see."

"Okay," I said. "I just wanted you to hear that story."

"Yeah."

"I don't want you to think that I'm taking advantage of you."

"I know what I'm getting into."

"Good," I said. "Okay. That's settled. That's okay, then. We won't say anything more about it. That's that. Enough said. Done. It's a done deal. Case closed. Good night."

Suspicions Confirmed

Chance, my friend and master, will surely deign to send again, to help me, the familiar devils of his unruly kingdom! I have no faith, except in him—and in myself. Particularly in him, for, when I sink, he fishes me up again, and grips and shakes me like a rescuing dog . . . So that every time I sink, I do not expect a final catastrophe, but only some adventure, some trivial, commonplace miracle which, like a sparkling link, may close up again the necklace of my days.

    Renée Néré, in Colette's *La Vagabonde*

YOU MAY SUSPECT that you have no real friends, and yet when you die, if you could somehow arrange to attend your own wake—disguised, perhaps, as a shadow in a corner or a mist drifting in through an open window—you might be surprised and delighted to see how many people show up. Of course, it is equally likely—at least equally likely, probably more likely—that your suspicions would be confirmed, and that the room where your corpse lay a-moldering would be empty except for a melancholy shade or a dispirited fog, so it's best not to leave such matters to chance. Make arrangements now for an open bar, hot hors d'oeuvres, and a jazz band. That'll bring them in.

I was thinking along those lines, and consequently sinking into self-pity, when I happened to bump into Lou at the coffee urn, where I thought I would probably find him at that time of the morning. "You know, Lou," I said, in a casual tone meant to catch him off guard, "I've been thinking."

"Uh-oh," he said.

"I've been thinking that we ought to celebrate your acquisition."

"Great idea."

"I was figuring that Small's Affairs could handle the catering, and Nancy and Elaine could take care of promotion and public relations."

"Sure. Sounds fine."

"Tony T could put the whole fleet of runabouts into service, perhaps decorate them a bit."

"Decorate?"

"I was thinking of a special pennant of some kind."

"A pennant?"

"Something like—oh—how about, 'Happy Birthday Peter'?"

"What?"

"Only kidding."

"Uh-huh."

"If we all pitch in, we could erect enough tents by tomorrow, I think."

"Tents?"

"Well, my guess is that if we turn Artie loose with a list of my closest friends we'll have an invasion on our hands by tomorrow morning—if he remembers to mention the open bar, the free food, and the jazz band."

"Jazz band?"

"Loretta can make it happen. I'm sure she can."

He looked at me for a minute, then asked; "Is it okay if some of the pennants say 'Good Luck Lou'?"

"Of course," I said.

"We'd better get Cutie working on those."

"Right," I said. "No time to lose."

THE AUDIENCE THAT NIGHT for my reading of episode forty-six of *Dead Air,* "Suspicions Confirmed," was a good one, a Friday crowd, but, looking out at them and beginning to read, I savored the pleasant expectation that Saturday's turnout would be even better.

BECAUSE I was attracted to Mrs. Jerrold, but she was attracted to Mr. Yummy, I was frustrated and jealous, jealous enough to build an electronic eavesdropping device and install it in Mrs. Jerrold's bedroom. I set up a secret listening post in a cave in my back yard, and I spent every spare hour in that cave, with my radio tuned to the eavesdropper in Mrs. Jerrold's bedroom, waiting to hear the details of her tumbles with Mr. Yummy, so that I would know just what I was missing, but hour after hour I heard nothing.

My parents began to wonder what I was doing during these absences, and I had begun to wonder myself. To camouflage my real occupation, spy, I offered them a cover that was nearly the truth.

I interrupted myself to say, "I have since learned, by the way, largely from this experience, that a cover that is nearly the truth is the best sort of cover to use. Convincing people that you are someone they already think you are is far easier than starting from scratch and convincing them that you are what you wish you were, what you want to be, or what you have been struggling all your life to become. In my case, I have put so much effort into disguising myself as a country bumpkin, assistant innkeeper at a small hotel on a small island, have done the job so thoroughly and so well, that I'm convinced that that is what I have become at last, just at the time when I have sold the job out from under myself."

"Peter," my father said at dinner one evening, in a casual tone meant to catch me off guard, "what are you doing with yourself these days?"

"Me?"

"No. The man in the moon."

"Well," I said, "that old man in the moon, he's just sitting there, watching us down here, spying on us while we do the crazy things we do, shaking his head, smiling that enigmatic smile."

"Don't get smart with me, Peter."

"But—I thought that was the point of my going to school, so that I'd—"

In a clipped, no-nonsense tone, he said, "I want to know what you've been doing and where you've been going every afternoon, young man. You've got your mother worried to death."

My mother pushed her plate away from her, lit a cigarette, and took a swallow of wine. She did look worried.

"I've been in my cave," I said.

"Your cave?" said my father, as if this were the last thing he had expected to hear.

"Yeah," I said. "Raskol and Marvin and Matthew and Spike and I dug a cave in the back yard, and I've got a radio transmitter out there, and I'm going to go on the air tomorrow."

"Don't mock me, young man," said my father, reddening, clenching his fists.

Turning to my mother, I said, "You'll be able to listen to me on the kitchen radio, and then you'll know where I am."

"Listen, Peter—" my father began, raising a finger to tick off the first of the points he planned to make.

"Come on out in the back," I said, cutting him off, "and I'll show you."

They followed close behind me, though I set a sprightly pace. Suddenly, having been forced to tear away the camouflage and reveal what lay beneath it, I found that I was eager to do so, eager to show them my handiwork, and I was growing more eager with every step. I knew what responses to expect; that is to say, I had imagined their responses and I'd come to believe what I had imagined. Previously, the supposed certainty of those expectations had kept me from showing the cave to my parents, but now I found that I wanted to check my assumptions. I imagined that my mother would be amazed by what I'd done and proud of the skill I displayed in doing it, that she would understand the effort that had gone into the work, and that she would find in it evidence that I was going to amount to something someday. My father would be annoyed that I had been so presumptuous as to tunnel through a section of his back yard without his permission, would interpret my tunneling as a metaphor for my undermining his authority, would wonder why I couldn't put this kind of effort into mowing the lawn, and would find in what I'd done evidence that I was never going to amount to anything.

We stopped at the place where my landscaping camouflaged the entrance to the cave, and my mother said, "Oh, this is that spot I was telling you about, Bert! Isn't it perfect? Those birches, that clump of wildflowers, the mossy hill, the stump—"

On that cue, I flipped the stump back on its hinges to reveal the entrance to the tunnel that led to the cave. My mother was amazed. My father was annoyed. How satisfyingly predictable they were—

people you could count on! I was glad to see my beliefs, my expectations, confirmed. It made me think that I had become the kind of savvy guy who really knows what's going on.

IN BED, Albertine rolled over onto me and made love to me slowly and thoroughly. She was so tender and affectionate that I began to suspect that she was administering delight as a preventive analgesic against some disappointment.

Spent, we lay awhile in a silent embrace. Then I said, "Forgive me for asking this, but there isn't anything wrong, is there?"

"No," she said. "Not really wrong, but—"

"Oh, those tormenting buts."

"You got a fax."

"From?"

"Well, it was signed 'Rockwell Kingman.'"

"*Rockwell Kingman?*"

"In quotation marks."

"Where is it?"

"I burned it."

"Burned it? That's dramatic."

"Oh, I didn't want you to see it—ever. But now I feel disloyal about it—overprotective or something."

"What did it say?"

"It said, 'I just sold the screen rights to my hideous urges. Thanks for everything.'"

Still No News from Outer Space

Life can never be anything but joyless without the consolations and companionship of friends.
    Marcus Tullius Cicero, *On Friendship*

MY FRIENDS DID SHOW UP, and Albertine's mother, all of her siblings, all of her aunts and uncles, and most of her cousins, so all the tents were full. I wished that Albertine's father could have been there, but wishing couldn't make it so, since he was among the dead, along with my parents, my grandparents, and many others that I would have liked to see again, and many more that I would not.

Dinner that night was a medley of my favorites: clams casino, clam fritters Harold, baked stuffed clams, clam chowder, fried clams the way my grandfather used to make them, linguini with clam sauce (white and red), and sautéed spinach with onions and ginger. For Albertine, who does not care for clams, there was *petti di pollo alla Bolognese*. The jazz band was actually just a piano player—Albertine, to tell the truth—but it was a treat to have a piano in the lounge again, and she was very good, and she knew my favorite tunes.

WHEN THE TIME ARRIVED for my reading, I thought of saying something sentimental about the comforts of friends and family, but the crowd had become boisterous to the point of riot, so, instead, I took a deep breath and delivered episode forty-seven of *Dead Air,* "Still No News from Outer Space," without a pause.

IF YOU HAD BEEN LIVING in Babbington, New York, Clam Capital of America, about thirty-seven years ago, a few days before my thirteenth birthday, and had tuned your radio to almost any spot on the AM dial, you might have heard me say, in my radio voice, not in the voice that I would have used if you and I had been sitting side by side and talking as friends, but in the voice that I had decided to use to emulate the professional friendliness that I heard on radio programs, a condescending warmth that kept the listeners in their place, "Good afternoon, Babbington, and welcome to the Peter Leroy Show. Unfortunately, Peter can't be here today. He's on vacation—lucky guy—so I'll be sitting in for him. You can call me Larry. I've got a little secret that I want to confess to you. Lean in closer, and I'll whisper it to you. Shh. Ready? Here it is. Don't tell anybody, but this is my first time on the radio. I've had a little practice talking into a tape recorder, with my lovely assistant, Betty, but she couldn't be here today, either, so I guess it's just you and me. You know, I've always been interested in radio. I used to listen to 'Bob Balducci's Breakfast Bunch,' and after Bob went on permanent vacation—lucky guy—I started listening to his dummy's show, 'Baldy's Nightcap,' and I'm a regular listener to Baldy now. So here I am in the broadcasting cave of WPLR, talking into my microphone, and you're out there, listening to your radio, which makes my microphone something like your ear, and your radio something like my mouth, doesn't it? Well, thanks for lending me your ear—and thanks for letting my mouth into your home. You know, speaking of letting people into your home, you wouldn't want to let just anybody into your home, would you? Of course not, and you wouldn't want flying saucers hovering over your home and spying on you either, would you? No, sir. And you wouldn't want an ICBM landing in your back yard without your permission, would you? No, sirree! Well, you'll be happy to know that you can get relief from saucer and missile anxiety with the Magnetomic Electronic Five-Stage Distant Early Warning Saucer-and-Warhead Detector. I've got one right here beside me. Let's see what it says. Good news! According to my detector, there is currently no danger whatsoever. That's a relief, isn't it? Of course, I can't be sure that my detector reaches as far as your house, so if you really want worry-free living, you should get a detector of your own. You'll find them in bedrooms all over Babbington—bedrooms where people say 'good night'—and mean it. Say! Do you want to see a Magnetomic Detector in action? Well, get on down to Kap'n Klam, the Home of Happy Diners. You'll find a Deluxe Model right there on the counter, and while you're there you can sample their new Klamburger. It's a delicious clam cake on a bun, but get this—the bun is shaped like a clamshell! You'll love it. It'll make you happy. And if it makes you happy enough they'll snap your picture and put it up on the Wall of Happy Diners. Be sure to tell them Peter sent you. I mean Larry. Peter's not here. He's on vacation—lucky guy. Anyway, let them know that you heard about the new Klamburger on WPLR, so they'll know you were listening, because otherwise I don't really have any way of telling whether anybody's out there. I mean, I keep talking, but I never hear anything back. It's a one-way street. You can detect me, but I can't detect you. Speaking of detecting things—let's take a look at the saucer detector. Still quiet! No flying saucers in the area. No nuclear warheads falling on us. And that reminds me—while you're at Kap'n Klam enjoying your Klamburger or a Klam Salad Sandwich, keep your eye on the Magnetomic Saucer Detector on the counter, because at Kap'n Klam you get your money back if saucers attack! I'm not sure about warheads. Ask them about that, but to tell you the truth, I don't think you get anything if a warhead lands on the place. I think your money will be vaporized. So will you. So will the whole clam bar—Babbington—everything. I'm in a cave, so I might be safe. Baldy the Dummy always says, 'Stay in the cave.' Well, that's where I am—in my cave. And it's a good cave, a very good cave. I've got all the comforts of home—most of the comforts of home, anyway. Some of the comforts of home. I hope you're comfortable there in your home, or your cave, or your car, or wherever you're listening to me. Thanks for tuning me in, and thanks for letting me into your home—or your cave—or your car. You may not know that our signal reaches all the way across Babbington on the WPLR Radio Broadcasting Network. Our 106 network affiliates are strung out like pearls from our secret underground headquarters all the way to Kap'n Klam, the Home of Happy Diners, just a stone's

throw from the town dock." I was exhausted and breathless from
the effort of talking without a pause, but the idea of leaving a moment of empty silence threw me into a panic, so I pressed on: "Let's
see—still no news from our saucer detector, and no news from our
new top-secret experimental detector, either. This one is so secret
that I can't even tell you what it detects." And on I went, until the
WPLR broadcast day came to a close.

ANARCHY REIGNED around the bar, with Albertine's relatives invading Lou's territory to make their own drinks and gathering in knots of
three and four to sing the bits and pieces of old songs that they found almost unforgettable. Lou threw in the towel. He also untied his apron,
came out from behind the bar, and said to me, "Come for a walk with me,
Peter. I got a little business proposition for you."

"Okay," I said. "Sure."

He elbowed his way back behind the bar, grabbed a bottle of cognac
and two snifters, and elbowed his way back to me.

"Let's go down to the dock," he said.

We did. It was a pleasant night, warmer than it ought to have been,
still, with half a moon. We sat at the end of the dock with our legs dangling, and Lou poured each of us a puddle of cognac. He raised his glass
to me and said, "Three days in advance, happy birthday, Peter."

"Good luck, Lou," I said.

He snorted. "Lou?" he said, as if he doubted that I'd meant to say it.
"You mean you really haven't figured out who I am?"

"No. Cedric R. Abbot. 'Call me Lou.' That's not who you are?"

Laughing, he said, "Yes and no. See if this helps." He looked at me
and he grinned his bizarre grin, and he said, "File that under Brilliant Dis-
guises, okay, Bob?"

In the moonlight the truth gleamed.

"You're Baldy the Dummy!" I said.

"Not quite," he said, shaking his head, "not unless I'm crazier than I
think, but you're close."

"If you're not Baldy the Dummy—"

"Yeah?" he said, in a voice I'd known for years.

"My God, you're Bob Balducci."

Laughing: "You got it, kid."

"But who's Cedric R. Abbot?"

"That's me. Balducci is my stage name."

"Your radio name."

"Yeah. My radio name, and my radio voice."

"And Baldy?"

"Bob is the voice of Baldy, and Bob controls Baldy, despite what may seem to be the case when you tune in at night."

He shifted into Bob's voice and said, "For three decades now, more than three decades now, I've been playing second banana to that dummy. But I'm calling it quits. In a couple of days, Baldy is going to learn one of the little truths about life, namely that it's the ventriloquist who controls the dummy, and not the other way around."

In his everyday voice he said, "I wanted to ask you how you would feel about writing the memoirs of Baldy the Dummy."

"I think that among ghostwriters it is generally accepted as truth that dummies and dead people make the very best clients," I said.

The Lonely Housewife's Friend

Our imagination, and our dreams, are forever invading our memories; and since we are all apt to believe in the reality of our fantasies, we end up transforming our lies into truths.
  Luis Buñuel, *My Last Sigh*

OTTO AND ESTHER—parents of Louise, son and daughter-in-law of Artie the Demolition Man and his wife Nancy—returned to the island after nineteen days away and found themselves surrounded by a bunch of zombies walking around in a hangover haze. (I will confess to you, reader, since we are nearing the end of this memoir and the time for confessions is hard upon us, that, as a rule, a hangover makes me horny. This one was no exception. I began nuzzling Albertine before she was even awake, and I pestered her all day long, sometimes, I think, embarrassing her in the presence of her relatives, who are generally circumspect about their affections.)

Mark and I were standing at the bar, waiting for Lou to fix us a Bloody Mary, when Otto and Esther appeared in the doorway of the lounge. "Look at those two," said Mark, nodding in their direction. "They will be interesting to watch. Notice the way they are standing in the doorway exhibiting diffidence. They are deliberately staying on the edge of the group, because they recognize that the group shares a definition of itself that does not include them. Once I have my hangover tonic in hand, I think I'm going to find it quite interesting to see how they manage to enter the group—assuming, of course, that they try to enter the group and that they succeed at the effort, but looking at them I suspect that they will—because to insinuate themselves into the group at this late stage in its development they will in effect have to learn the language of the group, and at the *vernacular,* not merely the *formal* level. I mean that in the sense that language rests on shared experience, the shared experience of a culture—whether it is experience gained at first hand or at second hand, through the mediation of language itself—because it is those shared definitions—in this case a definition of last night as 'the night before' and this morning as 'the morning after'—that define a culture, which leads me to a point I wanted to make the other night after you finished reading 'Funny Peculiar,' but refrained from making because I sensed that direct commentary on the readings is generally not the practice among your listeners, possibly because people think of themselves as on vacation when they are out here, isolated as they are from the hurly-burly, the 'incumbering hurry of the world.' Isn't that how it goes? I think so. I think it's: 'Till we are persuaded to stop, and step a little aside, out of the noisy crowd and incumbering hurry of the world, and calmly take a prospect of things, it will be impossible we should be able to make a right judgment of our selves or know our own misery. But after we have made the just reckonings which retirement will help us to, we shall begin to think the world in great measure mad, and that we have been in a sort of bedlam all this while.' William Penn, unless my memory fails me, in 'Some Fruits of Solitude,' and I think that just that sort of thing must happen to people here, at the very moment when they arrive here, I would think. In stepping off the launch and onto the island they probably have a fully conscious awareness of stepping out of 'the noisy crowd and incumbering hurry of the world,' I expect, and yet, can they ever leave that 'bedlam' entirely behind? Or do they always carry something of it with them in their hearts and minds? Isn't it, in fact, one of the shared definitions of the mad world they have left behind that allows them to recognize this island as a refuge from it, just as—and you see I'm coming back around to the comment I meant to make about 'Funny Peculiar'—the idea of the ideal picnic spot was one of the shared ideas that defined the culture in which you and I grew up. However—and this strikes me as perhaps marking a pivotal redefinition for our culture, one that, judging from your reading last night and the claims that you made within it for the deceptive power of your camouflage on the surface of the cave, you may have been responsible for initiating—the original definition of the ideal picnic spot was essentially a miniature Arcadia, in the sense that it was presumed to have existed 'forever,' to be the creation solely of nature, to be, in fact and in essence, pastoral, not merely to lie outside the bedlam that mankind had made but to be utterly unrelated to it and wholly unaffected by it, to be a place where the lucky people who happened upon it might pass the hour or so required for the eating of their lunch in blissful Edenic innocence, isolated from civilization and its discontents by virtue of having stumbled on a little patch of anachronism, a pre-existing paradise, but at some time, and perhaps it was at about the time when you and I were coming to the end of our childhood, just coming to understand the definitions common to the noisy crowd in adult bedlam, our culture began to give up looking for the ideal picnic spot, that little Arcadia, and began instead to try *make* the ideal picnic spot, a little Utopia rather than a little Arcadia, but while Arcadia comes to us already defined by nature, Utopia must be defined by those who mean to make it, and if it is going to be a place where the whole culture can picnic, where the whole culture will *want* to picnic, where the whole culture will be willing to *pay* to picnic, then it must be a place that the entire culture recognizes as the perfect spot, and that kind of mass acceptance requires a culture stable enough to have a definition of the perfect spot that is stable enough to become the common coin of cultural exchange, whether we're considering a culture that is no larger than the three housewives who sat on the hillock you had constructed on the roof of your cave or our little band of crapulous imbibers here, in which case the group is small enough to allow the exchange of cultural commonplaces directly, in conversation over coffee, for example, or over a Bloody Mary, or a culture that is much larger, as large as a town, or a hemisphere, in which case the common coin must be exchanged through other media, which introduces a greater likelihood of garbling."

He paused to pay some attention to his Bloody Mary, and in the pause I said, "Hangovers always make me horny."

"Me, too," said Mark, after a moment's reflection.

"Why is that?"

"I don't know the physiological basis for the phenomenon, but I think that psychologically it is due at least in part to the fact that the abstraction or separation that we feel from the world is as great during the hangover phase of a binge as it is during the drunken phase. We have been irresponsible and *know* that we have been irresponsible and feel the full force and effect of *having been* irresponsible throughout our being and—which is the saving grace, the liberating factor—we are *paying* for it. Our coin is the pain of the hangover, so we feel not only a lingering license to set aside the rules of practical life, but the physical necessity to do so, and into the bargain we feel that the bargain has already been struck, that since we are paying for this time off, and paying plenty, we want every pleasure we can get, because, goddamn it, we've earned it!"

ALTHOUGH Otto and Esther tried their best to enter the hangover culture, they couldn't quite manage it. By mid-morning, those of us who had lived through the night before had returned to something like our everyday charm, but under the influence of the same Bloody Marys that we were drinking Otto and Esther became as ebullient as all of us had been the night before, with the result that we could hardly look at them without laughing, because they seemed not merely drunken and ridiculous but exactly as drunken and ridiculous as we had been. It seemed like a generous, self-effacing gesture on their part, and we loved them for it.

AFTER A MIDDAY BUFFET DINNER, I read episode forty-eight of *Dead Air,* "The Lonely Housewife's Friend."

IN INSTALLED my electronic eavesdropping device in Betty Jerrold's bedroom because I couldn't think of a way to install *myself* in her bedroom. A week went by before I heard anything at all. Then one night when I saw the light go on in the Jerrolds' bedroom I dressed quickly, slipped out of the house, ran to the cave, where I had my listening post set up, scrambled inside, and turned the receiver on. It took a while to warm up, but as it did Mrs. Jerrold's voice slowly filled my little corner of the cave.

"... leaking every time it rains," she was saying, "but what do you care? You're not even here most of the time."

"What is this now? You're annoyed with me for working? Do you want me to quit my job?"

"Oh, your job. Your job is—"

"My job is damned hard work, Betty. Necessary work. And dangerous."

"My job *isn't* necessary? Raising your child isn't necessary? I am the only one who *is* raising him, you know—not you. You've got me trapped in this little house—you've got me trapped in this little *life*."

"You've got every comfort here."

"Not quite. I don't have a man in the house."

"Oh, don't you?"

"What do you mean by that?"

"You seem to have your admirers—like the kid who sold you this piece of junk."

"You've got to be kidding!"

"It seems to me that there's something going on there."

"Don't be ridiculous. What gives you an idea like that?"

"I've got my reasons. Maybe I've heard something. Maybe I've got ways of hearing what you're up to when I'm away. Maybe I'm not always away when I say I'm away. Maybe I've heard you and that kid—"

"He is a *boy,* Roger, a little boy—not even a teenager. You're being ridiculous."

"Am I? Okay. Let's try someone else. How about the delivery boy—the guy from Yummy Good Baked Goods?"

"Where are you getting these ideas?"

"I'm not a spy for nothing."

"A spy! Oh! I forgot. You're a spy. Mr. Spy. You want to know something, Roger? I don't think you *are* a spy."

"What?"

"I think you're a salesman."

"That's my cover, of course—"

"A door-to-door salesman."

"A *traveling* salesman."

"Door-to-door, traveling, used-car—what's the difference?"

"The traveling salesman is the knight-errant of the salesman fraternity, while the door-to-door salesman has the image of a swindler, preying on housewives when their husbands are away, and besides—it's only my cover."

"Your cover," she said, and I could hear the sneer. "It's not your *cover*. It's your life. I think you've been lying to me ever since I first met you. You're no spy. Your glamorous spy life?—that's your cover. Underneath it, you're a traveling salesman."

"I am a cold warrior, Betty, and what I do—"

"I'm the cold one, Roger. You leave me here while you go out on the road, and you never can tell me what you've done or where you've been because it's supposed to be a secret, but I think that the only one you're keeping your secrets from is the woman you leave at home—me—a cold woman in a lonely bed—a traveling salesman's wife."

"And a door-to-door salesman's slut."

"Don't you call me a slut."

"Everything has its proper name."

"Salesman!"

There was a silence, and then Mr. Jerrold said, more calmly, "Look, Betty, maybe I can arrange for a transfer to Europe or—"

"Give it up, Roger. I don't believe you anymore. You're too boring to be a spy."

"That's the way the modern spy—"

"Oh, shut up."

"It's just that you're laboring under a common misconception—"

"Will you please just stop talking?"

"I am a spy."

"Shut up."

"And a damn good one."

A silence.

"Come on, admit it, Betty. You believe I'm a spy, don't you? Silence.

"Don't do this to me, Betty."

Silence.

"Just say it once, Betty. 'You're a spy, Roger.'"

"No."

"Say it!" There was a sound that I now think was a slap. At the time, I thought it was some kind of electromagnetic interference.

"No!"

"Say it!" Another sound, muted, meaty. This, I knew even back then, was a punch. "Say it!" Another punch.

There was a longer silence, then the rustling of bedclothes, and then Mrs. Jerrold said, "Don't touch me, you bastard."

"Come on, Betty—"

"If you touch me again, I'll scream."

Mr. Jerrold sighed and said, "I guess you're saving it for the kid across the street—"

"Go to hell."

"—and the bakery boy."

"He's not a *boy,* Roger," said Mrs. Jerrold with a bitter laugh. "He's a grown man. The lonely housewife's friend. The kids all call him Mr. Yummy. So do I."

There was silence, a threatening silence, and I leaned toward the radio, straining to hear, because I expected the silence to be broken by the sound of violence, but the silence lasted so long that I grew tired of listening and turned the radio off, so for all I know there was silence for the rest of the night.

AFTER THE READING came the quick exit. It was Sunday evening, and people had to be at work on Monday, so they gathered their things and said their goodbyes and crowded the launch and the runabouts, leaving us—all of us who stayed behind—to settle into that sense of impending disaster that's known as the Sunday Blues, but Albertine whispered in my ear, and, giggling, we retired upstairs to savor the perdurable pleasures of our connubial bed.

Shame on Me

My life is like a stroll upon the beach,
As near the ocean's edge as I can go.
  Henry David Thoreau, "My Life Is Like a Stroll upon the Beach"

We don't even know where "real life" is lived nowadays, or what it
is, what name it goes by. . . . We are born dead, and moreover we
have long ceased to be the sons of living fathers. . . . But that's
enough; I shall write no more from the underground.
  Fyodor Dostoyevsky, *Notes from Underground*

I TOOK A WALK around the rim of the island at dawn, walking along
the sand, with my shoes off, in the lapping water, through the stones, pebbles, and broken shells. The water was cold now, but I wanted to walk in
it, as I used to do on summer mornings, in the inch of water at the edge of
the island, where I leave no footprints, because I had decided that this
would be the last time I did so. Before I went back inside the hotel I
stopped and just stood there for a little while, with the wavelets lapping in
over my numb feet, the morning sunlight skipping on the water, and the
breeze shaking me by the shoulders and asking me whether life could
possibly be better than this.

THIS DAY, Monday, was the first real working day for Lou's takeover
team, and they spent the day in constant conference, proposing and plan-

ning, scheming and dreaming. They were still buzzing after dinner, when we gathered in the lounge, but I silenced them with my reading of "Shame on Me," episode forty-nine of *Dead Air*.

FOR MY THIRTEENTH BIRTHDAY, I bought myself a tape recorder. It took all the money I had, but I thought it was worth it. I had just launched my radio career, and I had immediately discovered how very difficult it is to keep talking without pausing longer than a breath. After a couple of days on the air, my voice had degenerated to a rasping croak. With a tape recorder, I could record myself for an hour and then broadcast the recording as often as I liked, filling time with no effort until I had rested my voice and thought of something new to say.

Because I was so eager to give the tape recorder a trial run, I spent the morning of my birthday in the backyard cave that housed my radio transmitter (and my flying-saucer detector, and a receiver tuned to the frequency of the electronic eavesdropper that I had planted in Betty Jerrold's bedroom). I spent some time recording a few tapes full of random observations about current events in my immediate neighborhood and the actors involved in them, and when I had used all the tape that I had bought I pulled a reel from the stack and put it on the recorder. With no further broadcasting responsibilities for a while, I left the recorder running, transmitting a tape over the vast WPLR network, and I went off to explore the rest of the cave, to see what my fellow troglodytes had done with their parts of it, to snoop, to spy.

The cave was divided into several rooms, dens, or lairs, so that each of us who had built it and used it could have a place of his own. Mine was my broadcasting studio, of course. Marvin's was nearly empty, a monkish cell that he used for quiet thinking. Spike's was intriguing, since it was well stocked with what was considered pornography at the time. Raskol's was full of treasures that he had found unattended during his rambles through Babbington, but after giving them a thorough examination I had to admit that one man's treasures may be another man's junk. Matthew's was the most fascinating den. He called it his sanctum. It was locked, and that was part of its fascination. With the tape recorder running and my voice broadcasting the length of Babbington to camouflage my espionage, I set about, deliberately, penetrating the secret of Matthew's sanctum—that is, breaking in. Its boy-built door was secured with a boy-built lock. I picked the lock and let myself inside.

It was a shrine. At first, I thought it was simply a shrine to his father, because what I noticed first were the pictures of his father hanging on the back wall. I had never seen any pictures of Matthew's father before, but I could tell at once that the man I saw in these pictures had to be his father, because he looked just like Matthew, an older Matthew, but not that much older, a man, but a man in whom the boy has been allowed to linger, has not yet been sent to his room once and for all. Most of the pictures were snapshots, but one, a remarkable one at the center, was a drawing in pastels of his father in his flight jacket. The dampness of the cave and a leak in its boy-built roof had damaged the picture: a water mark ran down the left side. Most of the pictures were of his father alone, but some were of his father and mother, and three of them had been altered to include Matthew with his father and mother. We all knew that Matthew's father had been killed in World War II without ever seeing his son, but here Matthew had created the photographs that might have been; he had cut himself from other snapshots and inserted his image in pictures of his parents. Interspersed with these pictures of affection and wishful thinking, he had arranged pictures of war and death. One showed a grimacing gunner shooting at something outside the frame of the photograph—shooting at anything or anyone—and another showed a young antiaircraft gunner, dead at his post, twisted unnaturally, thrown to the ground like a dummy tossed into a box. The room was a shrine not only to the memory of his father but to the mother-father-son family that his had never been, and it was also a subterranean reminder of the madness that had taken his father from him.

I didn't belong there. I had insinuated myself into a place where I did not belong, from which I and everyone else had been excluded, and I was ashamed of myself for doing it. I backed out of the room, shut the door, and reset its clever lock, covering my tracks as I went, so that I wouldn't leave a trace of my transgression.

THERE WAS A QUESTION after the reading. It came from Miranda. "You've kept that memory all these years," she began, "but do you feel free of it now?"

"No, no," I said, "not at all. I write to remember, not to forget."

LOU AND HIS CREW spread sketches and drawings and charts and graphs along the bar to show Al and me what they intended to do with Small's. Artie gave the presentation.

"To begin with," he said, pointing to a map of the island, "over here, just this side of the wildlife sanctuary, we're going to be building accommodations for the staff. This whole compound will be pretty well concealed by the bamboo, so the guests in the hotel will never really see it. The rooms will be quite comfortable, luxurious, on the level of a world-class resort. We haven't set the rates for them yet, but we figure—"

"The rates?" asked Albertine.

"Yeah, we haven't quite decided what to charge for the whole package, you know?"

"No," I said. "We don't know what you're talking about."

"I'm sorry," he said, shaking his head. "It's been such an intense time, with so many conversations going on at once, I forgot that you don't even know the concept."

Albertine and I shrugged to indicate that he was right about our not knowing the concept, and he dropped back to the beginning.

"You see, we're going to market the pleasure that we've found here, the concept of losing your cares in somebody else's problems."

"You mean—"

"I mean that people will come here to work here—to fix the roof, cook the meals, tinker with the boiler, pilot the launch—"

I was on the verge of saying "Why didn't I think of that?" but I never got the chance because everyone began talking at once, each of them explaining a pet part of the scheme. My personal favorite was Nancy and Elaine's specialty. They had turned the shortage of actual hotel guests into a virtue. Some of the paying staff would get to set their worries aside by finding ways to lure guests to "The Little Hotel Without a Clientele." They had to have some guests, so that the work of the people who were paying for the privilege of working wouldn't seem pointless, so they'd have to have an advertising department, athough if worse came to worst they were prepared to fill the place with people on complementary passes, actual guests.

"Amazing," I said, when they had finished laying it all out for us.

"There's something we want to ask of you," said Lou, "a favor."

"What's that?" I asked.

"We'd like to use your saucer-detector slogan, 'No Worries, No Kidding'—but we're willing to pay handsomely for it."

"How handsomely?" asked Albertine.

Lou handed her a slip of paper.

"It's a deal," she said.

Someone, Somewhere

In some ways these people (I am one) cannot exist without the oxygen of laughter.

   Dawn Powell, diary entry

The ability to burst out laughing is proof of a fine character. I mistrust those who avoid laughter and refuse its overtures. They are afraid to shake the tree, mindful of the fruits and birds, afraid that someone might notice that nothing comes off their branches.

   Jean Cocteau, "On Laughter"

ALBERTINE AND I spent the whole day packing, with help from Lou and all his friends and from professionals hired by Artie for the heavy work. By dinnertime all of our worldly goods were en route to a small apartment in Manhattan, to be delivered the next day.

MY BIRTHDAY "CAKE" was a pecan pie with fifty candles. Before I began reading the final installment of *Dead Air,* I yielded the floor to Lou, who said, "Listen—for the last forty-nine nights I've been sending my show in on tapes that Elaine's been shuttling to the studio—except for one piece of the Catalog of Human Misery a few nights ago that I phoned in from my room here—but tonight, right after Peter's reading, I'm going to the studio to do this one live, because tonight's my last show, the sign-off, the gala, the big finish—so tune in, will you? It's a once-in-a-lifetime opportunity! Don't miss it!" Then I read "Someone, Somewhere."

WE ALL MAKE MISTAKES. On my thirteenth birthday, I made one. I was, at the time, the sole supplier of flying-saucer detectors in Babbington, New York, clam capital of America, my home town; I also ran a broadcasting network from a cave in my back yard; and I had begun spying in a small way, planting an electronic eavesdropping device camouflaged as a flying-saucer detector in the bedroom of Mr. and Mrs. Roger Jerrold, a couple who lived down the block from me—or around the corner—in the hope that I might hear Mrs. Jerrold having sex with Mr. Yummy, a man who delivered baked goods and other joys to the housebound wives of Babbington.

As it so often does, curiosity led to my mistake. One day, instead of attending to my duties as broadcaster and announcer, I plugged my tape recorder—a birthday gift to myself—into my transmitter and let a tape play over the air while I went prowling into the secrets that my friends Raskol, Marvin, Spike, and Matthew kept in the cave. When I had snooped enough to make myself feel guilty about it, I returned to the transmitter and put my headphones on to see what point I'd reached in my prerecorded palaver. I discovered that, instead of a recording of myself acting the part of Larry Peters, the congenial substitute host of "The Peter Leroy Show," I had been broadcasting a tape that I had stolen from the Jerrolds, a recording of Mrs. Jerrold and Mr. Yummy that had probably been made in secret by Mr. Jerrold, who may have been a spy—not an amateur like me, but a professional, a soldier in the cold war. The tape was nearly at its end, and Mrs. Jerrold was screaming "Oh, Yummy, Yummy, Yummy!" her voice rising in a crescendo of pleasure.

When one is in a cave sitting in front of a radio transmitter broadcasting a signal into an unseen world, it is hard to tell whether anyone at all is out there listening, unless one has a feedback system of some sort that allows one to detect the effects of the signal on the outside world. I had one of those effect-detectors: the electronic eavesdropper that I had installed in the Jerrolds' bedroom. I bent my ear to the radio that I kept tuned to the eavesdropper, listening for any sound that might suggest that the Jerrolds had heard the tape that I'd been playing. At first, I didn't hear much, because the eavesdropper wasn't sensitive enough to pick up sounds beyond the bedroom, but then I heard Mr. Jerrold's voice, increasing in volume as he came within range: ". . . not a fit mother, you bitch! Junior—get your coat. We're going to Grandma's." Then some banging and thumping—a crash—the ringing of a bell—and then nothing. The persistence and spaciousness of the nothingness led me to conclude that someone had knocked my eavesdropper to the floor and that it was going to require some repairs before it would work again.

I shut the transmitter down, came up out of the cave, lowered the stump into place, and walked to the Jerrolds' house. The car was not in the driveway. I walked up the side of the driveway, at the edge of it, on the grass, so that my footsteps wouldn't make a sound on the gravel. When I got to the window at the end of the living room, I stood on my toes and peeked inside. I saw Mrs. Jerrold, at the opposite end of the room, sitting on the sofa, in the gray light of the television set. She was smoking a cigarette. I ducked immediately, fearful that she would see me. I went home.

I ate my dinner. I helped wash the dishes. I went out for a walk. I returned to the Jerrolds' house. It was dark downstairs, but there was a light on in the bedroom. I went around to the back door and stood there trying to work up the courage to knock. If there ever was a time when I could knock at the door and say to Mrs. Jerrold, "Let me in, let me in, let me in, I implore," and hope to be admitted, it seemed to me that this was it, but I didn't have the nerve, and so I turned away, and put my head down, and put my hands in my pockets, and went home and went to bed.

What happened after that I know only at second hand, from the Jerrolds' neighbor, Mrs. Breed, who got it from the cops. Following a domestic dispute, Mr. Jerrold drove off with his son to visit his parents in Minnesota. Sometime after he left, Mrs. Jerrold locked all the doors and windows in the house, stuffed towels under the doors and up the flue of the living room fireplace, taped the cracks around the windows, taped wrapping paper over the glass, and drew the blinds and curtains. She heaped combustibles in the center of the living room: paper and boxes, scrap wood, rags, wooden tables and chairs, Mr. Jerrold's clothing, and reels of recording tape. While she was heaping the combustibles, or perhaps after she had finished the work, while she was taking a look at the heap and congratulating herself on a job well done, she drank a pitcher of whiskey sours ("made with good Canadian whiskey," according to what Mrs. Breed said the police said) and took several sleeping pills. Sometime after finishing her whiskey sours and sleeping pills, or perhaps just before she finished her whiskey sours and sleeping pills, she doused the pile of combustibles with some cleaning fluid and kerosene and set fire to it, and sometime after that she passed out, and sometime after that she died, but the house was not destroyed. Mrs. Jerrold had gone to great lengths to ensure that there would be no drafts, no air to save her from the end that she had designed for herself, but in her agitated state she had forgotten that a fire needs air as much as an unhappy woman does.

Neither the police nor Mrs. Breed made any mention of a visitor who stood outside the kitchen door, thought of knocking, did not knock, and left.

Mr. Jerrold and Junior never returned to town. The house was put on the market, but it took a long time to sell, because it smelled of smoke and needed work.

Was it all my fault? It may have been. The effects of the things we do extend themselves, like a chain or a relay network, reaching farther than we suppose, so all our acts have unforeseen consequences, and I suspect that someone, somewhere, suffers for every mistake I make.

EVERYONE SAT IN SILENCE until Lou said, "I have to admit that I was expecting a happy ending." Then he looked at his watch and said, "Hey, I've got to go."

BALDY'S SHOW that night was unremarkable until the end, when he announced that it was time to look into the Catalog of Human Misery. After the sound of the creaking cover of the catalog, there was the sound of rustling paper, turning pages, and then a long sigh from Baldy, and then the creaking cover again, and a thud when the catalog closed.

"Boys and girls," he said, "I know you think that I can't hear you, but I can. I have my ways. I have my devices. I know what you say, and I even know what you think. I know what goes through your minds each time I read to you from the Catalog of Human Misery. I can hear your little voices, even your inner voices. I can hear you asking, 'Baldy, how can those of us out here in radioland go on living when we know that we are responsible for every entry in the catalog, every one, that we're all guilty, that these things are our fault, that *nous avons tous les mains sales,* that we are all *monsters?*' That's what we hear them asking, isn't it, Bob?"

"Yeah."

"Lean in here, boys and girls. Lean in toward the radio. Lean in toward Baldy. Put your hands on the radio, boys and girls. Feel the power of the radio. Feel the hum and heat of the radio. Do you feel the hum and the heat? Do you feel the *tingle* in your fingers? That's the evil coming out of you. *Feel* the evil coming out of you. Feel the *guilt* coming out of you. *Give* it to me, boys and girls. Give me all the evil in you. You will *never* have to feel ashamed of your hideous evil urges ever again. The urges are gone. *Baldy's* got 'em. The *shame* is gone. *Baldy's* got it. Don't be embarrassed—*do* it! I see some of you out there are not putting your hands on that radio. You there, you boys and girls at that old hotel! Baldy sees you looking into your drinks and chuckling as if Baldy were just joking. Put those drinks down and get yourselves over to that radio and put your *hands* on it!"

Those of us in the lounge looked uneasily at one another to see whether we all agreed that Baldy was talking to us, and when he said, "Do it, boys and girls—don't be embarrassed—do it for old Baldy," we decided, unanimously, that he was talking to us, and though it embarrassed us to do so, we put our glasses down and circled the radio, laying our hands on it, as Baldy had asked us to.

"Feel the power of the radio waves!" said Baldy. "Feel the guilt coming out of you. Let me have it all! Give me all your nastiness. Give me your gluttony, your lust, your sloth, and all the rest of that stuff. I feel it! I feel it coming to me, boys and girls. I've got it! I've got it all. You're *free,* boys and girls! Baldy's got all the nastiness! Now you can be happy! Your hands are clean. Mine are dirty. I've got your guilt. I've got your evil urges. You can be happy at last!"

His wooden laugh rattled from the radio, rising and rasping until it became a hysterical shriek, and then a shot rang out, and then there was a moment of stunned silence, and then what was left of Baldy's wooden head struck his wooden table, then another silence, and then Bob shouted, "There! *That* ought to make the bastards happy," and he began to laugh

Baldy's disturbing laugh, in the same mad, rasping way, and then the microphone was switched off, leaving what would have been a permanent silence if all the inmates of Small's Hotel hadn't burst out laughing.

IN BED, Albertine and I squirreled under the covers, and she took my hand. "Did you always intend to have her kill herself?" she asked.

"No," I said, "not at all. When I started, I just wanted to explore the erotic attractions of all of the young matrons in my neighborhood, to make something out of a twelve-year-old's feelings for the mothers of his little friends, and to elaborate a bit on the way the existence of his little friends made their mothers all the more attractive, because it meant that they were sexually active."

"Or had been, anyway."

"Right. Very good. I didn't think of that distinction when I started, because I was looking at them only from the man's—or the boy's—point of view. I didn't even think about their disappointments, and I didn't expect Mrs. Jerrold to stand out particularly from the others, but, more and more, she did, and as she began to elbow all the other mothers aside I began to see how disappointed and lonely and isolated she was, and I began to use her—deliberately—to find out how it feels to be an unhappy woman, and—well—she got away from me. Her unhappiness metastasized beyond my control." I turned toward Albertine and held her and kissed her. "I used Mrs. Jerrold," I said, "to find out what it felt like to be unhappy, because when I tried to get into *your* mind I couldn't go very far. You're too real."

"Peter," she said, "I am *not* an unhappy woman."

"You were."

"I—"

"You were."

"All right, I was, but I was only unhappy in the way that anyone would be unhappy if she were worried about money, and—"

"You were feeling hopeless."

"I—I guess I was. But it happens to everyone sometimes. Hope and happiness come and go. *Unhappiness* is a human trait, just as curiosity and hope and happiness are. It also comes and goes."

"Are you happy now?" I asked her.

"I would be if you were," she said.

Afterword

Oh, dearest friend . . . save you, I think I scarce know any one that is happy in the world: I trust you may continue so . . . you in whose sweet serene happiness I am thankful to be allowed to repose sometimes. You are the island in the desert . . . and the birds sing there, and the fountain flows; and we come and repose by you for a little while, and to-morrow the march begins again, and the toil, and the struggle, and the desert. Good-bye, fountain!

    Ethel Newcome to Laura Pendennis, in
    William Makepeace Thackeray's *The Newcomes*

It needs a wild steersman when we voyage through chaos! The anchor is up—farewell!"

    Zenobia, in Nathaniel Hawthorne's *The Blithedale Romance*

IN THE MORNING, BEFORE DAWN, Eric slipped out of the hotel as silently as a shadow, made his way to the dock in the dark, patted the flank of the Chris-Craft triple-cockpit barrel-back mahogany runabout, and drifted across the bay like a patch of fog. He walked into town, walked to the train station, and caught the next train back into his life, where he and his wife, Madeline, were heavily in debt, living in a house that they could no longer afford, isolated on the east end of Long Island, dependent on an automobile for every social contact, sinking into the cesspool of popular culture. He was sitting at his computer in his workroom on the top floor of the house. He read the last chapter, changed "leaving a permanent silence" to "leaving what would have been a permanent silence if all the inmates of

Small's Hotel hadn't burst out laughing," and then wrote the last scene, which he found required no changes at all. He stood. He stretched. He rolled his head from side to side to get the kinks out of his neck. He had been away for quite a while. Three years had passed since he had stowed away aboard the leaking launch for the trip to Small's Hotel. He felt wonderfully refreshed by his visit, because time spent in another place, in another life, is the perfect vacation, the ideal.

Not until later in the morning, when he was walking along the edge of the ocean, did he fully appreciate the implications of what he had done, of what was about to happen.

AT THAT TIME, Albertine and I were standing on the dock, about to board the runabout and make our way across the bay.

Albertine put her hand on my arm.

"Peter," she said, "we don't have to go. We can stay here."

"Al—" I said.

"Really," she said. "We could. Lou would be happy to have us stay. We can play the parts we've been playing, but he'll be paying the bills, so it will be a carefree life, an easy imitation of the life we've been living."

I held both her hands and said, "My darling, sometime in the night I realized something about us."

She said nothing.

"Do you want to know what it is?" I asked.

"Maybe," she said.

I gave a sardonic grin and said, "We are among the very few people who *can* be happy, and I think that, since we have the ability, we have an obligation to use it."

"You do?"

"I do."

"And how do we do this?"

"First, we step aboard the boat."

"Oh, I don't know, Peter. I don't think you want to go."

"Listen," I said, and then went on to say what I had composed during the night. "Our two happinesses are forever linked. I love you, and you love me, and I want to make you happy, and you want to make me happy, so we are caught in a vicious circle, but it's not *really* a circle. It's a helix, a directed spiral, like the cutting edges of a screw, and if the helix is turning the wrong way, then when I see that you are a little unhappy I blame myself for it, and that makes me unhappy, and you see my unhappiness and blame yourself for it, which makes you unhappy, and so on, and if the turn of the screw is not reversed, then we will go on spiraling downward, narrower and narrower, until we are screwed down tight into our misery, and we will end up like Mrs. Jerrold or the people in Baldy the Dummy's catalog." I paused.

"'But'?" she said.

"What?"

"There is a 'but' coming, isn't there?"

"*But*," I said, "if we reverse the twist of the thing, make a change, shift gears, then the process begins working in our favor. You will see a little smile on my face, and you will smile to see it, and I will catch you smiling, and I will smile all the more to see it, and we will begin to spiral up and out, and we will rise, turn by turn, in a delicious circle of multiplied love, doubling daily, elevated and expansive, rising even above the petty preoccupations of our painful times, until we have sent ourselves off the chart, off the map, beyond the gravitational grip of human misery, and into the realm of immortal hilarity."

"No kidding?"

"No kidding. But it takes a reversal, a change of direction, to get that process started."

She wrinkled her brow.

"If you are in earnest, begin this very minute," I said.

She sighed and said, "Oh, Peter."

"One of us has to shift gears. One of us has to reverse the spiral. I'm asking you to be the one. I'm asking you to board the boat."

"I love you," she said, taking a step toward me, away from the boat.

"If you love me, you will take what I'm trying to give you."

She smiled, nodded her head once, and stepped aboard, and I followed her, and we settled into the third cockpit and covered ourselves with a blanket. Modesty ought to prevent me from telling you what she said to me next, reader, but it won't. She said, "Thank you for loving me. You are my happiness, and I am a lucky woman."

ERIC STOOD ON THE BEACH, looking out at the rolling waves, dictating Albertine's words into his microcassette recorder, and when, after a pause, he decided that not another word was needed, he snapped the stop button, put the recorder into his pocket, and stood there a moment longer, savoring the sensation, the tingle spreading within his mind, accompanied by a muted rumble, a ripple, a setting off, the embarkation of his imagination, released from its isolation, escaping the region of his mind to which it had been confined, slipping across the bay to insinuate itself into the rational regions, and there to run about. A shiver ran down his spine, just as people say it does in a moment of panic and doubt. "What have I done?" he asked himself, then shook himself and turned and began the walk back home, where, that night, he began reading this book to his wife, Madeline, one chapter a night.

Peter Leroy
Manhattan
February 19, 1998